Plight of the
Lions

Plight of the Lions

Roberto J Ramos

Plight of the Lions
Copyright © 2015 by Roberto J Ramos

Book design by Maureen Cutajar
www.gopublished.com

ISBN-13: 978-0-9968606-0-4

Dedication

I dedicate this book to the memory of my mother, Yolanda Ramos. She was unwavering in her support and belief in me. I only hope that she forgives me for not having finished the book before she left us. Her commitment to her children, grandchildren, and extended family was a lesson in pure and unconditional love.

Author's Note

I want to thank Diana Ramos for first recognizing that this was a novel that needed to be written.

I also want to thank Diana Meraz for reading the draft several times and making invaluable suggestions. Without her help, I would still be reviewing the manuscript.

I also wish to thank Mayela Salazar for taking the time to help shape and format the manuscript.

This is a work of fiction. While historical and biblical characters, as well as historical settings, are referenced throughout the book, it remains a work of fiction.

Finally, I thoroughly enjoyed writing this book, and if it brings even the smallest pleasure to the reader, then I will have succeeded in my endeavor.

Roberto J Ramos
December 9, 2014

Prologue

Nothing seemed to bother the boy as he slept on a wooded hill, beside the thick, twisted trunk of an olive tree. Streaks of light from a radiant, full moon spilled across his dark face, but that did not disturb his sleep, nor did the slight chill in the wind, nor did the persistent chirping of crickets hidden out of sight somewhere in the brush.

Normally, runaways could not afford to sleep so soundly, because sleeping in the streets required alertness at all times. But Akiva was just nine years old, and he had been on the road all day. Thus, the moment he had arrived at the hill and curled next to the olive tree, he had fallen fast asleep.

Yet, a different sound, a rumbling of sorts, emerged from somewhere in the distance. At first, Akiva merely stirred, but when the ground beneath his body shook, and leaves rustled and branches broke, he scrambled to his knees, and listened intently. *What was it? What was that noise?* "Feet," he whispered to himself. "Marching feet." He was certain of it, and this terrified him.

Akiva quickly fumbled for his sandals. "Dirty old rags," he murmured when one of the leather straps shredded in his hands. He tied what was left of the leather strap, and then slithered on his belly, like a snake, toward the sound. He reached a cluster of bushes and carefully peered down into the valley below. Two rows of torches steadily made their way up the hill. They had to be soldiers. Worse, only Roman soldiers marched in such neat rows. Akiva hated Roman soldiers. Earlier in the day in Bethlehem, two of those cowards had chased him out of an alley. He had gotten lost and was wondering the streets, trying to find a way out of the city, when the soldiers spotted him. They called him a thief and ordered him to stop, but Akiva had not listened and ran away.

Now here they were again and more of them. Akiva looked nervously across the hill at Jerusalem. At this late hour dim lights still flickered beyond the walls of the city. He was very thin but strong and quick on his feet. *Had he not outrun the soldiers in Bethlehem?* Besides, Jerusalem was just a stone's throw away. He was certain that he could reach the gates of the city in the blink of an eye. He scrambled to his feet. Nervous and scared, sweat poured from his brow. Akiva brushed it away, and as he did, he cringed. Akiva had a red welt across his left eyebrow that deformed the eyebrow. Every time that he touched it, it reminded him of how ugly he looked. The welt was so thick that it even partially obscured his vision from that eye. Back in the city of Petra, where he was from, the boys always made fun of his eyebrow, and that had been the main reason why he had decided to run away. The marching feet grew louder, and Akiva looked down the hill and gasped. The torches were now much closer. There was not another moment to lose. He took a deep breath, and like a wild desert hare, he charged out of the bushes and started down the hill through the trees. He had not gone far when he collided with a man, who had emerged from behind one of the trees, and landed hard on his back.

Startled, the man dropped down to a knee beside Akiva. He had long hair spread across his shoulders, and he wore a simple white tunic and white cloak that glistened in the moonlight. "Are you hurt, my child?" he whispered. "I did not see you coming." He helped Akiva to a sitting position.

"I-I am fine, sire" Akiva said, struggling to catch his breath.

"You should not be here," the man said "There is danger on this hill tonight. Can you stand?"

Akiva nodded and with the help of the man he got to his feet. He could not make out the man's face clearly, for light from the moon was coming from somewhere behind the man, causing a shadow to conceal his appearance.

"I know there is danger," Akiva said, dusting himself off. "Soldiers are coming, and I do not like them. They scare me."

"They will not harm you," the man said, "but it is better if you leave this hill. You will find a place to sleep in Jerusalem."

"Roman soldiers are mean," Akiva said. "Perhaps you should come with me?"

The man smiled and affectionately tousled Akiva's hair. "I shall be fine. Now run along, my child."

The trees thundered with noise, and Akiva's heart trembled with fear. Wild-eyed, he turned in the direction of the sounds. *The soldiers had to be upon them.* When his gaze returned to the man, he was no longer there. He was gone. Akiva turned in every direction, but the man had vanished. Alone again, Akiva backed away from the increasing noise, turned around and broke into a wild run. He ran as fast as he could. Even when his lungs burned and he thought he could not take another step, he still kept running. At last, he reached the bottom of the hill, but suddenly he lost his footing and tumbled forward.

Lying on his back gasping for air, Akiva gazed at the night sky. He had never seen it so clear and so full of bright stars. There had to be a millions stars. Akiva suddenly blinked. Something was wrong, something was terribly wrong. He blinked again and stared at the moon. It was dipping out of sight behind a distant hill, but what he could see of it was so radiant it nearly blinded him. He looked at the stars again. They somehow looked different. Everything looked different. Everything looked clearer. Akiva scrambled to his feet. The gates to the city were just ahead. Torches that hung from the walls illuminated the entrance. Strangely, those gates and those torches also looked clearer. Akiva suddenly realized that his eyes also felt differently. With trembling hands, he touched his left eyebrow. The welt was gone! He rubbed both eyes and shook his head, and again he touched his eyebrow. The welt had vanished. "But how?" he cried. "How had this happened?"

He looked toward the hill. The torches were coming down the hill. They looked like a trail of dancing fireflies. The soldiers were coming. Confused and shaken, Akiva started slowly toward the city. Just beyond the gates he found a dark alley between two buildings and dropped down. He touched his eyebrow again in disbelief. How, how had it happened? His mother had sacrificed many a gold piece to consult the best physicians she could find and none had given her any hope that the scar could be removed or even trimmed to allow her son to see better—and now, now it was gone!

The soldiers reached the gates of the city. Akiva huddled closer into his corner and watched them. They marched into the cobble stone streets of Jerusalem in pairs, with their shields and lances held in one hand and their torches in the other. Soon they were upon him, and Akiva held his breath while they filed past him.

Their faces were solemn. Akiva stared at their armaments, their uniforms and their capes, and he wondered why they were so mean. Akiva suddenly jerked back. He could not believe his eyes. The man whom he had collided with on the hill was in the middle of the column. He was walking with great difficulty between two soldiers. Akiva leaned forward to have a better look and then realized that the man's hands and feet were chained. *The Romans had arrested him! But why? What had he done?*

Curious about what was happening, Akiva stepped out of the shadows when the last soldier passed him and followed the procession from a distance. He ran from building to building and kept out of sight by hiding in the shadows. Here and there a window shutter cracked open, and a dark form would appear at the window and then disappear.

A dog bolted out of an alley and bared its teeth and barked noisily at the soldiers until one of them chased it away with his spear.

The soldiers stopped in front of a large but rather unassuming stone house and knocked on the door. A heavy man answered the door and spoke to the soldier in whispers. The conversation was brief and the man disappeared back inside the house and closed the door behind him.

The soldiers spoke amongst themselves and then continued their march through the city. On a slight hill, they stopped in front of a large two-story house that towered over a high wall. The house had two balconies that were lined with short pillars. One of the soldiers banged on a pair of wide, wooden doors. A light flickered from one of the balcony windows and then burned steadily. Moments later, one of the wooden doors creaked partially open and a man, accompanied by two dark half-naked men, emerged. The man had a conversation with the soldiers and then stepped to one side while his men dragged the doors wide open. The prisoner and several soldiers went inside. Before the doors closed, Akiva managed to look inside the courtyard of the house. Thick trees were scattered throughout the spacious grounds and columns and arches ran along the back wall.

Akiva did not know what to make of any of this. He walked to the opposite side of the street and dejectedly dropped down into a dark corner. Men began to gather in the middle of the street. One group whispered in the darkness, while another group started a fire and gathered around it.

Akiva clasped his hands around his knees and rested his chin on his kneecaps. Tears filled his eyes when he recalled how strangers and even his own friends had stared at his face. But now, now he was normal. One of the men who stood with the others around the fire suddenly raised his voice. "Why have the Romans gone through so much trouble to arrest Yeshua, a man who preaches peace?" he asked.

"Bah," another said. "I hear that Yeshua is a quite a magician. They say he can heal the sick with the touch of his hand. I would not be surprised if he has vanished from the hands of the Romans, and they are at this very moment guarding an empty cell, without realizing it."

Stunned, Akiva slowly rose to his feet and touched his eyebrow. He looked across the street at the wall that surrounded the house where they had taken him. *Had the man known as Yeshua cured him? Had he removed his scar using magic?*

Guards were stationed along the wall and one of them paused and eyed Akiva. It was only then that Akiva realized that he had walked across the street and was upon the wall. The guard lost interest in Akiva and walked away.

Akiva placed a hand on the wall and saw that it would not be difficult to climb, and without dwelling on it, he swallowed hard and scaled it. When he reached the top, he flung himself into the courtyard. There were trees scattered throughout the courtyard and he ducked behind the closest one. The tree smelled of sweet figs. There was an enormous house set back from rows of columns and arches that almost encircled the entire courtyard. Dim torches burned from some of the arches. Lights flickered from several windows on the first and second floor. To the right of the house there was a small square building with two wide, wooden doors. One of the doors was slightly ajar. Akiva found that he was breathing hard and that his heart was pounding heavily against his chest. For a fleeting moment, he considered abandoning his quest, but instead, he took a deep breath and tore across the courtyard toward the wooden doors. He slipped inside the door that was ajar and froze. He was almost in total darkness. He could barely see his feet. But as his eyes adjusted to the darkness, he realized that there was a very dim light burning from somewhere inside the building. He discovered that he was inside an enormous cave-like room. It even smelled of cool dirt. Akiva blinked. Stone steps leading to a lower chamber were directly in front of him. Trembling with excitement, he edged forward and stopped at the top of the steps. The light was coming from somewhere below the steps. Akiva hesitated, but he had come this far. He slowly started down. On the third step he paused and bent down to have a look. In the middle of the lower chamber, two guards sat at a table with a dim lamp burning between them. They were so still, Akiva was certain that they were asleep. His attention was drawn to the far left side of the room, to the dark entrance into another chamber. Was Yeshua being held prisoner in that dark room? Akiva hesitated again. What would happen to him if he were caught? He looked at the dark chamber off to the left and could not help himself. He started down. When he reached the lower chamber, he crouched low and with his eyes glued on the guards and his heart at his throat, he quietly made his way across the chamber. He reached the dark entrance and pressed his sweaty hands against one side of the rock wall in bitter disappointment. The chamber was too dark. He could not see a thing. He was about to turn and go back up the stairs, but froze. *Had he just heard the sound of shuffling feet, coming from inside the dark chamber?* He looked in that direction but could not see a thing. But suddenly there was a light, dim and barley visible. Encouraged, Akiva hugged the wall with his back and balancing himself with his arms spread out, he began to edge toward the light. But suddenly the ground beneath his right heel disappeared and Akiva lost his balance. He tried to push off the wall but could not hold on and fell sideways into a hole. In the darkness, he landed in the arms of a man, a man who gently set him down.

"Young one," the man whispered, " you should not have come down here."

Akiva struggled to catch his breath. Behind the man burned a very small torch and Akiva could not see his face clearly. Akiva tried to speak but was too choked with emotion. "Sire," he said at last, " Are you the man they call Yeshua?"

"I am. You have found me. It is the second time we meet tonight, my child, but you are again in danger."

"Then you remember me, sire."

Yeshua sighed and lifted Akiva's chin with his hand. "Of course. What is your name?"

"Akiva, sire…"

Yeshua put a finger to the boy's lips and moved him out of the way just as a bright light illuminated a small section of the dark pit.

Akiva held his breath and did not flinch a muscle. From where he stood, he could see the feet of the guard only. The guard, holding a torch that flickered in the darkness, towered over the hole.

"You still awake down there?" the guard said, yawning. "I do not blame you. This is your last night alive."

Akiva's eyes filled with tears. *What did the soldier mean? Were they going to kill Yeshua?* With tears rolling down his cheeks, he stared at Yeshua. He had stepped back away from the bright light so his face remained in the shadows. The guard left and everything turned black again, except for the feeble light that burned in one corner of the small cave-like room.

"Akiva," Yeshua whispered, pointing to the flickering light, "in a few moments that light is going to burn out and you will not be able to see your way out of here. As soon as the guard sits on his chair he will be fast asleep again. It is safe for you to go."

Akiva flung himself into Yeshua's arms and held him tightly. "Sire, why are they doing this to you? Can you leave with me? They are going to harm you."

Yeshua gently stroked Akiva's hair. "Do not worry about me, Akiva. In time, if you seek the answers, all of your questions shall be answered. But, you must be patient and never abandon your quest."

He lifted Akiva with gentle but strong hands, and Akiva reluctantly gripped the edges of the hole and pulled himself out. Still in tears, at the edge of the entrance to the next room, he paused to see what the guards were doing. One guard was fast asleep with his head hanging back over the back of the chair. The other had folded his arms on the table and rested his head upon them. Both were snoring loudly. Akiva quickly walked to the stone steps, climbed out of the lower chamber, and slipped back out into the courtyard.

He raced to the wall and climbed it. There was no sign of the guards or of the men who had gathered across the street. Everything was quiet. Akiva climbed back down and crossed the street.

He walked aimlessly through the streets of Jerusalem not knowing what to do and not knowing where he was going. He walked until his feet grew tired and it felt as if he could not take another step. Somewhere on a dark street he took refuge next to a small house and lowered his head into his arms. As his eyes grew heavy, he recalled how his mother used to sit with him on many nights and how she used to stroke his hair until he fell asleep. In those days, nothing seemed to matter but the warmth of her hands. Now that he no longer had a welt on his eyebrow, there was no reason not to go home, but how would he explain to his mother what had happened? Would she ever believe that a man he had accidentally encountered in the hills of Jerusalem had cured him? Akiva fell asleep and dreamed of being back at Petra with his mother, and his sister, and his little mutt. A loud banging almost roused him from his sleep, but he was too tired to open his eyes. The banging persisted, but Akiva slept soundly. Perhaps the raucous was a part of his dream. It did not matter. This time, nothing awakened him.

Lezinia bolted to a sitting position. The pounding at the door was so loud, so forceful that she feared the door would tear apart from the very hinges that secured it to its frame. Amazingly, the loud noise did not seem to disturb her husband in the least. Jarek was dead to the world and it was no wonder. He was the best carpenter in all of Judea and he had worked hard all day on a pair of chairs for the governor, Pontius Pilate. Normally, it might take over a week to complete such elaborate chairs, but Jarek had worked from dawn to dusk on the chairs so he could deliver them in three days.

Of course, she had worked hard too. She had cleaned Jarek's tools, helped bring in the special wood required for the project and swept the floor of his shop. She had also prepared his meals of fresh bread and cheese. But unlike Jarek, she was a light sleeper. No matter how tired she might be, the slightest noise would awaken her.

"Jarek!" she cried, shaking him violently. "Wake up, my husband. Someone is beating down the door."

Jarek slowly opened his eyes, heard the noise and jumped from the bed. He kept a short hammer beneath the bed for protection, and he reached for it and wielded it in front of him. "Wait here, Lezinia," he said.

"Jarek! In the name of your emperor Tiberius Caesar, open the door."

Jarek lowered his hammer. "Did you hear that?" Jarek said. "It is Petronius the Centurion."

"At this hour?" Lezinia cried. "He must be mad, frightening us like this." She wrapped a blanket around her shoulders and followed her husband to the door. She detested Petronius. Roman soldiers were arrogant and brutish, and as far as she was concerned, Petronius was the worst of them all.

Jarek unhinged the leather latch he had personally designed for the door and the door flew open.

Petronius burst into the room and planted his feet in front of Jarek. "Have you gone deaf, Jarek? Do you know how long I have been knocking on that door?" He glared briefly at Lezinia, and then took the hammer that Jarek held in his hands and looked at it with mild amusement. "Bah! Never mind that. I have work for you, Jarek."

"It could not have waited until the morning?" Lezinia cried.

Petronius flashed her a contemptuous look. "I am speaking to Jarek." He handed the hammer back to Jarek. "I need a cross bar, Jarek."

"You frightened us out of bed just for that?" Lezinia cried. "Who are you Romans crucifying this time?"

Petronius glared at her. "In a Roman household, such an outburst from a woman, even one from Germania, would not be tolerated, Jarek. You are fortunate that we are friends," he glared at Lezinia, "otherwise, I would drag her out of this house as an enemy of Rome."

Lezinia tightened the blanket around herself. "This is not Rome, even though you think you own Judea, and we are not Romans."

Jarek yawned and rubbed his eyes. "Lezinia is right, Petronius. This could not wait until morning? You have never made such a request of me at this hour."

Petronius retrieved a purse of money from his belt and held it tightly in the palm of one hand. "The business of Rome is no concern of yours, Jarek." He glared at Lezinia again. "Nor of your wife's!" Petronius juggled the purse from one hand to the other. "You shall be paid handsomely for your work, as always."

"Jarek is a skilled carpenter. Making the parts of one of your horrible crosses requires no skill," Lezinia said. "Today he worked all day on a pair of chairs for Pontius Pilate. That is real work."

Petronius ignored her. "What do you say, Jarek? Can you have one ready for me in a few hours?"

Jarek sighed. "Yes, of course, I shall began work on it at once."

"Excellent," Petronius said, tossing him the purse of money. "My men shall come for it at daybreak. Use your finest wood. It needs to be well-built."

"Everything Jarek makes is well-built," Lezinia said.

Petronius turned to leave but paused in front of her. "Who do you think recommended Jarek to Pilate, you foolish woman?" He slapped the air with a backhand and walked to the door. He was met there by one of his men, who whispered into his ear.

"Jarek," Petronius said, "I am told that there is a child, a boy asleep at the side of your house. He is probably a vagrant or a thief. I shall have him chased away."

"No!" Lezinia cried. "Let him sleep. I shall go and see for myself who he is."

"Do as you please," Petronius said, stepping out of the house. I have matters to attend to."

Lezinia reached for a lantern and rushed out the door. "Hurry, Jarek. Let us go and see the boy."

Lezinia raised the lantern over the child. He was fast asleep in a curled position. He was sweaty but not dirty and Lezinia thought him handsome. She reached down and brushed his hair. The boy did not so much as stir.

"He cannot be more than ten years old." Lezinia said, "and he must be terribly tired." She removed the blanket from her shoulders and covered him. "We cannot leave him out here, Jarek. Can you pick him up and bring him into the house."

Jarek looked at her. "Are you certain you want to do that? What if he is a thief?"

Lezinia frowned. "You sound as foolish as Petronius. Come, pick him up and bring him into the house. In the morning, he shall surely be hungry. While you work on your cross, I shall begin to prepare fresh bread and a warm meal."

One

Marcellius Kaelus Augustus arrived at the gates of his country-side villa in a whirl of dust and sweat. Riding his favorite black stallion, Kita, he flew past a pair of guards who were stationed under a marble arch that marked the beginning of his property. He raced across a heavily wooded garden on a path that was bordered on both sides by nude male and female statues. Torches lit the path that curved slightly to the right. As soon as he cleared the curve, the circular fountain that abutted the front of his house came into view. Water still poured from the mouths of a circle of lions that occupied the middle of the fountain. Marcellius loved the fountain. His private quarters were on the second floor facing the fountain and the sound of trickling water usually lulled him to sleep. He slowed Kita to a trot and skirted the fountain and palm trees that towered over it.

At the steps to the front portico of the house he dismounted and affectionately slapped Kita on the neck. Kita had brought him back from Brundisium in just a day and a half, and from the looks of the heavy dark clouds in the sky, he could not have arrived at a more propitious time. He tossed the reins to an alert guard who had emerged from behind one of the white columns that aligned the edge of the portico.

"Welcome home, my lord," the guard said, wrapping the reins around one hand and affectionately slapping Kita with the other. "I see that Kita has brought you safely home. Ah, and well before midnight."

"She did well, as usual," Marcellius said, "but she must be terribly thirsty and hungry."

"I shall have one of the stable boys take care of her at once, my lord" the guard said.

Marcellius stretched his arms and legs. The weeklong trip to Brundisium had been exhausting but well worth it. One of the wealthiest merchants in all of Rome, and one with the reputation of importing the finest rugs, paintings and other arts and crafts from around the world, Marcellius was always on the lookout for new quality products to sell. He had reliable agents and buyers who knew how to do his bidding, but there was still no substitute for handling some matters personally. He was almost forty years old, but still lean and muscular like in the days when he had been a fierce young commander in the emperor's army. Marcellius yawned and stepped inside his house.

A female servant sat at the edge of the atrium pool with her feet dangling in the water. In his household, servants were permitted to greet him, and this they usually did with a great deal of enthusiasm. This time, however, the dark-haired girl took one look at him and scrambled to her feet and hurriedly dried herself without a word.

"My lord," she finally said, avoiding his gaze. "Felicia thought you might arrive tonight. She instructed me to wait here for a few hours. Shall I prepare you a hot bath, something to eat perhaps?"

Marcellius shook his head. "I am fine," he said thoughtfully. He untied his blue cloak and let it drop into the girl's waiting hands. She fumbled it and nearly dropped it. Marcellius attributed her clumsiness to the late hour. Felicia, the freedwoman who was like a sister to him, had the servants polishing floors and cleaning rooms and fountains and pools at daybreak. The early hour was necessary due to the enormous size of the house. Greek in design, with red-orange cascading tiles on the roof, an open atrium, and an abundance of marbled columns, terraces and porticos, the house made Nero's Domus Transitoria look like a beggar's inn, at least that is the way Marcellius had once heard a senator describe his house. Indeed, Marcellius had also heard that Nero had dispatched architectural spies to monitor its construction. In addition, Marcellius's wife, Servia, to whom he had presented the house on her twentieth birthday, had lavishly decorated the fifty rooms and separate guest quarters with imported furniture, rugs, and curtains from the Far East.

Marcellius unbuckled the leather breastplate that he usually wore on long trips. "My wife and son," he said, casually, "how are they?"

The girl's face darkened, and her eyes widened as if the question had taken her by complete surprise.

"What is it?" Marcellius said. "Has something happened in my absence?"

The woman pressed the cloak against her chest, "No, no, my lord. Forgive me, it is just that, well——." She fell silent and clutched the cloak tightly.

"What is it?" Marcellius demanded. "Speak."

"My lord, it is just that, the Lady Servia left this afternoon, and she has not returned."

"Oh?" Marcellius' chiseled face, hardened. Servia was never out at this late hour. The streets of Rome were not safe at night. "Where did she go? Who accompanied her?"

The young girl trembled. "Forgive me, my lord, but I know none of those details."

Marcellius sighed. This was hardly what he had expected to find upon his arrival. "Where is Kemnebi? Is he aware of Servia's absence?"

As children, he and his brother had brought Kemnebi home from a carnival one day, and they had begged their father, Talorius Augustus, to let the young Egyptian slave live with them. Kemnebi, whose skin was as dark as molasses, had amused Talorius with his broken Latin and enthusiastic spirit. He was not only allowed to stay, but he had also been raised as a member of the household. His legal status had at first been a problem since Kemnebi's master had abandoned him in Rome without papers. But, in the end, Talorius's lawyers had managed to legalize him and make him a freedman. Kemnebi was like a brother to Marcellius.

"My lord, Kemnebi returned from Rome just moments ago, and he was immediately told of Servia's absence"

"Very, well," Marcellius said. "You may go."

The girl bowed slightly and without a word she quickly walked around the pool and disappeared down the corridor. Marcellius tossed his breastplate on a chair and also set out down the hall in swift, long strides. His riding boots glided noisily across the marble floor, and his short tunic clung to his muscular legs and chest. A bright flash of lightning suddenly illuminated the entire hall, and that was followed by loud crackling thunder that shook the walls. Marcellius paused and clenched his fists. The storm had arrived. This heightened his anxiety and further darkened his mood.

He exited the back of the house through wide double doors and walked down a set of marble steps. He walked around a circular pool and headed for Kemnebi's private quarters.

Kemnebi was at the door to his apartment pacing. He looked relieved to see Marcellius. "Marcellius! I thank the gods that you are safely home."

Marcellius worriedly shook his head. "This is hardly the home-coming that I expected, Kemnebi. I am worried. Where is Servia?"

Kemnebi placed a hand on the shoulder of Marcellius and led him into a spacious room elaborately decorated with golden drapes and green plants sprouting from huge golden pots. He exhaled. "I was told that three women visited her late this afternoon. They arrived in a well-guarded litter. One of them, Dometia, was a childhood acquaintance of Servia's. They had supper and then Dometia begged Servia to go to Rome with her to see her new house."

Unlike old-fashioned Romans who kept their wives caged at home, Marcellius made no such demands of his wife. She was free to come and go as she pleased and it had never been a problem. But now, now the hour was late, and Servia was always anxious to see him after one of his trips. Something was wrong. "But that was hours ago, was it not, Kemnebi? Servia would not have stayed long, especially since she knew I would arrive tonight."

"I agree and that is why I instructed Felicia to awaken the servants who served them a light meal and interrogate them. Perhaps one of them heard where this woman lives."

"I see," Marcellius said. He walked silently to one of the back windows of the apartment. This room was one of his favorite places in the entire house. In here, he and Kemnebi discussed business and quarreled over the decisions of the senate, or laughed about Nero's antics, usually over a cup of wine. Marcellius lifted one of the window shutters and peered at the dark skies. "It is a terrible night altogether." He released the shutter and began to pace. "What is taking Felicia so long?"

"Patience, Marcellius. She will be here any moment. In the meantime, tell me, how was Brundisium? Was your trip a success?"

Marcellius nodded absently. "Next week three dozen Greek paintings and sculptures will be delivered to our warehouses in Ostia. Were you able to secure additional warehouse space?"

"I did, but not as close to the Tiber as you requested. The warehouses I found are just west of the Via Ostiensis."

Marcellius gripped the rim of a vase that was on a table. "That will do. We will make a fortune satisfying the Roman thirst for Greek art."

"It would not surprise me if Nero, your biggest customer, depleted the imperial treasury trying to satisfy his own extravagances," Kemnebi said.

"I would not be surprised either. The imported marble his architects have ordered is going to be even more expensive than I had realized. It will have to come from Egypt."

Marcellius walked to the door and sighed. "I am going to look in on my son. Come and get me as soon as you hear from Felicia."

"I will," Kemnebi said.

It always amused Marcellius to see how peaceful Tessius Trulius slept. His eight-year-old son was rolled into a ball in one corner of his bed. Awake, he was a ball of fire—full of mischief. If he was not hanging upside down from some tree branch, he was racing down the hall with his wooden sword, stabbing the wind and challenging the guards to a sword match. Marcellius smiled. Even as a toddler Trulius had been incorrigible. At three or four years old he would jump from his bed in the middle of the night and run down the hall, evading and laughing at the guards and servants who tried to catch him. They never did, and he always seemed to make it into his father and mother's chambers and somersault onto their bed, terrifying his surprised mother.

Marcellius stroked Trulius's black curls and ran his rough hand gently across his smooth cheeks. Trulius stirred and stretched his legs. His eyes fluttered open.

"Father, is that you?" he whispered.

"Shush, sleep, Trulius. I shall see you in the morning."

At the sound of brisk steps out in the corridor, Marcellius turned toward the door. The steps sounded urgent, and he sensed trouble. He gently caressed Trulius one more time, and then stepped out into the corridor.

Kemnebi was as white as one of the columns that lined the hall, but before he could utter a word, Marcellius placed a finger to his lips, silencing him. "Trulius might hear us," he whispered, as he led Kemnebi down the hall and paused at the door of his quarters. "What did you discover, Kemnebi? You are trembling," Marcellius said.

Kemnebi gripped Marcellius's arm. "One of Dometia's guards just made it to the gates, Marcellius. He is mortally wounded but the brave man came to warn us. Servia was on her way back hours ago when the litter that carried her was attacked by a pack of drunken soldiers. They over-powered the guards and the slaves who carried the litter and took Servia. The drunken fools took Servia," Kemnebi said, raising his voice.

"No!" Marcellius cried.

"There is more," Kemnebi said. "As the soldiers rode away, the guard overheard one of them say that they should return to Tarian's house."

"Tarian's house!" Marcellius clenched his hands into tight fists and looked in the direction of Rome. "I know who Tarian is," he said bitterly. "He is a spoiled child. His father is wealthy and bought him an enormous house on the western slope of the Palatine. I know where it is." He started into his quarters. "I shall get my cloak. Ask that a horse be readied for me."

"How many men are we taking with us?" Kemnebi asked.

Marcellius paused. "You are not going with me, Kemnebi. I would feel better knowing you were here looking after Tessius Trulius and the rest of the household."

"But you will need my help. I can awaken all of our guards and place them around the property."

"No, it is not the same. I want you to stay."

Kemnebi started to protest again, but he deferred to Marcellius. "Very well, it shall be as you say, Marcellius. How many men are you taking with you?"

Marcellius thought a moment. Riding into Rome with half a dozen men could cause alarm. The last thing he wanted was all of Rome involved in his affairs. "I shall take two men."

"Two men!" Kemnebi cried. "But you are going to a house full of drunken soldiers."

"Two men," Marcellius said, and then disappeared into his quarters.

Two

Cerudotus, the Greek tutor, paused and looked back. He was tall and slender and dressed in a long white toga. He assessed their position and nodded with satisfaction. They had walked quite a distance from the fortress gates and were now safely out of the sight of the guards and any other potential onlookers. With his long, delicate fingers, he wiped the sweat from his brow. It was well past the noon hour and the sun was bearing down on them. The Syrian Desert was an inferno at this hour, and Cerudotus considered it madness to be out in this sweltering heat. After all, he was a scholar, accustomed to tending to his scholarly duties within the confines of his cool quarters. This insane venture into the desert had not been his idea, and it was very much against his better judgment. They were out here because his nine-year-old pupil, Farrenthias, had requested it, and there was nothing Cerudotus would not do for Farrenthias. He had taught him his very first words when Farrenthias had barely been a few months old. Cerudotus was also very proud of the fact that while Farrenthias was still in his mother's arms, Cerudotus had placed a writing instrument in his tiny hands. It did not matter that Farrenthias happened to be the son of Gaios, a wealthy Greek lord who had immigrated to Syria and constructed an enormous fortress in the Syrian Desert. No, Cerudotus would have loved his brilliant pupil even if he had been the son of a blacksmith. On the other hand, instilling reason into the young boy was also a part of Cerudotus's responsibility and at the moment there was nothing more important than that.

Shielding his eyes from the desert sun with one hand and fanning himself with the other, Cerudotus summoned Farrenthias to his side. Farrenthias was fair-skinned and a little short and thin for his age. Cerudotus bent down and brushed Farrenthias's golden hair away from the boy's eyes and took his hands. "My dear child," he said. "I must again protest this insane idea of yours. I implore you to reconsider this insane idea of yours so that we can retreat from this abominable heat and go back into a more suitable environment." He gazed with contempt at the young squire who accompanied them. He was perhaps a year or two older than Farrenthias, and he possessed an enormous belly for a child his age. Cerudotus then turned his attention to the horse the squire had brought along and shuttered. "Farrenthias, my dear child, how can you ask me to stand here and watch you climb aboard that abominable creature? Do you not understand that some men are born to toil the land with their hands, and other men are born to fight battles with horrific weapons, sometimes astride four-legged beasts. You, my child, were born for neither. You are refined and erudite."

Farrenthias laughed, and his dark green eyes sparkled. "Erudite, Cerudotus? What does that word mean?"

"It means," Cerudotus cried, "that since you were born I have tutored you in languages, science, mathematics and now you want to risk your precious little neck by attempting to ride that beast," he said pointing to the horse. "Instead of assuming your place at your study table, here we are."

Farrenthias laughed again and then waved the squire over. "I do not like it either, Cerudotus, but I want to surprise Father by showing him that I can ride a horse just like the other boys my age. And with Father and Mother in Antioch, this is the perfect time to learn to ride."

"Then at least consider an ass. They are more docile and lower to the ground," Cerudotus cried. "They are less dangerous."

Farrenthias laughed. "An ass? The boys say that only old men and women ride asses. Besides, Father says that most boys my age are already excellent riders. They all ride horses."

"Bah!" Cerudotus cried, throwing his arms into the air. "But you possess a brilliant mind, my child. You speak and write three languages—Greek, Latin, and Hebrew. What other child in this fortress can make that claim? For that matter, what other nine-year-old child in all of Syria can make that claim?" He reluctantly stepped back as the squire passed in front of him, pulling the horse along. "Just because we live in the barbarous desert of Syria does not mean that we must behave like savages," Cerudotus cried. "We are Greeks. Yes, some Greeks are brave warriors, but, more importantly, Greeks are artists, writers, teachers, thinkers."

"I have to try, Cerudotus. I want to please Father." Farrenthias touched the horse, but leaped back when the horse snorted.

Cerudotus screamed and pinched the squire's belly. "Child! Please hold the beast steady. Can't you see Farrenthias is trying to mount it?"

The squire giggled. "The horse did not move. It just snorted." He urged Farrenthias to step forward. "Nothing to it, Farrenthias," he said. "Here, I will help you." He handed the reins to Cerudotus, who reluctantly took them and held them away from his body at arm's length.

"I warn you," Cerudotus cried. "I shall personally skin your hide if so much as one hair is ruffled from the head of Farrenthias."

The squire laughed then laced his fingers and formed a cup with them. "Put your foot in here, Farrenthias," he said, "hold on to my neck and jump onto the horse's back. Nothing to it."

"I can do that," Farrenthias said. He slipped a foot into the boy's hands and pushed off, but the horse buckled away and Farrenthias flew into the arms of the squire. Both boys crashed to the ground and landed on their backs laughing.

"Enough!" Cerudotus cried. "I have seen enough." He helped Farrenthias to his feet and brushed the dirt from his hair. "I am not going to stand here and watch you break your neck, my child." He led Farrenthias to a lone withering tree that provided very little shade. He dusted the dirt from Farrenthias's tunic and ordered the squire to hand him the jug of water they had brought along. "Drink, Farrenthias," he said. "Perhaps the water will make you regain your senses."

Cerudotus angrily shook his head. As he had feared, this venture had been a disaster. Yet it amused Cerudotus that Farrenthias wished to please his father. He too continually found himself always trying to please the great man. Lord Gaios commanded utter loyalty from all his servants and small private army due to his kindness and devotion to them. He too was indebted to the kind man. At a relatively young age for a tutor, Cerudotus had been brought from Greece by a wealthy family to tutor their children in Antioch. When that family failed to adjust to life outside of Greece and chose to return to their motherland, Lord Gaios, a friend of the family, brought Cerudotus to his fortress specifically to tutor Farrenthias. At the time Farrenthias had just been born. And although he loved Farrenthias's twin sisters, Erisa and Clisa, he felt a special bond to his student. Still, he detested living in the desert. He preferred the much more civilized streets of Antioch and secretly dreamed that one day he and his pupil would be allowed to relocate to that city, which he considered a much more suitable environment for teaching and learning.

Farrenthias handed the jug of water back to Cerudotus. "I am ready to try again," he said, but Cerudotus barely heard him. His attention was drawn to the sound of horses. Cerudotus hooded his eyes and squinted in the direction of the sound. Like a mirage in the desert, a small band of men materialized out of the steaming dunes. There were twenty maybe thirty of them.

"Cerudotus," Farrenthias whispered, gripping his tutor's hand tightly. "Are they soldiers?"

"I do not know, my child," Cerudotus said. "They look more like savages."

"What do we do?" the squire asked.

"We wait until they pass us and then we head back home," Cerudotus said.

Cerudotus sighed with relief when it became clear that they were not in the direct path of the band of men. But to his horror, one of the men broke away and headed towards them, followed by a wagon.

"Ha!" the man shouted as he reached them and circled them on his horse. "What have we here? Three lost souls in the desert."

"Sire," Cerudotus said, "we are not lost. We reside in the fortress that you no doubt just passed."

The man ignored him. Instead he said, "We are off to do battle on behalf of the Roman Empire, and we can always use another horse and extra hands to feed and water the horses at night and collect wood for the campfires."

Cerudotus gasped and wrapped his arms protectively around Farrenthias and the squire. "You must be mad," he cried. "These are just children."

The man laughed. "You and the boy with the yellow hair are going with us. Now get on the wagon." He took the reins of the horse from the squire. You can go."

"Sire," Cerudotus cried. "Just take me. The boy's mother will be worried. I will work twice as hard."

The man laughed again. "We all have mothers that worry. Now hurry, get on the wagon."

"I am not afraid," Farrenthias whispered to Cerudotus in a trembling voice. "I—I would rather stay with you than go home."

Aghast, Cerudotus stared at him, then placed an arm around him and led him toward the wagon. "Of course you should not be afraid, my child. I shall never let anything happen to you."

Three

With his cloak blowing wildly in the wind, Marcellius rode his horse towards Rome like a man possessed. The two men who accompanied him could barely keep up. Marcellius did not slow down until he crossed the gates of Rome. Once inside the city he followed the old battered Servian wall toward the east side of the Aventine. He skirted the Pyramid of Cestus. Just past the temple of Diana he was forced to halt his horse while a few lonely souls crossed the street in front of him. No doubt they were homeless beggars, and though such poverty moved him, this night the only emotion he felt was anger. How dare those drunken fools take advantage of his wife. When the last wretched soul cleared out of his path, he tore down the street. He had lost precious time. He took the Via Ostiensis, and as the street looped around the Circus Maximus, he reached an intersection that was cluttered with empty shops on all sides. A small group of men sat around a fire, loudly arguing over the results of the day's chariot races. To his left, a short distance away was the Forum Boarium, dark and quiet. He reached the Palatine, but rather than remain on the street that he traveled on, he decided to take a shorter route through a dark alley.

Rome was famous for its dark alleys and for the thieves who hovered in and around them like wild street cats, waiting to seize those foolish enough to venture in. On any other night Marcellius would have avoided taking such a risk, but given the urgency of his mission, he steadied his horse and entered the narrow street with one hand wrapped tightly around the handle of his sword. The alley was empty. Still, Marcellius proceeded cautiously. He reached the other end, and just as he exited the alley, a man stepped out of the shadows, startling his horse. The stallion hurled its front legs into the air, and to avoid trampling the man, Marcellius pulled hard and to the left on the reins. The stranger stumbled backwards, slammed into a wall and fell forward onto his knees.

Marcellius vaulted from his horse and helped the man to his feet. "Are you hurt?" he said. "I did not see you."

The man shook his head. "No, no, I'm fine. It was my fault. I stepped out in front of your horse." Suddenly, he looked down. "My satchel!" He sprung to his feet. "I dropped my satchel."

Marcellius walked to a puddle of water and carefully lifted a leather satchel out of the muddy water with two fingers. "Here it is. I saw you drop it." Water poured from one corner of the leather bag. "I am afraid that whatever documents you have inside are ruined," he said.

"No!" the man cried. He took the satchel from Marcellius and let the water finish draining. "I should have been more careful." He shook the satchel until no more water dripped from its corner and then he placed it under his arm. He glanced at Marcellius as though he was about to speak, but instead he bowed his head slightly and set out down the street. He looked back, and when he did, he nearly collided with a broken cart that had been abandoned on the side of the street. He looked back several more times as if afraid that Marcellius might pursue him. Marcellius thought him most peculiar, but he had wasted enough time. He mounted his horse, motioned to his men, and they set out again.

He reached the residential area of the Palatine and hastily made his way down a long street and then turned onto a wide street on which stood three large houses. The center two-story house belonged to Tarian. A half-erected stone wall surrounded its green gardens. Light glowed from the dozen or so windows. There were no guards around. Inside the wall, Marcellius and his men dismounted and walked across the garden toward the entrance of the house.

Marcellius froze when the sky thundered. A cool breeze that blew the collar of his cloak into his face followed the thunder. Marcellius cursed. It was about to pour and that was the last thing that he needed. He walked briskly toward the house, and the closer he got, the louder muffled laughter could be heard. By the time he reached the front steps of the portico, Marcellius was besieged with anger. To make matters worse, a crack in one of the window curtains enabled him to look inside. None of what he saw shocked him. Orgies were quite common in Rome, but the thought that his wife might be inside sickened him. He tried the door. Fortunately it was unlocked.

"The two of you wait here for me," Marcellius said to his men.

He slipped inside unnoticed. Tall columns divided an enormous room into three sections, and every room was filled to capacity with drunken soldiers and women. The laughter and music were deafening. Discarded garments were strewn about on the white marble floor. It seemed as if everyone was engaged in some type of sexual act. Nude bodies of all shapes, glistening with sweat, lay in every position imaginable, and neither the loud music nor laughter could drown out the unmistakable sounds of passionate lovemaking. The house smelled of wine, of food, of sweat, and of cheap perfume. Just to the right of Marcellius, three naked men were kneeled at the feet of a naked woman who was gyrating and kicking them in the head with the bottom of her foot. Shaken with anger at the thought that his wife had been brought here, Marcellius started slowly into the house.

He walked from room to room around dark and light-skinned bodies that were sprawled on the floor and on red and purple couches. Never had he seen so many red and yellow-haired women, who no doubt used German dyes to color their hair. Servia had dark hair. Clinging desperately to the hope that his wife was safe, Marcellius sought out every dark-haired woman. As he entered the third room, he froze. For an instant he could not move as he took in the revolting scene that was unfolding before him. Lying on the floor against a couch, Servia was struggling with a young soldier who had her dress ripped to well below her hips. Even as Servia kicked and hit him, the soldier tried desperately to suckle her bare breasts. With the swiftness of a leopard, Marcellius flew across the room and pounced upon the soldier. He lifted the drunken man clean off the floor with a powerful grip and flung him across the room.

"Marcellius!" Servia cried, trying to cover herself with her shredded dress. Marcellius removed his cloak and covered her nakedness. He bent down to pick her up when a wild, piercing cry brought the entire house to a powerful silence. Marcellius turned to have a look. The young soldier he had just pulled from Servia stood in the middle of the room with the tip of a sword protruding from his belly. The lower half of his body was drenched in blood. All eyes were on the soldier who looked down at his body. He studied the tip of the sword with a strange expression on his face and then collapsed forward without a sound. The sword dislodged from his midsection and crashed on the marble floor shattering the silence in the house.

For a moment, no one moved or made a sound. Finally, a man approached the body, which was sprawled in a pool of blood, and turned it over. Several women screamed.

"Halius is dead!" one of them cried. "The nephew of Septimus has been murdered."

Marcellius had seen enough. He quickly lifted Servia into his arms and started out of the room, but a soldier quickly blocked his path.

"Have a look!" He shouted. "Here is your assassin. This man killed Halius."

"You must be mad!" Marcellius cried. "I did not kill that man. Look for yourself. He was struck from behind."

A handful of soldiers half-dressed and half-drunk staggered toward Marcellius. "Don't let him get away," one of them shouted. "We must arrest him."

"Marcellius," Servia cried. "I am afraid."

"Shh, Servia," Marcellius whispered. "Everything will be fine." He carefully lowered her down and drew his sword. "Do not move," he said. Marcellius studied the drunken, foolish faces of the soldiers, and he pitied what had become of Roman soldiers. Still, he wanted no trouble. "Let me pass," Marcellius said. "I killed no one, and I want no trouble."

"It is too late for that," one of the soldiers blurted out. "Look what you have done," he said, pointing to the man lying in the pool of blood. The soldier suddenly flung himself at Marcellius, swinging his sword wildly. Marcellius deflected his advancement and struck him with so much force that the soldier's sword flew from his hands. The soldier crashed on the floor at the feet of Marcellius. He attempted to get to his feet, but Marcellius slammed the gold handle of his sword on the soldier's head, sending him to the floor. Another soldier rushed Marcellius. Marcellius drew his sword back, ready to strike him, but Servia suddenly screamed. She screamed so loudly that Marcellius and his attacker turned to look at her. Servia was bleeding profusely from her midsection. It took a moment before Marcellius realized that she was clutching a dagger with both hands, a dagger that had been buried deep into her belly by the soldier who lay at his feet.

"No!" Marcellius shouted.

"There!" The soldier shouted. "I have avenged the death of Halius."

Servia moaned, sighed deeply and then her blood-soaked hands fell away from her lifeless body. Marcellius, choking back tears, stared numbly at her in disbelief, and then he raised his eyes to the man who had just killed his wife. The man stared back at Marcellius, his eyes suddenly filled with terror. Marcellius had killed many men in the battlefields, men from different countries and men in different uniforms, but he had never killed a Roman citizen, let alone a Roman soldier. Yet, while the man weakly wiped his mouth with a trembling hand, Marcellius struck him so fiercely with his sword that he nearly decapitated the man. Amid the screams that erupted, the other soldiers nervously tightened the circle around Marcellius.

"Drop your armament," one of them shouted. "You have now killed two soldiers."

"Fool!" Marcellius shouted. "Are you blind? That man just took my wife's life before my very eyes. Now get out of my way, all of you."

The soldier lunged at Marcellius without warning. Marcellius ducked and surprised his attacker by wielding his sword to his right while he spun to his left. The sword entered the man's chest from the side and Marcellius thrust it deeply. The other soldiers now backed away, and Marcellius became aware that the room had become utterly quiet. Without losing another moment, he hurriedly lifted the body of Servia into his arms and started out of the room. This time no one tried to stop him. Instead, stunned onlookers parted to let him pass. At the front door Marcellius kicked open the door and his two men fell in step behind him with their swords drawn.

"Marcellius!" one of them shouted. "Lady Servia? What happened?"

"Hurry, to the horses," Marcellius shouted. "There is no time for explanations!"

A crowd poured out of the house behind Marcellius. They cursed him and shouted insults at him. But no one gave chase, and for that Marcellius was grateful. For in spite of the adrenalin that raced through his veins, he was exhausted. A steady rain now fell, and the street was muddy, but that did not slow him down. One of the guards helped him with the body of Servia while he jumped on his horse, and with her limp body back in his arms he looked over his shoulder. Someone had just shouted his name. He had been recognized, and even though that did not surprise him, for he was a man well known in the city, he nonetheless cursed the gods. His wife was dead. He had been called an assassin, and now, because they knew who he was, he no doubt had placed Tessius Trulius in danger. He and his men disappeared down the street, and by the time they cleared the gates of Rome, Marcellius was soaked. Worse, the body of Servia, his beloved wife, had grown cold.

Barefooted and with a silk sheet wrapped around his frail shoulders to cover his nakedness, Tarian inventoried the bloody scene in the room. Three men were sprawled on the marble floor like torn puppets, soaked in blood, and no one seemed to care. The room was in an uproar as women and men dressed. Tarian flung his cup of wine across the room, and cried out in a high-pitched voice. "One man did this? And why here? Why in my house?"

A woman who had followed him out of his private quarters tried to comfort him, but Tarian slapped her hand away. "Leave me alone," he shouted. "I'm trying to think."

"But, why are you so angry," the woman cried. "This was not your fault."

Tarian grabbed her by the hair and twisted her head away from his face. "Do you see that man lying over there?"

The woman's eyes rolled in the direction of Halius. "Halius? Do you mean Halius?"

"Yes, Halius. He put a finger in her face. "One, his father is a madman, who is going to seek revenge for this killing." He raised a second finger. "Two, Halius is the nephew of the magistrate, Septimus." He raised another finger. "Three, his grandfather is Aurelius, proconsul at large to Syria. Nero, our lunatic emperor loves him. Everybody loves Aurelius. He was chummy with Claudius, and he fought alongside Tiberius in the Alps and Germania before Tiberius became emperor. Do you realize what all that means? Do you understand now?"

He released her hair and pushed her away when he spotted a ranking officer. "You there," he said, "no one leaves this house. I am going to get dressed now, and when I return I intend to find out how a man walks into my house, kills three soldiers, and then walks out of here untouched."

Four

Demarious edged closer to the window and carefully peaked through a crack in the thick curtain. The night was unusually dark, but from where he stood, he had a good look at the stranger who had just knocked at his door. The man wore a long toga, and a loose, dark cloak draped across his shoulders. He was not Roman, of that Demarious was certain. Romans preferred shorter togas. Their hair was cropped short, and they were generally more muscular than men from other regions. This man was not entirely unattractive. His hair was long but neatly pulled back. His face was thin and dark. And although his eyes were expressionless, he did not look particularly dangerous. But, Rome was full of shady characters, especially at night and in this area of the Aventine. Demarious tapped on the windowsill. "Over here," he whispered. "Who are you? Don't you know that no one opens a door to a stranger at this hour of the night?"

The man stepped away from the door and turned toward the window. "I am indeed a stranger to this great city, sire, but you need not fear me. My name is Akiva. I am not from Rome."

"Akiva? Ha! You are Hebrew. I knew you were not Roman the moment I laid eyes on you."

The man bowed his head slightly. "It is as you say. I am from Petra."

"The rock city. You are far away from home."

"I arrived in Rome just yesterday and was quite surprised to find a large community of Hebrews living here. By chance, I discovered that one Demarious, nephew of Nicodemus of Judea, was here in the city, earning a living drawing sketches in the streets of Rome. I was told that I might find him at this house."

Demarious stared suspiciously at the stranger. Who would be looking for him, a relatively unknown in this city? "Why do you seek Demarious? You could not wait for the morning? What is your urgency?"

"Sire," Akiva said, "Forgive the late hour. But you see, I am a man who has traveled considerably, and if I have learned one thing, it is that important matters are not to be left for another day. They should be pursued at once, lest the moment be lost."

"I see, and what important matters are you seeking out, Akiva?"

Akiva lowered his gaze. "As a child, I once had a strange encounter with Nicodemus and Yousef of Arimethea in Judea." He paused and raised his gaze.

Demarious's curiosity was instantly aroused. First, the man had mentioned his uncle's name, Nicodemus. Now, he also mentioned Yousef of Arimethea, a man whom he also considered an uncle, not by blood but by sentimentality, for Demarious had grown very close to Yousef, his uncle's close friend.

Akiva placed a hand on the windowsill. "If you are Demarious, the nephew of Nicodemus, perhaps you knew Yeshua, the Nazorean."

"Yeshua? The Hebrew Master?" Demarious cried. His thick, brown eyebrows flickered, and his cheeks trembled. "No doubt you have guessed by now that I am Demarious. Just a moment."

Demarious unlatched the door. He lived a frugal but comfortable life in Rome. A table and a few chairs are all the furniture that occupied the tiny room and that is all that he needed. He greeted Akiva by taking his forearm and leading him to the table. "Please, have a seat. May I offer you a cup of wine and a piece of bread?"

"No thank you."

Demarious edged an oil lamp closer to the middle of the table and sat opposite his guest. Light from lamp flickered and danced across the face of Akiva, and for the first time, Demarious noticed sparkling eyes that looked distant, perhaps contemplative.

"I must tell you," Akiva said, "that I am surprised to find such a well-organized community of Hebrews living here in Rome, so far away from Judea."

"I suppose it does sound strange, but people from all over the world come to this wondrous city. And a man, even a Hebrew man, can do well in this city if he works hard. What brings you to Rome?"

Akiva smiled quietly. "I am a restless soul, dear friend, who has yet to find a place where I might wish to permanently stay. I, too, have heard about the marvels of this city and thought that I should like to see for myself."

"I see, so tell me, Akiva. What brings you to my doorstep at this hour?"

Akiva's hands fumbled through his garments from where he produced a scroll, which was neatly rolled and tied with a thin, dark piece of leather. He played with it for a moment before setting it on the table. "I am aware that your uncle died a few years ago, and Yousef of Arimethea vanished from Judea years ago." He eyed the scroll. "I would have liked for them to read this."

Demarious touched the scroll with the tip of his finger. The scroll was pale, too pale to be Egyptian papyrus. The material was very thin. "It is not Egyptian papyrus," he said.

"Silk," the Akiva answered.

"What is it about?"

"Years ago, as a child, Demarious, I had an encounter with Yeshua in the hills across from Jerusalem. Later I saw him again, this time inside of a tomb—where your uncle and Yousef of Arimethea tended to his wounds."

"You—you were there?" Demarious said. "But...but"

"Did your uncle ever speak of those events to you?" Akiva said, interrupting his guest.

"I too was there, but I was outside of the tomb. I was not allowed to enter."

"I see." Akiva said. He carefully pushed the scroll toward Demarious. "I would be very grateful if you read this. I think it will interest you. And then perhaps you will help me to fill some of the gaps in the story, if you are able to."

Demarious stared at the scroll with great interest. Like his uncle and Yousef he, too, had been a great admirer of Yeshua, although his love of the great master had been restricted to what little he understood at the time—which was that he was a great healer and a very kind man. "Then this scroll is about Yeshua?"

Akiva nodded.

Demarious untied the scroll and gently spread the silk document across the table and studied it briefly. "It is written in Aramaic. I assume that it is your work?" he asked, lifting an eyebrow.

"It is," Akiva said.

Demarious positioned the lamp so that its dim light glowed steadily across the words written on the scroll. He leaned forward onto the table and placed a forearm on each side of the document. Silently he read the first few lines and then immediately recalled those days long ago when, as a child, he had followed his uncle all over Judea, observing and listening to events he would understand only much later. He continued to read silently. His eyes absorbed every word, every detail written in the document.

Many moments later a gush of wind blasted through the window, causing the wooden shutters to rattle and the lamp on the table to flicker. Demarious barely noticed. He continued to read, frequently shaking his head in amazement. At last he tapped the last line of the scroll with a finger and raised his weary eyes. "This—this is astonishing," he said. "You speak very well of events that profoundly touched me as a child and that I still frequently recall as an adult."

Akiva leaned across the table toward him, his eyes sparkling in the light of the oil lamp. "Then my words are accurate? Does this scroll speak the truth?"

Another gush of wind swept through the room, this time bringing the smell of rain. The lamp on the table rocked and nearly tipped over. "A storm," Demarious whispered. He walked to the window and secured the shutters with a piece of twine. "I am thirsty. May I offer you a cup of wine, water perhaps?"

Akiva shook his head. "I am not thirsty."

Demarious uncorked a brown jug and poured himself a cup of wine and raised it to his lips. "Other than Yousef and my uncle I did not think that there had been another witness," he said. He sipped from the cup. "Of the events of which I am familiar, indeed you have written the truth. But tell me, why did you write it? What is your interest in Yeshua? Are you one of his followers?"

Akiva touched his left eyebrow. "I was born with this eyebrow deformed. People could barely look at me without their gaze turning into a gaze of either pity or revulsion. And then one night, across from Jerusalem, I happened upon Yeshua by pure chance." Akiva sighed. "I bumped into him, and the next thing that I knew the deformity was gone. That chance encounter changed my life."

Demarious nodded. "I am not surprised. Yeshua possessed many strange abilities, curing the sick was one of them."

"Then you understand why I was intrigued." Akiva said. "At first, I merely wanted to know who he was and how he performed such magic, but the more I learned about him the more mysterious and fascinated I found his life to be. How was it that he came to possess such powers?"

"That truly was a mystery," Demarious said.

Akiva shrugged. "And then I was quite surprised to discover that his fame as a great teacher had spread to well beyond the borders of Judea and Galilee."

Demarious returned to the table and sat down. "His fame spread because of men like Paulous of Tarsus. Surely you have heard of him."

"I have."

"You are quite correct, his life was quite mysterious."

Akiva took the scroll and put it back into his satchel. "Indeed, many questions about his life remain unanswered. Even about what exactly occurred the day of the crucifixion."

Demarious stared solemnly at his guest. He had never discussed such matters with an outsider before, but something about Akiva struck him as tragically sincere. Demarious closed his eyes. "It is odd," he said, "but almost twenty-two years later, I can still smell the sweetness of the perfumes and aloe, and the myrrh that was in my uncle's satchel. I can feel the soft linen sheets that were folded and placed on a wagon." Tears filled his eyes. "Yousef had it all planned." Demarious opened his eyes and rapped the table with a knuckle. "He was determined not to let Yeshua die at the hands of the Romans. He was even prepared to storm the cross, had that been necessary. In any case, Pilate gave him permission to take the body of Yeshua and you saw what happened when Yousef arrived at the sight of the crucifixion...."

Five

Kemnebi dropped to one knee beside the cold, lifeless body of Servia and wept like a child. Marcellius had carried her to his private quarters and had laid her on a couch. Kemnebi had last seen her alive in this very room just hours before, and now she was unrecognizable. This could not possibly be the woman whose beauty rivaled the beauty of the most beautiful Greek goddesses. Her skin, which had once glistened like lilies in a pond, was pale, gray, and dull. Her lips—once bright red and as delicate as the sweetest strawberry were now purple and dry. And her hair, her long beautiful brown hair, was wet and wilted like the fallen limbs of a dying tree.

Kemnebi took one of her hands, cold and wet, and held it as he whispered prayers to the gods that they receive her soul and treat her well. Marcellius paced behind him as he spoke. He recounted everything that had happened in Rome. When he finished speaking, he and Kemnebi stared at each other in silence, listening to the outside rain and the thunder that shook the house.

"Drunken fools," Kemnebi finally whispered. "Did they not know that you were once a distinguished officer? Is there no longer any loyalty among the ranks?"

Marcellius shook his head. "Those imbeciles were young, Kemnebi. Their loyalties will be to their own friends. No doubt they will twist the facts and conspire against me. I am afraid that I will be arrested."

"For what crime? For defending yourself? We will hire the best lawyers! And you have friends in the senate, friends who owe you many favors for the expensive merchandise you have sold to them for scraps. They must come to your defense. They must!"

Marcellius sighed. "Kemnebi, you are not Roman, but have you not learned a thing living in Rome all of these years? Yes, I have friends, but I also have enemies, enemies who are driven by their envy of me. They are envious of my business, of my properties and of my house. They too are powerful and dangerous." Marcellius shook his head. "And then there is Nestor. He will seek to avenge the death of his son the old fashioned way—by killing mine. I am afraid that I have placed the life of my son in terrible danger."

Kemnebi rose quickly to his feet. "I must agree with you. Nestor knows no reason. With him it is an eye for an eye." He placed a hand on Marcellius. "But do not fear. This very night I will summon all the men who have worked for you. We will build a fortress around the house. Tessius Trulius will be safe."

"I considered that all the way back from Rome, Kemnebi, but that would only be a temporary solution."

Kemnebi thought a moment and then nodded. "Perhaps you are right. Then leave Rome with Tessius Trulius for a few weeks. I shall look after things around here."

"Getting Trulius out of the city is exactly the conclusion that I reached, but if I leave I will have the entire Roman army looking for me. Besides, if I do not stay and defend myself I risk losing everything."

"Then I shall go. I shall take Tessius Trulius out of the city for his safety."

Marcellius stared at Kemnebi. "You will be risking your life over a mess I created."

Kemnebi hardened his eyes. "You insult me, Marcellius. Are we not brothers? Have we not overcome many obstacles together? The blood that runs through my veins may not be the same as yours, but it will surely bleed for you." He looked at Servia. "I too loved Servia. You and Servia and my dear Trulius are the only family I have. Now, have you any suggestions on where Trulius and I might go?"

Marcellius sighed wearily. "I do, Kemnebi. Armenia."

"Armenia?" Kemnebi cried. "Why Armenia?"

Marcellius walked to one of the coffers he kept beside his bed and took out two papyrus scrolls. He stared at them as he held them in his hands and scrutinized them. "The day that I left for Brundisium I received a letter from Erasmus Harel."

"What? We have not heard from him in years. What did he write? Where is he?" Kemnebi said.

"My half-brother is in Armenia."

"Armenia?" Kemnebi cried. "Why Armenia?"

"I am not quite certain why he is there," Marcellius said. He unrolled one of the scrolls. "He sent this map." He tapped the right hand corner of the map. "According to the letter, on these high cliffs you will find a fortress. Erasmus Harel tells me that they call it Clivus. You and Trulius will find refuge there." Marcellius ran his finger along the map. "You should find a passage through these cliffs." Marcellius handed him the map. "After that, according to

Erasmus Harel, you will see a path that snakes around one of these cliffs. It will lead you straight to Clivus. According to Erasmus Harel, the path is on a very high cliff and it narrows considerably, so be careful."

"How strange," Kemnebi said. "We have not heard from Erasmus Harel in years, and, suddenly, I am out to look for him." He took the map and slipped it into his belt. "I shall get Trulius safely to Clivus and then return as soon as possible."

"No, Kemnebi! You must not leave Trulius alone. Stay at Clivus until you hear from me."

"But Marcellius, Trulius will be in good hands with Erasmus Harel. You will need me here. At times like these who else can you trust, and what of the household? What of Felicia, and Gianina? What will Gianina do without Trulius?"

Marcellius cringed as if he had just been struck with a dagger. Gianina was Felicia's daughter, Trulius's playmate. She and Trulius played together, studied together, ate together, and took naps together. Marcellius adored her. She was like a daughter to him, and he had already considered her situation. In Rome, a man's life was infinitely more valuable than a woman's. Nestor would go after Trulius not Gianina. But, Gianina was sure to be devastated by the absence of Trulius. "I am sending Felicia and Gianina to one of my houses in Rome. Felicia can summon guards if she feels like she will need them, but I do not believe that they will be in the same danger as Trulius from those who may wish to harm me. As you know, a son is everything in a Roman household."

"Very well, Marcellius. It shall be as you ask." Kemnebi brushed his chin with a look of great concern in his eyes. "Trulius is a bright boy, Marcellius. If we do not see you in…well he will be asking questions."

Marcellius nodded sadly. He was aware of that. He was also aware that there was no way of keeping the truth from him. "For now, I don't think we should tell Trulius about his mother or what happened tonight. Exactly when he must be told I leave entirely up to you, Kemnebi."

Marcellius opened another coffer and retrieved several purses filed with gold coins. He placed them in a satchel and handed it to Kemnebi. "That should carry you very well."

Kemnebi lifted a portion of his cloak and placed the satchel around his neck, hidden from sight. "Be careful in Armenia," Marcellius said. "The struggle against the Parthians continues, and the roads could be dangerous."

Kemnebi squeezed one of Marcellius's shoulders. "I will protect Trulius with my life. Now, shall we take Servia to the family mausoleum?"

"We don't have time. You and Trulius should leave at once. "Marcellius held his breath, then sighed bitterly. "After you are gone, I shall take care of the matter myself."

"You are certain?"

"Yes." He led Kemnebi to the door. "Go, prepare your things. I shall go and get Trulius ready for the trip."

With a lump in his throat, Marcellius stood by the bed of Trulius and watched his son sleep. His puppy, Pharaoh, a gift from one of his Egyptian merchant friends slept beside him. Since he had been given the puppy three months before, Trulius, Gianina and Pharaoh had been inseparable. A few days ago he and Servia had laughed when they saw Gianina and Pharaoh chase Trulius into the atrium pool. The memory crushed Marcellius, and he angrily clenched his fists. Nothing in the world was more precious to him than his wife and son, and now he had lost them both. He gently shook Trulius and tried to speak, but choked. Trulius moaned but did not open his eyes. Marcellius shook him again. "Trulius," he finally whispered. "Wake up, son."

Trulius opened his eyes, briefly looked at his father, and then closed them again.

Trulius loved to hear about his father's adventures in the battle-fields and dreamed of the day when he would turn seventeen and wear the cape and helmet of a Roman soldier. Marcellius shook him again. "Trulius, a Roman soldier is always quick to rise," he said.

The boy's eyes flew open. He reached for his wooden sword that he had placed on the other side of Pharaoh. "What is it, Father?" he cried. "Are we going into battle? Is the enemy at the gates?" He flung his thin legs over the bed. "I am ready to march, Father."

In spite of his bitter pain, Marcellius could not help but to smile. It was just like Trulius to always make him smile and bring joy to his heart. "No, my son, you are not going into battle. You and Kemnebi are taking a trip, and you must leave at once."

"Are you and Mother coming?"

Marcellius tensed. "No, Trulius, your mother and I are not going."

Trulius shrugged in disappointment, but his head suddenly snapped back. "Is Gianina coming with me and Kemnebi?"

"She can't go, Trulius. Now hurry, on your feet."

"But why? Gianina goes everywhere with me."

"She cannot go with you this time."

Trulius caressed his puppy. "At least I will have Pharaoh with me."

Marcellius sighed heavily. "Trulius, the journey would not be safe for Pharaoh. Gianina will look after him."

Trulius burst into tears. "Gianina is not going with me and nei-ther is Pharaoh? What will they do without me? What will I do without them? Can't they please go with me?"

Marcellius sighed. "My son, I am sorry. They cannot go. Now hurry."

"Where are Kemnebi and I going anyway?"

Marcellius poured water into a large white basin. "You are going to a beautiful place where you will study with tutors. Now rinse your mouth and face."

Trulius tied his tunic together and slipped his sword through his belt. "I already have tutors. They bore me." He splashed water on his face, rinsed his mouth, and brushed back his black wavy hair with his hands. "Will we be back soon?"

Marcellius paused from packing a satchel with some of Trulius's clothes. "I do not know. You may be gone for a while."

Trulius dried his face. "But Kemnebi is taking me to the Circus Maximus next week to ride a chariot. He promised."

"You can do that when you return."

Trulius returned to his bed and caressed Pharaoh. "And you have been promising to take me to a gladiator school to meet a real gladiator."

"Trulius, all of that is going to have to wait until you return," Marcellius said.

"Mother is going to miss me, and I will miss her," Trulius said, fumbling with the handle of his sword. "May I go and see her before I leave and can I say good-bye to Gianina?"

Marcellius stared at his son. He detested lying to him and considered telling him the truth. For an instant, he also considered leaving Rome with him and Kemnebi, but no, that would not be wise. It would only endanger his son. He took Trulius affectionately into his arms. "We should probably not disturb them, son. They are both asleep and, besides, women are delicate about certain matters. It might be too painful for them to see you go. Now hurry. Kemnebi is waiting."

Six

Septimus Cassis, dressed in the short toga that he slept in, staggered into the atrium of his house. He yawned. It was not uncommon for him to be awakened in the middle of the night to address some legal issue that could not wait until morning. Usually, it was to make a ruling on the arrest of some drunken senator who had broken the peace or who had gone home and beat his wife over some trivial matter. He greeted Tarian and the soldier who accompanied him with a courteous but tired nod. Dressed in full military regalia, the two soldiers stood at full attention.

"So" Septimus said, yawning again and settling back into his chair, "why have you dragged me from by warm bed at this hour, Captain Tarian?"

Tarian looked briefly at him and then fixed his gaze on a dark bust of Mars that sat directly behind Septimus on a marble table. "Excellency, a terrible tragedy has occurred this evening at my house." His eyes had been lowered, and he now raised them and momentarily met the eyes of Septimus. "Your nephew Halius."

Septimus nearly bolted from his chair. Halius was like a son to him. He was actually the son of Laecidia, his wife Varelia's sister. But ever since Halius had been born, he had felt a special attachment to the bright boy, especially since his own wife could not bare children. He had visited Septimus late yesterday afternoon with the promise that tomorrow he would visit again, this time to discuss the possibility of his abandoning his military commission in order to pursue the study of law. The news had thrilled Septimus.

"What about Halius? Has something happened to him?" His eyes were ablaze.

Tarian nervously cleared his throat. "Sire, he—he was killed. He was murdered."

Septimus rose slowly to his feet and staggered slightly forward. Only his full inner strength prevented him from collapsing back into the chair. He stared at one soldier and then the other. This was absurd. Halius could not possibly be dead. Impossible! Tarian nervously cleared his throat and continued. "I—I had a house full of guests, Excellency. I had food, drinks, and music. The witnesses say that one Marcellius Kaelus—"

"Marcellius Kaelus Augustus, the wealthy merchant?" Septimus asked.

"Yes, Excellency, that very one."

"Go on," Septimus whispered, his voice stricken with pain and sudden anger.

"Apparently, his wife was at my house," Tarian said. He shook his head. "I did not invite her, Excellency, nor did I personally see her. But I am told that she was quite attractive, and that she was very drunk and behaving promiscuously. Her husband arrived and—she, well, Marcellius found her almost completely disrobed, in the arms of Halius." Tarian exchanged tight glances with the other soldier. "According to the witnesses, Marcellius went into a rage. He plunged a dagger into the back of Halius and then flung him across the room. After Marcellius killed Halius my men tried to subdue him, but he went on a rampage. He was like a madman. He killed two more men before he made his escape." Tarian again exchanged glances with the other soldier. "Also, Excellency, during the scuffle the wife of Marcellius was also killed." He cleared his throat. "My men are outside awaiting your orders." Tarian fixed his eyes on the bust again.

Septimus walked around the chair and slumped down. His beloved Halius was dead, killed by a man he knew. Septimus smiled bitterly. But of course, decadence was a way of life in Rome, but what decent husband could endure the spectacle of his wife in the arms of another man? "Frankly," he said shaking his head. "I am surprised that more killings don't occur at Roman orgies."

"Excellency, as I have already explained. I did not invite her, and she was drunk."

"I heard you," Septimus shouted, "but you have only described for me what happened. I am trying to understand why it had to happen. What married man would not draw his sword in anger at the sight of his wife being defiled in public?"

"Sire," Tarian said. "The house was full of married women, and most were without their husbands. And they...."

"But of course," Septimus said, cutting him off and gripping the sides of his chair, "the women are out playing while their husbands are off on military campaigns. And someone has to accommodate their needs, is that it? Well, someone also has to assume responsibility for this terrible mess, Tarian, and it happened in your house!" Septimus shifted uncomfortably in his chair. "Has Nestor been notified?"

Tarian flinched. "No, Excellency."

"He will be screaming for blood. Have one of your men bring him to me at once. I had better be the one to break the news to him." He paused. "Arrest Marcellius. I do not want him harmed. He must be brought to justice. I also want the witnesses who saw the incident brought here to be interrogated by my secretaries." He waved the soldiers away. "Go now. I wish to be alone to mourn the loss of my nephew."

Septimus sighed. "Halius," he murmured. Having no children of his own, it had always been his wish that one day his nephew would hang up his military uniform and join him in the hall of justice, perhaps as a magistrate or lawyer—but that was no longer to be.

Seven

Marcellius removed the chain he always wore around his neck and wiped it dry. Depicted on the small medallion that hung from the gold chain was a bearded man. Marcellius placed it around the neck of Trulius. "This is yours now, Trulius. My father gave it to me. It once belonged to his father. They stood behind the house, where the grass sloped toward a thick, wooded area. The first hour of daylight was not far off, and the rain had slowed to a drizzle.

Trulius lifted the medallion from his chest and inspected it in the darkness. "Who is the bearded man, Father?"

"I do not know. I asked my father once, and he did not know either."

"I have always believed," Kemnebi said, from behind Trulius, "that it came from Egypt."

Marcellius embraced Trulius, then lifted him into the air and placed him on a horse. "Study your lessons, Trulius, and be obedient. I shall see you soon."

"Father," Trulius said, wiping his tears with his forearm. "Tell Mother I hope she feels better. I shall miss her. And tell Gianina and Felicia that I shall miss them, too. Oh, and tell Gianina that Pharaoh will keep her company until I return."

Marcellius nodded and took a few steps away from the horses with Kemnebi at his side.

"He is in your hands now, Kemnebi," Marcellius said. "When you feel the time is right, tell him the truth." Marcellius sighed. "He will learn much at Clivus, but you must also resume his lessons on how to use the sword. One day he must fulfill his duty to the empire, and he must be prepared." Marcellius squeezed one of Kemnebi's arms. "Look after yourself, Kemnebi."

Kemnebi covered the hand of Marcellius with his own. "May Montu, the warrior god of Egypt, look after you."

The two men embraced and returned to the horses. While Kemnebi mounted his horse, Marcellius gently slapped Trulius on the leg and then stepped back. The two horses turned together and set out at in a brisk walk toward the wooded hill. Marcellius watched them for a moment. It began to thunder and he had work to do, but he found that he was paralyzed with grief. He could not take his eyes off of Trulius, who grew smaller the higher he and Kemnebi climbed. Finally, he blinked and snapped out of his stupor. He looked around, found a branch and set about the task of erasing whatever tracks he could see. A good scout would not be fooled, but the precaution made him feel better.

When he finished, he searched the hill. Kemnebi and Trulius were now nothing more than a pair of blurry shadows on the hill. Still, it crushed the heart of Marcellius to see the tiny arm of Trulius wave his wooden sword. He lifted his own arm, which felt as heavy as a block of marble, and waved back. He wondered, would he ever see his son again? Kemnebi and Trulius disappeared into the trees just as it began to rain again. Marcellius raised his chin and closed his eyes. Rain splashed onto his face and mixed with his tears. The tears washed away, but not the blistering pain in his heart. No, that pain lingered and it nearly rendered him powerless to move. Yet, he somehow found the strength to return to the house. He still had to do the unthinkable—inter Servia in a shallow grave as if she had been the wife of a plebian, a common man of no means. The idea repulsed Marcellius, but what choice did he have? Today, he had become an accused murderer, and no amount of wealth ever protected a Roman citizen from a fickle government that often feared, resented, and ultimately thrived on destroying the affluent. His life as he had once enjoyed it was finished, and who knew what other terrible fate awaited him.

Eight

Septimus glared angrily at his brother-in-law, Nestor. Nestor was ranting incessantly like a lunatic, pacing the floor of the back portico of the house with clenched fists. He was not grieving over the loss of his son, Halius. No, he spoke only of revenge, and this further incensed Septimus. More than once, Septimus wanted to cut him off—but Septimus let him continue. Let the fool spill his anger here with him where he could do no harm. Nevertheless, Septimus had had enough. He stopped listening. He stared at the sun as it crept along the red and purple tiles of the marble floor. He recalled sadly that at this very spot he had last spoken to Halius and the very thought of never seeing him again brought enormous pain. Behind him the Palatine was a fury of early morning activity. His neighbor's servants noisily scoured their master's lavish gardens, assessing what work needed to be done that morning. Horses snorted and buckled beneath the heavy brushes of the slaves who groomed them. Farther away, female servants armed with satchels and baskets headed down the hill in their loose dresses and light sandals toward the Forum to collect fresh eggs and sweet delicacies for their master's table. Septimus had not had his breakfast yet and the thought of a freshly baked sugar roll stirred his appetite and further fueled his impatience with Nestor. He stared at Nestor. Tall and muscular, he suddenly paused in front of a small table and slammed his fist into it, sending a bowl of dates crashing to the floor. "Damn it, Septimus," he shouted. Thick veins swelled along his neck, threatening to burst. "Am I talking to the walls? Are you not listening to me? That rich maggot must pay for what he has done—I will make him pay. Do you hear me? I will make him pay, my way."

Septimus cringed with anger. In truth, his intense dislike of Nestor had recently grown into genuine hatred, for Nestor had been a terrible father and was a terrible husband to Laecidia, the mother of Halius. Exactly what Laecidia saw in him truly baffled Septimus. Laecidia was sweet and kind, sweeter than his own wife, Varelia, and she was not in the least unattractive. Septimus sighed impatiently. He tolerated Nestor only because of his father-in-law Atenuar, a man Septimus truly loved and admired. And it was at moments like this, therefore, that Septimus restrained the anger he held for Nestor. "Do not be a fool, Nestor. I have already told you. I have ordered the arrest of Marcellius. He shall stand trial for what he has done."

"A trial? Bah!" Nestor cried. "You would deny me the satisfaction of killing the bastard myself? Let me put a sword through his back. Is that not what he did to Halius? Only a swine attacks a man from behind."

Septimus smiled without humor. He expected no less from Nestor. The concept of justice was completely foreign to him, beyond his comprehension. "I suggest that you not interfere with my orders or I will have you arrested as well." Septimus rose from his chair and turned his back to Nestor. "It may surprise you, Nestor, but Rome has laws and those laws afford every citizen of Rome, including Marcellius, certain rights." Septimus turned to look at Nestor. "Tell me, Nestor, have you thought at all about the actions of Halius that night. Are you not troubled by the fact that he was drunk and was seducing the wife of a well-known man in public?"

Nestor laughed. "You must be mad, Septimus. Do you know how many married women make fools of their husbands? Should I tell you how many married whores I have bedded myself?" He pretended to spit on the floor. "That's what I think of stupid and weak men who cannot keep their whores at home."

Septimus's nostrils flared. "Do not pretend to lecture me on the pitiful morals of Rome, Nestor. I am well aware that this city has its darker side. But do you not understand that in those dark moments it is the walls of justice that keep the empire from collapsing into complete chaos?"

Nestor laughed hard. "You are dreaming, brother-in-law. I have seen Nero with my own eyes in the filthy alleys of the Aventine looking for pleasure, and he doesn't give a pig's ass if he finds it with a married whore or a bratty boy of ten. Is that the Rome you want to protect?"

"Nero's personal habits are none of my business. As long as it is within my power, I will uphold the laws of Rome. Now, as I have repeatedly told you, Marcellius will get a fair trial. He will not be murdered by you, or by one of your men. Enough corruption exists in the city and I will not be a part of it. Besides, vengeance has no place in a court of justice."

Nestor glared at Septimus. "Then tell me this, oh pious Septimus, exactly how will you punish the merchant? Will you banish him like all the other rich maggots who commit crimes? Ha! He will laugh in your face. He has enough money to live like an emperor anywhere in the world." He waved his fisted hands. "He will buy his freedom. What fat official of Rome has not purchased goods from that rat? Even those roaches that call themselves senators are in his debt. All of Rome treats him as if he were Mars himself."

Septimus looked past Nestor at the sound of footsteps coming from behind his brother-in-law. When his wife emerged out of the shadows of the room, he angrily clenched his jaw. No doubt she had been listening. He detested her deplorable habit of eavesdropping on his conversations.

Leaving a trail of the scent of Jasmine behind her, Varelia walked past the two men. Her eyes were ablaze with fire. She paused at the balcony and pretended to gaze at the Palatine hill. "Nestor," she said, without turning to look at him. "You are wasting your breath. All of Italy will burn to ashes before Septimus will violate one of his precious little laws." She finally turned and looked at her husband. "He won't break one of his laws even for Halius, who supposedly was so precious to him."

Septimus gathered the folds of his long toga. "I have said enough about the matter for now. I am hungry. I owe neither one of you any further explanations." He turned to leave.

"I will never understand," Varelia said, "why Father favors you so much, Septimus."

Septimus paused and turned to her. "How many times have you and I had this conversation about your father, Varelia?"

Varelia laughed sarcastically and tossed her head from side to side. "But of course, tell me again how both of you struggled out of the ashes of childhood poverty. Tell me again how you both labored in sweat to make names for yourselves." Varelia stopped laughing and glared at her husband. "And how many times have I reminded you that neither you, my dear husband, nor my father wears a crown? What riches do you really possess? Do either of you own a private ship that can carry you across the world on a whim? Of course, you both enjoy an excellent reputation." Varelia laughed. "But what is a frivolous and meaningless reputation worth?"

Septimus sighed. "Varelia, you, in turn, truly amaze me. Is it possible that you grow more shallow every day? Your father is one of the noblest and wisest men in Rome and—bah! I see that I am wasting my breath." He started out of the room.

"Septimus," Nestor said, falling in step beside him. "Nero's henchman, Anicetus, he is a friend of mine. We both know what he did to Agrippina on the orders of Nero. If Nero can have his own mother murdered, then why can't I have my revenge? Kill Marcellius or I will."

Septimus stopped abruptly, his face suddenly ashen. "I warn you again, Nestor, disobey me about this matter and I will forget that you are my brother-in-law." He turned and walked away, feeling the eyes of Varelia and Nestor burning holes into his back.

He, too, was devastated and outraged at the death of Halius. And worse¬Marcellius had killed him. How ironic. Of all the men in Rome why had fate brought Marcellius in such a cruel fashion back into his life? No, he did not know him personally. Strangely, he had never made an effort to get to know the man whose quick actions in the battlefield had saved his life years ago. Could he really sit in judgment of that man's actions? Could he really order his execution if such was the will of the people? Septimus quickened his pace. Maybe Nestor was right. Maybe he was a fool to believe that justice could prevail in a world filled with nothing but the barbarous and deplorable habits of man.

Nine

Marcellius stood, looking intensely out of a window of his quarters. From this window he could clearly see the dusty road used for travel to and from Rome. Daybreak had arrived with a blinding orange sunrise that spanned the horizon, and the sight of it caused Marcellius bitter pain. Many times, he and Servia had stood at this very window enjoying such sunrises in each other's arms. Now all was lost. Yet for all his grief, he winced at the sight of a cloud of dust far off in the distance. They had wasted no time. They were coming for him. He estimated that there were at least a dozen riders, maybe more.

In an act of personal defiance, he had changed into his old military uniform. If he was going to be dragged from his house in shackles, let the cowards see that he had once served the empire with pride. After all, he had once been a commander with the fifth legion and that legion still existed today. Nero had recently sent it to Syria. He turned away from the window. Felicia sat on a couch sobbing quietly.

"They are coming," Marcellius whispered.

Normally a woman of little words and little emotion, Felicia rushed to the window, saw the soldiers and then threw her arms around Marcellius. "For the love of the gods, Marcellius, leave now. There is time. Do not let them take you." She took his hands and held them tightly. "Please. I will tell them that you never returned from Rome last night. I will send them away."

Marcellius almost smiled. He expected nothing less of Felicia. She was two years younger than he, and much like Trulius and Gianina, they too had played together as children. He loved her and realized now more than ever that aside from Kemnebi there was no one else in this world that he trusted more. "No, Felicia. They will tear the house apart looking for me. And even if I did escape and went into voluntary exile, I could lose my citizenship and have all my property confiscated."

Felicia lowered her head against his chest and sobbed quietly. "How could this have happened to our beloved Servia, and now I cannot bear the thought of your being arrested and taken away. There is not a more honest man in Rome."

"Felicia listen to me," Marcellius said, taking her by the arms. "You must be strong, and you must follow my instructions exactly as I have outlined them to you. Farron is a smart accountant and good friend. You can trust him. He will help you deal with the lawyers and bankers and anyone else who might pry into my financial affairs."

"I understand," Felicia said nodding.

"But even Farron must not know about the hidden assets that I have disclosed to you. The less people know about my true worth, the better it will be for everyone."

"Shall I ask Farron to hire lawyers for your defense?"

"No! It will be a waste of time and money. And tell him that I do not want the slaves auctioned in a slave market. I want him to find them good homes. They should all be sold at private sales."

At Marcellius's request Felicia had brought Gianina into his quarters. She was sound asleep on the couch. Marcellius kneeled beside her and kissed her on the cheek. Tears filled his eyes. Gianina had no legal father, but as far as Marcellius was concerned, she did not need one. He loved her as much as he loved Trulius. She was the daughter he and Servia never had. "Take good care of my precious little pearl, Felicia," he said, getting to his feet. "I could not bear it if something happened to her." He took Felicia's hand. "Leave with her tonight. In spite of the guards, it is too dangerous for you to stay here. Go to one of my houses in Rome. I do not mean to frighten you, but men, other than soldiers, may come prowling around here tonight. And I assure you that they will be looking to hurt those that I love." He affectionately lifted Felicia's chin with a bent finger. "And remember my instructions, no matter what happens, do not try and communicate with me. It will be too risky for you and Gianina."

Felicia nodded. "When should I expect Kemnebi and Trulius to return?"

A sick feeling returned to the pit of Marcellius' belly, for he too wondered when indeed his son might once again roam the halls of this house. "It is better that you know nothing about that, Felicia."

They both froze at the sound of horses thundering across the garden. Earlier this morning, Marcellius had instructed his guards to lay down their arms should soldiers arrive and allow them onto his property without obstruction. That moment had now arrived.

"Stay here," Marcellius said. "Do not come downstairs unless you are asked to."

Marcellius hurried down to the first floor of his house and whisked down the main hall, past his collection of rugs and paintings. He turned the corner and walked around the atrium pool to the front door to greet the men who had come to arrest him. As soon as he stepped out of the house, the soldiers halted their horses and drew their swords. Never taking their eyes from Marcellius, they dismounted but they did not approach him.

Marcellius could barely contain his anger. Every fiber of his being wanted to offer them violent resistance, every inch of his skin swelled in defiance, but, instead, he controlled his anger and offered no resistance. He unsheathed his sword and let it drop. The soldiers did not move. They waited, and when Marcellius did not move, one of them spoke. "You are wise to offer no resistance, sire. We have orders to arrest you for the murder of several Roman soldiers." He turned to his men and nodded. Two of them cautiously approached Marcellius and chained his wrists as if he were a common criminal, an enemy of Rome. A horse was brought around and Marcellius was instructed to mount it. At least he was spared the humiliation of being dragged on his feet all the way to Rome.

Halfway down the garden, Marcellius looked back. Felicia was at one of the windows, with her hands in her face, quietly weeping. The soldiers had not bothered her. In fact, they had not even entered his house, and for that, at least, Marcellius was grateful.

Ten

The night was bitterly cold, and although Cerudotus was exhausted, the cold and his aching muscles made it impossible for him to sleep. He was still young, but his body was unaccustomed to the rigors that he had endured the last seven days. His back, arms and legs were throbbing with pain, and it is no wonder he was so miserable. The men had kept a maddening pace across the flat, dry Syrian Desert, and they had continued their relentless pace until they had reached the outskirts of Armenia, where they were now camped. The nights in Syria could get cold, but nothing like this. Here, the nights could be brutal, sometimes year around.

Farrenthias lay asleep beside him, and at least for that Cerudotus was grateful. He reached down and made sure that the cloak that he had placed over Farrenthias covered his entire body.

"Where are we?" Farrenthias suddenly asked.

"I thought you were asleep?"

"I am too cold to sleep."

Cerudotus pitched the last few sticks into the campfire in an effort to rouse the fire, but the sticks he was using were too thin.

Farrenthias lowered the cloak away from his face and huddled closer to Cerudotus. "Where are we?" he repeated, shivering slightly. "I have never seen so many trees."

"Somewhere in Armenia, my child." Cerudotus poked at the fire with a stick, but this effort produced only thick smoke. "I cannot deny that this is a beautiful country but it is cold, too cold for my bones." He stood and surveyed the other fires around the camp. Most had died down, but by the sound of snoring men it seemed as if no one had noticed. "I am going for more wood," he said. "Would you like to accompany me or are you too cold?"

Farrenthias quickly jumped to his feet. "I am coming with you."

Cerudotus raised a finger to his lips, indicating to Farrenthias that they should be as quiet as possible, lest they disturb the men. He carefully led Farrenthias through the camp, careful not to step on a body or a discarded piece of garment or armament. At the edge of the camp a sleepy guard snapped his head back when he heard them. By now, most of the men knew that Cerudotus and Farrenthias gathered wood nightly, and keeping an eye on them was no longer a priority. They had been warned early on that if they tried to escape, they would be caught and killed.

"Do not go too far," the guard muttered and then lowered his head and almost instantly began to snore.

Cerudotus and Farrenthias walked into the trees, but it quickly became apparent that it was too dark to see a thing.

"Do you think Father is looking for us," Farrenthias whispered.

"I have no doubt," Cerudotus said, bending down to pick up a piece of wood. He inspected it then let it drop from his hands. "And I feel sorry for theses barbarians when he catches up to us."

"I hope Mother—"

"Sshh," Cerudotus whispered. He pulled Farrenthias closer into the folds of his cloak and ducked. Cerudotus was no outdoorsman, but he had heard something, which made him uneasy. No telling what vile creatures inhabited these woods at night.

A twig snapped and then another and another and the trees, which moments before had been as still as the night, appeared to be moving. Cerudotus blinked. The entire forest seemed to come alive before his very eyes. Shadows and dark forms scurried and crawled about.

"Devils!" A man cried in a loud voice. He started to yell something else but his voice died out, followed by a muted thud.

Instantly, the dark, quiet forest erupted into total chaos. Men on horses raced into the camp. There was shouting and cursing and sounds of clashing swords and shields. Torches lit up the trees, giving light to the attack.

Cerudotus suddenly felt the full weight of a man plow into him and drag him down.

"Keep your head down, tutor," the man whispered to Cerudotus. He had also managed to grab Farrenthias and had him collared with one arm. "Are you both all right?"

"Yes," Cerudotus cried. "But who…Lord Gaois?"

The man nodded. "Two of us were about to sneak into the camp to snatch you both, but you made it easier on all of us when you walked out of the camp on your own."

"You were watching us?" Cerudotus asked.

The man nodded again then turned in the direction of the commotion. "The fighting has escalated. Follow me, Lord Gaios has designated a place where we are to meet."

Cerudotus did not move. Instead, his eyes remained fixed on the wild commotion. From what he could tell, the men who had taken him and Farrenthias prisoners were being slaughtered. "Is, is all the killing necessary," he whispered.

The man pulled Cerudotus along. "You are naive, tutor. Those men are cutthroats. They sell their skill to the highest bidder. Every last one of them must die or they will seek revenge on all of us. Now hurry."

"Where is Father?" Farrenthias asked.

The man lifted him into the air and placed him on his back. "You shall see him soon enough."

Cerudotus awakened with a start. Farrenthias had fallen asleep in his arms last night and now he was gone. But Cerudotus sighed with relief when he recalled that he and Farrenthias had been rescued last night. They were no longer prisoners. Indeed, Lord Gaios's armed guards were scattered all around him. Most were still asleep.

The morning was cold, and although it was light, the sun had not yet appeared in the sky. Cerudotus found that they had camped at the edge of an enormous ravine that dropped down and away for as far as he could see. He stretched and then made his way to a circle of guards who were gathered around Lord Gaios.

"Cerudotus," Lord Gaios said, "I trust that you slept reasonably well."

Cerudotus yawned. "Sire, I have not slept well since I have been away from Syria, but I am indeed happy that you found us when you did." He folded his arms to keep warm. "As I told you last night, I trust that you will forgive me for the trouble that I have brought upon you."

Lord Gaios shook his head. "It is not your fault that we live in a world where armies and bandits think that they can take whatever liberties they like with the lives of people. I am happy I found you both alive." He turned his attention to Tavius, the captain of his guard. "So, we lost five men last night, five good men, and three of our wounded died overnight and one this morning is that correct?"

"Yes, my lord, that leaves us with four wounded men and two of the four are not doing well. The cold was brutal last night. Another night like that and we are going to lose all four."

Lord Gaios frowned. He had left Syria with twenty of his best men. He was now down to eleven and the wounded. Of course, in spite of having been heavily outnumbered, they had killed every last one of those cowards.

"Father!"

Farrenthias was running back from the edge of the ravine, where he had ventured off with one of the men.

"Father, we saw smoke! We saw smoke in the distance!" Farrenthias said excitedly.

The soldier who accompanied Farrenthias nodded. "The lad is right, my lord. There is some type of structure just across the ravine. From a distance it is difficult to tell what it is."

"Oh?" Lord Gaios said, getting to his feet and following Farrenthias who was pulling him by the hand. "What can possibly be out here in these mountains made of solid rock?"

The sun was barely clearing the horizon, and in the faint light of dawn, he looked across the enormous wide ravine. They were high on the ridge of a shear cliff that overlooked more cliffs and green patches of forests.

"Over there," Farrenthias said, pointing far into the distance.

Lord Gaios squinted. Was the sun playing games with its glare, or was he staring at a series of towers atop a faraway peak? He hooded his eyes with his hands. He could barely discern their shape, but squinting hard, he counted three towers dangling from a cliff. And, indeed, from one of the towers rose a hazy feeble cloud of smoke that, had it not been pointed out to him, he would not have noticed. Someone either had a fire going to keep warm or was preparing a warm meal.

"I am amazed that you saw the smoke," Lord Gaios said.

"We have Farrenthias to thank for that, my lord," Tavius said.

"What is it?" Lord Gaios said. "A fortress? Out here? In this rough part of the country?"

"It is difficult to say," Tavius said. "We know there is fighting to the north of here. Did we not speculate that is where the men who kidnapped Cerudotus and Farrenthias were headed? Is it possible that we are looking at a Roman or Parthian stronghold?"

Lord Gaios silently rubbed his chin. "Perhaps," he murmured. "The towers are well hidden, barely visible from this distance." Lord Giaos looked at Tavius. "But have we not also heard that the people of these lands are tired of the fighting. It could be that someone has taken refuge there." He gripped the handle of his sword tightly. "Either way we must investigate. We have the wounded to think about. They need shelter and rest."

"I know what you are thinking, my lord," Tavius said. "Taking into account the terrain that must be crossed, with some luck I could probably reach those towers in a few hours."

"Good," Lord Gaios said. "Take two men with you. Stay out of sight, but move quickly. The rest of us will follow slowly until you report back."

Eleven

Nero leaned back against the sculptured headboard of his enormous bed and happily clapped his hands. He giggled at the news that was brought to him, much like a child giggles at the silliest thing. Nothing delighted him like the stinging gossip of his subordinates. He stared at Seneca and Burrus, his two closest confidants. Why, this morning's news was even more interesting than last week's confession from his astrologer that the wives of three senators were, not just his clients, but his mistresses as well. Nero slapped the bare bottom of Lanera, his favorite concubine, who was asleep beside him. When she did not wake up, he shoved her out of the way. "Come, come and sit beside me, my dear friends," he said to Seneca and Burrus. In a fit of annoyance, he ripped the canopy from one of the bedposts and tossed it to the floor.

The two men eased onto the edge of the bed, glancing discreetly at Lanera, whose entire backside was exposed to them.

Lanera suddenly stirred turned and raised herself to a sitting position. "My pet," she said, stretching her arms and yawning. "What are Seneca and Burrus doing in our bed?"

Nero affectionately brushed her cheek. "Quiet, my irascible little fool. I am trying to think."

He folded his thin legs up to his chest and wrapped his arms around his knees. "Now, let me see if I understand the news that you have brought me this morning. A prominent citizen of Rome, a man of wealth, finds his beautiful wife in the arms of a young soldier. He goes into a rage and kills her lover and all those who tried to stop him." Nero's dark eyes grew wide. "And, the magistrate is the uncle of the lover, and he is here right now, wanting me to rule on whether he should remove himself from the case because he served in the military at the same time as the accused murderer—a man he apparently holds in high esteem." Nero threw his head back and laughed. "Oh, but wait, there is more. The lover's grandfather is one of my advisors. Ha! What an excellent script. The best writers in Rome could not have written a better drama," he shouted. "This would make an excellent play for my new amphitheater at the Campus Martius." Nero reached for his lyre, strummed a few notes and hummed a few versus of an old Roman ballad. Then, he abruptly stopped and stared at his two confidants.

Lanera burst into applause. "That was lovely, my pet. I want to hear more."

Seneca also burst into applause and elbowed Burrus in the ribs.

"Delightful," Burrus cried, clapping. "Your voice is in excellent condition this morning, Excellency."

Nero smiled and set his lyre down. "Do you really think so, Burrus?"

"But of course, great Caesar." Burrus cleared his throat. "Now, I was thinking, sire, perhaps you should personally handle the case against the merchant. You have ordered the execution of men for having committed crimes much less severe than what he did."

Nero frowned. He looked around and reached into a bowl of figs and threw one at Burrus. "Imbecile! Have you not been listening?" He eyed Seneca with contempt. "Tell him, Seneca. Tell him I cannot interfere in this great play."

"Why, Burrus," Seneca said, feigning shock and surprise. "The people of Rome are speaking of nothing else this morning. If our dear emperor removes the case from the hands of Septimus, what intrigue will be left in the drama?"

"Exactly!" Nero cried. He reclined on the bed and stared at the ceiling through the thin veil that still remained. He reached for his lyre, and stroked it again and hummed along with the notes. "Continue, Seneca. I am listening."

Seneca nervously cleared his throat. "Well, the people of Rome love their emperor and their emperor must not disappoint them. I shall tell Septimus that his Caesar wants him to preside over the case. Next, the masses must be told that it is their emperor's wish that they witness Roman justice under his rule. Burrus and I will write a proclamation to that effect and have it read at the Forum at once."

Nero stopped playing. Tears welled in his eyes, and he kissed Seneca on the lips. "My dear, Seneca, I can always count on you to voice my very thoughts."

Suddenly, Nero threw the covers from the bed and vaulted from the bed. "I do, however, see a problem. I do wish to see this drama played out, but how? How can I, the god of Rome, lower myself to make an appearance at the justice hall? How can I mix with slobs and filthy women and children who will fill the gallery? Slimy senators who resent my popularity with the people will gawk at me and look for some reason to later speak about me behind my back. I cannot bear such a thought." He walked around the room wearing nothing but a crooked crown of grass, which he had hastily placed on his head.

Seneca left the bed and pulled at his chin. "The solution is really quite simple, great Caesar."

Nero paused. "I am listening."

Seneca smiled. "You shall attend in disguise."

"But of course!" Nero cried. "What a brilliant suggestion—which I had to drag out of you, Seneca."

Burrus also left the bed. "Tell us, great one. Will the great emperor disguise himself as a man or as a woman?"

"As a woman? Burrus!" Nero shouted. "At last a brilliant idea from that empty head of yours! I shall dress as a woman, of course."

Lanera clapped her hands. "My pet, I have the perfect dress for you and you can pick from one of my wigs. We shall attend as two friends."

Nero placed his hands on his hips and angrily faced his two guests. "Well? What are you two still doing here? Can I have some privacy? Get out! I have things to do! I have to choose a wig to wear. I have to select a dress and sandals to wear. Out of my chambers!"

Twelve

"Only five men you say?" Lord Gaios asked Tavius. "And you think they are priests?"

"The men we saw wear the robes of a priest," Tavius said. "But, without doubt, it was once a well-fortified palace to a king and his private army. Two or three hundred men could have lived there at one time. There are enough stables to house two hundred horses. Yet, only five assess are in the stables."

Lord Gaios looked past Tavius and studied the fortress. The entire structure was built at the very edge of a very high peak. The tops of the three towers were so tall they vanished into low clouds that hovered over them. As a defense against an attack, it looked difficult to reach indeed, but it could also be a death trap if an attacking army was persistent. Perhaps that is why it was abandoned.

"Where are the gates, how can it be reached?" Lord Gaios asked.

Tavius pointed to his left. "In that direction is a wide path coming out of the mountains that leads straight to the gates. From here we can reach the gates through a very narrow path that snakes around the mountains."

"What you did was discover the back way to get there," Lord Gaios said.

"I realized that once we reached the gates," Tavius said, nodding.

"And priests are now living there," Lord Gaios said. "What you are telling me is that they converted a stronghold into some type of cloister for their worship."

"Exactly, my lord," Tavius said. "They have goats and chickens and other animals. They have vegetable gardens. It looks like they are well-settled."

Lord Gaios turned on his horse. Farrenthias rode with one of his men and Cerudotus with another. The two more seriously wounded men were pulled along on wooden pallets his men had made from tree branches. The pallets were thin but sturdy, and that was good; otherwise, in this terrain they would have come apart by now. All of the men looked tired and hungry, and the wounded needed care and peaceful rest. "Will the pallets carrying the wounded make it though?" he asked.

"Yes," Tavius said. "We go straight. There is a small, wooded area just ahead. Once we get past that, we turn to the left and follow a path into the mountains. As we climb, the path will narrow considerably, but it is manageable."

Lord Gaios motioned with his head. "Let us go, only move slowly. We do not want to further aggravate the injuries of our wounded."

Lord Gaios waited until the last man passed him and then he followed last. He kept an eye on Farrenthias who had said very little since his rescue. Even Cerudotus seemed resigned to the difficult conditions they found themselves in. Both rode silently behind the men who guided their horses. After they emerged from the wooded area, Tavius stopped for a moment. "We now start the climb," he shouted.

At first, the path was wide enough so that two men could ride side by side but soon, as Tavius had warned, the road grew narrow. Soon, the path could only be traversed in single file around tight spiraling turns that ascended drastically around a sheer cliff. It seemed as though they were barely clinging to the mountain. Lord Gaios, worried, looked up ahead. If a man took a misstep to the right, he would plunge to his death into an abyss, the bottom of which was not visible. Fortunately, both Farrenthias and Cerudotus had their heads turned toward the mountain. No doubt they had been told by Tavius not to look down. Of course, Lord Gaios, who had been living for a long time in the Syrian Desert, could not help but to notice how beautiful the scenery was. The sky was dark blue and filled with thick, white clouds. The air was fresh and crisp, and the entire landscape was filled with stunning snow-capped mountains.

As they climbed, it grew colder and the wind picked up. There was no place to stop and rest, but at least the road had not gotten any narrower. They climbed in this manner for what seemed like hours, but, at last, the road opened into a wide-open plateau. They had reached the very top of the mountain.

The right side of the fortress was straight ahead through a sparse tree area. Lord Gaios dismounted and studied the fortress. The three towers were located on three of the four corners of the structure. Each tower was slightly taller than the next and layers of roofs and smaller structures that had many windows connected all three towers. But, what amazed Lord Gaios the most was that the entire structure was carved into the very edge of the cliff with several balconies appearing to hang over the edge. The roof of the highest tower vanished into thick, white clouds, clouds that looked so close, Lord Gaios thought he could touch them with his hands. He stood with one hand holding the reins of his horse and the other resting on the handle of his sword. He did not for a moment doubt Tavius's report; nevertheless, with his experienced eyes he instinctively scrutinized every crevice where a man could hide. He could discern nobody hiding in the shadows.

"It is an architectural wonder," Cerudotus said, suddenly standing next to him. "It must have taken a very brilliant architect to design such a structure and a very clever and persistent army of engineers to have built such a wonder."

"Indeed," Lord Gaios said. "If I did not know any better, I would have guessed that this was the palace of Zeus." His eyes remained fixed on the towers. "The labor must have been difficult and dangerous."

Cerudotus shivered loudly. "It is freezing up here. It is hard to believe that a few days ago we were baking in the Syrian Desert." He inhaled deeply. "Of course, this cold and thin air is good for the lungs and the soul, but not so good for the bones."

"Father! Cerudotus!" Farrenthias cried. "How high are we? I wish Erisa and Clisa could see this." He took Cerudotus by the hand and pulled him along toward the edge of the cliff. "Come, Cerudotus. Let us look around."

"You two be careful," Lord Gaios said.

"Have a look, my lord," one of Lord Gaios's men said.

Lord Gaios squinted. Four men, leading a flock of goats, sheep, and chickens, were heading in their direction. They were dressed in long, white robes with hoods hanging from the back of their necks. The first man was of average height and of a slight build. He walked with a slow deliberate stride with his hands clasped behind his back, as if on a casual stroll. He had long, dark hair and a swarthy complexion. He had a serious and pensive expression. Walking beside him was a much thinner and slightly shorter man. The two were obviously engaged in a deep discussion. The third man was short and heavy, and he suddenly placed a flute to his lips and began to play. His jowls swayed from side to side as he moved his head back and forth to the sweet sound that he produced with his wooden instrument. The fourth man was much older then the others and moved much slower. He carried a bowl of feed for the chickens that surrounded him, and as he sprinkled it to the ground, the chickens scrambled wildly and pecked at the food.

All at once, the four men noticed Lord Gaios and his men walking towards them. The flute player stopped playing and lowered his wooden instrument. The four stared at Lord Gaios, at first, with blank expressions on their faces that quickly turned to looks of concern.

Tavius walked to Lord Gaios. "Those are the men I spoke to you about," he said. "What do you think, my lord?"

"You were correct. They are priests," Lord Gaios said, "and I am afraid that we have frightened them. Let us go and greet them." Lord Gaios raised a hand in salutation and started slowly toward them. Within a few feet of them he stopped. "Greetings," he said. "We mean you no harm. My name is Gaios and these are my men. I am from Athens but reside in Syria."

"Greetings to you, my lord," the man with the long, dark hair said. "My name is Ya'ir." He looked past Lord Gaios. "You are a long way from Syria and it looks like you have wounded."

"It is as you say," Lord Gaios said. "We have wounded, and my men need shelter and food."

"We can offer you both," Ya'ir said. He turned to the oldest priest. "This is Abiel. His experienced and gentle hands are very good at cleaning and dressing wounds." He turned to the man who had walked beside him. "This is Ezri, and our flute playing friend is Adin. Welcome to Clivus."

"I am very grateful to you," Lord Gaios said. "There are many of us, but do not be alarmed. My men are excellent hunters and will hunt these cliffs for wild game. Surely even in this climate, there must be wild game."

"We have plenty of bread, vegetables, and fruits." Ya'ir said. "However, if you wish to eat meat, then indeed your men will have to hunt for game since we do not consume it."

"We also do not consume fish," Ezri added. "But I can show you a stream where you can fish."

Abiel, who had made his way to inspect the wounded, returned. "Your men have serious wounds. I will clean and dress the wounds. If they do not suffer nausea or fever in the next day or two then we can assume that there are no internal injuries and they will recover."

"Excellent," Lord Gaios said. "Will they then be able to travel?"

"No," Abiel said. "The wounds will require at the very least two to three weeks to heal. Traveling before that will risk making matters worse."

"I see," Lord Gaios said, frowning with disappointment.

"Please do not worry about the longer stay," Ya'ir said. "You are welcome here for as long as it takes your men to recover."

"Very well then," Lord Gaios said. "I again thank you for your willingness to help us. Perhaps my men will find some work to do while we wait for my men to recover."

Ya'ir began to protest, but Lord Gaios cut him off by raising a hand. "I would feel much better about our extended stay here if we were of some assistance to you."

Ya'ir bowed his head slightly. "Then it is settled. If you are ready, we shall escort you into Clivus and find accommodations for you and your men."

Lord Gaios summoned Farrenthias and Cerudotus to his side while he walked beside Ya'ir.

"Ya'ir, this is my son and his tutor, Cerudotus," he said.

Ya'ir smiled. "I am very pleased to meet both of you, and I am very impressed. A child who travels with his tutor must be very serious about his studies. Tell me, Farrenthias, do you enjoy your studies?"

"Very much, sire," Farrenthias said, blushing.

"And he is an excellent student," Cerudotus said.

"I think you will both enjoy your stay here at Clivus," Ya'ir said.

"What is this place?" Lord Gaios asked. "At first, we thought it might be a fortress, or a stronghold for an army, or a palace."

"Once, it was all three" Ya'ir said. "It was built by Tigranus, the Great King of Armenia, who died many years ago. Shortly after we discovered this place, a small garrison of men from the current government arrived one day. They questioned us, and when they realized that we were peaceful men, they had a meal with us then left. They never returned. That was five years ago."

"You have not had any other visitors?" Lord Gaios asked.

Ya'ir slowly shook his head. "No, that is why we were quite surprised to see you."

"What is the closest city from here?" Cerudotus asked.

"Tigranocerta, Cerudotus. It is not too far from here, but it can only be reached through heavy forests," Ya'ir said.

The moment he set foot inside the gates of Clivus Lord Gaios was struck by the oddest sensation. Farrenthias, who had taken his hand, squeezed it hard. His eyes were filled with tears, and he could barely speak he seemed so excited.

"Father," he whispered. "This, this place is so beautiful."

Each building, as well as the wall that surrounded the courtyard, was built of solid stone, which showed no erosion. There was a fountain near the center of the courtyard with a statue of a warrior in the middle. The warrior held a round shield in one hand and a sword in the other. Fish encircled the entire fountain at the feet of the warrior, and although apparently designed for water to pour from their mouths, the fountain was dry. A few stone benches were scattered near the buildings beneath a tree or arch.

"Ah, I see that Ezri has shown your men the stables," Ya'ir said. "Excellent."

The men emerged from the stables, and under the supervision of Abiel, they carried the wounded into one of the buildings.

Ya'ir said to Lord Gaios, "If you, Cerudotus and Farrenthias, accompany me, I will take you to meet the man who guides us, Erasmus Harel." He paused. "You have something in common with him. Although his father was Roman, he was raised in Greece by his Greek mother."

Inside the tallest tower, Ya'ir led the way up a wide circular stairway made of uneven stone. Along the left wall, lanterns burned from holes that were placed several steps apart. Farrenthias took a deep whiff. He loved the smell of stone. It smelled crisp and cool. It almost felt as if they were outside in the woods. Besides counting the lanterns, Farrenthias counted the steps. On the fifth floor Ya'ir led them down a narrow hall. He stopped in front of a simple wooden door and knocked. He did not wait for a response. He opened the door and stepped aside to let Lord Gaios and Cerudotus step inside the room first. Cerudotus took Farrenthias by the hand and led him inside.

They were in a small chamber, and from where Farrenthias stood, he could see into the next room. Dim light from various windows allowed him to see the man they had come to meet. He sat at a large desk writing furiously, but the moment he saw Ya'ir, he set his writing instrument down and rose to his feet. "If you will wait here for just a moment," Ya'ir said. "I will explain your presence to Erasmus Harel."

Farrenthias was fascinated with Erasmus Harel. He looked very much like the scholars from the Greek school he and Cerudotus often visited in Antioch, but his hair was a bit lighter and longer than the other men. He was thin and had dark, sparkling eyes. He also moved differently than other men he had met. This man moved with a certain grace and elegance that was lacking in the other scholars back at Antioch.

He walked towards them and held out a hand in greeting.

"Greetings to all of you, my dear friends. Welcome to Clivus." His voice was soft but firm. "I am Erasmus Harel, he said, bowing his head slightly before Lord Gaios. "Ya'ir tells me that you arrived with wounded men and that Abiel is tending to them. I am sorry for your misfortune, but we will do everything possible to make you comfortable while you are here at Clivus."

"I am very grateful for your understanding and assistance," Lord Gaios said. "I hope we will not be much trouble to you while we are here."

"I assure you that your presence is no trouble at all, my lord. On the contrary, I hope that you and your men will be comfortable during your stay here."

Erasmus Harel turned his attention to Farrenthias and Cerudotus and smiled. "A tutor and his pupil." He clasped his hands in front of him and spoke to Cerudotus. "At Clivus you will find many rooms that will provide you with the solitude needed for studying, should you and Farrenthias decide to resume your lessons while you are here."

"We have scrolls and writing instruments should you need them," Ya'ir added.

"I must confess," Cerudotus said. "The thought did occur to me, and Farrenthias has already asked me if we can review some of his lessons. He has a gift for languages. Aside from Greek, he speaks Latin, Hebrew and Aramaic."

Lord Gaios cleared his throat. "I am very proud of these two, but at times I worry that for one so young, Farrenthias is much too serious about his studies. He would rather be discussing numbers with Cerudotus in different languages than playing with children his age."

Erasmus Harel smiled assuredly. "I would not hold that against him, my lord. Such is the conduct of a truly gifted child." He turned to Farrenthias. "So, my child, you like numbers and languages. Numbers hold the key to many mysteries of the universe, and every language unlocks the door to another world."

Erasmus Harel stopped speaking in Greek and spoke to Farrenthias in Latin. "What did you think of the cliffs, Farrenthias? Are they not beautiful?"

"Very beautiful, sire. We do not have mountains like that in Syria. Syria is mostly flat," Farrenthias answered in perfect Latin.

Erasmus then spoke in Hebrew. "Why did you wish to learn Hebrew and Aramaic?"

"Cerudotus thinks that besides Greek and Latin, Hebrew and Aramaic are two important languages in Syria and the Mediterranean."

Erasmus Harel folded his arms and nodded approvingly. His eyes shifted toward Cerudotus. "You are an excellent tutor, Cerudotus. Farrenthias speaks flawlessly in all these languages."

Cerudotus blushed. "I cannot take credit for the gifts our child possesses, for they are considerable. Upon our return I plan to enlist the services of an Egyptian teacher to teach Farrenthias Hieroglyphics."

"Excellent. The language of the Egyptians holds many secrets. All of us here at Clivus have mastered it," Erasmus Harel said. "Perhaps we can start him here, that is, if you and Lord Gaios would allow it."

"I have no objection," Lord Gaios said. "I leave such matters to Cerudotus. However, forgive me for asking but what are you doing out here in the mountains so far away from people? What deity do you worship? What religion do you follow?"

Erasmus Harel smiled benevolently and his eyes sparkled. "We are indeed very far from home."

"Far away from home?" Lord Gaios asked. "Where are you from?"

"We are part of a sect which resides mostly outside of Jerusalem. We worship one God but have chosen a life of seclusion in order to meditate upon divine matters. But we also seek truth and knowledge, and truth and knowledge has been contemplated and written about by brilliant men from all over the world. We pursue and study those works."

"Then you have certainly studied the writings of Aristotle and Plato?" Lord Gaios asked.

"We have," Erasmus Harel said. "But Aristotle and Plato are merely two men. As I say, truths can be found from wise men from all parts of the world and in all cultures. Thus, we have travelled to many places in search of these truths. That is how we happened to find this place. At first, we had contemplated staying just a few months; that was over four years ago."

Cerudotus's eyes widened with excitement. "Have you also visited Egypt?"

Erasmus smiled in amusement. "I have visited Egypt twice, Cerudotus."

"Then you have visited the Great Pyramid?"

Farrenthias looked excitedly at Erasmus Harel. Cerudotus had told him all about the Great Pyramid. He knew that the most brilliant engineers in all of Egypt had designed it and that many hardworking slaves had lost their lives building it. Cerudotus believed that it was the greatest structure on earth, and he dreamed of one day seeing it.

Erasmus Harel nodded. "On both occasions I visited the Great Pyramid. It is a spectacular structure, a wonder to behold."

Lord Gaois cleared his throat again. "Very well then. I think that we have taken enough of your time, Erasmus Harel."

"Oh, but of course," Cerudotus said. "Forgive me."

"On the contrary," Erasmus Harel said. "It is I who has taken too much of your time. You must be tired and hungry. Ya'ir will escort you back to the dining hall. I am certain that Adin has something prepared to eat by now." He turned to Ya'ir. "Perhaps tomorrow, after our guests have rested fully, we shall give them a tour of Clivus so that they will be familiar with it during their stay here."

"An excellent suggestion," Ya'ir said. "I think they will enjoy seeing this beautiful structure."

Thirteen

By the noon hour, the Justice Hall was filled to capacity. Every space where a man could stand was occupied. The galleries were a tight mass of humanity, and the noise was deafening. Men and women argued loudly about the facts of the case, and they speculated about the possible outcome. Seated in a chair in the middle of the hall, Septimus silently and discreetly surveyed the crowd. He sighed cynically. Never had he seen the justice hall so packed with spectators, but that did not surprise him. Romans loved a good drama. Even senators, lawyers, and other dignitaries, who normally hated to mix with the common people, were present. They were dressed in their finest silk and linen togas, befitting their positions, and they sat, of course, in a reserved area.

Fortunately, Nameya, Septimus' beloved concubine, had dressed him for the occasion. Such matters did not concern Septimus in the least, but Nameya would have none of it. She knew that he would be scrutinized closely not just for the words he would utter this morning but, also, for the way he presented himself. He would no doubt be judged on everything from the sandals that he wore to the belt around his waist. Thus, Nameya had chosen a sparkling, white silk toga that had gold embroidery around the hem and sleeves, and she had wrapped a wide golden belt around his thin waist.

Septimus discreetly glanced to his right. Varelia, Nestor, and Laecidia were seated in the front row seats usually reserved for the families of victims. Septimus cringed. As usual, his wife was inappropriately dressed. She wore a tight evening gown with a plunging neckline and excessive sparkling jewels around her neck, fingers, and hair. Her makeup was also excessive and especially heavy around the eyes. She did not look like an aunt in mourning. Instead, her eyes were ablaze. She was obviously seething. Nestor was even less discreet. For a father who had just lost a beloved son, he looked openly hostile rather than aggrieved. Only Laecidia quietly wept.

Finally, from the far end of the hall, a pair of doors flew open with a thunder. A silence rippled though the crowd until the entire room was utterly silent. Those who had seats jumped to their feet to get a better look, and those already standing edged forward, their chins thrust in the direction of the action. A squadron of guards made their way across the floor with Marcellius, hands bound in front of him, walking in the middle of the tight group. The only sound in the room was the echo of marching feet.

Septimus flinched at the sight of Marcellius, who looked exactly as he last remembered him. He even wore his military toga. He looked shaken and pale but his face betrayed no fear. There was only resolve in his stare, and for a fleeting moment Septimus almost wished Marcellius had fled the country. The guards stopped in front of Septimus, and before they walked away from their prisoner, they bowed slightly. The silence in the great hall became almost unbearably thick.

Septimus cleared his throat. "Marcellius, Marcellius Kaelus Augustus," he said, in a deep voice that resonated throughout the hall. "Our emperor, Nero, has authorized me to preside over the case against you. Therefore, let me advise you that you stand accused of murdering a Roman soldier by stabbing him in the back and then of killing two other soldiers when you made your escape. These are capital crimes that could result in your execution." Septimus studied Marcellius's expressionless face while he spoke. He still showed no fear, and yet, his eyes, Septimus was certain, were ablaze with defiance, or perhaps contempt. "As a citizen of Rome, you have the right to plead your case before a judicial tribunal and to representation by a lawyer. However, if you wish to dispose of this matter expeditiously, I am prepared to do that now if you so choose."

"I am an innocent man," Marcellius said, in a surprisingly firm and steady voice, "but how can I defend myself against what will not doubt be perjured testimony. You decide my fate, Septimus. I do not wish to prolong this matter longer than is necessary."

"You question the ability of Rome to offer you a fair trial?"

Marcellius turned and looked intently at Nestor. "I am a man in custody. Yet, rumors have already reached me that my son is in danger. Since when do relatives of Roman officials take matters into their own hands? Is that the Roman justice you refer to?"

The audience erupted into gasps, hisses, boos, and even some cheers. Septimus felt the blood rush to his cheeks. His head snapped sideways, and he glared at Nestor, who had jumped to his feet and was being restrained by Varelia and Laecidia. "Murderer!" Nestor shouted. "Filthy murderer."

Septimus seethed with anger. Much as he had pleaded with him, Nestor had disobeyed him and, worse, his sloppy plotting was now out in the open. Ignoring Nestor's outburst, Septimus said, "You are in no position to be making accusations, Marcellius. Three soldiers are dead, killed by your hand, and you had a motive, a motive driven by your domestic problems."

"The soldiers were drunk, too drunk to know what was happening. They attacked me," Marcellius said, his voice forceful but still calm, "and one of those drunks murdered my wife while I held her in my arms."

"You provoked the entire matter," Septimus said, pointing a finger at Marcellius. "I would say that makes you guilty of having caused her death as well. Now, what have you to say about the sword you plunged into Halius's back?"

"I cannot explain what happened to him, but I will tell you this. I am no coward. I have never ever struck a man from behind."

"I have written statements by witnesses who say otherwise," Septimus said.

"They are lying," Marcellius said, raising his voice in anger.

"Do you deny that you went into a rage when you discovered your wife in the arms of Halius?"

"What man would not?" Marcellius said. "But I did not kill the young man. I flung him away from my wife."

"We have sworn witness statements that say otherwise."

"They lie, but, again, you decide my fate, Septimus."

The grand hall erupted again with loud whispers of men and women who pondered Marcellius's testimony. Septimus leaned back in his chair and stared at Marcellius. He had spoken well in his own defense. He too agreed that a man of his integrity and skill would never strike a man from behind, but given the circumstances of last night, any man's judgment might falter. Septimus sighed. "What should I do with you, Marcellius, put you to death? Send you into exile and strip you of everything you own? Should I send you abroad to hard labor in one of our silver mines, or perhaps deliver you to one of our gladiator schools?"

Septimus rose to his feet. His decision was not going to be a popular one, but judicial decrees rarely ever were. "Taking notice of the circumstances and of your excellent military record, you shall be exiled to an undisclosed location for a period no less than ten years. You shall remain in custody until the appropriate arrangements are made for the carrying out of your sentence."

The crowd erupted into an uproar. There was no reaction from Marcellius, although his eyes remained fixed on Septimus, and they were cold and hard.

Nestor jumped to his feet and cursed Septimus, and, again, Varelia and Laecidia had to restrain him. Septimus frowned angrily. Marcellius had probably heard correctly. In spite of the warning he had given him, Nestor was no doubt meddling in the affairs of the state. He would have another word with him, but it would do no good. Nestor would stop at nothing to avenge the death of Halius, and there was only so much Septimus could do to prevent it. Septimus waved to the guards, and they escorted Marcellius out of the room amidst an uproar.

Fourteen

"Damn it!" Belfore murmured under his breath. Night was almost upon them, and he and his companions were barely leaving Rome. He had promised Nestor that by sundown the son of Marcellius would be dead. He slowed his horse and jerked around to look back. Delerin and Bentore had fallen far behind again and Bentore was the reason. He was drunk. Bentore was always slowing them down and Nestor detested him. But, Delerin loved his simpleminded brother, and Delerin was an excellent man with the sword and dagger. Belfore needed him. He slowed down. "Hurry! You two pieces of swine. The house of the merchant is just ahead," he shouted. "We got less than an hour of daylight left."

Bentore laughed. "So we kill the little bastard in the darkness. What is the difference?" He belched. "Then it is back to Rome to collect the rest of our pay. I want to get back to that tavern. Did you see the wench I had in my arms?"

"Fool. She made a mule's ass out of you," Delerin shouted at his brother. "She took every last silver denarii from your purse. And you can forget her. Her grimy hands are probably all over another poor bastard's purse this very moment." He pulled closer to Bentore and kicked his horse. "Belfore is right you drunken fool. If we had left that tavern when I wanted to, we would be back in Rome by now."

"There!" Belfore shouted pointing to a distant clump of trees. "That has got to be it. That has to be the merchant's villa." He dug his heels in, and his horse lurched forward into a full gallop again. "Stay with me, I expect that we will have to wrestle a guard or two to the ground when we get there."

Belfore eased his horse to a halt and spit on the ground. There had been no guards at the gates and the enormous house was utterly still and dark. Even its white walls and columns were dark. Yellow and light-green leaves were scattered about the porch. Belfore jumped from his horse. "Curses! I knew it. We are too late! The place is empty."

"What now?" Delerin asked.

Belfore glared at him. "We look around. We still have some light. Let us hope we find some tracks."

Bentore, who had dipped his face into the pool, dried his face with the sleeve of his brown, dirty tunic. "I say we loot the place and look for the child tomorrow."

"Imbecile!" Belfore yelled. "Nestor warned me that this was a palace, and he warned me that if we did not find the child, we had better not be distracted by greed. We kill the son of Marcellius first and then we return to ransack the place."

"But the house is empty," Bentore said. "Who would notice if a few pieces of gold are missing?"

"Shut up," Delerin said. "I am with Belfore. We have no time right now."

"Come on," Belfore said. "Let us look around for tracks."

With Gianina tucked beneath one of her trembling arms, Felicia stood paralyzed at one of the upstairs windows of the house. The three strange men looked dangerous, frightening. One of them was dark, and although large and robust, he took quick steps while he pointed at the ground and at the house. The second man stood beside him also looking down. He had a deep scar running down the left side of his face. The third man was heavy and disheveled, and he walked with a stagger. Felicia held her breath. Marcellius had warned her that men might come looking around, but why? Why had she not listened to him and left with the others? At the very least she should not have so abruptly dismissed the guards.

"Who are they, Mother?" Gianina whispered.

"Quiet, my little one."

The large man suddenly raised his voice. "Bah, this is a minor setback. Soon enough the son of the merchant shall be dead. Come to the back!"

Felicia gasped and Gianina wilted in her arms. Felicia took her daughter into her arms and raced to one of the back windows. The men were gathered around the burly man, who was on his knees prying the ground.

Gianina awakened with a scream, but Felicia had anticipated it. She immediately covered her mouth and muffled it.

"Mother," Gianina cried, pulling her mother's hand away. "Do those men want to hurt Trulius?"

"Do not worry, my little one," Felicia said, brushing the tears from her daughter's face with the back of her hand. "Kemnebi will never let anything happen to Trulius. I promise."

"Then what is happening Mother? Why is the house empty? Where is Trulius? Where are Lady Servia and Lord Marcellius? I want to see them."

"Silent, my child, I shall explain everything to you later."

Belfore wiped his muddy hands on his tunic. That damned merchant was not going to fool him. "Two horses," he said. "And someone tried to cover these tracks." He looked in the direction of the wooded hill to where the tracks led. "They went that way."

"So," Delerin said. "Marcellius sent his son away."

"Why take the back hills?" Bentore asked, "why not the Via Appia to Capua. It is faster."

"Idiot," Delerin said. "They are on the run. A child cannot ride fast."

Belfore got to his feet and stretched his thick legs. He glared at Delerin with seething eyes. "Nestor mentioned an Egyptian who lives with Marcellius. Kemnebi. That Egyptian bastard must have taken the boy."

"To where?" Bentore said. "Where are they going?"

"They are traveling south," Delerin said, staring at the hill. "Puteoli is in that direction. You will not find any stone *miliaria*, milestones, in those trees, telling how many leagues to Puteoli. I say at least three days ride, but first they must pass through Capua."

"Puteoli?" Belfore shouted. "Why Puteoli?"

Delerin tightened his jaw and slowly nodded. "It makes sense. Capua is a rat hole. No one can hide there, but Puteoli is a port city. He must be planning to take the child out of the country by sea."

"What?" Belfore cried, making a tight fist and waving it in front of his face. "Never!"

"Then why did they not travel through Ostia?" Bentore said. "It is closer."

"Ostia is in the wrong direction," Delerin said, shaking his head. "No, Kemnebi is going to take a ship at Puteoli and head east."

"Brundisium is also in that direction. Could they be going there?" Bentore said.

"Perhaps," Delerin answered, pensively. "But if he passes through Capua, my guess is that Kemnebi is headed for Puteoli."

Belfore gripped the handle of his sword. "If Kemnebi gets on a ship we are finished, and how will that look to Anicetus if we fail? It is he who sent Nestor to us. We will have made a fool of him and us."

"We must be more cunning than this Kemnebi," Delerin said, scratching the thick scar on his face. "I will take the main road, the Via Appia to Puteoli. You two track him through the woods. If they are going to Puteoli I should arrive ahead of them. If they stop at Capua you will overtake them there."

Belfore mounted his horse. "Agreed. We meet at Puteoli in a few days." He pulled his horse around. "Come on, Bentore, that slimy Egyptian is not going to make pigs' asses out of us. Let us overtake him and be done with this."

Fifteen

At dawn one morning, a few days after his arrival at Clivus, Farrenthias realized that he had never been happier in his life. He shoved to one side the pile of blankets that had kept him warm throughout the night and got out of bed. He threw a blanket across his shoulders and dragged a stool to the small window in his room and jumped on top of the stool. He had quickly discovered that nothing was as beautiful as watching the sunrise across the towering cliffs that surrounded Clivus. He removed the thick cloth that covered the window and inhaled deeply. A rush of cold air burned through his nose and lungs, but he loved the feeling and the smell of the breeze. In the distance, behind towering cliffs whose jagged peaks were white with snow, a dim red, orange and yellow sunrise cast its meager light across cliffs and dark green valleys that stretched in all directions for as far as he could see. Farrenthias stretched and hung his head out of the square window and looked down. The shear drop from his room was so terrifying it made him dizzy, but he also loved the idea of being so high in the sky. Clivus was so high, in fact, that thick clouds often surrounded the cliffs and prevented him from seeing all the way down.

Farrenthias inhaled again and then lowered his chin into his arms. Yes, he had never been so happy in his life. He especially loved the men of Clivus. They were fascinating men who were extremely knowledgeable about everything from the farthest point in the sky to the habits of the smallest insects that crawled on the ground. Farrenthias had never met men like these before. Even Cerudotus agreed that he had never been in the company of men who were so intelligent and yet lived such a simple and modest existence. Cerudotus had remarked that these men were probably going to spend the rest of their lives studying and writing scrolls at Clivus.

Every night right after supper the men would disappear into a room that they entered through a sunken door behind one of the towers. They would remain inside that room until very late and Farrenthias would not see them again until the next morning. This routine became so familiar to Farrenthias that the first few nights at Clivus, while he studied his own lessons, he instinctively paused to look out of a window that overlooked the courtyard, and he watched the men march across the courtyard and vanish into their tower to work.

Of course, there was also Clivus itself. It had taken Adin days to give him and Cerudotus a complete tour of this marvel in the sky. Each tower was filled with stairways that opened into narrow hallways, some straight and some that curved around many doors that led into rooms of all shapes and sizes. No two towers were alike, and there were many passages that could be explored only with the use of torches and lamps, even in the daylight. Adin had also shown them his gardens, where he planted wild vegetables, and a small fenced pen, where he kept his goats and pigs and chickens.

There was the slightest knock at the door, and then the door opened. Cerudotus walked in, carrying a wooden bowl of water.

"Ah, I knew that I would find you awake, and once again hanging out that window," Cerudotus said. "You love Clivus do you not my irrepressible little scholar?"

Farrenthias jumped from the stool and hurriedly changed into his long toga. "Very much, Cerudotus. I have never seen anything like this place before."

Cerudotus set the bowl of water down on a small table and shivered. "Well, it is rather unique and spectacular, but you are going to get sick if you keep hanging your head out of that window. Fortunately, I warmed the water for you, now lets get clean."

Farrenthias dipped his hands into the bowl and rinsed his face. The water was indeed warm and soothing.

"Do not forget to wash behind your ears," Cerudotus said, walking to the window. "What a magnificent view. I can see why you enjoy hanging out this window so much."

"Cerudotus," Farrenthias said. "What god do you think Erasmus Harel and the others worship?"

Cerudotus placed a hand on the windowsill and frowned. "Ah, your mind is working very early this morning, my child. I approve. The early morning is a very good time for man to contemplate life. Now, let me think. It appears that Erasmus Harel and the others worship the one Hebrew God. But they are also scholars, and true scholars have an unquenchable thirst for knowledge."

"Is that what Erasmus Harel meant when he said that they pursue truths?"

Cerudotus nodded. "Exactly." Cerudotus thought a moment and then said, "Of course, the pursuit of truths can sometimes lead a man to a spiritual quest."

"What is a truth, anyway, Cerudotus?"

Cerudotus turned to face Farrenthias with a wry smile on his face. "Ah! I have always known that you are too mature and perceptive for your age, my child. You ask questions many adults do not even contemplate." He folded his arms and leaned against the window. "It is like this, my dear Farrenthias. There are certain principles that govern the world, principles that man has no control over. For example, the sun rises in the morning and sets at night. Consequently, we have night and day. It rains, it shines, it is cold, it is warm, and man has no authority over such matters because they are set in nature. On the other hand, questions such as why did our world and the stars come into existence in the first place? What is the purpose of life? Exactly what conclusions man reaches when attempting to answer these questions he sometimes defines as truths."

Cerudotus turned slightly and stared out the window again, as if drawing inspiration from the natural beauty that surrounded them. "Unfortunately, man is influenced by a variety of beliefs, Farrenthias, such as cultural beliefs and spiritual beliefs. Those beliefs can sometimes distort man's perception of the world and, therefore, his perception of the truth. Therefore, what one man may perceive as a truth another will define as a folly."

Farrenthias frowned. "In Antioch, we met many people who worshipped different gods."

"Exactly, which is why they each possess their own ideas about what a truth is, and we must learn to respect their beliefs even though they may be wrong." Cerudotus walked to Farrenthias and placed a gentle hand on his shoulder. "It is good that at your young age you are contemplating such matters. That is a part of your learning, but do not let such queries trouble you. In truth, such matters are quite complicated. There will be time enough for you to better understand such passions." Cerudotus pointed to a washcloth. "Now bring me that washcloth."

Cerudotus lifted Farrenthias's chin and inspected first the left side of his face and ear and then the right. He then brushed back a few strands of hair away from his forehead with the towel. Farrenthias was used to this type of inspection. Cerudotus always told him that Greek scholars had to be presentable at all times.

"Good," Cerudotus said, handing him back the washcloth. "You are now ready to face another day at Clivus."

Cerudotus paused at the door. "It is still very early. We have time to stroll across the courtyard before breakfast. How does that sound?"

Farrenthias rushed to his side. "I would like that very much, Cerudotus."

The morning was cold and the air fresh and crisp and Farrenthias could not be happier. He and Cerudotus walked to one edge of the courtyard that overlooked a deep and extended valley that seemed to vanish into the horizon. As usual, the highest mountain peaks disappeared into scattered clouds. A few jagged peaks, covered in snow, protruded out of the clouds.

Cerudotus sighed heavily. "What a magnificent sight," he whispered. "What do you think my dear, Farrenthias? Have you ever seen such beauty?" When Farrenthias failed to answer him, the thin tutor turned to him and smiled. Farrenthias was so deep in thought that he was almost in a trance. His bright eyes were locked on the beauty that lay before them. Then suddenly, Farrenthias drew his breath and exhaled slowly and watched the little clouds form and then dissipate before his eyes.

Cerudotus cleared his throat and Farrenthias blinked and looked at him. "Cerudotus," he said, "I have never seen such beautiful mountains and valleys and forests. How is such beauty possible?"

Cerudotus laughed and pressed Farrenthias's thin shoulder. "It pleases me to see you enjoy nature like this, Farrenthias. It is good to appreciate such natural beauty and try to understand it."

Cerudotus's attention was drawn to the sound of someone approaching. Erasmus Harel and Ya'ir were slowing walking toward them. They were deep in conversation. They walked with their heads bowed and their hands clasped behind them. Each took turns nodding slowly while the other spoke. They seemed completely oblivious of the world that surrounded them. Cerudotus smiled. With each new day at Clivus, he came to admire all these men more and more. They were, without a doubt, the most brilliant men he had ever encountered. It seemed as if between these two men and the others, they had every academic subject mastered. They also had interesting practices. They practiced fasting and ate frugally and often breakfasted in total silence.

Erasmus Harel suddenly noticed Cerudotus and Farrenthias. "Good morning, dear friends," he said. "I see that you have chosen an excellent location from where you can enjoy this glorious morning."

"The view is truly spectacular," Cerudotus said.

"The morning is my favorite part of the day," Erasmus Harel said. "If you listen and watch carefully you will hear and see the day begin to unravel before your very eyes."

"Farrenthias and I are astounded at how beautiful it is up here," Cerudotus said.

"Ya'ir and I are headed for our study chamber," Erasmus Harel said. "Perhaps you and Farrenthias would like to accompany us. We have a few moments before Adin serves breakfast."

"Ah," Cerudotus murmured. "Farrenthias and I would be most honored to accompany you."

"Excellent," Erasmus Harel said. He placed an arm around the shoulder of Farrenthias as they walked. "What you will see in our study are scrolls that we have gathered from India, Tibet, Persia, Greece, Egypt and, of course, from ancient Hebrew tribes."

"We bargained for them, and in some cases, bartered for them with our own works," Ya'ir added.

"A library!" Cerudotus cried. "You are putting together a library of knowledge."

Ya'ir smiled. "The scrolls have been written by scribes, teachers, and masters."

"You have travelled to all those places?" Cerudotus asked.

"We have," Erasmus Harel said, "And because the scrolls are written in the language native to the country from where we gathered them, in the evenings, we transcribe them into Greek if we are able, and we ponder their meaning."

"But there are many scrolls that we do not understand because we are not familiar with all dialects," Ya'ir added.

Behind one of the towers they stepped down into a sunken stairway and entered the building. At the end of a short hall, Cerudotus and Farrenthias followed Erasmus Harel and Ya'ir into a room nearly the size of the room where they took their meals. Two long, wooden tables stood in the middle of the spacious room that had no windows and whose walls were made of solid rock. On top of one of the tables was a pile of scrolls, and against one wall were two short, wooden shelves that were filled with stacks of neatly rolled scrolls.

Erasmus Harel pointed to the shelves. "These scrolls speak about everything from the creation of the world to life after death, and of the men and women who have studied those mysteries."

"It is our hope," Ya'ir said, "that one day man will read what is in this room and learn from its wisdom."

Nodding slowly, Cerudotus affectionately placed a hand on the shoulder of Farrenthias, encouraging him to look around. "I am extremely impressed," he said. "I can only imagine what knowledge is hidden in these scrolls."

"As our guests," Erasmus Harel said, "This room is open to the two of you. You are welcome here anytime."

Farrenthias, who had stepped away from Cerudotus, stood in front of one of the shelves and sighed out loud. "Sire, " he said looking at Erasmus Harel, "teach me how to read these scrolls. I want to learn what they speak about."

Cerudotus frowned. "Farrenthias," he said, "With the little time that we have left here at Clivus, I am not certain how much you will be able to read."

Erasmus Harel smiled wryly and drew a scroll from the shelf and handed it to Farrenthias. "Have we not established that our young scholar has a gift for languages? It would take him no time to master at least Hieroglyphics." He glanced at Cerudotus. "You are also welcomed to accompany us to our work session tonight."

"Tonight," Ya'ir said. "We are going to review a set of scrolls from Egypt."

Farrenthias could hardly contain himself. "May we come back tonight, Cerudotus?"

Cerudotus had never seen such excitement in the eyes of Farrenthias, had never seen his face glow with so much joy, and for a strange moment, he almost did not recognize his dear pupil. "Yes we can come back, but as I have already said, Farrenthias, we will not be here at Clivus very long. Do not set your heart at reading many of these scrolls."

Sixteen

The merchant Canario stood at the top of the stairs leading down into Rome's Mamertine Prison and gagged from the terrible stench. The prison was just beneath sewers, and even though he was not a man with a weak stomach, the stench nearly made him sick. Nevertheless, he reminded himself that he was on an important mission and that this venture into the hell of Rome was not about him. He was robust and heavy but he could be agile and quick when the need arose. Thus, without giving it another thought he held his breath and hastily set out down the narrow steps.

The first guard that Canario encountered stepped in front of him and raised his torch. Without speaking a word, Canario handed him the document that he had obtained from the office of Septimus. It authorized him to enter the prison. The guard saw the seal of Septimus and looked at Canario. "You carrying any weapons?"

"No weapons," Canario said.

"You are also not allowed to bring anything to the prisoners. I shall have to search you."

"Ah, well," Canario said. "I am in a hurry and well…" He produced a small bag of coins. "This is yours if I can just hurry through."

The guard took the bag, squeezed it in his hand and then smiled. "Very well, the man you are here to see is at the very end of this corridor. Take no turns, just keep going straight and when you get to the end, show this document to the guard."

There was another guard halfway down the dark corridor but he barely glanced at Canario.

At last, Canario reached the end. There was a heavy iron door and seated next to it was a guard. He got to his feet when he saw Canario.

"I have a sealed order from Septimus," Canario said. The man merely glanced at the scroll and then unbolted the heavy iron door and dragged it open. A powerful stench buckled Canario's knees. He coughed and lifted a piece of his garment to cover his mouth and nose.

The guard chuckled without humor. "You will get used to it." He held a torch high. "Stay close to me."

Canario followed him down narrow steps that spiraled steeply to the left and disappeared into darkness. When they reached the bottom they entered a chamber through another bolted door. The stench was worse. The long hall was humid, and it smelled of sweat mixed with other repulsive bodily odors. The snoring from the cells that lined both sides of the room was loud; other men cried softly from either tormenting dreams or from beatings they might have received earlier in the day. When they reached another door, they encountered a guard, fast asleep on a chair that was propped against a rock wall. The man who accompanied Canario kicked the chair, and the guard flew to his feet. The keys that hung from his belt on a chain rattled.

"Scared me to death damn you," he said, rubbing his eyes. "Got another one for me?"

"Nah, he is here to see the prisoner."

The guard yawned. "I thought he was not allowed visitors."

"He has an order from Septimus."

"Come then," the guard said, glaring at Canario. He unlocked the door with a long key and dragged it open. The door screeched loudly. It led into a short corridor at the end of which was another door. The wooden door had a very small window with flat iron bars.

The guard took a torch from the wall and handed it to Canario. He inserted another key and opened the door. "Go on," he said. "Call out to me when you are ready to go."

Canario held the torch in front of him and stepped into a large cell that was divided into three small sections by several wide pillars. "Marcellius," he whispered. "Where are you?"

Canario took another step, but a thin strong arm collared him from behind.

"Canario?" Marcellius released him and swung him around. "Canario, you devil. It really is you!"

Canario raised the torch. Marcellius was pale and gaunt and his hair long, but otherwise he looked well. "Marcellius, my friend." He leaned the torch against a wall and threw his arms around his old friend. "I thank the gods of this wicked world that you are well. You smell like swine and you are a bit thin, but you look well."

Marcellius laughed. "How did you ever manage to get into this wretched place?"

"Bah! Nothing was going to keep me from seeing my old friend. It was not easy. You have become somewhat of an infamous celebrity, but here I am."

Marcellius stepped back. "You have risked your life coming to see me. Nestor has many spies."

"Bah! What is life if a man is not willing to gamble it for a true friend." He eyed the door, and then opened his cloak and pulled out a satchel. "And what kind of a friend would I be if I did not come bearing gifts?"

Marcellius laughed again. "Your spirit is irrepressible, Canario." He led him to a stone bench built against one corner of the cell.

Canario fumbled through the satchel. "Let us see, I brought fruit, a slab of cheese, fresh bread, and this my good friend." He lifted a pouch made of goat's skin to his lips and kissed it.

Marcellius stared at the animal skin and moistened his lips. "You are amazing, Canario."

Canario unsealed the pouch and handed it to Marcellius. "It is the finest wine in Italy. Not even Nero himself serves this at his table."

Marcellius nodded and smiled. "I believe you." He sipped the wine and smacked his lips. "I thought I would never savor the taste of such fine wine again." He took a full drink, but this time the smile vanished from his face. He leaned closer to Canario. "What news do you bring me, old friend? Have you heard anything?"

"I knew you would ask, but I warn you, you will not like what I have to tell you."

Marcellius's eyes hardened. "Speak, Canario, and hold nothing back."

Canario nibbled nervously on a piece of bread. "I have nothing but terrible news. Nero's men emptied your house and auctioned it off. A Greek investor bought it, but so far he has not taken possession of it. Also, the emperor confiscated the assets from every warehouse that you own. He is a pervert and a thief." Canario pressed a hand on Marcellius's arm. "But, our dear and trusted accountant Farron assures me that you are not completely destitute. He did not give me details. He only told me to tell you that your dear and loyal Felicia is smarter than any man alive. In any case, Felicia and Gianina are fine. They are terribly worried about you, but they are fine."

Marcellius nodded silently. "I knew those vultures would fight over my assets. I do not care about that. I care only about Felicia and Gianina. Please look after them."

"Of course, but you and I both know that when threatened Felicia can be as conniving as a serpent. At times, even Farron does not know what she is up to. I would not like to cross her when it comes to protecting her own. She can run circles around any man."

"I agree with you," Marcellius said. "I agree with you completely. I am very fortunate to have her." He clutched Canario by the arm. "What else, Canario? I know you have more to convey to me. I can see it in your eyes. What is it?"

Canario sighed heavily. "And now the worst news, my friend." He nervously brushed his chin. "Nestor sent three assassins after Trulius. A certain Belfore and two brothers."

Marcellius angrily sprung to his feet. "I knew it! Damned Nestor. I knew he would do something like that!"

"Do not despair, my friend. Belfore and the two brothers have not been heard from, and the word is that they were…" Canario abruptly fell silent.

"Go on, Canario. Were those bastards to kill my son and return with some sort of proof in order to collect their payment?"

Canario slowly shook his head. "As I say, they have not been heard from." He nervously bit into the piece of bread. "Forgive me, Marcellius, but as you very well know, Romans make sport of everything. The bets are that Belfore and his two brothers took Nestor's money and made an ass out of him. Others have bet that you sent

Trulius into hiding with Kemnebi and that Kemnebi is too cunning for those assassins."

Marcellius sat back down and leaned forward, placing his elbows on his knees. "I do not know what to think. I know only that Nestor will stop at nothing to get his revenge."

Canario nodded. "I am afraid that you are correct about that. And you know of course that the witnesses who declared against you were either threatened or bribed by him." He stood to leave. "There is one final matter. My spies tell me that before the week is out you will be taken out of here in the middle of the night to board a ship. You will be shipped to Malta."

"Malta?" Marcellius cried. He sprung to his feet again and began to pace. "Malta," he repeated.

Canario struggled to his feet. "Do not despair, Marcellius. Farron and I are already working to make things bearable for you when you arrive there. As you well know, guards are not paid well, and it should not come as a surprise to you that you are well-known and still held in high regard by many people, people who believe you were guilty of nothing but defending your honor."

Marcellius stopped pacing and regarded Canario with a humbling expression. "I am indebted to you and Farron for all that you have done for me," he said.

"Nonsense," Canario said. "It is I who am forever indebted to you, great Marcellius. Did you not open your money coffers to me when I made foolish investments and was at the brink of losing everything? Did you not come to my defense more than once when robbers held a dagger to my throat?"

"Bah," Marcellius murmured. "That was nothing. Now, please be careful. Nestor has many spies and people talk. By tomorrow news of your visit will be known throughout the Forum."

"I am not easily frightened," Canario said. "I will even visit you in Malta."

"No, Canario," Marcellius said. "It would be too much of a risk."

"We shall see. I am a sentimental fool. I hate to see you shipped to Malta, but it has to be better than this rat hole."

Marcellius smiled and slapped his friend on the back. "I will be fine."

Canario adjusted his cloak and banged on the door. A key rattled the lock and Canario placed a hand on Marcellius. "Take care of yourself, dear friend."

Marcellius stood at the small window and watched the guard and Canario disappear down the small corridor. He closed his eyes and sighed wearily. He wondered what Trulius and Kemnebi might be doing this very moment. And then, the face of Servia came to him so vividly that he slid to the floor and leaned against the door. He recalled with great detail the last time he and his family had all been together. They had taken a ride into the woods early one morning. He and Servia had spread out a blanket on some soft grass and he had rested his head across her lap. Trulius and Gianina had run off and were chasing each other. Suddenly, Gianina had screamed.

"Trulius!" she cried. "You are frightening me. Come down from there before you fall and hurt yourself."

Servia screamed when she saw Trulius hanging upside down from a tree branch. "Marcellius!" she cried. "Trulius will hurt himself. Please tell him to come down!"

Marcellius chuckled. "Come down from there, Trulius. You are frightening the women."

Trulius laughed and released his legs. Servia and Gianina screamed. Trulius somersaulted in the air and landed on his feet next to Gianina.

"Marcellius did you see that?" Servia cried. "He could have hurt himself."

"He has done that many times," Marcellius said, lying down on the blanket again. "That was nothing compared to what I have seen him do." He laughed. "Our son knows no bounds."

Marcellius blinked and he was back in his dark dreary cell. He sipped despondently from the wine that Canario had brought him. The sweet hot taste burned his mouth and throat. He sipped again, but this time, he took a long deep swig. He continued to drink until his head and eyelids felt heavy. He stretched across the cold hard cement floor. Maybe tonight sleep would not elude him as it often did these days. As he dozed in and out of sleep his mind swirled with thoughts of the miserable rat Nestor and what he had set out to do. But Marcellius had faith in Kemnebi. No matter how conniving the men Nestor had sent after Trulius were, they were no match for Kemnebi. Still, Marcellius agonized, for of one thing he was certain. From this moment forward there could be no peace in his heart ever again, that is, not until the day he would once again hold Trulius safely in his arms.

Seventeen

E rasmus Harel raised a torch to the statue and studied it with great interest and curiosity. The statue was of a soldier, a warrior, and it was the size of a normal man. The warrior wore a short toga and held a small round shield in its right hand and a short sword in its left hand. Between its elbow and torso was a helmet with a full-face shield. A look of defiance was depicted on the statue's face.

"Not only have I never seen this statue," he said, "I did not even know this room existed." He studied the obscure room that was hidden behind a spiraling stairwell. Except for the statue, it was empty and the ceiling was rather low. "How did your men ever find this room, Lord Gaios," Erasmus Harel asked.

"I am not surprised that they did," Lord Gaios said. "My men are fascinated with Clivus. I think they have explored every corner of this place."

Erasmus Harel turned to Ya'ir and Ezri. "Were either of you aware of this room?"

Ya'ir ran a hand along the shoulder of the statue. "I was not, and although we hardly ever enter this tower, I have been in here on more than one occasion. The last time I was in here Ezri accompanied me."

"Indeed," Ezri said. "And we did not even see the door leading into this room."

"It is apparent," Lord Gaios said, "that this room was to be hidden."

"I would say," Erasmus Harel said, returning his attention to the statue, "that this is the face of a Roman, and these powerful arms and legs are the features of a Roman gladiator. What do you think, Lord Gaios?"

"You are very perceptive," Lord Gaios said. "I concluded the same thing. But it is curious, did you not tell us that Tigranus the Great built this fortress?"

"That is what we were told," Erasmus Harel said.

"Hum," Lord Gaios murmured. "Perhaps this statue was built to honor the Romans, but there is something else I want you to look at." He motioned to the wall behind the statue with a nod. "Have a look behind the statue."

Erasmus Harel edged around the monument he raised his torch to have a look. A hole, perfectly round and large enough so that a man could crawl into it, was built into the wall. "Is there something behind this wall?"

"That hole is the entrance to a passageway, that leads into lower tunnels," Lord Gaios said.

"Tunnels?" Ya'ir said. "But how is that possible? We are on a cliff that is made of solid rock. The section we are in is already several feet below ground level. We have to be surrounded by solid rock."

"You are quite correct," Lord Gaios said, pensively. "No tools could have dug what we found inside. This hole is man-made, but what we found inside is a natural crevice in the earth. At the end of the passageway there is a ladder, made of rope, dangling down to a lower chamber that leads to other tunnels."

"And what did you find down there?" Erasmus Harel asked.

"We did not go down," Lord Gaios said. "We needed to replenish our torches and I thought I might give you an opportunity to join us."

"Of course," Erasmus Harel said. "Hum, this is most curious."

Lord Gaios motioned to Tavius. "We are right behind you," he said.

Tavius entered the hole followed by Erasmus Harel, Ya'ir, Ezri and then Lord Gaios.

Moving in a crouched position and in single file they quickly reached the edge of the passageway and the ladder that Lord Gaios had described.

Lord Gaios lifted his torch. "Behold this natural wonder," he said. The chamber below was enormous, but as Lord Gaios stood admiring the cavernous room, he noticed something he had not noticed earlier. From somewhere below there was the faint but unmistakable sound of trickling water.

"Do you hear that, my lord?" Tavius asked.

"Water," Lord Gaios said.

"It is amazing," Erasmus Harel said. "What are we about to discover down there, my lord?"

"Whatever it is, we are not the first," Lord Gaios said. "Someone placed this ladder here and used it to get down there."

"I shall go first," Tavius said. He handed his torch to Lord Gaios and swung around onto the ladder. Taking back the torch, he started down. The ladder wobbled but his feet felt secure. It was much further down than he realized. When he reached the bottom, he lowered the torch. Rodents and insects scattered away from the light. Tavius leaned the torch against the wall and took hold of the ladder.

"I shall hold it steady, my lord, while all of you come down," he said.

The chamber was much larger than it looked from above and much colder. The walls were made of solid rock with pointed edges protruding out of the wall. Lord Gaios walked slowly around a series of large boulders and quickly realized that they were on a man-made path. He followed it to the entrance of a tunnel and discovered that the sound of trickling water was coming from somewhere within this tunnel."

"What do you think, my lord?" Tavius asked raising his torch to the entrance. "Shall we go in?"

Lord Gaios nodded. "We are right behind you, Tavius."

Crouched low, Lord Gaios and the others followed Tavius slowly into the passageway, which resembled one of the corridors of Clivus. In some sections the ceiling was very low but passable, and it was cold and dark. Lord Gaios was about to suggest that they turn around, when they suddenly reached a small chamber from which they were all able to gather.

"This is it?" Tavius whispered. "A dead end?"

"Water," Lord Gaios said. He pointed to the far wall of the small chamber. "I hear water coming from the other side of that wall. He walked to the wall and raised his torch. "This wall is not solid rock," he said. He placed a hand on it. "It is man made."

Tavius leaned into the wall and placed his ear against it. "You are correct, my lord," he murmured. "I hear running water on the other side."

Lord Gaios unsheathed his dagger and dropped to one knee. He began to dig into the right lower corner of the wall.

Tavius unsheathed his own dagger and helped Lord Gaios dig. Before long, they had dug a small hole through the wall.

Tavius took a whiff of the air and coughed. "Whew! What a ghastly smell," he said.

Lord Gaios also coughed. "I have smelled this before. It is the smell of death."

"I can smell it from here," Erasmus Harel said. "Are there dead animals in there?"

Lord Gaios looked briefly at him and then looked with dread at the hole. "I am afraid we might have uncovered a tomb, but not of dead animals." He moved Tavius out of the way and kicked at the hole with the sole of his thick-leathered heel. A section collapsed forward, making a hole the size of a round shield.

Lord Gaios covered his mouth with the collar of his shirt and slipped the upper part of his body inside the hole and raised his torch. The chamber was small and in the right corner was a pile of scattered skeletons. To his left, two more skeletons, partially wrapped in torn clothing, dangled from a wall. There was faded scribbling and carvings on all the chamber walls. Lord Gaios squinted. The bottom section of the far wall looked moist. Lord Gaios pulled back. "As I feared, we have uncovered a tomb," he said.

He studied the low ceiling and sides of the tunnel where they were standing. "I am amazed at the length of this tunnel. We are on top of a mountain made of solid rock or so I thought. This tunnel and this chamber we just uncovered, is mostly natural terrain, although I do see the work of man in some parts. What do you think is above us? Where are we?"

Erasmus Harel looked at the ceiling. "I think we might be past the courtyard, possibly past the gates of Clivus. What do you think, Ya'ir?"

"If I were to guess," Ya'ir said, "I believe that we have walked well past the gates of Clivus."

Lord Gaios looked into the chamber again and studied it quietly. "There is something odd about that far wall," he said. "The bottom of it is moist," he said pensively, "I think we should go in and have a look."

"I agree," Erasmus Harel said.

Lord Gaios stood next to one of the hung skeletons and studied it carefully. "These men quite possibly took their own lives."

"Why do you say that, my lord," Ezri asked.

Lord Gaios looked solemnly at him. "I think these men were buried alive," he said.

"Why did they not just dig their way out?" Ya'ri asked.

Lord Gaios pointed to a rusted pair of short swords that lay at the feet of the skeletons. "They could have, but guards were probably posted on the other side," he said. He walked to the far wall and pressed his hands up and down against the wall. "The upper part of the wall is solid rock but this lower section is damp." He took his dagger and scraped the lower section, which almost formed a perfect square. "Mud," he said.

Lord Gaios stepped back and studied the wall. "Tavius," he said.

"I know what you are thinking, my lord," Tavius said. "We need to dig through the lower half of this wall."

He dropped to his knees and unsheathed his dagger and buried it into the wall. He moved the dagger to the left and to the right as if he were carving out a piece of wood. Lord Gaios did the same with his dagger.

Soon light pierced into the lower half of the dark room. A breeze slipped into the room and the soft sounds of birds filled the dark quiet room.

"We have almost broken through," Lord Gaios said, digging faster.

At last they stopped digging and Tavius kicked away what little remained of the small section of the wall. He scrambled forward on his knees and disappeared into the hole. He returned a few moments later dripping wet. "There is a small cavern at the other side of this wall, and there is a stream in the middle of the cavern that flows to the outside through an exit that is covered by bushes. We are all going to get wet."

One by one they followed Tavius into the cavern, and one by one they waded into the stream, until they reached the outside.

Lord Gaios was the last, and dripping wet, he studied the hole from where they had just emerged. It had vanished behind bushes and water. The stream was natural, of course, but he was certain that the bushes had been deliberately planted at the exit to conceal it. The stream emptied into a pond that was just off the path that led straight into Clivus.

"What are we to make of this," Erasmus Harel said.

"I do not know," Lord Gaios said. "But this is a very well-concealed exit and entrance."

Erasmus Harel sighed. "Those men who lost their lives in there. We cannot just leave them in there."

Lord Gaios nodded. "I shall have my men remove the bones and burn them," he said. "And if you like, my men can attempt to seal this exit and the entrance we discovered inside Clivus."

"Hum," Erasmus Harel murmured. "Before you do that, my lord, I think we should further explore the cave-like tunnels and passageways, at least what is right beneath Clivus."

"I agree," Ezri said. "We should study the natural terrain. It is fascinating."

Eighteen

arrenthias stood at the top of the sunken stairs that led down into the study chamber where the men worked and looked around. A full, yellow moon, partially hidden behind thick clouds, barely lit the enormous courtyard. The trees along two walls and scattered benches were barely visible in the darkness. Farrenthias sighed. Back home Erisa and Clisa were always complaining that they were afraid of the dark, but he loved quiet, dark settings. A slight wind swept through the trees and Farrenthias shivered. It was cold, colder than the night before, but still not so cold that he could not huddle in some corner of the courtyard with a blanket, a lantern, and a scroll. He had done that the last two nights and had enjoyed it thoroughly. He also loved the cold in spite of being raised in the middle of a desert. He finally set out down the stairs and let himself into the chamber.

All the priests and Cerudotus were gathered around a long table talking quietly but enthusiastically. Lanterns that burned brightly from all corners of the room caused their shadows to dance on the walls. Farrenthias greeted them with a slight nod and a shy smile.

"Ah," Adin said. "Our little student is here with his lamp, ready to continue his studies. Find yourself a scroll or two, my child, and perhaps I will join you outside in a little while."

"I would like that very much," Farrenthias said. He walked to the shelves and studied the racks. They were filled with neatly stacked scrolls. He wanted to read them all at once and so found it difficult to choose what to read first. Of course, some were written in a language unfamiliar to him and Farrenthias wished that he knew the language so he could read those too. His attention was drawn to three scrolls that were neatly rolled and tied together. They were on one corner of a shelf, separate from the other scrolls. Farrenthias had not noticed them before. Unlike the other scrolls, which were loosely tied and thick, these three scrolls were very thin and tightly rolled into thin tubes. The material was also much lighter in color than the other scrolls. Farrenthias touched one of them. It did not feel like typical papyrus. It was very thin and brittle along the edges, as if someone had ripped a section off. The three tubes were tied together with a thin leather ribbon.

"Farrenthias," Erasmus Harel said, from where he sat at the table. "I see that you have discovered our three mysterious fragments. I brought them into this room just this evening."

"Fragments, sire?" Farrenthias said.

"Yes, they are part of one scroll, but that scroll is not complete," Erasmus Harel said. "Come, bring them here and I will show you."

"You have aroused my curiosity," Cerudotus said. "Why are they mysterious?"

Erasmus Harel took the fragments from Farrenthias and untied them. He unrolled each one and set them down flat on the table.

"They are mysterious, my dear Cerudotus," Erasmus Harel said, "because these fragments, written in an Asian dialect, speak about a great Hebrew master and his visit to the Far East. We concluded that it could only have been Yeshua, the wise and great master from Galilee. They were given to us by Asian priests who were living in a remote convent at the foot of the Himalayas."

Erasmus Harel rearranged them until all three lay side by side. "They are part of one scroll and this is their order."

"Are you referring to the same Yeshua whom the Romans hung from a tree about thirty years ago?" Cerudotus asked.

"I am," Erasmus Harel. "Are you are familiar with his story?"

"I know that in his day he roamed the countryside preaching. And to this day he has followers in Antioch who now refer to themselves as Christians. Apparently they continue to grow in numbers."

"They do indeed," Erasmus Harel said. "An eloquent man by the name of Paulous has rallied people from across Judea, including non-Hebrews, to look upon Yeshua as a great messiah for all the people."

"Was Yeshua as wise as Pythagoras and Plato?" Farrenthias asked.

"Ah," Erasmus Harel murmured. "A clever question. How would you answer the young lad, Ya'ir?"

Ya'ir gently stroked the head of Farrenthias. "Yeshua, my lad, was a teacher of wisdom who interacted with his disciples in different ways than Pythagoras and Plato. Those two men spent their lives studying the art of science and philosophy. Yeshua, on the other hand, spent his life roaming the plains learning and teaching man the way to a better existence."

"Love and forgiveness," Ezri added. "That is what he taught—that was his message to whomever would listen to him."

"Ezri is correct," Erasmus Harel said. "Yeshua taught a very simple lesson, do no harm to any living creature and learn to forgive, no matter the transgression against you."

"Why did the Romans hang him from a tree?" Farrenthias asked. "What did he do to upset them?"

"Another excellent question," Erasmus Harel said. "A certain sect of Hebrew leaders accused him of blasphemy and inciting the people against Rome," Erasmus Harel said. "But because they did not have the authority to order his execution they went to the Romans and asked them to punish Yeshua and put him to death."

Cerudotus lifted one of the scroll fragments and studied it. What do these speak about?"

"They speak about Yeshua's arrival to the Himalayas. He almost did not make it. He was found on the side of an unmarked road, half-starved and half-frozen, by a small caravan of hunters. Upon regaining his health, he was questioned about what he was doing out in the mountains and his answer was that he had traveled from the west to seek out the eastern masters and to learn from them."

Farrenthias took the scrolls from Cerudotus. "I wish that I could learn to read these." He eyed Cerudotus. "I wish that you and I could stay at Clivus, Cerudotus," he blurted out. "I wish that we could stay here so I can learn to read all of these scrolls."

Cerudotus gasped. Speechless, he glanced helplessly at Erasmus Harel and frowned in embarrassment. "Farrenthias," he cried. "What are you saying, my child? Even if an invitation was extended for us to stay, what you ask is completely out of the question. Your father would never allow it!"

Suddenly embarrassed by his outburst, Farrenthias's eyes swelled with tears. "Forgive me, Cerudotus. Forgive me for speaking out of turn."

The room became utterly still until Erasmus Harel cleared his throat and spoke. "Do not be so surprised, Cerudotus. I am afraid that we have overwhelmed the curious mind of Farrenthias with many learning possibilities, and I speak for all of us when I tell you that nothing would please us more than to have you and Farrenthias join our family here at Clivus."

Shocked, Cerudotus slowly shook his head. What was Farrenthias thinking? What was Erasmus Harel proposing? Lord Gaios would never hear of it. He would never allow it. Never! "I am grateful for the invitation, Erasmus Harel, but what Farrenthias proposes is impossible. There are excellent private schools in Antioch, but Lord Gaios refused to consider matriculating Farrenthias in one of them; that is why I was retained as his private tutor. Lord Gaios never considered allowing Farrenthias to leave his home to attend such a school. To suggest that he allow his son to stay here, so far away from Syria, is preposterous."

Erasmus Harel nodded as did Ya'ir, but neither said a word. Farrenthias stood with his eyes full of tears staring sadly at the three fragments on the table. Cerudotus's heart swelled with pride and sadness, pride because his student was clearly making a decision based on all that he as his tutor had instilled in him about the pursuit of learning, and sadness, because clearly there would be no happy solution to what Farrenthais was proposing. Yes, Farrenthias did not go riding with his father the way other boys did with their fathers, nor did he know how to use a weapon, much less know how to hunt, but Farrenthias was Lord Gaios's only son. He would never part with him. And what of his mother, Lady Oralia? She adored Farrenthias and spent considerable hours listening to her son read and speak about his lessons. And then there was Erisa and Clisa? Farrenthias loved reading Greek stories to them and then patiently explain to them what the stories meant when they did not understand. They would surely be crushed by their brother's absence, as would his mother. "My child," Cerudotus said. "I have lived to please you and to try and do what is best for your education, but this—what you ask is impossible." He affectionately took the hand of Farrenthias and squeezed it. "Please understand."

Farrenthias smiled weakly and it was such a tender smile that Cerudotus sighed with self-doubt. Had he not always encouraged his pupil to speak his mind without fear? Had he not instilled in him a need to always speak the truth? "Farrenthias," Cerudotus said, going against all of his instincts. "We have just been here a few days, are you certain about your feelings? Would you like me to have a word with your father?"

Farrenthias shook with excitement and eagerly nodded. "I am certain, Cerudotus. Will you tell Father that I wish to stay at Clivus to study?"

"It would have to be soon," Erasmus Harel said. "Abiel tells me that he has advised Lord Gaios that his men have been recuperating much quicker than he had anticipated. They will be ready to travel in just over a week. Would you like me to accompany you?"

Cerudotus thought a moment. Under normal circumstances he would have instantly rejected the idea since he considered this to be a family matter, but this was a highly unusual circumstance. "Perhaps it might help."

Nineteen

Belfore studied the rocky terrain just ahead of him with little interest and then laughed out loud. He and Bentore had slept just a few hours last night but that is all that he needed. The chase had aroused an unexpected excitement in him. He was the hunter and the hunter was beginning to smell his prey. He leaned forward on his horse and looked down into the gully again. The drop was steep and full of loose rocks, but he dismissed the danger with another laugh. "Bentore!" he shouted. "Hurry, and stop falling behind you lazy swine. Can you not see that we are closing in on them? Capua is not far now and soon the brat and the Egyptian will be carcasses. I feel it in my blood."

Belfore spat and dug his heels into the belly of his horse. The horse snorted and jerked its head sideways refusing to budge. Belfore slammed his heels down again, this time harder. The horse jerked to the side and then started down slowly. Belfore laughed again. "Damn you, Egyptian, I am at your heels," he shouted. "I am at your heels and soon you shall join your forefathers in hell!"

The horse slipped slightly but Belfore held him tightly and guided him expertly to the bottom. Safely down, he turned and watched Bentore come down. He laughed at the sight of his pathetic companion, whose eyes were threatening to spring from their sockets with fear. He was leaning so far back he looked like he was about to fall off the rear of the horse. "This is child's play you terrified old woman," Belfore shouted. "Why, I am of a mind to climb back up and do it again!"

"You are mad," Bentore cried. He reached the bottom gasping for air. "We could have found an easier way down."

"No time," Belfore said. "Kemnebi and the child took this very path. Capua is just ahead." He pulled out his pouch of water, gulped thirstily and wiped his mouth. "I bet Kemnebi stopped at Capua last night to let the child rest. He might still be there, and if we hurry we will catch them." He slapped Bentore on the shoulder. "Let us go. Tonight we get drunk and sleep with whores."

❖ PUTEOLI ❖

Delerin nervously rubbed his chin as he looked up and down the empty road that led straight into Puteoli. Puteoli was a busy port city, and this main road was usually crowded with traffic, especially at this hour of the morning. Once, it had taken him and his brother hours to reach the gates of the city from this very spot where he now looked around. Yet, the road was now strangely empty. It is true that he preferred traveling in the evenings when the roads were cool and less crowded, but merchants had wares to move and that meant crowded roads. At last, some figures appeared in the distance, coming from the direction of Puteoli. Relieved to finally see somebody on the road, Delerin started down the road slowly. It was a caravan of carts, each being pulled by a pair of oxen. When they got close, the driver of the leading cart looked nervously at Delerin, and Delerin understood his fear. Thieves were quite common on all Roman roads, and he and his brother had on many occasions filled their purses with someone else's gold.

Delerin raised his hand in greeting. "Good morning, friend," he said. "You need not fear me. I merely want to know why this busy road is empty today? Would you happen to know?"

The driver halted his cart. The rest of the caravan stopped behind him. The man briefly glanced back over his shoulder. "It is because the port is closed and the streets of the city are packed with merchants waiting for their goods from the sea, and others are waiting to take a ship."

"The port closed? Why?"

"A ship pulled in from Ostia last night. The passengers got some sort of plague. Last I heard they were washing down the ship's decks and loading medicine."

Delerin looked toward Puteoli and chewed on his lower lip. Nothing frightened him more than plagues and diseases. Once, he had watched an old friend of his rot to death before his very eyes. Clumps of flesh had peeled from his bones like torn pieces of a tunic. Why should he risk entering Puteoli? Kemnebi would not take such a chance. He would not endanger the child's life.

"It's safe to enter the city," the driver said, as if sensing Delerin's reluctance. "Just stay away from the docks until the ship leaves."

Delerin pulled his horse back out of the way of the caravan. "I am grateful for the information," he said.

The driver whistled and shook the reins that he held in his hands. The two heavy oxen set out slowly, struggling with every step.

Delerin watched them pass while he pondered his predicament. At last he decided that he would take the driver's word that it was safe to enter the city. But, if he smelled trouble, he would turn around and wait for his brother and Bentore at the outskirts to the city.

Puteoli was a crowded mess. Long lines of people, carts, wagons, horses, mules, oxen, and other animals filled the streets. And the lines were not moving. Delerin also noticed that, while the people looked restless and frustrated, no one looked particularly scared or worried. Children were even playing on the street with their toys and trinkets. Delerin carefully weaved his way through the congested traffic. People had set out blankets on the dirt road and many were still stretched out on their makeshift beds. Delerin had no idea where he was going. He took a narrow side street and headed down its winding path. Fortunately, the street barely had any traffic, and it was all moving against him. Soon the air became thick and muggy and it smelled of water from the sea. He was near the port. But, the street dead-ended into an old, abandoned building. Delerin now understood why there had been so little traffic on this street. He searched for a way around the building and found an alley so narrow that Delerin had to struggle to keep his horse moving forward, instead of backing out of the alley as he wanted to do. At last Delerin exited to the other side. The sea was a blazing dark blue, and the port, crowded with ships, was to his immediate left. To his right, a few steps away, was an old inn bursting at the seams with people. Delerin grinned and scratched his scar. From that inn he had a clear view of the ships a weary traveler would have to board if he planned to travel by sea. Indeed, at that inn he would wet his dry throat and wait for his brother and Belfore. And, if Kemnebi were fool enough to enter the city with the boy and try to leave the country by sea, he would be ready for him. Delerin started for the inn, and out of habit, he fumbled for his knife with his right hand and squeezed its handle.

Belfore reached over the counter, grabbed the terrified innkeeper by the collar, and pulled him off his feet. This rat hole was at the very entrance to Capua and since the morning sun still hung low, maybe—just maybe, they were in luck. "See here," Belfore said. "Do I have to pound your face in to jar your memory? The Egyptian is a dark man and he is probably wearing eccentric rags. The child is Roman about seven or eight years old. Think!"

"Sire," the man cried, "Look around you, this is a very busy inn. Merchants do not travel alone. Slaves sometimes carry..." the man's eyes widened. "Wait, last night a very dark man dressed in a splendid robe did come in, but he was alone. He asked for a back room with a window, and when I advised him that on crowded days the room had to be shared, he paid me extra to be left alone."

"Ha! I knew it!" Belfore cried. He released the man and slammed a hand on the counter. "It has to be Kemnebi. Is he still here?"

"As far as I know, yes sire."

"But he was alone." Bentore said.

"No child," the man said, agreeing with him.

Belfore glared at Bentore then jabbed the side of his temple with a finger. "Think, you piece of swine, lest I put a hole in that empty head of yours. Kemnebi walked in through the front door alone, but in the room, he slipped the boy in through the window. It has to be him. We have him I tell you." Belfore withdrew his sword. "Take us to the room," he said to the innkeeper.

The innkeeper stared at the sword without moving.

"Move!" Belfore shouted.

The man stumbled around the counter and led them to a narrow hall to the right of the main area of the inn. He stopped halfway down the hall. "Three doors from the end of this hall," the innkeeper whispered. "On the left."

Belfore pushed him out of the way. "Come on, Bentore," he said. "We have him!"

Belfore reached the door first and quietly crossed over to the other side. He turned to look at Bentore, whose eyes were wild with anticipation. Bentore knew exactly what to do. They had surprised many a man in a similar way. "Now!" Belfore shouted. Bentore stepped in front of the door and kicked it with all of his strength. The door shattered into pieces, and he charged into the tiny room. Belfore was right behind him, ready to pounce on the Egyptian, the Egyptian who had caused them so much trouble. But the room was empty.

Belfore kicked a pile of mats across the floor. "We had him. We had that filthy Egyptian rat."

"It could have been somebody else," Bentore said.

Belfore stepped to the window and ripped the thin window cover to one side. "No, my gut tells me it was Kemnebi, and what worries me is that he is taking precautions," he glanced at Bentore and his stare turned into a glare. "He is taking precautions as if he suspects that he is being followed."

The innkeeper was suddenly at the door with his hands at his cheeks. "Look," he screamed. "Look what you have done to my door, and window covering! You have destroyed this room."

Belfore started out of the room but paused in front of the innkeeper, who looked up at him in terror. Belfore buried his fist into the man's belly with so much force that the man doubled over and dropped to his knees. As the man lay on the floor gasping for air, Belfore kicked him out of the way and stepped out of the room. He had not slept very well last night, and he was famished. None of that mattered now, however. What mattered is that Kemnebi was proving to be a bigger annoyance than what he had anticipated. Suddenly, Belfore lost his appetite for the hunt, and for that, he would make the Egyptian pay.

Twenty

Romans loved public bathhouses. A bathhouse was a place where a man could relax, get caught up with the day's gossip, get drunk with his friends, or perhaps chase naked nymphets about the halls. A bathhouse was not for the modest, for no conduct was too outrageous or too lascivious with a willing partner. At high noon, the Agrippa bathhouse was packed to capacity. Unlike Nero's more popular baths, which could accommodate as many as sixteen hundred men and women at the same time, the Agrippa bathhouse was smaller, more discreet. A mere three hundred occupied this bathhouse, which had high ceilings, beautiful columns and lavish murals of oceans and sunsets on the ceilings and walls.

Parsino Laggetous made his way through the crowded bathhouse half an hour before his scheduled appointment with Felicia. It had been years since he had last been here, but not much had changed. He knew his way around well. He walked past three large pools full of scantily clad people who laughed and danced in the water and, generally, made fools of themselves. His favorite pool was in a secluded corner of the large complex, and when he got there, he was pleased to discover that it still remained the one pool where a man could soak in relative peace and quiet. Only two couples and a man, who was floating on his back staring at the ceiling, occupied the pool. Parsino stripped down to a loincloth and lowered his body into one corner of the pool and closed his eyes. The water was warm and soothing. Parsino tried to remember the last time he had been here but could not recall when that had been. Memories had kept him away, memories of the days when he and Felicia would spend entire afternoons in each other's arms in this very pool. It was sad that it had to be the arrest of his good friend Marcellius that was about to bring them together again. Without question, the arrest of Marcellius had been the talk of Rome for weeks, and since Parsino was a soldier assigned to the city guard, he knew she would be contacting him to inquire about Marcellius's well being. The note had not been a surprise, but his reaction to it did surprise him. They had not spoken in years, but that did not matter. In spite of the years that had passed and in spite of all of his traveling abroad, his love for her had not diminished in the least. Seeing her writing on that note had made him realize that, and it had made him tremble with excitement.

Felicia was also early. Parsino opened his eyes just in time to see her enter this area of the bathhouse. She was dressed in a short, white, flimsy tunic, and her dark hair was tied back in curls. She was slim yet full-figured. She had not aged a day. She was, quite possibly, even more beautiful than the last time he had seen her. He instantly lamented his foolish pride, a pride that had allowed so many years to slip by without speaking to her again. He had ended their relationship after a frivolous argument, and when she had gotten pregnant one year later, it doomed their relationship even though she never married the father of her child—a father whom she had refused to name.

"Parsino," Felicia said. "Is it really you? I am delighted to see you!"

Parsino jumped out of the water and kissed her on the cheek. "Felicia, what a joy it is to see you. You are more beautiful than ever."

He took her hand while she lowered herself onto the edge of the pool and dipped her feet into the water and then he dropped back into the pool.

"How many years has it been since we were last here?" she asked, looking around.

"For me a lifetime, Felicia, and yet you have not aged a day since I first laid eyes on you at the Forum Square."

Felicia blushed. "You are being overly generous with your compliments, Parsino, but, I agree, that was another lifetime. Marcellius often spoke of you and of how well your military career was going."

Parsino folded his arms over the edge of the pool and rested his chin on them. "Nonsense. I have been nothing but a servant of the empire, sent from one end of the empire to the other, that has been my life the last seven years. I have never stayed at a single place long enough to buy a home, to settle down. I returned less than six months ago from Germania, and in six months I leave for Judea for at least a year, maybe two, who knows."

"Judea?" Felicia cried. "The last time I heard Marcellius speak of Judea he predicted that the Hebrews would one day revolt against the Roman occupation."

"Marcellius was right. Sooner or later all colonized people revolt. The Hebrew people are a proud and smart people. I think they are fed up with Roman interference in their country."

"Then you must be careful, Parsino," Felicia said. "You may not have a home but you have plenty of people who care about you."

Parsino waved a dismissive hand in the air. "I shall be fine." He lightly cleared his throat. "Enough about me, I know why you called, Felicia. You are worried about Marcellius."

Felicia's eyes filled with tears. "Have you seen him, Parsino? Have you any news about how he is doing?"

Parsino pulled himself out of the water and sat next to her. "I spoke to him briefly when he was first arrested, but I was out of the city when he was taken away."

Felicia gasped and then covered her lips. "Taken away?" she cried. "I had heard rumors that he might be moved out of the city, but I have heard nothing more about it. Where to?"

"He has been quietly banished to the island of Malta but do not worry. I heard from one of my men that he arrived safely."

"Malta?"

"Malta." Parsino leaned back and brushed his wet hair back away from his face. "The island is actually a paradise, but I do not suppose that a man banished from his country will see it that way."

Felicia lowered her eyes and shook her head. "Malta? What will he do on that island? How long will he be there?"

"Who knows, but remember, Septimus sentenced him into exile for no less then ten years."

Felicia turned away, fighting back tears. "He is an innocent man. How could this have happened to him?"

Parsino comforted her by placing a hand over one of hers and squeezing it lightly. "I know how much you love him, Felicia. But do not worry. Marcellius is strong and resilient and brilliant. He will survive this terrible ordeal."

Tears streamed down Felicia's face and her voice trembled "I do love him, Parsino. Marcellius has been so kind to me. In his house and his father's house I was never treated like a servant, not even before I was legally freed. I was always a member of the family. Marcellius has always been like a brother to me."

"I know, " Parsino said.

Felicia quietly looked at Parsino, her eyes still glistening with tears. "When Gianina was born, at first, he wanted to adopt her. He wanted to giver her a name, his name, but he and Servia hoped that one day Gianina and Trulius might..." her voice trailed off and she grew quiet. "So, instead of adopting her, he legally freed me and allowed me to keep her. Now, Gianina misses Trulius terribly and it has not been that long since he has been gone."

"Trulius!" Parisino frowned. "I do not mean to alarm you, but it is Trulius I am worried about. Is he safe?"

Felicia sighed and clenched his arm. "I have no idea where Trulius is, but Kemnebi would never let anything happen to him. Never."

Parsino nodded. "I agree. Trulius could not be in better hands." Parsino looked at her. "Where are you staying? I heard that Nero seized Marcellius's beautiful estate and other properties and sold everything."

Felicia grew quiet. "I am fine, but what a nightmare this has been. Servia gone and Marcellius convicted of murder and poor Trulius sent out into the night to flee from his home."

Loud shrieks, shouts and laughter broke out at the opposite end of the pool. Men, many of whom Parsino recognized as senators, with their huge bellies and sagging chests, rushed in from another room and began to take turns tossing naked women into the water. Parsino shook his head. The upper class, the better educated, were at times the worst behaved in public. "They are a distinguished bunch, are they not?" Parsino said.

Felicia pulled her legs out of the water. "I should be going. Gianina is taking all of this very hard. She weeps two or three times a day and cannot be consoled. She misses Trulius terribly."

Parsino looked idly across the room at the senators. Several were now openly fondling and kissing the women. "She must be very beautiful. I am so sorry for her."

He fell silent, then suddenly and unexpectedly said, "Do you ever wonder what might have happened if you and I…"

Felicia smiled quietly and placed a gentle hand on his face. "Of course I have wondered how our lives might have turned out had we stayed together. What woman does not dream?"

"Why haven't you married, Felicia? You are after all a freedwoman, and you are so beautiful and so kind. Surely there have been men who have expressed an interest. Marcellius would want that for you."

"Yes, Marcellius was always looking after my best interest, but he has never pressed me to find a man and marry. I have always been content with my love for Gianina and Trulius. They kept me busy those two, and I had a big house to run."

"What about you, Parsino?"

"Me, marriage? Bah, what woman would want a soldier who never stops moving around?"

She started to get to her feet and Parsino helped her. "Will you please let me know if you hear anything about Marcellius, Parsino?" she said. "Will money help?"

"No, keep your money. Septimus was at least generous enough to appoint him guards that are familiar with his military record. Guards who respect him."

"Very well then. Take care of yourself in Judea."

"Felicia, I know a place just around the corner that specializes in confections. Will you accompany me so that I can send some to Gianina?"

Felicia smiled and then nodded. "That is very kind of you, Parino. I think Gianina might enjoy that. I will get dressed and meet you outside."

Twenty-One

Kemnebi studied the Navis Oneraria, the Roman merchant vessel that was the cause of all the trouble at Puteoli, from a safe distance. He estimated that it had three decks with a capacity to carry two maybe three hundred men. He had heard that the quarantined ship was about to depart for Rhegium, a coastal city to the south of Puteoli, at any moment, and all the activity in and around the ship confirmed this.

The ship's sails were hoisted and wrapped around the masts. On the peer, slaves clad in filthy loincloths formed an assembly line and passed small boxes onto the Navis Oneraria. They worked diligently, seemingly oblivious of the hot afternoon sun that baked and furthered darkened their skin. Supervising the activity was a lean man. He wore a long white toga with the sleeves rolled to his elbows. He walked back and forth inspecting the cargo that the slaves were loading on board, his golden hair glistening in the sunlight. His skin, also burned from the sun, was rich and golden. No doubt he was the physician in charge. To the right of the ship a large group of men, women, and a few children formed a circle between several guards who watched over them. These had to be the passengers, and even though a few coughed here and there, none looked terribly ill. Farther down the dock, other ships were also moored, and they too were full of activity. Kemnebi speculated that he would have no trouble finding a passage out of the country.

Trulius stood beside Kemnebi. He was quietly chewing on a piece of bread Kemnebi had bought for him from a merchant who had set up a temporary bakery in the middle of a busy intersection. Trulius had repeatedly told Kemnebi that he was not hungry, and Kemnebi could hardly blame him. Food was also the last thing on his mind too, but Trulius needed his strength. They still had quite a ways to go before reaching their destination.

"Now that you have had your breakfast," Kemnebi said. "We shall sell the horses and then wait for the ships to start sailing."

Across the street, a small mob noisily poured out of a tavern. They cheered two men who circled each other with daggers drawn. One of them had a thick scar running down the length of his right cheek. By the way he moved and held his dagger, Kemnebi knew the other man was done for.

"Fool!" the one with the scar shouted. "If I had wanted to steal your purse, I would have slit your throat and taken it."

"Thief," the other cried. "I saw your filthy hands reach for it."

The crowd urged them to fight, and while they continued to circle each other, Kemnebi became distracted by the activity on the *Navis Oneraria*. A group of slaves walked down the ship's plank carrying buckets and wet rags. Obviously they had scrubbed the decks and were now finished. "We must hurry," Kemnebi said. "They are cleaning the deck. It will sail soon."

Above the shouts of the mob a woman screamed loudly. The

man with the scar now stood over his fallen accuser with his dagger dripping with blood.

"Who is he?" Trulius whispered.

Kemnebi blinked. "What, Trulius?"

"The man with the scar, you are staring at him."

Kemnebi gently squeezed one of Trulius's ear lobes. "You are too perceptive for your age, dear child. Come now. We've got to get rid of these horses."

The activity on the docks intensified as news of the imminent departure of the Navis Oneraria spread. Merchants and traders formed a line with their cargo and luggage. Farmers gathered their small animals and cages, and families huddled with their children. Kemnebi bickered with a local merchant about the price of the horses and, at last, agreed on a sum. Suddenly a cheer erupted. The passengers were boarding the *Navis Oneraria*. Kemnebi put away his purse of money, but suddenly looked about. Trulius had vanished from his side. He looked in every direction and froze when he spotted Trulius talking to a child who was in line to board the *Navis Oneraria*.

Kemnebi hurried to him. "Tessius Trulius," he cried. "Get over here."

Trulius turned, but an armed guard blocked his path.

"Where do you think you are going?" the man said. "Stay in line."

"No, no!" Kemnebi cried, reaching for Trulius's hand. "My ward was not on that ship. He slipped away from my side."

The man roughly grabbed Kemnebi by the collar. "If he is your ward then you belong in this line too."

"But you don't understand. We just arrived in Puteoli by horseback. We were not on that ship."

The guard released Kemnebi with a shove and a laugh. "Do you know how many times I have heard that story in the last few minutes? Now move along. You're not going anywhere."

Kemnebi considered grabbing Trulius and running, but how far would he get? A few people heard the guard, and they yelled at Kemnebi to stay in line.

"Forgive me, Kemnebi," Trulius whispered.

Kemnebi protectively placed both arms around Trulius and pushed him along up the plank. "We will be fine, my child," Kemnebi said. "Just don't leave my side again."

Twenty-Two

Lord Gaios's teeth flashed in anger and his face became dark and flushed. He glared at Cerudotus, then at Erasmus Harel, and then returned his gaze to Cerudotus. "That is a preposterous suggestion, Cerudotus!" he cried. He rose from his chair so forcefully that the chair flew backwards and crashed onto the floor with a thundering noise. "Farrenthias, stay here? Why, I have just made the arrangements for our departure. We leave the day after tomorrow. His eyes narrowed and his nose flared. "I know you well enough to know that this idea could not have come from you, Cerudotus. Farrenthias put you up to this, did he not?"

Cerudotus nervously bit his lip. He had never lied to Lord Gaios, not even about the most insignificant matter. Yet, the thought of betraying his beloved student mortified him.

"Hum," Lord Gaios murmured. "Do not say another word, Cerudotus. Your hesitation has answered my question." He stared at the fallen chair as if unaware that he had caused it to tip over. The color returned to his face, and he was suddenly embarrassed.

"Forgive my outburst, Erasmus Harel," he said. He lifted the chair with one hand. "But I must admit I am rather puzzled and surprised that Farrenthias would be willing to stay here so far away from his family."

"There is no need to apologize, my lord," Erasmus Hariel said. "I understand your confusion and anger."

"Cerudotus," Lord Gaios said. "I have always conceded to your every request when it came to my son, beginning with your request that he be excused from the activities required of the other boys his age. I have also allowed you to take him to Antioch to study with your scholarly acquaintances. But this...this is absurd. We are in the middle of nowhere. How can I seriously consider leaving my son here?"

"My lord," Cerudotus said. "When the discussion first arose I too was at first aghast. But then I realized two things. One, I have never seen Farrenthias so happy and so full of life. Why, in the short days that he has been here, he has spent countless hours in a room full of scrolls wanting to read them all, and he has taken so quickly to understanding Hieroglyphics that he is already reading Egyptian scrolls as well. Two, at the risk of jeopardizing my position as his tutor, I fear that in a few short years Farrenthias will be years ahead of any knowledge that I or any scholar in Antioch can impart to him. In just days he masters lessons that it takes other boys his age months to understand. Here at Clivus, with brilliant men, such as Erasmus Harel and Ya'ir and the others, that is not likely to happen soon. They have a special room where they dedicate hours translating and studying the works of brilliant men, men who lived in various parts of the world. I lost count of the many languages and dialects that they speak. I might also add that they have all expressed surprise at how quickly Farrenthias has taken to what they have taught him."

Lord Gaios frowned in exasperation, and turning to Erasmus Harel said, "Forgive me, Erasmus, but I must confess that I find your existence here rather bleak. You have isolated yourself from the rest of the world and that is not the type of life I want for my son."

Erasmus Harel smiled. "You do not offend me, my lord. We do not expect people to either understand or agree with our motives. While we have travelled extensively, we do indeed prefer our quiet moments within these walls where we can pray and meditate. We have no interest in the material world. Here our existence is simple. We seek knowledge and spiritual growth."

Lord Gaios sighed. "Are you suggesting, Erasmus Harel, that this is the life that awaits my son? But he is just a child, how would he know what benefits him the most. As his father I must assume certain decisions on his behalf until he is old enough to make those decisions for himself."

"Agreed, my lord," Erasmus Harel said. "A father must certainly guide a son on the path he must take, but men of learning are different. They discover their true passion very early in their lives. Even as children they are driven by intellectual pursuits that most people do not comprehend. You can guide Farrenthias and point him in the direction of your choosing, but you will never remove what truly lies in his heart. In time you will discover that for yourself."

Lord Gaios fell silent. "Tell me, Cerudotus," he finally said. "You know Farrenthias more than anyone else. Is he really the type of child that Erasmus has just described? Would staying here really make him happy?"

Cerudotus nodded slowly and without hesitation. "He is a special child, my lord. I have always said that. If you allowed him to stay, with your permission, I would stay with him."

Lord Gaios exhaled and quietly stared at Erasmus Harel and then at Cerudotus. "It pains me to even consider it, but against my better judgment, I shall give it some consideration." He sighed. "I shall let both of you know in a few days of my decision."

Twenty-Three

Kemnebi gazed across the crowded deck of the ship and was seized by shock. Yesterday, when they had been forced onto the ship, a few sick souls had meandered about the deck. Nothing about them had alarmed him. Now after a night of restless activity that had ended only a few hours before, the deck was a sea of ailing men, women, and children. Their faces were pale and dripping with perspiration. Legs and arms were sprawled and entangled with one another like vines on a tree. The sick moaned in pain. They vomited and, worse, they looked and smelled of death. The stench from human waste and from the corpses that were stacked on one corner of the ship like wooden boards made breathing difficult.

Kemnebi collapsed back into the corner where he and Trulius were huddled together in utter despair. The sick had never left the ship back at Puteoli. They had been forced onto one of the decks below, and now here they were, a few feet away spreading whatever deadly ailment had invaded their bodies. The crew was working tirelessly, raising buckets of water from the sea and dousing the deck, but it was to no avail. There were too many bodies. There was too much filth, and the stench was unbearable.

"Kemnebi," Trulius whispered, coughing and gagging. "What is wrong with all those people? They look very sick. It smells terrible."

Kemnebi looked at Trulius and realized that he had to keep his composure and not alarm him. "I do not know what disease ails them," Kemnebi said. "But you have nothing to worry about." He rinsed Trulius's mouth and face with water from a pouch that he carried. "Cover your mouth with the sleeve of your tunic," Kemnebi said. "It will help you breathe easier. We will be fine."

But Kemnebi worried. The situation was grim. Aside from the smell, sleep was nearly impossible. The sick moaned loudly and incessantly, and what if he or Trulius got ill?

Slumped behind a pair of wooden barrels, Kemnebi and Trulius dozed off and on for hours. At last, when night fell and darkened the wretched scene, both fell asleep. But an hour later the ship anchored, and Kemnebi's eyes flashed open. Shadows scurried about the deck, carrying dim torches, and the moaning of the sick was replaced by nervous whispers. A strange tension spread along the deck as the shadows continued to move about the crowded deck.

Finally, all activity on the deck came to an abrupt halt and the deck fell eerily silent. But then a single cry pierced the air. "No!" a man screamed. "She is not dead! She is not dead I tell you!" He sobbed loudly and then, as if a single blow had cut him down, his cries stopped. Shortly after, the sounds of distant splashing could be heard. Kemnebi tensed as soon as he realized what was happening.

Trulius squirmed out of his arms. "What is happening, Kemnebi?"

Kemnebi pulled Trulius back down and cuddled him. "Go back to sleep, my child. They are disposing of the dead bodies." But the man's cry still rang in his ears, and it terrified him. Were they also tossing the living? The living who were too ill to defend themselves?

The following morning a basket of dried fruit and a jug of water were passed from hand to hand, and when it reached Kemnebi, he refused it. He still had some dry meat and two leather pouches full of water. Perhaps that was not enough, but it would have to do for now. Kemnebi wet his lips with water, but he insisted that Trulius quench his thirst. Trulius barely had a sip and then he sealed the pouch. Kemnebi sighed. Trulius had become aware of their dilemma. Soon they would be out of fresh water.

By the late afternoon the crew had pulled out more corpses from the lower deck and stacked them at one end of the deck like a pile of wood. That night the previous night's activity was repeated: the moving about the deck by the ship's crew, the hushed whispers and the splashing—almost until dawn. This abominable routine was followed day after day.

One morning, about a week after they had boarded the ship, panic seized Kemnebi. Trulius's skin glistened with perspiration, his dark, thick hair was damp and limp and his lips had grown dry and purple. Kemnebi wiped the perspiration from Trulius's face and then tried to waken him.

"Trulius," he whispered. "Wake up, my son." He shook him lightly, and at last Trulius barely opened his eyes. They were dazed and distant. "How do you feel, Trulius?" Kemnebi whispered.

Trulius did not respond. Instead, he smiled at Kemnebi as if he were smiling at a total stranger.

"Trulius," Kemnebi said again. "How do you feel?"

Trulius's dry lips parted. "Kemnebi," he said weakly, "I-I am fine, just tired," and then he closed his eyes and fell asleep again.

Kemnebi stared at him in horror. *Had Trulius contracted the mysterious illness? But how could this have happened?* "I have not let him out of my sight." Kemnebi whispered to himself. He looked over the ship's railing. For days now the ship had been drifting slowly, almost aimlessly, close to the coastline and Kemnebi wondered if they truly intended to reach Rhegium. At this rate, the plague or illness was going to kill everyone on board. No one was going to survive.

Trulius drank very little water throughout the day, and he complained that the dry fruit Kemnebi forced him to eat had given him cramps. In just a few short hours Trulius's health had deteriorated drastically.

Kemnebi slumped down and closed his eyes. He had to do something. He was not going to sit back and watch Trulius die. Trulius had his whole life ahead of him. With his mind still in a quandary, Kemnebi got up, and for the first time since they had boarded the ship, he left Trulius alone and walked slowly across the deck. Unsure of what he was doing he stepped around the sick, almost in a daze, when a hand gripped his foot and then let it go. Kemnebi stopped and looked down.

"Forgive me," the man said. "You were about to step on this lady."

Kemnebi could not believe his eyes. It was the man he had seen supervising the slaves. The man he believed to be a physician. His hair was disheveled beneath his hood. His face looked haggard. His white tunic was stained and dirty, and his sandals were worn. He was huddled over an old man, obviously attending to him.

"Are you a physician?" Kemnebi whispered.

The man nodded quietly without saying a word.

"Please," Kemnebi whispered. "My name is Kemnebi. I need your help. A child that I have been charged to protect has fallen ill. I do not want these barbaric seamen to discover that he is ill."

The physician looked down at the old man that he held in his arms and gently set him down.

"I am finished here," he said to Kemnebi. He looked discreetly around. "I do not have much time. Go, I am right behind you."

The physician uncovered Trulius with long, thin hands that moved swiftly, expertly. "What is his name?" he asked in a gentle, compassionate voice.

"Trulius," Kemnebi said anxiously.

"When did you first notice his symptoms?"

"This morning. He must have gotten sick overnight, but I do not know how," Kemnebi said.

The physician scrubbed Trulius's forehead with a damp cloth that he produced from a pouch. He pressed his hand on his chest to feel the rhythm of his heart.

"I saw you on the pier," Kemnebi said. "Why have I not seen you on the deck more often, treating the sick?"

The physician raised his eyes to Kemnebi though his hands remained on Trulius. "I was warned not to come up to the deck, so I have come up here mostly at night. But, this morning I had to see someone I have been treating. You are fortunate you saw me."

"Then there are many below who are also sick?" Kemnebi asked.

The physician sighed. "Below there is a very sick commander and about one hundred of his men are also sick."

"Of what?" Kemnebi said. "What is this ailment? How did it start?"

The physician looked patiently at Kemnebi. "I believe they caught this disease in the marshes near Rome." He wiped the dampness from his face with the inside of his elbow. "I have seen this disease before, but I do not know how to treat it. I ordered herbs and potions in Puteoli, but so far my treatment merely slows down the symptoms."

"You are Greek?"

"Yes, but I must confess that I have never really lived in Greece." He produced a pouch and handed it to Kemnebi. "This mixture of wild herbs will help him retain his fluids, which should help keep his strength. Unfortunately, the sick on this ship will not get well without fresh water and freshly cut herbs and roots that can cleanse the body."

The physician paused and stared at Trulius, this time, not with the eyes of a physician but with the eyes of a good and caring man. "He is a special child. I sense that a fire drives him in. What is this handsome young man's full name?"

"Tessius Trulius Augustus," Kemnebi said.

"He is much stronger than other boys his age that I have treated, and that is good." He rose to leave. "He will need all of his strength to fight this ailment."

The physician placed a hand on Kemnebi's shoulder. "Try and get some rest. I shall come tomorrow and see how Tessius Trulius is doing. I am Lucanus," he said.

"I am grateful to you, Lucanus. I shall pray to the gods that they forever illuminate your path."

Lucanus nodded. "A man can always use the prayers of others, Kemnebi. I welcome your thoughtfulness."

Twenty-Four

Erasmus Harel looked up from the scroll he was reading and smiled. He was seated at his desk in his quarters. The window was wide open, and he could clearly hear Adin. He was outside in the courtyard, pleading with an ass, begging the animal to get up. Erasmus Harel walked to the window and peered down into the courtyard. Adin was standing in front of an ass that had completely lowered itself in the middle of the courtyard, refusing to move. Adin gently tugged at the rope he had placed around the animal's neck, but the animal did not budge.

Farrenthias stood next to Adin. He was carefully studying a flute that he held in his hands. Farrenthias placed the flute up to his mouth and blew into it. No sound came out from the flute.

Adin stopped tugging at the rope and looked at Farrenthias. "Take one deep breath and blow steady and gently, my son."

Farrenthias tried it again and this time a feeble sound filled the air.

"There!" Adin cried. "You have it!"

"But it does not sound very good," Farrenthias said.

Adin tugged at the rope again. "Patience, Farrenthias. You must have patience. See how much patience I am demonstrating now with our little friend." He sighed. "I just hope that one day soon we make it to the stables."

Farrenthias laughed and caressed the ass. "Does she have a name, Adin?"

Adin scratched his head. "Now that I think about it, no she does not. You can name her if you like."

Farrenthias looked into the animal's eyes and then gently stroked her. "Dolce is her name because she is sweet." Farrenthias looked at Adin. "Adin, I beg you not to tell anyone, but I would rather ride Dolce than a horse. I am afraid of horses."

Adin laughed. "Your secret is safe with me, my dear child. Why, Dolce here may be slow and capricious at times, but she will never toss you." He tugged at the rope again, "and it might take an eternity, but she will eventually get you to your destination in one piece. But, is it not better to arrive late than on time with broken bones?"

Farrenthias laughed again. "I once tried to ride a horse, and just trying to mount it, I almost broke my bones."

Erasmus smiled. He too had been afraid of horses when he had been young and he too had fallen the first time he had tried to ride one. He folded his arms and watched Adin and Farrenthias finally start toward the stables again with Dolce. Indeed he had failed miserably the first time he had tried to ride. He closed his eyes and recalled that day in great detail. His father had taken him to Rome to spend another summer with his half-brother, Marcellius Kaelus. He had been twelve years old and his younger brother, ten. He was thin and awkward and his tunic hung loosely around his body as if it were too large for him. Marcellius was slightly shorter, but his small frame was already filled with developing muscles. Marcellius had already expertly mounted his horse and was shouting at him.

"What are you waiting for, Erasmus Harel? The carnival awaits us." He laughed. "Tiberius has banned soothsayers, but since he is not in Rome, I bet we can get our fortunes told."

"I do not want to know my future," Erasmus Harel said, looking nervously at the horse he was supposed to ride.

"Erasmus Harel!" His brother yelled. "Stop staring at the horse and mount him. Do not be afraid. Show him who is master!"

Erasmus Harel took hold of the horse, jumped, and tried to throw a leg across the back of the horse but stumbled backwards and landed on his back.

"You almost had it that time," Marcellius yelled. "Try it again. Do not give up."

In a fit of anger, Erasmus Harel jumped to his feet and grasped the horse's mane. He jumped again, and this time, landed squarely on the horse's back.

"That is it!" Marcellius cried. "You did it!"

But suddenly, the horse buckled wildly, and Erasmus Harel flew from its back and hit the ground hard. He rolled onto his back with his arms spread wide. "I give up," he cried. "I am not going, Marcellius! Go without me!"

Marcellius walked his horse over to where Erasmus Harel lay and reached down and offered him a hand. "Come, Erasmus, we will ride together."

Erasmus Harel slowly got to his feet and dusted off his tunic. "I said I was not going, Marcellius, please do not insist."

Marcellius did not withdraw his hand. "I will not go without you, Erasmus Harel. I have been looking forward to this carnival for weeks but I am not going without you. Either we both go, or neither one of us goes."

Erasmus Harel sighed. In the few short summer months he would spend with his brother in Rome, Marcellius always managed to get his way with him, but Erasmus Harel loved him and secretly enjoyed the mischief he got them into. He reached for his brother's hand. "Very well, but you better not let me fall."

With Marcellius's assistance, he mounted the horse and wrapped his hands around his younger brother. "I am ready, and I warn you, you had better not go fast."

Marcellius laughed and dug his heels into the horse. "Hang on brother, I will have us at the gates of Rome in no time."

Erasmus Harel tightened his arms around his brother's waist, and Marcellius coughed and gagged. "You are squeezing me to death, brother," he shouted.

"And you are frightening me to death, slow down."

Marcellius roared with laughter, and it was such an infectious laughter that Erasmus Harel also laughed. They did not stop laughing until they reached the many red, orange, purple and yellow tents that were aligned just outside the gates of Rome.

They entrusted the horse to a squire and walked among the hundreds of people who were jammed on the carnival grounds. Children competed in frivolous games and grownups played board games and dice. There were exquisite foods, music, and other festivities. Actors, dressed in outrageous costumes, and wearing painted faces, entertained the crowds on temporary wooden stages. Mimes and clowns walked the grounds and entertained along the way. Rows and rows of booths were lined beneath a beautiful clear sky. Some booths housed philosophers who matched wits with those who dropped by and wished to engage in polemics, and other tents had writers selling their latest works, or artists selling their sketches. Men dressed in long cloaks sat patiently listening to dreams and interpreting them. Fortunetellers entertained the curious and magicians dazzled the gullible.

"We are passing the fortuneteller tents," Erasmus Harel said. "Are you not going into one of them?"

Marcellius shrugged. "We have no time for that right now. Hurry, I see an interesting gathering just ahead." He pointed to an area where a large crowd was gathered. "That," Marcellius said, "is where the real men are gathered."

Erasmus Harel knew very well what Marcellius was talking about. Marcellius loved to wrestle. Their father was an excellent wrestler, and he might have taken the sport more seriously were he not such a busy man. Nevertheless, he always had time to wrestle with Marcellius, and when he was away, Marcellius would practice with the servants or anyone else he could get his hands on. Usually it was somebody bigger than he.

"Hurry," Marcellius shouted, running ahead of Erasmus Harel. "They are letting boys wrestle."

They pushed through the crowd until they had a clear view of a man holding up the arm of a tall muscular boy whose dark skin glistened like molasses.

"We have a champion. I will allow one more match in this category, and then we return to the men. So come now, who is next? Who will challenge our valiant champion?"

"I will!" Marcellius shouted. The crowd turned to look at Marcellius, and when they saw his small stature they went wild with laughter and cheers.

The blood drained from Erasmus Harel's face. He stared at his brother, who had removed his outer tunic and wore nothing but a short undergarment. Marcellius's opponent was taller and he looked like he was about thirteen years old. His dark skin glistened like black molasses and he had a much stronger build. Erasmus Harel caught his elbow.

"You have gone mad, Marcellius. That boy is twice your size. He is going to hurt you."

"Wrestling," whispered Marcellius, "is not always won by the larger or stronger man." He tapped the left side of his temple. "If your opponent is bigger than you, then the victory lies in outwitting him."

"Be serious, Marcellius. What will I tell Father if you get hurt? As your older brother I am responsible for you."

Marcellius grinned. "Tell Father? If I get hurt, how will you ever get home, brother?"

Marcellius stepped forward confident and fearless and flexed his muscles to the delight of the crowd.

"The rules are simple, lads," the man who was officiating said, "just pin your opponent, or force him into submission, oh, and be content that we do not make you wrestle naked like the Greeks often do."

The crowd erupted into laughter and began to shout words of encouragement to the two boys.

Marcellius approached the much taller boy, and when the crowd saw how disproportionate they were in size, they burst into laughter again but cheered Marcellius on.

The older boy folded his arms. "Are you certain you want to do this? I do not want to hurt you," he said.

Marcellius frowned and crouched into a fighting position. "You will not hurt me. Perhaps it is I who will hurt you."

"Begin," the official shouted and stepped out of the way.

Like a lion stalking its prey, Marcellius crouched even lower and began to circle his opponent, waiting for an opening to attack. The older boy also assumed the fighting position. He glared at Marcellius, and then, without warning, he lunged at him. His swiftness surprised Marcellius, but he had anticipated the move. He countered the move by dropping to the ground and rolling out of the way. As the boy flew past him, Marcellius stuck out his foot and tripped him. The crowd went wild with applause and cheers. But to the surprise of Marcellius, the boy was quickly on his feet and charging him again. Marcellius danced to the left, then to the right, but the boy did not take the bait. He plowed into Marcellius and pinned him between his knees. Then, he reached down and cleanly picked up Marcellius by his feet and swung him in a full circle and released him. Marcellius flew into the air and landed hard, but instead of withering in pain, he somersaulted to his feet and charged the boy. But, instead of crashing into him, Marcellius, swiftly dropped in front of the boy and curled his legs around the boy's legs. The boy tried to keep his balance but failed. He fell forward, and Marcellius jumped on his back.

"Have you had enough?" Marcellius yelled. The crowd screamed with laughter.

The boy struggled to his feet, but he too found humor in the words of Marcellius and laughed so hard Marcellius easily knocked him down again.

"Enough!" cried the official. He helped Marcellius to his feet. "This young lad has made his point. He is a brave one. We shall call this match a draw."

Erasmus Harel rushed to his brother's side. "Marcellius, are you alright? Are you hurt?" he asked.

Marcellius gasped for air and stretched his arms high above his head. "I am fine. Did you see how well I did? I almost had him," he cried. "They should not have stopped the match."

The boy he had just wrestled walked up to him. "Bah, I might have hurt you had I not started laughing so much."

Marcellius slapped his belly. "I have developed quite an appetite. Shall we get something to eat?"

"Are you also hungry?" Erasmus Harel asked the boy.

"I am starving." The boy said. "But I have nothing to buy food with."

"Then," Erasmus Harel said, "we shall treat you. I am Erasmus Harel and my brother's name is Marcellius."

"My name is Kemnebi," the boy said. He placed a strong arm around the shoulders of Marcellius. "So, little friend, who taught you how to wrestle so well?"

Erasmus Harel turned at the sound of steps approaching, and the memory faded. Lord Gaios stopped at the open door. His face was ashen and his lips tight, his eyes intense.

"Forgive me for interrupting you," he said, in a surprisingly calm voice.

"You are not interrupting me, Lord Gaios. Please come in," Erasmus Harel said. He pointed to a chair. "Please have a seat." Erasmus Harel walked to a table on which was a small jug of wine surrounded by several clay cups. "May I offer you a cup of wine, Lord Gaios?" he said. "I assure you that it is excellent wine. Ya'ir brought it with him from your part of the country several months ago."

Lord Gaios nodded and silently took a cup from Erasmus Harel and sipped from it. He stared quietly out the window.

"Tell me, Erasmus Harel," he said, "Are there really any answers to the mysteries of life? I am not as educated as you and your companions, nor am I a brilliant thinker. I do know, however, that the Greeks have their gods, the Hebrew worship their mysterious one god, and the Romans have their beliefs. In truth, I suppose the people of every country have their own beliefs." He nodded pensively. "Where then, I ask myself, does the truth lie, and why would a man wish to spend an entire life seeking answers that will always elude him or that perhaps do not even exist?"

Erasmus Harel frowned delightfully. "For a man who claims not to be a brilliant thinker, you pose very thoughtful questions, my lord," he said. He sat in front of Lord Gaios and looked solemnly at him. He reclined back and sighed. "Lord Gaios, in many ways, the truth has nothing to do with the beliefs of man for the reasons you have just set out. In the Far East, a wise man once told me that it is easier to move a mountain, pebble by pebble, than it is to convince just one man that his beliefs are false. Here, we have studied the beliefs of many spiritual and philosophical thinkers, and what we have learned is that there are many roads that can lead a man to resolve the questions that dwell within his heart about his purpose, about his existence. On the other hand, the pursuit of knowledge, my lord, includes not just the words of man, it also includes his deeds and an understanding of the land we live on, of the stars above, the air we breathe, the trees and plants that surround us, all of those things must be understood and contemplated. And, I might add that not all men possess either the patience or the desire to think about such matters. Those of us that do wish to do nothing else with our lives."

Lord Gaios sat silently pondering those words. "I see," he finally said. "Well spoken." He became pensive again. He clenched his hands and stared at them. "With these hands, I converted the hundreds of acres of land that I own into a fortress, surrounded by a protective wall, where many people have come to live and raise their families." He smiled sarcastically. "Truly I am a wealthy man. Yet, it is clear to me that Farrenthias, my only son and heir, has no interest in all that he will inherit from me."

Erasmus Harel considered Lord Gaios' pain. "My lord, just now when you walked in, I was recalling my youth. I was raised in Greece and when I was old enough my father, a Roman official, made arrangements for me to return permanently to Rome with him. Although I loved him and loved my half-brother, I begged him to let me stay in Greece and allow me to study with a group of local priests. After much pleading on my part I was able to persuade him. Devout priests who would burn candles and incense to the gods day and night educated me. They fasted and spent days in silent prayer, and they instilled in me a desire to pursue what was in my heart, even if it went against traditional Greek thinking. That is the life I chose as a child, my lord."

Lord Gaios sat silent for a long time with a troubling expression on his face. At last, he sighed and set his cup of wine down and stood. "Very well then, tomorrow, when my men and I leave, a part of my very soul shall remain behind, Erasmus Harel." He paused at the door. "I shall return in about six or ten months. I want to make certain that Farrenthias is doing well. In the meantime, Tavius, one of the members of my personal guard shall remain here."

"I understand. Also, my lord, Ya'ir will be returning to Jerusalem shortly. Were Farrenthias to change his mind about staying here, he and Cerudotus could return with him."

Lord Gaios winced and tried to smile. "I do not have such hopes. It is clear to me that my son has found something here that was clearly missing in his life back home."

Erasmus Harel nodded slowly. "I know it is of little comfort to you, but I tell you, truly, that you have made a wise decision, a decision that will please Farrenthias and make him very happy."

Lord Gaios nodded sadly. "Yes, unfortunately I think I have made the right decision."

Twenty-Five

As darkness fell across the ship, the tension on the deck heightened with nervous anticipation. Every night since the ship had left Puteoli, the crew combed the deck and callously tore the covers off of those who slept and kicked and poked them. Those who did not respond quickly enough were immediately hauled away to the corner of the ship where they kept a pile of dead bodies, bodies that would be dumped into the sea.

Kemnebi watched them anxiously. Trulius had not gotten worse, but neither had he improved. When a tall, dark man reached him, Kemnebi stiffened and wrapped one of his hidden hands tightly around the handle of his dagger. No one was going to take Trulius from him, no matter the consequences. But as the man reached down to uncover Trulius, an old man, a few paces away, began to struggle with two crewmen.

"No!" the old man shouted. "Let go of her. She is just asleep! My wife is just asleep" He wrapped his arms protectively around her.

"Release her, old man." One of the men with whom he struggled kicked him hard, but the old man clung to his wife. "She is
not dead. I will not let you take her," he cried.

The man leaning over Kemnebi hesitated for a moment then
dropped his hands and ran to help. The crewmen took turns kicking the old man until Kemnebi could no longer bear to watch. He
set Trulius down and angrily pushed his way through those who
had gathered to watch. He was about to step in front of the old
man to stop the beating, when a strong hand grabbed him from
behind.

"Kemnebi," Lucanus whispered, still holding onto him. "Let me
take care of this."

He released Kemnebi and stepped ahead of him. The men had
finally wrestled the woman from the old man, but Lucanus blocked
their path.

"Move, physician," one of the men said. "This does not concern
you."

"Set the woman down," Lucanus said. Suddenly, he seemed taller,
stronger and full of confidence. "If she is not dead, like her husband claims, then as the ship's physician the matter does concern
me."

The crewman stared at the woman and then motioned to the
others to set her down. "Go on," he said. "See for yourself. She is
not breathing."

Lucanus crouched over her and placed a cheek to her lips. He
detected the faintest breathing—barely. Still crouched over her, he
quickly placed a hand beneath the woman's nose. She gagged and
then coughed.

"Bah!" the crewman said. "By morning she will be dead, and by
tomorrow night she will be at the bottom of the sea." He pushed

the old man out of the way. "Give us trouble again and you will join her."

Lucanus rose to his feet and placed a hand on the shoulder of the old man. "What is your name?"

"Pableus, sire." He rubbed his wrists where the men had squeezed them. "I am very grateful to you, for what you have done."

"And your wife, what is her name?"

"Grecia." He lowered his voice and spoke in a whisper. "How did you get her to cough?"

Lucanus opened his fingers and showed him a small vial. "Vinegar," he whispered. He frowned and shook his head. "Of course, she is terribly ill and may not survive another night or two."

Pableus nodded sadly. "I am aware of her critical condition, but I could not let them take her so that she could die alone like an animal in one corner of the ship." He stared at the covered face of his wife. "I am aware of our dire situation and am not opposed to a burial at sea, but I had hoped for at least a day of mourning."

"I understand," Lucanus said.

Lucanus started to leave but paused in front of Kemnebi. "I am afraid," he glanced over his shoulder to make certain that no one was listening. "I am afraid that I just discovered the first case of leprosy below deck. I am obliged to report it to the captain of the ship, and when I do, I fear that he and his men will panic."

"Leprosy?" Kemnebi cried. "Am I correct that it is a highly contagious disease?"

"It is, and that is why I expect that the captain of the ship will panic."

"Why does he not dock at some isolated location and let us off the ship?"

"I begged him to do that before we even arrived at Puteoli, but he would not consider it. I am afraid he is under orders to rid the ship of all the sick. They want no ailing stragglers venturing onto land." Lucanus turned to leave. "Of course, after he learns of the leprosy, he might even start tossing the living overboard. To stay on this ship means certain death."

Kemnebi stood pensively looking at Lucanus as he weaved through the sea of people and disappeared below deck. He then turned his attention to the deck, and this time he studied the masts, the lines and sails, and the pile of wood between sacks of grain and large clay jars. He decided that he had all that he needed. Moreover, the ship remained close to the coastline. This last detail encouraged him even more.

Kemnebi quietly sought out Pableus and eased next to him. Pableus had taken his wife back into his arms. "Pableus," Kemnebi whispered. "I have a child in my care who is also sick, and I have no intention of letting him die on this ship." He leaned closer to the old man. "I am taking him off this floating tomb—tonight. Would you like to come with us?"

Pableus stared at Kemnebi. "What do you mean?"

"I am jumping ship with my ward."

"And you would be willing to take Grecia and me along with you? We would only slow you down."

"It does not matter. I could use your help."

"But if we are caught…"

"If we are caught what? Staying on this ship means certain death. Every man deserves a chance to live and a chance to die with dignity if he can help it."

Pableus nodded. "I agree." He pressed a hand against his wife. "How—how do we do it?"

Kemnebi looked discreetly in the direction of the cargo. "We build a raft with those boards over there." He then looked toward the sky and at the darkening clouds. "I think it is going to rain tonight. If it does, it will be our perfect cover. As soon as the ship anchors to toss the corpses overboard, we go."

Twenty-Six

The ship drifted to a stop, and Kemnebi scrambled to his knees and waited anxiously for the anchor to hit the water. Rain clouds had formed and there was a slight breeze, but the weather was not going to deter Kemnebi's plans. He was determined to get Trulius off of this floating tomb, and he was going to do it today, right now. He heard a loud splash and raised his head to have a look. Six maybe seven men approached the pile of corpses with the sleeves of their tunics rolled high above their elbows. They were about to start the grim task of dumping the bodies overboard. A cold wind, followed by a flash of lightening, gushed across the deck. It thundered and then suddenly began to pour. The crew abandoned their task and ran for cover, and all across the deck, people raised rags, shirts or any other loose garment they could get their hands on and placed them over their heads.

Kemnebi looked down. As planned, Pableus and Grecia were now next to Trulius. Pableus had covered her and Trulius from the rain, and he was looking anxiously at Kemnebi, waiting for a signal.

The rain intensified, and for a fleeting moment, Kemnebi nearly lost his nerve. Would the rain prove too big of an obstacle? But, the look of willingness in the eyes of Pableus encouraged Kemnebi and erased all doubts. He was about to spring into action when he spotted a lone figure weaving quickly through the huddled throngs, seemingly oblivious of the hard rain that drenched him. Kemnebi breathed easier when he recognized Lucanus's long stride.

Lucanus ducked down beside Kemnebi and wiped the water from his face. "I thought I might be too late."

Kemnebi glared at him in surprise. "You—you know what we are about to do?"

Lucanus nodded. "I figured you had no choice." He looked at Pableus and his wife. "I see that you are taking them with you. Such kindness can yield many rewards."

"Do you want to go?"

Lucanus shook his head. "I cannot abandon the sick." He uncovered the forehead of Grecia and placed the palm of his hand on it. "Her fever remains dangerously high." He then turned to Trulius and did the same. "He too is burning. They both need fresh water."

"Then we have no time to lose," Kemnebi said. He looked at Pableus. "We have got to move fast."

"I am right behind you, Kemnebi," he said.

"How can I help?" Lucanus said.

Kemnebi crouched low. "Follow us."

Kemnebi moved quickly but cautiously across the deck. He stopped at the foot of the first mast. It towered over them. The rain remained steady but was less intense, and for that Kemnebi was grateful. He was going to climb the mast and cut some lines, but first, Kemnebi carefully studied the sail. He had to be careful not to cut the main lines and collapse the sail.

Convinced that he knew which two he would cut, Kemnebi turned to Pableus and Lucanus. "I am going to cut the lines that we will need."

The climb was difficult, and with the rain splashing across his face, seeing was also difficult. Nevertheless, Kemnebi reached the lines and cut them. The two lines dropped down and Kemnebi quickly scrambled down and helped coil the ropes. He then squinted in the darkness and pointed to a corner of the ship. "The boards we will need are somewhere over there."

"I too have seen them," Lucanus said. "Follow me."

Kemnebi looked around. They remained inconspicuous, but the rain was beginning to slow down significantly. This meant that the ship's men would be on the deck soon, disposing of the bodies. They had to hurry.

Lucanus lifted a board. "Are these the ones?"

"Yes," Kemnebi said. "We need six."

All of a sudden, a man grabbed Pableus by the ankle and pulled him to his knees. The man was drenched and his eyes were wild and glued on Pableus.

"Think I do not know what you are up to?" he said, coughing. He grabbed the rope that Pableus had around his chest. "A rope and boards? You are fixing to leave the ship, and I am going with you."

Pableus tensed. "You are mad. Let go of me!" he whispered.

"I am going with you I tell you." The man started to struggle to his feet, still clinging to the rope around Pableus.

Kemnebi gripped the man's hand. "Let go of him," he said in a low but stern voice.

The man raised his other hand in which he held a dagger and placed it at the throat of Pableus. "I said I was going."

Above the sound of the rain came a splashing sound. The crew was on the deck again and had started to dispose of the bodies. They had no more time to lose. Kemnebi released his grip on the man. "Very well then, you can come. Now hurry," he said.

The man chuckled triumphantly and let go of Pableus. Kemnebi moved so swiftly that no one realized what had happened until the man coughed out blood. He opened his mouth wide, as if he were about to scream, but no sound came out of his mouth. He dropped his dagger and reached for his throat and tried desperately to stop the flow of blood pouring from the clean sliver Kemnebi's dagger had made across his throat, but the gesture proved futile. The man gasped and choked and then collapsed to one side.

Lucanus and Pableus stared in horror at the dead man, but Kemnebi urged them along. "Hurry!" he whispered. "We have wasted enough time."

Kemnebi spread out five of the boards and quickly weaved the three ropes through them and tied all but one of the boards together at both ends. He did this expertly from years of tying merchandize that he and Marcellius frequently transported across Rome on carts to their warehouses. Certain that the rope was secure around each board, he cut another piece of rope and loosely tied the last board to the raft. "This last board we break in half and use as an oar," he said to Pableus and then placed both hands on him.

"You go down first, my friend. When you reach the water untie yourself. Lucanus and I will pull up the rope and lower the raft into the water. After that we will lower Grecia into your arms."

"I understand," Pableus said.

"Good, now raise your arms so I can tie the rope around your waist," Kemnebi said.

Pableus raised his arms but Kemnebi paused. The rain had abruptly stopped, and worse, at the other end of the ship the splashing sounds slowed drastically. They were almost finished disposing of the bodies. Kemnebi and Lucanus looked at each other, and even in the darkness, Kemnebi could clearly see the worried expression on the physician's face. If they were caught they would lose their lives.

"I know," Kemnebi whispered. "We have to hurry."

Kemnebi swiftly tied the rope around Pableus and he and Lucanus helped Pableus over the edge and slowly lowered him into the water. To the surprise of Kemnebi, Pableus moved quickly. He untied the rope and waved that he was fine. Without a word spoken between them they lowered the raft and waited while Pableus untied the rope and crawled onto the raft. Kemnebi held his breath, but to his relief, their crude boat floated.

"Hopefully the raft will float long enough to carry us to the coast, Lucanus," he said

Lucanus placed an arm around his shoulders. "I have faith, my friend, that soon you will be on land."

They swiftly, but delicately, tied the rope beneath the arms of Grecia and carefully lowered her into Pableus's arms. They froze, however, when a woman suddenly wailed that her husband be spared and not be tossed into the sea. Others around her tried to calm her down and keep her quiet, but the woman only screamed louder.

"She is going to wake everybody up," Kemnebi whispered to Lucanus. "Go, dear friend, and keep her quiet. I can do the rest by myself."

"I think that is best," Lucanus said. He squeezed the arm of Kemnebi. "Good luck to all of you. I shall pray that you are guided to safety."

As soon as Pableus freed the rope, Kemnebi retrieved it as fast as he could then dropped down beside Trulius. The woman's screams had awakened him.

"Kemnebi," Trulius whispered, "why is that woman crying?"

"Hush, my child," Kemnebi said. "And listen carefully. Do you have the strength to climb onto my back? We are getting off the ship, but we must climb down a rope to do it."

Trulius lifted his head and slowly nodded. Kemnebi was much relieved to see some semblance of the old Trulius, the Trulius who was always full of adventure and fire. He prayed that soon he would see that Trulius again.

"Hurry then and whatever you do, do not let go."

Trulius threw the covers away and crawled onto the back of Kemnebi and locked his arms around his neck.

"I know you are weak," Kemnebi said. "But you must try and hang on." He swung over the side of the ship, and standing on a small ledge, he gripped the rope. "Are you ready?"

"Yes," Trulius said. "I am ready."

Kemnebi dropped one foot off the ledge and then the other. He and Trulius were now dangling off the side of the ship on the rope. Kemnebi started down the rope but stopped when he felt Trulius's hold around his neck and shoulders slacken.

"Hold me tight, Trulius. Do not let go."

"Forgive me, Kemnebi," Trulius whispered, his feeble voice filled with fear. "I started to slip."

The arms of Trulius tightened around Kemnebi's neck, but the rope in Kemnebi's hands jerked savagely. Kemnebi looked up. A few men were gathered at the side of the ship looking down at him.

"Help me pull them up!" one of them shouted.

Kemnebi felt a hard tug on the rope and he and Trulius bounced upwards. "Trulius," he whispered, "take a deep breath, take a deep breath and let go of me."

"Kemnebi," Trulius cried, "do you want me to jump into the water?"

"Yes, Trulius. Do it now! Let go!" Kemnebi shouted.

Kemnebi felt his back free of the weight of Trulius. He looked down, saw Trulius hit the water, and he released his grip on the rope. The rope danced away from his face and flew upward. The moment Kemnebi hit the water he spread out his arms and kicked his legs to stop his downward momentum. When he broke the surface he frantically searched for Trulius. Fortunately, Pableus was pulling him out of the water and onto the raft. Kemnebi quickly swam to the raft and crawled onto it. He took one of the broken pieces of boards from Pableus and rowed as hard as he could.

Torches lit the side of the ship, and amid shouting and cursing the torches were soon raining down on them like fiery spears.

"Row, Pableus!" Kemnebi cried above the shouting and chaos that had erupted from the ship.

The raft moved oddly and threatened to fall apart, but it held together and cut through the water. Soon, they were beyond the range of the torches and Kemnebi paused to catch his breath. Grecia it appeared had slept through the entire incident, and although Trulius was awake, he lay quiet and still. Pableus was still rowing madly and Kemnebi placed a hand on him to slow him down.

"Pableus, you can relax," Kemnebi said to him. "We did it. We really did it."

The raft glided silently through choppy waters in the direction of the coast. Kemnebi looked back. The ship was nothing more than a dark form in the distance, and soon, it evaporated into the darkness altogether.

"What a nightmare," Kemnebi said.

"May Neptune look after the souls of those who were tossed into the sea tonight," Pableus said. "And of those souls who will follow tomorrow."

Twenty-Seven

Belfore leaped to his feet, and then angrily flung his plate of roasted boar across the room. "Damn it!" He shouted. "How can you expect me to eat?" He stared at his hands. "We had him! We had that Egyptian maggot and the boy. We had them in the palm of our hands and lost them." He pounded the table and pushed his chair out of the way. "Now look at us. We are in Puteoli sitting around like stupid fools, with no idea of where they might be." He pounded the table again and looked at Delerin and then at Bentore. "Where are they? Where did that scoundrel Kemnebi go when he left Capua? How could he have fooled us? Did he head east toward Brundisium? Bentore and I must have lost his trail."

"Impossible," Delerin said. "If they went through Capua he was coming here to Puteoli. It only makes sense."

Bentore, who was chewing loudly, spoke with his mouth full. "How can you be sure it was Kemnebi in Capua at that inn? Remember, the innkeeper never saw a child with that man you suspect was Kemnebi."

Belfore glared at him. "Fool! Do you know nothing about track-ing prey? Of course it was Kemnebi! A hunter has to have instincts and he must learn to rely and trust those instincts. I would bet my life on it!" He slapped Bentore on the shoulder as he walked past him. "Bah! What do you know about such matters." He walked to the window and stared out at the crowded peer. It was in total chaos. Merchants, looking ridiculous in their expensive gowns, watched as their slaves rushed to load their precious goods onto the ships, and the seamen aboard those ships scuttled about the decks like blind ants tending to every last minute detail before their departure. Worst of all, men, women, and children desperate to get on board the ships crowded onto the planks, and those planks threatened to collapse from the weight. Belfore laughed at them all. "Maggots," he cried. "Look at all those maggots." But suddenly his amusement turned into horror. "Delerin," he shouted. "Tell me again about that ship from Ostia?"

"What?" Delerin said. "I told you what happened. Why do you ask me again?"

Belfore ignored him and continued to stare out the window again. The crowds were getting worse. They kept pushing forward on the planks, and now seamen were trying to control the flow of the traffic. "Listen to me, Delerin," Belfore said. "It was Kemnebi in Capua I tell you, and he left that inn by crawling out of the window rather than walking out the front door. So, he is taking no chances, just in case he is being followed." He looked over his shoulder and gave Delerin a menacing look. "If he was willing to do that, then perhaps he was willing to climb aboard a ship full of diseased fools, just so he could leave the country as quickly as possible."

"I am no fool," Delerin cried, "that thought also occurred to me, so I made inquiries. The passengers aboard that ship were doomed. A physician was charged with keeping the crew of that ship from getting ill. The ship was to be out at sea for just one week. And anyone with the slightest symptom of an illness was going to be tossed into the sea."

Bentore laughed. "Then Kemnebi and the boy are surely dead if they boarded that ship! Let us return to Rome and report this news to Nestor."

"Fool!" Belfore shouted. "What evidence do we have that the boy is dead? It is just our luck that the Egyptian boarded that ship and survived. We have nothing to report. Nestor will laugh in our faces and demand his money back." He glared at Delerin. "Where was the ship going to dock?"

"Rhegium."

Belfore returned to the table and gulped the rest of his wine and slammed the cup down. "Then we go to Rhegium. That is better than sitting around here like a pig's ass doing nothing. Let us go and find that Egyptian piece of manure before he has us chasing him all over the empire."

Twenty-Eight

Kemnebi rose to his feet and brushed the sweat from his brow. He had never buried anyone, much less with nothing but sticks and rocks. He dusted off his hands and knees and inspected his work. He and Pableus had agreed that Grecia's grave should not be detectable, so after burying her, Kemnebi had smoothed out the dirt and scattered shrubs and rocks on top, thereby removing all traces that it was a grave. Pableus stood solemnly at the foot of his wife's grave with his eyes cast down and his hands clasped in front of him. Trulius was on one knee quietly watching Kemnebi. Behind them, a short distance away, the dark blue waters of the Mediterranean Sea glistened beneath what was left of a late afternoon sun, dipping out of sight.

"You did all that you could to save her," Kemnebi said, trying feebly to comfort the old man. "I did not know her, but I know she was a brave woman. The few days that she was here with us she did not complain once."

"That was my Grecia. She never complained about anything,"

Pableus said sadly. "We had been together since we were children playing in the streets."

"She is in the hands of the gods now," Kemnebi said. "May she travel safely in the next world." He considered the irony that just days before he had offered to help Marcellius bury Servia and now this. "It will be dark soon," he said. "I shall start a fire."

"May I start the fire, Kemnebi?" Trulius asked, jumping to his feet.

"Yes, but be careful." Kemnebi marveled at how well Trulius was doing. He had lost weight, but otherwise he had recovered well enough to have insisted on helping Kemnebi dig Grecia's grave.

"On the ship you never mentioned that you were a physician," Kemnebi said. "What you did for Trulius in just one week is re-markable. Lucanus would have been proud of you."

"I am no physician," Pableus said, his voice sounding fatigued from the sleepless nights during which he had looked after his two patients. "It was actually Grecia's father who first placed a vial of boiled herbs in my hands one day. He told me that it would cure me of the terrible stomach ache that I was suffering from. It worked, and I was intrigued. Now, I am just familiar with a few wild herbs and their power to heal."

"Is that not what a physician does, cure the ill with wild herbs? I have seen physicians that do not heal people as quickly and as well as you do. Why do you not carry the title?"

Pableus shrugged. "Wearing the toga of a physician has never appealed to me. Besides, it is only a matter of time before Rome regulates physicians, and I am too old to comply with regulations."

"I thought anyone could acquire the title by merely acquiring the experience."

"It was like that once. Men of different professions would mix their own potions and call it medicine. But then the Greeks arrived, and Augustus was so impressed with their medical knowledge that he exempted the profession from taxation. Suddenly, everyone wanted to be a physician."

"In Egypt," Kemnebi said, "most physicians learn other methods of treating the sick. I once witnessed a man who awoke one morning with the inability to walk. He had been quite healthy the morning before and there was no apparent reason for his sudden and unexplained paralysis. His wife knew immediately that her husband was under some terrible hex. The physicians prayed over him continually for three days before the man was finally able to regain the use of his legs."

Pableus nodded. "I am familiar with Egyptian practices. While I have never been to Egypt, I knew an Egyptian once who went to Rome and spent three years there before he returned to his country. He taught me many things."

"Come," Kemenbi said. "I see that Trulius has started an excellent fire. You must rest."

The two men sat next to the fire and quietly watched Trulius poke it with a stick.

"So," Kemnebi said, reclining back on his elbows. "Where do you go from here, Pableus?"

Pableus tossed a twig into the fire. "I considered just returning to Rome, but I suppose I should go on to Sicilia. Grecia and I have a son there. I will have to be the bearer of the sad news."

"Would you not consider just staying in Sicilia with your son?"

Pableus thought a moment. "My son is a good man. He will insist that I do just that, but I will refuse. He and his wife have two small children. I do not want him worrying about me. Besides, I have an apartment in the Aventine. Grecia and I had lived there for over thirty years. It is small, but in one room, I am able to tend to some patients."

Kemnebi laid out a handful of silver coins on the grass. "This should cover your travel expenses to Sicilia."

Pableus looked at the coins but made no effort to pick them up. "You are kind to offer me money, but I would not feel very good about accepting it. I am indebted to you for taking Grecia and me off that ship." He sighed and then quietly said, "Here, at least she died with dignity and has come to rest at a beautiful place."

Kemnebi lifted the coins and placed them on Pableus's lap. "Please take them. Perhaps one day when Trulius and I return to Rome we might need your services again."

"Hum," Pableus murmured. "What about you and Trulius? Where are you going from here?"

"We must still cross the great sea."

"I see," Pableus said. "You will find plenty of ships in Rhegium."

"Kemnebi," Trulius said. "I am hungry. Is it too late to fish? I could eat a whole fish."

"It is the best time to fish, Trulius," Kemnebi said. "No hot sun, no pesky bugs to worry about." He stood and turned to Pableus. "Is it a good sign that Trulius is hungry?"

Pableus managed a sad smile. "Yes, it is a sign that our boy has completely recovered."

Twenty-Nine

Lucanus paused at the top of the ship's gangplank and surveyed the crowded dock of Rhegium. The sight of so many people going about their morning business filled him with rage as if they were to blame for the terrible nightmare he had just endured. By his estimate, there had been over three hundred people on board the ship. Now, a few weeks later, fewer than a hundred had survived and half were part of the ship's crew. He had done all that he could. He had held many women and children and old men in his arms and listened as their last breath escaped from their lips. He had prayed to every god imaginable, every Greek and Roman god. He had even prayed to the Hebrew God, but in the end, all of his efforts, everything that he had tried, had been in vain. What kind of a god or gods, would allow this to happen?

He angrily clutched his satchel, flung it across his back, and started down the gangplank. Three men caught his attention because of the loud manner in which they were interrogating two members of the crew. The largest of the three men suddenly grabbed one of the crewmen and nearly lifted him from his feet. Lucanus slowed his stride at this gesture of violence.

"A raft left the ship?" The man shouted. "Who was on that raft?" Was it an Egyptian and a Roman boy?" He squeezed the crewman's throat. "Speak!"

The man gagged and his eyes bulged. "I—I saw nothing I tell you." He coughed. "I just heard that it happened. I was below deck."

"Belfore," one of his companions said, tugging at his arm. "You are choking him. Let him speak."

Belfore released the man with a shove. "Then you make him talk, Delerin. He is lying. He saw who got on that raft."

"There!" the crewman shouted. "There is the ship's physician. He will tell you what happened."

Belfore and his companions confronted Lucanus and blocked his path. "I want to have a word with you," Belfore said.

Lucanus tried to walk around him, but Belfore grabbed him by the arm. "Are you deaf? I said I want to have a word with you."

Lucanus lowered his eyes to the hold Belfore had on him. "Sire, I am terribly exhausted and I am famished. I wish to be on my way." He raised his eyes and angrily stared at Belfore. "I heard your inquiries. The whole pier heard you."

Belfore let his hand drop with a grunt. "Then what have you to say? Did you see the Egyptian and the boy? Were they the ones who got away on the raft?"

His dear friend Paulous had instilled in Lucanus a deep sense of honesty, an attribute that Lucanus agreed was highly desirable and sorely lacking in the world, but not all men were worthy of the truth. What was to be lost by lying to a scoundrel, especially if it meant saving a life? "I do recall several men of dark skin," Lucanus said, frowning. "Perhaps they were Egyptian, and one or two of them might have been traveling with a boy, as I recall. In any case, none survived. I personally closed their eyes and offered their souls to the gods."

Lucanus reached around his back and adjusted his satchel. "I, too, heard rumblings from the crewmen that several men might have escaped from the ship on a raft. No one knows for sure who they were, but I assure you that they too are dead. All who were on the deck were deathly sick and none survived. He started to step around Belfore then paused. "Surely those men had the ailment and probably died on some shore somewhere between here and Ostia."

Lucanus stepped around Belfore and quickly disappeared into the throngs of people.

"Ha!" Bentore cried. "We now know for sure that the boy is dead."

"You fool," Belfore said, looking idly in the direction in which Lucanus had disappeared. "We are done for."

"We are done for?" Bentore cried. "Why? Let us take this news to Nestor and collect the rest of our money?"

"You imbecile," Belfore shouted. "Nestor needs proof! I promised him that I would throw the boy's carcass at his feet. I bragged about it. Now we have nothing. We are done for I tell you."

"Then if we return to Rome," Bentore said, "Nestor will laugh in our faces and demand that we return his money."

Delerin laughed sarcastically. "Belfore is right, brother, you are a fool. If that were the worst of it I would not care. If we go back to Rome now, Nestor will have our heads. We made fools of ourselves and we made a fool of him. We are dead men."

"So what now?" Bentore asked.

Belfore brushed the stubble around his chin and pondered the mess they were in, and the more he thought about it, the angrier he got. At last he said, "The Egyptian maggot defeated us after all. It is better if the three of us are not seen together again, and I suggest that none of us return to Rome anytime soon."

"I agree," Delerin said. "Rome is not safe. Maybe someday we can return there, but not now."

"I have a cousin in northern Italy that I have not seen in years," Belfore said. "Perhaps it is time I pay him a visit. It is far way from Rome."

Bentore turned to his brother. "Where do we go, Delerin?"

Delerin shrugged his shoulders. "Where do a couple of thieves like us go? I am suddenly thirsty. Let us go and find a tavern where we can think about this some more." He held out a hand to Belfore and gripped his forearm, and without a word, he motioned to his brother to follow.

Belfore watched Delerin and Bentore disappear into the crowds like Lucanus had just done minutes before, and his fury returned. He angrily glanced at the ship. Rome suited him, with its many taverns, where a man could get drunk and steal away a wench, and its ample dark alleys, where a man could rob an idiot and not get caught. But Delerin had been right. Maybe one day it would be safe to return, but not now. "No," he murmured out loud. "Not now."

Thirty

"**P**lease!" Kemnebi cried. "Let us on board. I will pay for our passage. We have been sent by an acquaintance of yours, Pableus."

"Hold it!" Esio shouted to his men, who were hoisting the ship's plank. "Pableus sent you to me? Why, no man can cure a soul like Pableus. How is that old rascal? How is Grecia?"

Kemnebi's face grew dark, and he winced as if in pain. "I am afraid that we come from a terrible tragedy." He told Esio of what they had just been through and how they had buried Grecia.

Esio stood motionless looking down at Kemnebi. "That is a terrible tragedy," he said. He silently motioned for his men to lower the plank. "You and the child come on board," Esio said.

Kemnebi removed his money pouch but Esio shook his head.

"Put away your money," he said. "You have brought me sad news, but at least I welcome the opportunity to pray for the soul of Grecia."

Late one afternoon, days later, Esio stood beneath his ship's sails with a puzzled expression on his face. The winds had been especially good all day and they were moving at an excellent pace. The gods had never abandoned him on his frequent trips back and forth across the Great Sea of the Philistines. At this rate, this was sure to be the fastest trip he had ever taken across the Great Sea, but something troubled Esio. The sea looked unusually calm in a strange sort of way, and even with all his experience, he did not know what to make of it.

"What luck you have, my friend," Kemnebi said, joining Esio on the deck. "The gods favor you."

Esio gripped the line of one of the masts and tugged on it. It was firm and secure. "We are indeed doing very well. You shall be on the shores of Adana in a few days. What will you do after that?"

"Trulius and I will head for Tarsus. What about you? Will you stay in Adana long?"

"I will stay docked for one evening. I have cargo to deliver in Caesarea to greedy merchants who have no understanding of how fickle the seas can be."

Esio jumped from his position. "I shall see you later," he said to Kemnebi, and hollered to one of his men. "Follow me, let us check the rest of the masts."

"Kemnebi?" Trulius cried. He was at the ship's railing, looking at the sky. "Come," he said, waving at Kemnebi to join him.

"Be careful, Trulius," Kemnebi said. "I thought you were asleep below."

"I could not sleep so I came to see the stars," Trulius said. "Gianina and I used to count them."

The sky was lit with millions of lights. It reminded Kemnebi of Egypt, where as a child, he to had enjoyed many nights in the desert gazing at the stars. Egypt had beautiful clear nights. It was no wonder that Egyptians were excellent astronomers. "Some day your father and I will have to take you to Egypt, Trulius. You will not believe those skies." He leaned against the wooden rail next to Trulius and placed an arm around him. "So, my child, you are thinking about Gianina?"

Trulius shrugged. "Do you think she misses me? I miss her, and it has only been a few days."

Kemnebi affectionately pinched one of Trulius's earlobes. "Of course she misses you. Women are the most sentimental creatures in the world. But do not worry about Gianina. Even though she is just a child, women of any age are much stronger than men, and smarter I might add. She is probably counting the days until you return."

"Kemnebi," Trulius said, frowning. "One day in the Forum, I heard two merchants talking about Gianina. She and Felicia were with us, and as all of you walked ahead of me, I heard one of them wonder out loud who her father was. They said she was a beautiful child, but that since no one knows who her father was, he could be a slave. And they said that she would never possess a fine dowry for marriage. What did all that mean?"

"Rodents," Kemnebi said. "Do not listen to the words of rodents. Gianina is no slave." He squeezed Trulius's shoulders. "As for the matter of her father, I can tell you that Gianina is of excellent stock. Besides, Felicia is kind, refined and educated, and she has passed those excellent qualities to Gianina."

A sudden gust of wind swept across the ship causing it to rock hard.

"Have a look at what is coming our way," Esio said, suddenly standing next to Kemnebi.

Esio gripped a line that danced in front of him from one of the masts and hoisted himself onto an observational deck. Heavy, dark clouds had moved into the area. They were low and ominous. His instincts had been correct. The sea was now restless and threatening. "A storm," he whispered.

"What do you think, Esio?" Kemnebi said.

"I have seen those clouds before," Esio said, "and I do not like it." He looked at Trulius. "I do not wish to alarm Trulius, but I think you should ride out the storm down below." His expression softened. "Of course, the sea is very fickle. We could be in for a rough ride for just a few hours, maybe more maybe less. And I would not be surprised if tomorrow we wake up to a glorious morning."

A flash of light illuminated the sky and that was followed by a very strong and long gush of wind. Kemnebi had jumped off the observational deck and took the hand of Trulius. "An excellent suggestion, Esio" he said. "I think we shall do just that."

"Bah," Trulius murmured. "I am not afraid of a silly old storm, Kemnebi."

"None of us is, my child," Kemnebi said. "But out at sea it is always prudent to respect nature."

In the crammed quarters below, Kemnebi fixed a blanket for him in one corner of the small room. He lit a lamp and secured it to a wall.

"Try and sleep, Trulius," he said. "That is all we can do."

But the ship began to rock violently and water slapped heavily against the hull of the ship. There was shouting and the sounds of wild commotion coming from the deck. Kemnebi glanced at the short stairs leading to the deck and listened intently. A mast had broken in half and toppled over. Kemnebi inadvertently took a step in the direction of the stairs but paused to look at Trulius.

Trulius was looking at him intently. "Go, Kemnebi, I am not afraid to be alone."

Out on the deck, the ship was rocking so violently Kemnebi was barely able to stand. Sheets of rain were pouring down, the wind was blowing hard, and the sea was hurling wave after wave of water at the ship. Amidst the chaos, Kemnebi immediately saw the problem. The largest mast had broken nearly in two and a part of it was hanging over the side of the ship threatening to tip it over. Esio and his men were trying to break it off its base, and two other men were trying to cut the entangled lines.

Kemnebi rushed to help. He had barely reached the other men when a strong wave caused the ship to rock so severely that one of the men lost his grip and flew off the side of the ship. At the last minute, he managed to grip one of the lines of the broken mast. Kemnebi slid on his belly toward the man and managed to take a hold of his wrists. There was terror in the man's eyes.

"Please," he shouted, "do not let me go."

Esio slid next to Kemnebi and also took hold of the man. "Pull him in, Kemnebi" Esio shouted. "Pull him in, the mast is about to go!"

Kemnebi and Esio pulled hard, but they lost their grip on the man when the ship lifted out of the water and crashed back down so violently that it caused the mast to break off completely and fly off into the sea, taking the man with him.

Kemnebi and Esio helped each other take hold of what was left of the ship's railing. Neither spoke a word as both held on tightly for what seemed hours. At last, the rain slackened and the seas became calm. By then, the sun was piercing the horizon.

Kemnebi opened his eyes at the sound of his name. Someone was shaking him.

"Kemnebi," Trulius, said again. "Are you all right?"

Tarsus was not Rome, but the crowded streets, shops, and merchants on the streets reminded Trulius of the Forum. Vendors were everywhere selling sweets, clothes, sandals, and trinkets. And like at the Forum, men in long togas stood at the steps of tall buildings and argued loudly with one another. Kemnebi bought them breakfast of bread and honey from a mute vendor who kneeled in front of him and lifted his tray of goods. They stopped to eat at a public fountain where two comic actors were making everyone laugh. Trulius whispered to Kemnebi that he had never heard anyone speak Greek so rapidly.

"Now you understand why your father insisted that your tutors teach you Greek," Kemnebi said. "The Hellenistic language is the universal language of the Mediterranean world."

A loud mob suddenly came around a street corner and disrupted the flow of traffic. Men and women, and even children, cursed and poked fun of two men who were at the center of the crowd. One of them walked along acting as if he could not hear a thing. He was short and heavy around the middle. His white hair was long and his beard short. He reached the fountain a step ahead of the man who accompanied him and calmly retrieved a bucket that was tied to a rope. He scooped water from the fountain and offered the bucket to his companion.

"Behold," one of the comic actors said in a loud voice that quieted the crowd. "Here we have Paulous, who professes to have an easy solution to the despicable state of human affairs. He offers us a messiah—Yeshua, the Nazorean who was hung from a cross." The actor made a funny face. "Oh, Cilicia listen to me," Paulous cries. "Yeshua came to save the world. Believe in him and all will be well." The comic spread his arms. "Maybe life is not so bad after all. If I were a Roman, why would I want to be rescued from the arms of a beautiful mistress, a cup of excellent wine and a nagging wife?"

The crowd roared with laughter. But at that moment several Roman soldiers pushed their way through the crowd and ordered them to go about their business. One of them removed his helmet and shoved it into the chest of Paulous. "I should have known I would find you in the middle of this mob, Paulous. Yesterday I rescued you from the clutches of a man who wanted to slice your throat. Trouble seems to follow you."

Paulous leaned against the fountain. "I am sorry if my words offend some people. But do not worry, Silas and I are off to Lycaonia today."

"Good," the soldier said. "But it would be better if on the way wild boars had you for breakfast." He walked away shaking his head and pushing the crowd along.

Trulius got bored, and wielding his sword, he jumped on the fountain ledge.

"Ah," Paulous said, "a young soldier with his weapon. What is your name, lad?"

Trulius lowered his sword. "Tessius Trulius, sire. One day I am going to be a commander in the Roman army like my father was."

"Of course," Paulous said. "I have no doubt, but remember, my child, even Roman soldiers must one day answer to God for their actions."

Trulius shrugged. "Father says I must be good or I will anger the gods."

Paulous brushed his beard. "I am certain he is a wise man, your father, but without knowledge of Yeshua, the Savior, man will remain in darkness about God."

"Which God?" Trulius asked.

Paulous grinned. "Did you hear that, Silas? This young man asks more intelligent questions than the people do."

Silas set the bucket down. "One day the entire world will worship the one true God, young man," he said.

"I hope it is Mars, the god of war," Trulius said. "I like his sword."

Paulous laughed and was about to speak, when Kemnebi helped Trulius down. "We must be on our way," he said.

"Forgive me for delaying you," Paulous said. He smiled at Trulius. "You are an interesting young man. May God always enlighten your path."

Kemnebi hurried Trulius along, and a short distance away, Trulius looked back. Paulous was still talking to his friend. "Do you think there is only one God, Kemnebi?" Trulius asked.

Kemnebi shrugged. "In Egypt we worship many gods. In Rome, Romans love to worship Greek gods. At this moment let us hope that at least one of them is looking after us, my child."

Thrity-One

Kemnebi and Trulius emerged out of a wall of cliffs and found themselves high atop a ridge that overlooked an enormous canyon. Hidden from the rest of the world, the canyon was deep, wide, and dark. Kemnebi had lost track of the days, but he speculated that they had left Tarsus at least a dozen days before. But, he could not be certain. Exhausted, his feet swollen, and his brow dusty, he, nevertheless, was excited to finely reach the cliffs of Armenia that Marcellius had spoken about. Of course, the trip had not been easy. Armenia was beautiful, but mountainous and treacherous in many places. The days had been warm under a bright sun, but the nights had been cold, sometimes unbearably cold.

Kemnebi produced the map that Marcellius had given him and studied it. He then looked to his left. The chiseled rock walls looked impenetrable, but, without a doubt, there had to be a path that snaked into the rocks.

It was just past the noon hour, but the sun was hidden somewhere beyond the towering peaks. The canyon below was almost completely enshrined in an early afternoon shadow. It might have been totally dark except that a clear and magnificent stream of sun-rays shot through the peaks and lit up a dark, green lake below. Kemnebi figured that some underground river was feeding into it. Trees surrounded the lake, and some type of vegetation was grow-ing out of the near end of the lake.

Kemnebi suddenly became aware of Trulius. He had slipped down the mountain and was waving at him from the edge of the lake. Kemnebi laughed when Trulius dipped a foot into the water and then started to remove his clothes. Kemnebi started down. Oddly, the lower he climbed the less dense the air became and the warmer the canyon felt.

"Kemnebi," Trulius shouted. He was now naked and standing at the edge of the water. "Hurry! And jump in with me."

"Yes, yes," Kemnebi shouted back. "I am coming."

Kemnebi reached the water and stared incredulously at the short plant stalks peeking out of the far end of the lake. He immediately recognized what they were but could not believe his eyes. He stud-ied them carefully. They were short papyrus plants. Papyrus in Armenia? Papyrus plants were native to the fertile Nile valley, and they usually grew tall and in abundance in the warm climate of Egypt. Armenia was too cold. On the other hand, these were not typical papyrus plants. They were much shorter than usual. He reached down and easily pulled one of the plants out of the water, root and all.

Trulius laughed and hollered at him. He dipped below the water and disappeared. When his head emerged, he was a short distance from Kemnebi. "What are you doing, Kemnebi?" he cried. "Are you not going to get in the water? It is not the Tiberius but it is nice and warm."

"I will join you in a moment," Kemnebi said. He studied the canyon and noted how it was much warmer than the top of the canyon.

Trulius jumped out of the water and joined him. "What are those?" he asked.

"Papyrus plants, Trulius, and I am trying to figure out how these plants got here." He shook his head. "They are supposed to grow only in warm weather."

"They look healthy to me," Trulius said.

"Shush!" Kemnebi whispered, and flung around. The rumbling noise had been ever so subtle, but it had not escaped his sharp and experienced ears. He bent down and placed his palms on the dirt allowing them to absorb even the faintest tremble from the ground, but he felt nothing. Nevertheless, he had heard it. "Horses," he whispered, "possibly asses. But I cannot tell from what direction they are coming."

Trulius looked anxiously at him. "What do we do?"

"Get dressed, hurry."

Trulius rushed for his clothes and started to dress. Suddenly, he looked at Kemnebi. "Do you hear that?"

Kemnebi cuffed his hands above his eyebrows and scanned the cliffs. "I do," he whispered. "It is a flute."

Kemnebi squinted. Coming down the cliffs along a narrow path was a small party of riders. They were indeed riding asses. He took Trulius by the hand and slipped into a crack inside the closest set of cliffs.

The party momentarily disappeared, and when they appeared again, they were much closer. There were three of them, two men and a boy. It was the boy who was playing the flute. All three wore hoods, and as they approached the lake, the three of them removed their hoods. Kemnebi stared at them and shook his head with excitement.

"What is it, Kemnebi?" Trulius asked. "You seem very excited."

Kemnebi took his hand and stepped out of their hiding place. "Come, Trulius," he said. "You are about to meet your uncle?"

"My uncle?" Trulius cried. "I have an uncle?"

Kemnebi smiled. "Yes, Trulius, you have an uncle, and you will never find a more brilliant and kinder man."

Kemnebi shrugged sadly. "I am truly sorry that after all these years of not seeing you, I am the bearer of such terrible news."

Erasmus Harel stared at him, unable to speak. He could do nothing but shake his head in despair. How could this have happened to Marcellius? He knew of no nobler man than his brother. He did not deserve such a cruel tragedy. At last Erasmus Harel found his voice, and he spoke softly. "Tell me, my dear Kemenbi, is there something that we can do for my brother? Rome is a city of laws. What about lawyers? Surely a successful and noble man like Marcellius must have many important friends who can help him?"

Kemnebi nodded. "Rome is a city of laws, but even more importantly it is a city full of ruthless politicians who will not stick their necks out for a friend if it is not in their political interest. Nevertheless, Marcellius does have many loyal friends, and I pray that one or two of them will help him in some capacity."

"Then what were his instructions to you, Kemnebi? Are you returning to Rome?"

"No, Marcellius forbade me from returning. His only concern was for the protection and safety of Tessius Trulius."

"Tessius Trulius," Ersamus Harel murmured. He glanced at Trulius. He was helping Farrenthias and Adin collect papyrus plants from the lake. "He is a handsome lad, and I can already see that he possesses his father's spirit and no doubt he also possesses his father's many skills. A boy such as that needs his father to properly educate him and keep him out of mischief." Erasmus Harel managed a strained smile. "Of course, Marcellius is fortunate to have you to look after him, Kemnebi."

"Your assessment of Trulius is quite correct, Erasmus Harel. Trulius is his father's son in many ways. He is absolutely fearless, and I have no doubt that one day he will march ahead of an army as his father once did." He nodded in the direction of Trulius. "And as you can clearly see, he makes friends very easily."

"Indeed," Erasmus Harel said. "It is ironic that my brother's trage-dy appears to have solved a problem that had begun to concern me."

"What problem is that?" Kemnebi asked.

"Farrenthias just joined our community to study with us, but as you can see, he is just a child and a child that age needs a companion his age. Of course, Farrenthias has never expressed an interest in run-ning around like other boys. Nevertheless, he needs a companion."

Trulius and Farrenthias were at the edge of the lake, dripping wet and full of mud. They were still pulling plants.

"Hum," Kemnebi murmured. "Trulius is left-handed like you, Erasmus Harel, and I notice that the young lad Farrenthias also favors his left hand. An interesting coincidence."

"How is Trulius with his studies?" Erasmus Harel asked.

"Back home, he would rather play with his wooden sword or wrestle with one of the guards than to sit with his tutors, but once forced to sit and study, he can be quite witty and bright. He is an intelligent young man."

"I think they will get along very well those two," Erasmus Harel said. He led Kemnebi back towards the others. "You must both be very tired. Fortunately, Clivus is not far from here. I think Adin and the boys have collected enough papyrus. We should start back."

"I must admit that I was quite surprised to find papyrus plants here in Armenia," Kemnebi said.

"I planted them myself," Erasmus said. "I carried several papyrus reeds out of Egypt and thought they were dead by the time we reached here. I dropped them in the water and never imagined that they would take root and flourish like they did."

They stopped and listened to Adin explain how they made scrolls.

"All we have to do is pull the reeds from the stalks, cut them and cross-layer them to make our writing leaves. But, not only do we make our writing papyri from these water plants, but like the Egyptians, we make sandals, ropes, mats, baskets and other things."

"Ah! Picking papyrus plants is great fun," Trulius said. "I want to learn how to make rope."

"Of course," Adin answered.

"We should be getting back," Erasmus Harel said. He looked at Farrenthias. "Farrenthias, you and Trulius can ride together, and once we arrive at Clivus, perhaps you and Adin can take Trulius to his new quarters, next to yours."

Thirty-Two

arrenthias inhaled deeply, held his breath for an instant and then exhaled softly into the mouth piece of his flute. The sound of a sweet prolonged note filled the small room, and Adin clapped enthusiastically.

"Each day you get better and better, my child," he said.

Trulius jumped off his new bed and sliced the air with his sword. His room was extremely small compared to his room back home, but that did not matter to Trulius. He was happy to have his room next to Farrenthias's room, and Kemnebi's quarters were just down the hall. He landed between Farrenthias and Adin and slipped his wooden sword into his belt.

"I like your flute, Farrenthias," Trulius said, "but you should also learn to play the horn. Horns blare out before Roman soldiers march into battle."

Adin laughed and affectionately stroked Trulius's arm. "If we had a horn, my little Roman soldier, I would surely teach Farrenthias how to play it." Adin struggled to his feet from the floor. "Very well, children, now that we have settled Tessius Trulius into his room and I have taught Farrenthias a new note on the flute, it is time that I get to the kitchen and prepare our evening meal." He paused. "Farrenthias, perhaps you would like to show Tessius Trulius around Clivus."

Farrenthias lowered his flute. "Would you like that, Trulius?"

"Ah, I would like that very much," Trulius said. He placed his sword inside his belt. "I am ready."

While they walked across the courtyard to the next tower, Trulius suddenly grew despondent. Clivus was beautiful, and he liked his uncle and Farrenthias. He liked everyone else, but he wished his father and mother could see this place. He wished Gianina was here. He also worried that Pharaoh would miss him if he stayed away from Rome for too long.

Farrenthias led him into the tallest tower, and the sight of the narrow spiraling stairway that disappeared into the ceiling somewhere above their head helped Trulius snap out of his melancholy mood. On the second floor, Trulius ran one hand along a rough wall while he and Farrenthias walked down a long, dark corridor. "I love this place," Trulius said. "We could get lost in here."

Farrenthias lifted a lamp to the face of Trulius. "You have not seen anything yet," he said. "Even the other two smaller towers are full of narrow stairways and secret passages."

Trulius drew his sword and jabbed the air with his sword. "One day I will wear the Roman cape of a Roman soldier and fight the enemy in a palace like this." He swung his sword up and down and back and forth, the way his father had taught him.

Farrenthias laughed and stopped to watch him. "You are really good with that sword, Trulius."

Trulius lowered his arms. "Father told me, not too long ago, that in another year I would be ready to handle a real sword."

"Well, my father has a collection of swords," Farrenthias said. "He loves swords. Maybe one day he will give you one."

"Does he come to visit you? Maybe he will bring some of his swords so I can look at them."

Farrenthias set the lamp down and sat beside it. "I do not know when he will return. He was not terribly happy when I asked him to allow me to stay here."

Trulius laid down his wooden armament and stretched out beside Farrenthias. He stared at the high sculptured ceiling with his hands behind his head and grew quiet and pensive. The mention of his father made him think of home again.

"Trulius," Farrenthias said, "do you have any brothers and sisters?"

Trulius shrugged. "No, but I have a friend, Gianina. She is a girl but she rides horses and climbs trees with me, and I have my dog, Pharaoh. Do you have any brothers and sisters? Do you have a dog?"

"I have twin sisters. Their names are Erisa and Clisa. But I do not have a dog. I wish we could ride horses together, but once, when I tried to ride one, I fell. And I have never climbed a tree."

Trulius bolted to a sitting position. "You have never climbed a tree? But there are hundreds of trees out here. Are you afraid of heights?"

"No, I do not think so. Some of these stairs are very high, and I am not afraid to climb them. Maybe one day we can climb a tree together."

"Yes, we will climb many trees together, and I will teach you how to ride a horse. I can even teach you tricks on horses." Trulius rolled onto his belly. "Do you like to wrestle? Gianina wrestles with me."

"I do not know how," Farrenthias said. "But I can show you a secret place. Do you want to see it?"

Trulius jumped to his feet. "A secret place? Where is it?"

"Come," Farrenthias said, getting to his feet. "I'll show you. Tavius showed it to me."

They ran down the stairs, out of the tower and across the courtyard to the outside gate. Farrenthias started down the path that lead into Clivus, but then veered off the main path to his left and started down the narrow path that led to the papyrus lake. Just a few paces down he stopped next to the pond Tavius and his father had discovered. Farrenthias pointed to the end of the pond that was filled with bushes. "Through those bushes is the entrance to a tunnel," he said. "Want to see it?"

Trulius eagerly nodded.

Farrenthias waded into the pond and crawled through the bushes. Trulius crawled in behind him and found Farrenthias standing inside a small cave that opened into a dark abyss.

"Ah," Trulius cried. He inhaled deeply. The cave was fresh and cool and dimly lit. "Have you ever been down there?" Trulius asked.

"No, Trulius. I could not even get Cerudotus to come in here. When I told him there was a stream down here he almost forbade me from coming back in. I had to promise him that I would never attempt to go down there if he let me come back in."

"Hum," Trulius murmured.

"Well, what do you think?" Farrenthias asked. "Is it not beautiful in here?"

"What a secret hideaway!" Trulius said. "Gianina would love this cave. Do you come here all the time?"

"Not all the time, but when I do, it is in the early evenings before the sun sets. I like the sound of the water."

Trulius raised his sword and pretended to scribble in the air with it. "What are you doing here at Clivus, anyway?"

"I study. I am learning Egyptian hieroglyphics, and I am learning the teachings of many wise men."

"I do not know how long I am going to be here, but do you want me to come with you when you come here?"

"I would love for you to come here with me, Trulius. It is now our secret place."

Trulius lowered his sword and smiled. "I have an idea. Maybe Kemnebi will help me make a sword for you. Would you like to have a sword like mine? We could form a legion, a Roman legion. The empire has the best fighting soldiers in the world."

Farrenthias paled and stared at Trulius's sword. "I—well if you think that I should have one, but I would not know what to do with it," he said.

"Hum, well I suppose I could practice with Kemnebi." Trulius frowned. "I am starving."

"Of course," Farrenthias cried. "I am certain Adin has something for us to eat. Shall we go?"

Trulius put away his sword. "I am right behind you."

In the months that followed, Trulius would study in the mornings, not because he wanted to, but because Kemnebi insisted that he take lessons from the priests. Then, after a frugal lunch, if he and Farrenthias were not in their secret place, Trulius would run rampant about Clivus waving his sword. He took turns sparring with Kemnebi and Tavius. First, he practiced his skills with the sword. Next, Kemnebi taught him how to use a dagger and toss a spear. Trulius would then strip down to his loincloth and beg the men to wrestle with him. He would tire Kemnebi and then wrestle Tavius. He would tire him too but still beg him for one more tumble on the ground. Trulius was indefatigable. He also loved to ride horses and took to performing daring tricks on them, much to the chagrin of Kemnebi. The afternoons were Trulius's favorite part of the day.

Trulius loved to pretend he was a charioteer. He would tie several goats together, and pretending that he was at the Circus Maximus, he would race them around the courtyard. One day, he even led the goats into a study room where everyone was gathered. Knocking over chairs and tables, the terrified goats trampled through the room. Cups and scrolls flew into the air, and everyone ran for cover.

"The child is mad!" Cerudotus cried, before ducking under a fallen table. Trulius raced twice around the room then disappeared out the door.

Another favorite game of Trulius's was hide-and-seek. One morning in the middle of breakfast, he abruptly disappeared out of the room and hollered at Farrenthias that he should come and find him in the next room. Erasmus Harel nodded at Farrenthias, giving his approval for him to leave the table and go and search for Trulius, but when Farrenthias returned and announced that he could not find Trulius, everyone joined in the search. Moments later, the men stood in the middle of the room where Trulius was hidden and shook their heads in amazement. They had searched every corner of the room but all their efforts had proved to be futile. They were perplexed.

"The child has vanished," cried Adin.

But at last, Trulius broke into laughter. "Underneath the table," he cried, still laughing. "Look carefully underneath the table again."

Everyone kneeled and stared in amazement at Trulius, who had wedged himself tightly up against the underside of the table.

Thirty-Three

One morning, Trulius sat on the floor of one of the study rooms staring intensely at Farrenthias and Erasmus Harel. Today, he and Farrenthias were going exploring and Trulius could not wait to get started. He and Farrenthias had finished this morning's assignments on the study of the Greek philosophers, Pythagoras, Socrates, and Plato, but as usual Farrenthias had drawn Erasmus Harel into a discussion that Trulius considered wholly trivial and pointless! Yet, even though he had grown restless and impatient he said nothing. Instead, he rested his chin on his bent knees and tried to be patient.

Erasmus Harel tapped the palm of one hand with a scroll that he was holding and looked thoughtfully at Farrenthias.

"What is it about the theory of rebirths that you like, Farrenthias," he said. "And what troubles you about the theory?"

Farrenthias lowered his gaze as he often did when he was deep in thought. "Well, I do believe that there is much suffering in the world, and life is more fair if we understand rebirths."

Erasmus Harel gazed proudly at Farrenthias. "Go on, explain why some men are born to a life of poverty, while others are born sometimes to undeserved wealth, or why some men are born healthy while others are born maimed or handicapped. Does that sound like the work of a good omnipotent god? What god would create such a world?"

"Hum," Farrenthias murmured. "I do not believe that God created such a world. God created everyone with the capacity to be equal, but because man makes his own decisions and some are poor decisions, it turns out that men may not be equal after all, at least not during the same lifetime. Reincarnation teaches that a man is born several times, and in each lifetime his soul will learn new lessons that will improve his life."

Adin clapped his hands. "Well stated, dear Farrenthias."

"Give us an example," Erasmus Harel said, his eyes and voice filled with pride.

"Well," Farrenthias said, "a blind beggar may be reborn an emperor in the next lifetime if he learned humility in his present life. On the other hand, a wealthy man may be reborn a homeless vagrant if he abused his wealth. He must learn compassion for others. Man sets his own destiny, depending on what good deeds he accomplishes and how much he is able to progress spiritually."

Trulius squirmed. Why were rebirths necessary? Was there no faster way for a man to learn. Unable to keep quiet any longer he cleared his throat to draw attention to himself. "Uncle," he said, when all eyes in the room were upon him. "What is a soul anyway and where did it come from? Which god created man's soul?"

"Ah," Erasmus Harel said. "An excellent question and observation, Trulius. It is good to question such matters, my child. Unfortunately, the problem of creation, Trulius, is one of those riddles that I do not believe man is capable of solving completely, but we do have clues about our existence, and of course different cultures throughout the world have their own theories and ideas. For example, what you just heard Farrenthias speak about are also the beliefs of many wise men from India and the Far East and they have held those beliefs for centuries. But who created man's soul you ask? Greeks and Romans believe in many gods and they believe that those gods must be worshipped in order that man may live a good existence. Also, the Hebrew people have taught that there is one God and that God is the creator of all things."

Trulius frowned. "One God? How can just one God create the sun and the moon and who would lead men into battle if not the god mars?"

Abiel said, "Some things are difficult to understand, Trulius, but the world is full of wise men and teachers, teachers such as Yeshua."

"Yeshua? Who was he?" Trulius asked.

"He was a great Hebrew master," Farrenthias said. "I shall have to tell you all about him, Trulius."

"Farrenthias," Cerudotus said. He rose from his chair and nodded approvingly and then looked worried. "You have learned more in just a few months than I could have taught you in years. But what am I to do if your father hears your recitation of so many varied beliefs? After all, he is very much a Greek."

Ezri cleared his throat. "I think Lord Gaios will understand that Farrenthias has become a seeker of truth, dear Cerudotus."

Erasmus Harel also rose to his feet. "I think our morning lessons are concluded and I am certain that Trulius and Farrenthias are ready for some fresh air."

Trulius grabbed his spear and dagger that Kemnebi had fashioned for him from scraps of metal. "May Farrenthias and I be excused?"

Thirty-Four

High on a slope, Trulius stopped and ceremoniously buried the tip of his spear into the ground. His eyes swept across the vast mountains that were composed of thick forests. He wiped the sweat from his brow and sighed with delight. Armenia fascinated him. He and Kemnebi had been at Clivus for over a year now and every other week he and Farrenthias would set out to explore some part of the surrounding country. Of course, since he and Farrenthias were allowed to leave Clivus alone, there were certain rules in place. Before each adventure, Kemnebi, with Cerudotus clinging to his cloak and muttering prayers to the gods, escorted them out of the gate. There, he and Trulius would agree in what direction he and Farrenthias were going to go. No deviation was allowed. Thus, if the boys did not return by nightfall, Kemnebi would know in what general direction to search. Also, the moment the sun began to dip toward the horizon they were to immediately head back.

From his location on the slope, Trulius hollered at Farrenthias, who had fallen slightly behind. "Hurry, Farrenthias," Trulius cried.

"It is a magnificent day. The sun is shining brightly. It is nice and cool, and we have much to see and far to go." He inhaled and exhaled loudly. "Is this not much better than being locked away at Clivus?" He laughed. "Why, I would rather smell pig manure than read another scroll!"

Panting and struggling to catch his breath, Farrenthias reached Trulius and started to laugh. "Pig manure, Trulius? You would rather smell pig manure than read another scroll?"

"Yes! Is that not terrible?" Trulius said. He lifted his spear and pointed toward the bottom of the mountain on which they stood. "I say we make our way down in that direction, towards that gully full of trees. There has to be an opening in the trees somewhere. What do you think?"

Farrenthias searched the gully. "Whatever you think, Trulius. I am ready." He looked around. "I agree with you that it is a magnificent day, but I would rather be enjoying it from a balcony back at Clivus, perhaps with a scroll on my lap."

"Nonsense!" Trulius cried. "Come on."

When they reached the gully, they disappeared into a corridor packed with thick brush and towering trees. The sky above them disappeared.

Farrenthias reached for Trulius's arm. "Have you ever seen anything like this, Trulius? Why, in here it is practically nightfall."

"I like it," Trulius said. "I can barely see, but I like it."

They walked through the trees for what seemed like an eternity, but at last they finally emerged into a wide-open area.

"Aha!" Trulius cried. He extended his arms and sucked in the cool fresh air. But just as quickly as he had raised his arms, he dropped them to his sides and stared in disbelief at the thick, dark clouds that now filled the sky.

"What happened to the clear blue skies?" Farrenthias asked. "What happened to the sun?"

Trulius shook his head. "I do not know." It was also eerily quiet. There was not even a hint of a slight wind and this worried Trulius. The last time he had seen calm weather like this a sudden storm had turned the great sea into a nightmare. "A storm is upon us, Farrenthias," he whispered. "It is about to pour."

"What should we do?" Farrenthias said. "Should we seek cover or start back to Clivus? Erasmus Harel and the others will be worried about us."

"We should start back right away," Trulius said. "I do not want to worry my uncle and Kemnebi. And Cerudotus is going to yell at me for getting you wet."

"Drenched, I would say," Farrenthias said.

"Let us go," Trulius said, but he did not move. Instead, he gripped the arm of Farrenthias. "Do not move, Farrenthias," he whispered. "Do not move a muscle." His eyes were ablaze and fixed on something in front of him. Farrenthias followed his gaze and gasped. A huge lion was blocking their path.

"Trulius," Farrenthias whispered, in a voice that quivered with fear, "what—what are we going to do?"

"Shssh" Trulius murmured. "Do not move," he said. His eyes narrowed, and he stared at the lion with so much intensity that his face darkened and contorted. He stood utterly still, and did not dare so much as blink. He had never seen a more powerful looking animal in his life, and it was so close he could see saliva dripping from its long, yellow fangs. The eyes of the lion sparkled and they were glued on Trulius. It was as if the lion were carefully studying its prey, and waiting for the right moment to charge.

Trulius did not wait another moment. Slowly he shifted his feet to a wider stance. The move seemed to agitate the lion. It growled and snarled beneath its breath. Then, without taking its eyes off of Trulius, it lowered its head and its shoulder muscles visibly tensed. Instinct told Trulius the lion was about to attack. Sweat poured from Trulius's brow. He tried to swallow, but found that his throat and mouth were too dry. Yet, his eyes remained wild and defiant, as if he dared the lion to charge.

Trulius drew his breath and slowly began to draw his spear back. The lion growled under its breath. Sweat continued to pour from Trulius's brow but he ignored it. At last, his arm was fully extended back. He was ready to launch his spear. The lion recoiled back, and its entire body was now nearly as low as the ground. For an instant all was quiet. But suddenly, the sky exploded with thunder. Startled, Trulius instinctively ducked. The lion, also startled, let out an enormous growl that nearly drowned out the thunder, and with its sharp claws protruding from its thick paws, it launched into the air toward Trulius. Trulius took a quick step back and then thrust his spear as hard as he could. It struck the lion squarely between its front legs. The lion shrieked and tumbled backwards in mid-air, breaking the spear in half. It squirmed and kicked and clutched the broken spear with its paws.

It thundered again and this time it began to pour.

"Run!" Trulius shouted at Farrenthias. "Run!" Farrenthias took off running with Trulius on his heels but Farrenthias tripped and fell into a puddle of mud. Trulius helped him to his feet and then froze. The wounded lion hobbled quickly toward Trulius and Farrenthias, with a piece of the spear protruding from its chest.

Trulius drew his short, crude dagger and flung it at the lion, striking it again almost at the same spot where the spear had struck it. The lion stumbled, squirmed, and growled for a few moments and then stopped moving.

Oblivious of the rain that was pounding him, Trulius walked slowly toward the fallen lion and stared silently at its massive shoulders and thick claws. He could not believe that he had killed such an enormous beast.

"Look at its size," Farrenthias said, in a voice still trembling with fear. He stood next to Trulius shaking his head. "I have never seen such a huge animal, Trulius. You saved our lives. Kemnebi is not going to believe this."

Trulius looked quickly at Farrenthias. "Should we tell him? He may not let us come out here again. I mean would you be afraid to accompany me again? You do not have to if this frightened you too much."

"You are not afraid to encounter another one of these lions, Trulius?"

"Well, sort of but...well, Father had always told me that a man has to overcome his fears or he might as well be a dead man."

Farrenthias continued to stare at the lion. "I know how much coming out here means to you, Trulius." It began to rain again and Farrenthias shivered from the cold. "You are right. We should not tell anyone what happened. They will only worry. And, if you want me to come out here with you again, I will."

Trulius motioned for them to start on their way. He shoved Farrenthias on the shoulder. "What an adventure! What do you think, Farrenthias? Are we brothers?"

Farrenthias smiled. "We will always be brothers, Trulius."

Thirty-Five

Abiel leaned into the face of Farrenthias and cringed with dread. Dark circles had formed around the boy's eyes. His forehead was drenched in sweat and his skin lacked color. Abiel placed the palm of his hand on Farrenthias's forehead. He was burning alive. Abiel motioned for the others to follow him out of the room.

Abiel addressed Erasmus Harel, but as he spoke, his eyes shifted to Ya'ir, then to Ezri, and then Adin, and finally to Kemnebi. "It has been three days now since Farrenthias fell ill, and I have done all that I can but nothing has worked. His fever is very high. I would feel much better if he were in the hands of a physician."

"Can he be moved?" Ya'ir asked. "We can take him to Tigranocerta."

Abiel looked through the open door at Farrenthias. Cerudotus was at his bedside, stroking his hand. "He is in a very delicate state, but we have no choice."

"We will have to be careful," Ezri said. "Soldiers might be in the area."

"I will take him," Kemnebi said.

"And I will go with you," Tavius said. "It is good that Lord Gaios left us some horses."

"I, too, will accompany you," Ezri said. "I can ride. Besides, I know a short route to Tigranocerta."

"I do not know how to ride a horse," Cerudotus said, stepping out into the hall. "But I should go."

Erasmus Harel affectionately pressed his arm. "It would be more prudent if you stayed. You will only slow them down. Kemnebi and Ezri will take good care of Farrenthias."

"But...but Farrenthias is my responsibilty? How can I just sit by and do nothing?"

"Erasmus Harel is right," Kemnebi said. "You will slow us down, Cerudotus, and that is not in the best interest of Farrenthias."

"This was my fault," Trulius said. "I should not have taken Farrenthias that far into the woods. Please let me go, Erasmus Harel."

Erasmus Harel glanced at Kemnebi, who assented with a nod.

"Then it is settled," Abiel said. "Come Cerudotus, let us prepare Farrenthias for the trip to Tigranocerta."

Kemnebi halted his horse just behind a thin curtain of trees and peered at the Roman soldiers who held the road. He counted six of them and two supply wagons. One of the supply wagons had a broken wheel. A very short young man with a crooked back was repairing the wheel. He worked diligently in spite of the fact that his hands were tied together with a short leather strap.

"I do not like it," Kemnebi whispered to Ezri and Tavius. "Do you know another place where we can connect to the road, Ezri? I would rather not explain to these soldiers who we are and what we are doing out here."

"I have always joined the road from here," Ezri said, "But I suppose that we can ride further down."

"I agree with you, Kemnebi," Tavius said. "I think we should try another route."

Kemnebi nodded and started to back his horse away when he was suddenly struck by the oddest feeling. There was a sudden stillness in the air that made him uneasy. The Romans sensed it too, for suddenly they drew their weapons then grew as still as the trees. One of them ordered the short man to stop working while they all looked around and waited.

The first to shout a warning was a soldier who was the closet to the edge of the trees. But, the armed men who poured out of the trees, shouting and cursing, drowned out his warning. The men swung their swords and hatchets wildly at the Romans but with precision.

"Parthians!" Ezri cried. "We should leave at once."

"Wait," Kemnebi said. "I want to be certain that there are no more surprises in the trees." Worried about Trulius, he quickly glanced past Ezri. Trulius looked more fascinated by the scene than frightened. His left hand was wrapped around the handle of a short sword that Kemnebi had fashioned for him from scrap metal. This instinctive reaction for one so young should have surprised Kemnebi, but nothing about Trulius surprised him anymore.

The Romans were heavily outnumbered but better prepared. They formed a tight circle and furiously fought the Parthians, until one by one the Parthian's numbers began to dwindle. Soon, the few Parthians who remained began to retreat back into the trees and the Romans gave chase. Kemnebi had seen enough. He waved to the others that they should go, but a movement in the trees caught his attention. Kemnebi sprang from his horse and pinned down the man just as he emerged from the trees.

Kemnebi stared into the terrified eyes of the short young man who had been working on the broken wheel of one of the Roman wagons. Kemnebi's dagger was at the young man's throat.

"Sire," the young man cried. "I am no criminal nor am I a slave. The Romans found me asleep under a tree."

Kemnebi took pity on him. He looked terrified and, though not a child, his body size was no bigger than a child of perhaps six years old. His legs and arms were very thin and his back more crooked than he had at first observed. Kemnebi withdrew his dagger from the man's throat and released the hold he had on him. "Who are you and why were you asleep under a tree out here? As you have just found out that is a dangerous thing to do."

"Quanarious is my name, sire. I—I have no home. I sleep where I can."

Kemnebi helped him to his feet and cut the long straps that bound Quanarious's hands together. "Go, Quanarious. The Romans will be looking for you."

"I am most grateful, sire," Quanarious said. He turned to leave, then paused. "I think you should leave too. The Romans are dangerous men."

"Indeed," Kemnebi said. "We have wasted enough time. We have a sick child and we must get to Tigranocerta as soon as possible. Are we on the right path, Quanarious? Do you know?"

Quanarious nodded furiously. "I know these parts very well. Tigranocerta is not far from here. From here I know a shorter route," he said. "If you like I will take you there." He nervously scratched his chin. "I know a physician. Would you like me to take you to him?"

"Yes!' Kemnebi said. "Take us to him at once!" He jumped back on his horse and offered a hand to Quanarious. "Come on."

Quanarious stared at his hand. "Sire, I prefer to walk. I can walk very fast."

"Very well then," Kemnebi said. "Go"

Quanarious walked with a slight limp but moved quickly through the trees. "Follow me," he said looking back, "we shall be there in no time."

Thirty-Six

A drenio, the Greek physician, poured a mixture of dry wild roots and flowers into a cup and handed the cup to Ezri. "Boil this in water and bring it to me, please," he whispered. Adrenio returned to the bed where Farrenthias slept and studied his patient silently. His fever remained dangerously high, but his breathing was steadier than when he had been brought to him a few hours ago. He dipped a cloth into a bowl of cold water and wiped Farrenthias's forehead, chest, and arms. When Ezri returned with the mixture, Adrenio moistened Farrenthias's lips with the roots and then resumed his treatment of applying cold water to Farrenthias's body. He repeatedly sent Trulius to a well to bring him fresh cold water.

After working for hours, Adrenio tossed the cloth into the bowl and dried his hands with another cloth. "His fever is finally going down. In the morning he should be much better." He rubbed the back of his neck and looked at Kemnebi. "You are lucky that our friend Quanarious brought you to me when he did. Farrenthias's fever was very high. Another hour and his mouth and face might have contorted, and he would have been in very serious danger of dying. Of course, it helped that he is in very good health. He is thin but strong."

Kemnebi looked at Trulius. "I suppose we owe that to Trulius here. He keeps Farrenthias quite active." He looked through the open door at Quanarious. He had helped Trulius draw water from a deep well so that the water was as cold as possible. Kemnebi thought it odd that he had not left. He now sat by the well alert and ready to draw more water, and for the first time, Kemnebi noticed that, except for his deformity, he was not a bad-looking young man. His tunic was ragged but not soiled, and he had tied his long dark hair back, giving him a neat appearance. Kemnebi turned to Adrenio and pointed to Quanarious with his chin. "Who is he?"

"Ah, our dear little friend, Quanarious. I first saw him on a street corner about a year ago. He was rubbing some old calluses on his knees. He told me he had just scrubbed the floor of some tavern for food. I gave him an ointment made of animal fat to rub on those calluses. No one knows where he came from."

"He told us that he had no home," Ezri said. "Is that true?"

"As far as I know, he sleeps where he can. Some people, including myself, have offered him a permanent place to sleep, but he prefers to keep to himself."

"The Romans had him trying to change the wheel of a wagon with his hands tied together," Ezri said.

"He is a good little worker," Adrenio said. "He goes from house to house asking for work, and when there is none, he is still offered a coin or two or a piece of bread but he refuses it. He is a proud young man." Adrenio stood and stretched his arms. "Farrenthias is breathing much easier. I think I will get some fresh air." He held out a hand to Trulius. "Go Trulius, you too could use some fresh air."

Kemnebi also walked to the door but did not step outside. He leaned against the door with folded arms and watched Adrenio and Trulius approach Quanarious. Trulius sat beside him and placed an arm around his shoulder. Quanarious seemed to enjoy the gesture of friendship. He slapped Trulius on a knee and smiled at Adrenio as if to show off his new friend.

"I am afraid to ask what you are thinking, Kemnebi," Ezri said. "I can see it in your eyes. You are a compassionate man, and I can also see that Trulius has become quite fond of Quanarious."

"It is more than being compassionate," Kemnebi said. "I know what it is like to be homeless, to have no place to rest your head at night except perhaps a cold, dark alley somewhere." He glanced at Ezri. "Could you not use an extra hand at Clivus?"

"Hum," Ezri murmured. "Erasmus Harel has always instilled in us the idea that there is not enough compassion in the world, and clearly this young man is in need of compassion. Still, I do not have the authority to invite him to stay."

"Suppose we take him with us," Kemnebi said. "If Erasmus Harel decides that he cannot stay, then I will personally bring him back. I am certain that we can trust Quanarious not to say a word about where he has been."

"I will accompany you if the trip becomes necessary," Tavius said.

Ezri summoned Quanarious and then watched as the small young man responded without hesitation and hastily walked towards him.

"Yes," sire," Quanarious said. "Do we need more water for the lad Farrenthias?"

"No," Ezri said. "Farrenthias is resting now. You and Trulius helped save his life. Now tell me, Quanarious. You say that you do not have a home?"

Quanarious lowered his chin. "It is true, I have no home."

Ezri sighed. "Well, would you consider returning into the woods with us? We are well established and have plenty of room. But before you speak, let me warn you that we all rise very early and there are many chores that need to be done. Would you consider going with us?"

Quanarious beamed with delight and swallowed. "Sire, I—I would like that very much." He looked happily around. "I—I am not afraid of hard work and most days I am awake even before the sun shows its face."

"What happened to your family?"

Quanarious lowered his chin again and blushed. "I used to travel with my mother, helping her clean taverns." He paused and swallowed sadly. "One morning in a village far from here, I woke up and she was gone. The innkeeper told me that she had left with a man." Quanarious raised his eyes and for an instant they almost sparkled with tears. He withdrew a small pouch from his belt. "When she left, she left me this pouch with the innkeeper. There were five coins in it and they are still here."

Ezri smiled and stroked his face. "I see. Now, I want you to understand, Quanarious, that I do not have the final word on whether you can stay where we are going. If you cannot stay, Kemnebi and Tavius here will bring you back, and we will ask you not to tell anyone about where we live."

Quanarious nodded sadly. "I understand, sire."

"Also, it is not a place where you can just come and go as you please," Ezri said. "Would you be willing to stay for a long period of time, years perhaps?"

Quanarious nodded enthusiastically. "I—I have never had a home. I have nothing else to do with my life."

"Very well, Quanarious, then it is settled. As soon as Farrenthias is able to travel, you will go back with us."

Quanarious dropped to his knees and took the hand of Ezri and attempted to kiss it, but Ezri gently pulled his hand back.

"On your feet, my dear Quanarious, that is not necessary."

Farrenthias suddenly stirred in his bed and opened his eyes. "Ezri," he said. "Where is Trulius?"

Thirty-Seven

✤ 61 AD ✤

"Father!" Farrenthias cried. He ran ahead of Tavius and the others and rushed into his father's outstretched arms. "Father!" He said again. "What a surprise! How good to see you!"

Lord Gaios arrived at the gates of Clivus with a small band of soldiers and squires, and three loaded carts of supplies, including sacks of wheat grain, vegetables, fruits, bottles of wine, blankets, cloaks, and other commodities. He held Farrenthias at arm's length and looked him over with an approving nod.

"You look well, son. Tavius," he said, "In just over a year Farrenthias has grown considerably. Of course, he could be heavier. He is too thin, but then he has never had much of an appetite."

"Of course he has grown, my lord," Tavius said. "And I assure you that I pester him daily about eating well and enough."

Farrenthias looked past his father, and when he did not see his mother or sisters, his eyes became moist with disappointment. Sensing his father's gaze, he immediately forced a smile.

"You look disappointed, my son," Lord Gaios said compassionately. "Perhaps you were expecting to see your mother and sisters."

Lord Gaios caressed his son's chin. "I believe this is a too difficult and dangerous of a journey for them, but they did beg me to bring them. They miss you terribly."

Farrenthias blushed. "I miss them too, but," he quickly added, "I have been happy here."

"In the supplies that I brought you will find a cloak your mother sent you and some trinkets your sisters made for you."

"Greetings, Lord Gaios," Erasmus Harel said, looking from cart to cart. "It must have been difficult pulling those carts along some of the narrow paths."

"Bah, children's play," Lord Gaios said. "If you were a little closer I would have brought even more supplies."

Erasmus Harel smiled. "These supplies will last us a year. You should not have troubled yourself. But I do thank you for your generosity."

"Go and find the cloak your mother sent," Lord Gaios said to Farrenthias. He watched Farrenthias as he and Adin helped unpack one of the carts. "He tells me that he is happy here," he said to Erasmus Harel.

"It pleases me to hear you say that, my lord." Eramus Harel said. "We love having him and Cerudotus here."

Lord Gaios looked around the courtyard. "Cerudotus. Where is that irascible tutor?"

"I sent Ezri to find him. The last time I saw him he was in one of the halls reading."

"Adin!" Farrenthias yelled from one of the carts. He held up a wooden figurine holding a tiny sword. "Look, my sisters sent me these wooden soldiers. This one looks like Trulius!"

"Who is Trulius," Lord Gaios asked.

"Tessius Trulius is my brother's son. He and his guardian Kemnebi, a close friend of the family, arrived shortly after you left," Erasmus Harel said. "He is Farrnthias's age and those two have become inseparable."

"Excellent," Lord Giaos said. "I never expected that Farrenthias would have a companion here."

"Indeed," Eramus Harel, "But I must tell you that as bright as Trulius is he can be a handful. A few months ago, Farrenthias was out exploring the forest with Trulius when they were caught in a violent storm. Farrenthias caught quite a fever. We had to take him to Tigranocerta to a physician for treatment, but as you can see, he has recovered completely."

"Hum," Lord Gaios murmured pensively. "Were I a different type of father that news might have alarmed me, but it would not be the first time Farrenthias has fallen ill enough to be taken to a physician. Besides, it pleases me to hear that Farrenthias was out in the forest exploring. I could never get him away from his studies in Syria. Where is Tessius Trulius now?"

"Out hunting with Kemnebi. They have been out for hours and should return shortly,"

Farrenthias and Tavius joined them, and Lord Gaios said, "Farrenthias, Erasmus Harel tells me that you have a companion now. Tessius Trulius."

"Yes, Father," Farrenthias said. "Trulius can swing a sword like a true soldier and he can ride a horse backwards and do flips on its back."

Tavius laughed. "Farrenthias does not exaggerate, my lord. The young man is quite talented and he does not tire easily. Why, Kemnebi and I have to take turns fencing with him, and after he tires us both, he still runs away looking for a horse to ride."

Lord Gaios nodded in amusement. "I see, then I can hardly wait to greet this amazing young man. Hopefully he will get here soon." Lord Gaios bellowed.

Erasmus Harel nodded and said, "In the meantime, Farrenthias, if your father is not too tired, perhaps you can escort him to your room and show him some of your work."

"An excellent suggestion," Lord Gaios said. "I am most anxious to hear about what you have accomplished since you have been here, Farrenthias."

As Farrenthias walked quietly beside his father, he started to say something then grew quiet again.

"What is it, Farrenthias?" Lord Gaios said. "Speak your mind, my son."

"May I speak freely, Father?" Farrenthias said.

Lord Gaios stopped walking. "Of course, I can see that you are quite anxious to tell me something. Could it be that it has something to do with Clivus and your desire to stay here?"

Farrenthias stared quietly at his father. It did not surprise him that he knew exactly what he wanted to tell him. At times, Farrenthias believed that his father knew him even better than he knew himself. "Yes, Father," he said, "that is what I wanted to tell you. While I have truly missed all of you, I wish to stay here. I have learned a great deal and I have a great deal more to learn. I hope you understand and permit me to stay."

Lord Gaios looked straight ahead with no expression on his face. "Your mother predicted that you would not want to return with me, and I must confess to you that deep in my heart I had hopes that she was wrong and that you were ready to come home."

Farrenthias cast his eyes down. "Do I disappoint you, Father?"

Lord Gaios looked warmly at his son. "No, Farrenthias. A son who pursues his dreams can never disappoint a father, especially when those dreams are noble and admirable."

They walked in silence and entered the tower where Farrenthias had his room. At the beginning of a long hall Farrenthias paused. The hall was lit by a few dim lanterns, which hung from a wall. The door to Farrenthias's room was open and from inside burned another dim light. They had just reached the small cubicle when Cerudotus came rushing down the hall.

"My lord!" he cried. "When they told me of your arrival I could not believe my ears, but it is true. Here you are. How good to see you!"

"It is good to see you, my dear Cerudotus," Lord Gaios said. "You could not have arrived at a better moment. Farrenthias and I just had a heart to heart talk."

Cerudotus paled and looked from Lord Gaios to Farrenthias, and then he smiled weakly. "Farrenthias has told you that—that he wishes to stay at Clivus?"

Lord Gaios folded his arms and nodded. "He has. What are your thoughts on the matter? Before you speak, let me say this. I am letting Farrenthias stay, but if you do not want to, I am prepared to release you of your obligation to stay with him. You can return to Syria with me and assume the education of Erisa and Clisa."

Cerudotus gasped and stared wildly at Lord Gaios. He looked at Farrenthias. By the expression on his face it was apparent that he too had been shocked by his father's comment.

"My lord," Cerudotus cried. "I adore Clisa and Erisa. There is not a thing I would not do for those two rose petals, but my place is with Farrenthias. I would never, I could never leave his side." Cerudotus inhaled. "Unless of course you ordered it and then I would beg you to change your mind."

Lord Gaios exhaled loudly. "Good. It pleases me to hear that. Then the matter is settled. You both stay." He looked at the scrolls that were neatly piled next to Farrenthias's bed. What is all that about, my son? What is written in those scrolls?"

Farrenthias picked up one of the scrolls and motioned for his father to sit beside him on the bed. "Many fascinating things are written in these scrolls, Father. Here, I shall read you from one written by a sage from the Far East ..."

Trulius blushed. His clothes were filthy and he smelled like the rotted carcass of a goat. But, that did not stop Lord Gaios from throwing his arms around him and squeezing him tightly.

"I have heard nothing but good things about you, young man," he said. "I hear that you handle a sword very well. That is good. You are at the perfect age to learn such skills. The Romans have the best army in the world and that is because they start training Roman boys at a young age."

"One day I should like to lead a legion into battle like my father once did," Trulius said, regaining some of his nerve.

Lord Gaios laughed. "I have no doubt that you will. He pointed to Trulius's sword. "I see that you carry your armament now. That looks like an excellent sword."

Trulius studied the sword. "It belongs to Kemnebi, my lord, but he promised that the next time we visit Tigranocerta he is going to buy me my own sword."

Lord Gaios walked to a large box and opened it. "That will not be necessary. I think we can outfit you now if Kemnebi will allow me. We always travel with an abundance of weapons."

"My lord," Kemnebi mumbled. "Are you certain that you can spare a sword?"

"Bah," Lord Gaios cried. "Not only can I spare a sword, I shall also outfit Trulius with a dagger and a spear as well. They are part of the equipment every good soldier should have."

"In that case, I am grateful to you," Kemnebi said. "If you like, Trulius can show you the skills he has learned."

"An excellent idea," Lord Gaios said.

Lord Gaios motioned to his men, and two of them removed an arsenal of weapons out of the box and set them out on the floor. Trulius stared incredulously at the armaments. He dropped to his knees to inspect them but caught himself and pulled back his hands.

"Go on, my son," Lord Gaios said. "See how they feel."

"I told you Father had many swords," Farrenthias said to Trulius.

Trulius picked up one sword and then another. "These are all magnificent," he said. "Kemnebi," he said. "These are as magnificent as the weapons Father stores."

"No doubt your father has an excellent collection of swords, Trulius," Lord Gaios said. He reached down and picked up a sword and handed it to Trulius. "This is what you want, my son. It is a Gladius Roman sword. It is light, yet strong, and balanced. It will serve you well for many years."

Trulius's hand trembled with excitement as he took the sword from Lord Gaios and studied its silver handle and sharp blade."

"It is a beautiful sword, Trulius," Kemnebi said. "And a most popular one with Romans."

Lord Gaios lifted the sheath that accompanied the sword and handed it to Trulius's belt. He then picked out a dagger and javelin.

"Do you know how to use these yet, Trulius?" he asked.

"Father," Farrenthias cried. "Why, Trulius is an expert at those weapons. He killed a lion with a wooden spear and a crude dagger."

The moment he had spoken the words, Farrenthias gasped and covered his mouth.

Lord Gaios flashed him a look, and then he turned to look at Tavius.

"Trulius!" Kemnebi cried. "What is Farrenthias talking about? You never..."

"I was afraid to tell you," Trulius cried. "It was the day Farrenthais and I got caught in the storm. I was afraid you would not let us go out again."

"A lion?" Lord Gaios bellowed. He eyed Tavius, who swallowed fearfully. "Did you know about this?"

"My lord," he cried, "I did not. Forgive me. I know you entrusted me with Farrenthias's safety. I do not know what to say."

Lord Gaios waved a hand and his harsh frown softened. "You are not to blame, Tavius. Boys cannot be kept in cages or looked after as women. Besides, a boy must learn how to hunt and there is danger in hunting. Do you agree, Kemnebi?"

Kemnebi sighed and slowly shook his head. "Yes, I suppose you are right, my lord."

"Good," Lord Gaios said. He eyed Farrenthias sternly. "You must never let this slip out of you in front of your mother. Do you understand?"

Red in the face, Farrenthias nodded. "Of course, Father."

Lord Gaios motioned for everyone to follow him. "Enough talk. Let us go outside. I want to see what Trulius can do with his new sword."

Although still small in stature, Trulius was developing well. His young chest, arms, and legs were already well defined with young muscles that glistened in the sun. The sword felt good in his grip and surprisingly light, and he knew why. For the last year, aside from using Kemnebi's sword, Kemnebi had also taken to making him wave his wooden sword over and over again after he had attached a set of heavy rocks with a leather strap to the blade. Trulius, however, was terribly nervous. He wanted to do well in front of Lord Gaios. He also wanted to make Kemnebi and Farrenthias proud. He did, however, find assurance in the broad smile Kemnebi gave him. Moreover, Kemnebi inhaled deeply and motioned for Trulius to do the same. Trulius took in a deep breath and exhaled slowly as instructed, raised his sword and assumed a defensive position.

"Ah, I already approve of the stance," Lord Gaios said, "and look at this, the lad is left handed like his friend Farrenthias." Lord Gaios spread his legs, bent his knees slightly, and raised his sword. "Attack, Trulius. Come at me."

Trulius charged, thrusting his sword from a high position to a low and then from side to side. He moved with speed and agility.

"Excellent, Trulius, excellent," Lord Gaios shouted. "Keep coming." Lord Gaios moved backwards and from side to side. "Kemnebi," he said. "You have taught Trulius well. I have never seen such speed and agility in a boy his size and age. Trulius is a natural."

"Now grip your sword like this," Lord Gaios said, gripping his sword with both hands, "and protect yourself." Lord Gaios moved forward, slashing and jabbing, carefully measuring the strength of his blows so as not to hurt Trulius. At last he paused and dug the point of his sword into the ground. "I am most impressed, indeed, Trulius. Tavius," he said, "take my lead, I want to see Trulius in action as a spectator."

Lord Gaios stepped to one side, next to Kemnebi. "You have done an outstanding job with the lad," Lord Gaios said. "I have never seen a boy his age with such skills. I also notice that he carries himself with a certain confidence and style that is the true mark of a leader."

"I cannot take all the credit, my lord," Kemnebi said. "Trulius comes from excellent lineage. His father, Marcellius Kaelus, was once a fierce and well-respected Roman commander. In the battlefield his skills were unmatched. Marcellius practiced with Trulius practically from the moment Trulius could walk and hold a wooden sword."

"Then that explains his remarkable skills," Lord Gaios said. He studied Trulius. "Cerudotus tells me that Trulius also has a good head on his shoulders. A bright man with such skill will know no bounds on what he can accomplish. Rome is lucky to have him."

"Agreed," Kemnebi said. "He is like a son to me and such praises make me proud. Nevertheless, Trulius also worries me. He will grow into a fierce warrior. His enemies will fear him and his friends will resent his superior skills. I worry that such men will never have a peaceful existence."

Thirty-Eight

Late one afternoon Kemnebi returned to the courtyard and happened upon Trulius and Farrenthias, where he had left them hours earlier. Kemnebi paused a short distance away and watched Trulius draw circles in the dirt with the tip of his sword. He was clearly in a sullen mood and all attempts by Farrenthias to engage him in conversation were of no avail. Earlier, at this very spot, everyone at Clivus had gathered to bid farewell to Lord Gaios. His departure had clearly affected Trulius, who had taken to practicing his sword fighting with Lord Gaios every day two or three times a day. Kemnebi knew, however, that something else troubled Trulius. The presence of the father of Farrenthias had clearly made it difficult for Trulius not think about his own father and wonder where he was and why they had not heard from him. In fact, on those days when he had not been practicing with Lord Gaios, Trulius had taken to longer and longer walks by himself. He would return subdued and quiet, and on those occasions not even Farrenthias could cheer him up.

Kemnebi was deeply saddened and knew that he could no longer keep the truth from young Trulius. He drew his breath and approached the two boys cautiously. "Trulius," he said, "Perhaps you and I should take a walk."

Trulius looked at Kemnebi with a drawn face, yet with eyes that told Kemnebi that Trulius knew he was about to be told something very important that had been kept from him. "Can Farrenthias accompany us?"

"No, no," Farrenthias said quickly, also grasping the importance of the moment.

"Of course he can walk with us," Kemnebi said. "I think it is an excellent suggestion."

Kemnebi led them slowly across the courtyard and out the gates in silence. He walked with his head cast down, obviously deep in thought, and neither Trulius nor Farrenthias attempted to break the silence. Just beyond the gates he at last raised his chin and glanced at Trulius. "My dear Trulius, you are still very young but quite intelligent for your age, and I think it is time that I tell you why your father sent us away from Rome in the middle of the night."

"Was there some sort of trouble?" Trulius asked. "Is that why we had to leave?"

Kemnebi stopped walking and affectionately placed an arm around Trulius. "My son," he said, "the night we left Rome, a terrible thing occurred in the city. Your mother was murdered. She was murdered by a Roman soldier. Your father killed the man who did that and he killed the man's companions when they tried to prevent your father from making his escape. As a result, your father was arrested. I believe he is still in custody somewhere, otherwise, he would have joined us by now."

Trulius stared at Kemnebi, his face pale and his eyes full of tears. Unable to speak, he wept quietly. "Mother," he finally said. "My mother is dead?"

"I am afraid so, my child." Kemnebi said.

Trulius wiped the tears from his face. "Roman soldiers did this?" he asked. Kemnebi did not answer him.

Trulius was suddenly in a rage. "Romans killed my mother and now they have my father, why?"

"Trulius," Kemnebi said. "Listen to me, my child. You cannot fill your heart with such rage."

Trulius unsheathed the sword Lord Gaios had given him and stared at it. "I once heard Cerudotus describe Tiberius as a mad man, and Caligula as a pig, and he said that Nero was both a mad man and a pig. Is that true, Kemnebi? Are all Roman emperors insane?"

"Cerudotus is a brilliant man with a colorful tongue, Trulius," Kemnebi said. "Yes, power sometimes corrupts men, but you must love and respect your country. Rome is a great empire."

"Will we ever see Father again?"

"I have faith that we will, Trulius. I pray to the gods that he is well."

"What gods?" Trulius cried. "He pointed to his sword. "This is the only thing that matters. Only foolish men waste their time kneeling before idols that do not exist." He turned and glared at Farrenthias, who stood quietly weeping. "Farrenthias, look at me and tell me I am wrong. You have told me that the Hebrew people believe in one God, a God who they say created the world, a God who is responsible for everything that happens? If that were true why would He allow so much killing?"

Farrenthias swallowed slowly. "Trulius there is much evil in the world. I agree with that, but man is responsible for his own actions. God cannot be blamed for the evil that men do."

Trulius shook his head "No, Farrenthias, you are wrong! Either God is responsible for everything that happens, good or bad, or he is not responsible for anything at all." He fought back tears. "Maybe everyone is wrong! The Romans, the Greeks, the Christians, they are all wrong. Maybe no gods exist at all."

"Trulius," Farrenthias said, "I am so sorry for what has happened to you. I cannot begin to feel your pain. I do not have the answers you seek, but my own belief is that all suffering is temporary and that it is designed for a purpose. Everything has a purpose."

"I do not care about any purpose," Trulius cried. "I just want to see my mother. I want to see my father. Will the God of the Hebrews, if he does exist, grant me that wish?" He glared at his sword. "I will never defend Rome with this sword! I do not ever want to wear the cape of a Roman soldier. I hate Rome and I hate everything it represents!"

Erasmus Harel peeked into Trulius's room and his heart ached. Trulius sat on his bed weeping. He resembled his father so much when he was that age that Erasmus Harel stared at him in awe.

"Trulius," he whispered.

Trulius quickly dried the tears from his eyes and tried to hide his grief-stricken face.

Erasmus Harel stepped into the room. "Kemnebi just told me that he has informed you about what happened in Rome the day you left." He sighed quietly. "I am sorry, Trulius, that you have suffered such a terrible tragedy."

Trulius shrugged. "I want to go home. I want to go back to Rome and find Father."

Erasmus Harel sat next to Trulius. "It would not be wise for you and Kemnebi to return to Rome just yet, my son. By sending you here your father believed that you were in danger, and if anything were to happen to you it would destroy him."

Trulius dejectedly lowered his head. "Do you think he is alright? You do not think the Romans have hurt him do you?"

"Your father is a remarkable man, Trulius. He knows how to take care of himself. In truth, you are much like him. When he was your age our father, Trabellius, had to assign one of his men to follow us around the Forum whenever we visited lest your father get into some mischief."

Trulius smiled through his pain and tears. "I never heard that. What kind of mischief would Father get into?"

Erasmus Harel smiled. "Well, once, I had just arrived in Rome from Greece and your father insisted that we visit the Forum the very next day. Father was against it for there were special tournaments going on adjacent to the Forum. There were visitors from all over the world. By then Kemnebi had already been adopted into the family, so the three of us set out for the Forum. It was a glorious sunny day and there were so many people we could barely walk through the crowds. We stuffed ourselves with confections and baked sweets, and your father and Kemnebi chased pigs and chickens along with the other boys. We were resting at a fountain at noon trying to decide what to do next when a troop of soldiers dismounted and began to cool off at the fountain. I know only that they were not Roman. One of them thought it funny to splash your father with water. A small crowd who saw it laughed. Actually, your father was one who did enjoy good humor, but the soldier clearly did it to humiliate him. When I saw the look on your father's face, I knew there was going to be trouble. Your father, who barely reached the man's shoulders, politely told the man that he did not appreciate the ridicule. "Were I bigger I would make you apologize," your father said to the soldier. The soldier's companions now laughed at their friend. "Ha," one of them cried. "The young lad has clearly scolded you. Now apologize before he tosses you into the fountain."

Highly embarrassed, the soldier roughly grabbed your father by the back of the neck and lifted him off the ground. "Ah, an excellent suggestion," the soldier yelled, laughing. "I think I will toss this lad into the fountain."

Erasmus Harel sighed. "Two things happened quickly. Marcellius was about thirteen but possessed the strength of someone much older. Well, while the man was looking at his companions still laughing, Marcellius dug one of his heels into the man's belly so hard that the man dropped him and doubled over with pain. At that point Marcellius shoved him so hard the man fell into the fountain headfirst. Fortunately, Father's guards arrived just in time to whisk us away as everyone laughed at the soldier."

Trulius laughed. "I never heard that story."

Erasmus Harel affectionately tapped him on the shoulder. "In time, I will tell you many more stories about your father." He stood. "Come, my son, Ya'ir is about to depart and we must wish him farewell."

"Ya'ir is leaving?" Trulius asked, also getting to his feet. "Why? Where is he going?"

"He is returning to Jerusalem," Erasmus Harel said.

"When will he return?" Trulius asked.

Erasmus Harel paused and frowned. "He will not be returning to Clivus, Trulius. He has much work to do in Jerusalem."

Thirty-Nine

Annais dug an elbow into Septimus's lower back and pressed down hard. Septimus winced with pain, stiffened and then relaxed. An effective massage had to include some measure of pain, and Annais knew just how much each of her clients could endure before the pain became unbearable. Annais was a stout woman, broad-shouldered and strong, and in her expert hands Septimus's muscles were like dough. Stretched across a long table on his belly, with a towel partially covering his nude body, Septimus was as firm and strong as a man half his age. It was high noon, but inside his private gymnasium, where there were no windows, the room was dark. A row of lamps burned dimly from two humid walls. The room smelled of the sweet flowery oils that Annais used to soften his muscles and moisten his skin. Annais shifted her elbow across his back and pressed down again and again. Septimus winced with pain. Annais was not just Septimus's masseuse, she was also a childhood friend and confidante. And because babbling senators and other politicians regularly summoned her to their private chambers in the Forum for a massage, Annais was privy to all the latest gossip in Rome. And, everything she heard she carried to Septimus.

Annais playfully slapped Septimus's partially exposed buttocks. "I will have you know that the Forum is rattling with rumors about the upcoming political elections and appointments, and as usual your name is at the top of every list, Septimus. A senate seat is yours for the asking."

Septimus kept his face hidden beneath his folded arms. "I am not interested," he murmured with no emotion.

"Yes, I know," Annias said. "You have told me that time and again and I still do not understand you. Are you not sick of listening to the lies of murdering thieves? Are you not sick of the bickering of neighbors over property disputes? Bah! It is time that you display your talents in the Senate."

"Resolving legal issues is a noble profession, my dear Annais," Septimus said. "A civilized community cannot exist without laws and the men who enforce them. On the other hand, politics can easily erode a man's morals. In severe cases, it can turn a good man into a predator, not unlike the reptiles that crawl in the desert lurking and ready to strike."

Annais laughed. "I would agree that most politicians are snakes but do not lie to me, Septimus. I have known you all my life. Were we not poor street urchins in the Aventine together? And now look at you? You have made a name for yourself. All that I have is because of you. You were born to speak for the poor. You were born for a senate seat." She drummed her fingers on his back. "It is that wife of yours, is it not? You deny yourself a senate seat because of that hussy. I hate her."

Septimus raised his head to protest, but Annais gently pushed it down. "You heard me. She is a hussy, even by Roman standards."

Annais glanced at a lamp that burned across the room. "Nameya, now there is a light that truly glows. You should have divorced Varelia a long time ago and married Nameya. Ha, I still remember that incident at the Tiber River last year. Why, the way Varelia frolicked naked in the water in front of her guards. And if that were not enough, she then ordered poor Nameya to disrobe and join her in the water. It served Varelia right that every single man, out of respect for you and for Nameya, turned away rather than gaze at your lovely concubine's nakedness. I have never seen a freed woman like Nameya command such respect. She would make an excellent wife for you." Annais wiped the excessive oil from Septimus's back with a cloth and announced that she was finished.

Septimus rolled onto his back and sat up on the table. Annais was right. Nameya was not just his concubine. She was his closest friend and ally, and he loved her. Septimus tried to step off the table but cringed with pain and pressed his temples.

"Aha!" Annais cried, "Another one of your mysterious headaches."

Septimus gave her a stern look. "Annais," he said. "I warn you, speak of this to no one, not even Nameya." He rubbed his temples but it did not help.

"You need not keep reminding me," Annais said. "My lips are sealed, but you really need to have someone examine you, someone other than your incompetent physician, Guardo." She opened her satchel and began to put away her oils. "The man is a comedian. He does not know the difference between a toe and a finger."

Septimus laughed. "You are vicious, Annais."

Annais took his chin and caressed it as a mother caresses the chin of her favorite child. "I have another appointment, Septimus, and were it not for that, I would stay here and do you the favor of finding your pompous wife and strangling her with my bare hands."

Septimus laughed again, only this time harder, and the effort made his head throb with more pain. "Go now, you silly woman, before you cause me more pain."

Septimus walked across the hall to his steam parlor and opened the door. A wave of hot, thick steam poured from the room and engulfed his body, and for an instant the shock of the heat soothed his headache. He stepped inside the room and stretched on a raised slab of stone and the headache returned. The door opened and he raised his head in anticipation. Only one other person was allowed in his steam parlor. Nameya stood at the threshold in a cloud of steam. She wore a short, thin dress that clung to her full breasts and round hips. Her light brown hair was disheveled around her soft, bare shoulders. Instantly, Septimus felt much better. Nameya had that effect on him. She was as lovely as Venus and, if possible, even lovelier.

"I saw Annais leaving," Nameya said. "How was your massage today, my lord?"

Septimus swung his legs around and kissed her on the cheek. Her skin was soft and moist and it tasted of sweet lilies. "Excellent. Annais has the hands of a mason, and as usual she left me as weak as a child."

He kissed her again on her neck, her cheeks and her lips. His fingers searched for the straps on her dress and untied them. He tugged at her dress until it dropped to the floor. He then ran a finger down between her lovely breasts to the dark mound just below her flat belly.

"Nameya," he whispered. For an instant, the pain threatened to return, but it quickly vanished when she touched him. He closed his eyes and at that moment, with his loins burning with desire, nothing else mattered, not his headaches and not his disastrous marriage. At this moment, the only thing that mattered was Nameya and the intoxicating pleasure only she was capable of giving him. Everything else was nothing.

Forty

June arrived in Rome with unusually heavy rains. It drizzled in the mornings, poured in the afternoons, and the nights were hot, humid, and wet. The downpours kept the Tiber River filled to capacity with its dark, green waters threatening to overrun its banks. Gardens throughout the city were green with fertile grass, and the gardens were filled with colorful flowers and excessive bushes and shrubs that kept gardeners busy. It was difficult to maneuver carriages and carts through the wet streets, some of which flooded easily, but that did not deter the heavy traffic.

Late one afternoon, Varelia stormed into her quarters and burst through the double doors that led to the veranda that overlooked the garden. She cursed the gods. It had been raining for hours and the incessant rain would not stop. She walked back into her room and paced in her expansive quarters. She cursed the gods again and dug her nails into the edge of a sofa. So this is what she had returned to after being out of Rome for a few months. Nameya was pregnant. What did that harlot mean by allowing herself to get pregnant? Every woman in Rome knew how to take care of herself. What was she thinking? How dare that wench embarrass and humiliate her in her own house? How dare Septimus allow this to happen! No, she did not love her husband. She detested him, and it suited her well that his precious little concubine kept him occupied. But the idea that she would bear him a child, his first child, was an insult to her status as his wife. She stopped pacing and glanced out the double doors. The rain had slackened into a steady drizzle. Varelia could wait no longer. She grabbed her cloak and flew out of her room. She had already arranged for her litter to be prepared, and as soon as the slaves saw her dash out of the house, they scrambled to their feet. "Quickly!" She shouted. She stepped into her litter and stuck her head out. "Hurry, you imbeciles," she shouted. "Get me to Father's house before it starts to pour again."

Four muscular slaves clad in loin clothes lifted her litter and started out at a medium pace in order not to rock the litter too much. But Varelia screamed at them.

"Imbeciles! Pick up the pace. We are never going to get to the Palatine at this pace."

Varelia reclined back into her litter. Suddenly, she had an excruciating headache. The streets were crowded, but her slaves were experts at maneuvering around throngs of people and puddles of water without slowing down. They managed to reach her father's house just as it began to pour again.

Varelia leaped out of her litter and stormed into the house. She brushed past her father's servants who offered to take her cloak and pushed open the doors to her father's private study. Atenuar was not alone. He had guests. Fortunately, he was concluding his business with them. Surprised and obviously irritated by her outburst, he nevertheless patiently introduced his daughter to his guests and then escorted them to the door and entrusted them to a servant who escorted them out of the house.

Atenuar turned his attention to his daughter. Her eyes were ablaze, and she was ashen and had begun to pace around the room. He knew exactly why she was here and why she was so angry. He certainly empathized with her, at least to some degree. Atenuar knew full well that most of Varelia's problems were a result of her own doing. "That was quite an entrance you just made, my dear," he said calmly. "No doubt you have become aware of Nameya's condition."

"So," Varelia shouted. "All of Rome knows? All of Rome is aware that your precious son-in-law has made a complete fool of your daughter. Tell me Father, are people laughing behind my back? Why was I not told? You could have sent a courier to warn me. Instead, I return to Rome, and as I walk down the halls of my own house, I have to endure the whispers and laughter behind my back from my own servants."

"No one is laughing at you, my dear," Atenuar said patiently. "Yes, Romans laugh and gossip, but I assure you, your marital problems are not the only gossip in the streets of Rome." Atenuar frowned. "Besides, how was I to reach you? You have been gone for six weeks and you were not very clear about where you were going. You merely sent me a note advising me that you would be out of the city for at least a month. When did you get back?"

"I got back last night and I saw her this afternoon." Varelia paused and glared at her father. "Why have you done nothing about this? Why do I have to return to my house and have to see my husband's concubine carrying his child? I demand that you forbid him from letting her have that child and that you order him to banish her from our house."

Atenuar stared at his daughter for a long moment. She was truly beautiful and he loved her. Yes, in spite of her selfish and manipulative nature he loved her, but he did not know her. He did not understand his own daughter. She was nothing like him and certainly nothing like her mother, who had died giving birth to their last child. "Varelia," he said patiently. "I have told you many times that Septimus is no different than any other Roman man when it comes to wanting an heir. He has always wanted a child. You saw one physician and then you refused to see another or to keep trying. Under such circumstances, do you blame him for what has happened?"

"Father!" Varelia shouted. Why do you side with him? Am I to blame for not being able to get pregnant? I came here for you to console me, not for you to chastise and hurt me. His concubine is pregnant and living under my roof! That might be acceptable in some households but not mine. I want her out of my house!"

"Need I remind you, my dear daughter, that you were the first to stray from your marital bed? You were not even discreet with the men whom you took as lovers. How many drunken soldiers have you slept with since you married Septimus? You have always detested him and have never passed an opportunity to hurt and embarrass him. He grew tired of you and turned to a woman who truly loves him."

"I do detest him! What do I care who he gets pregnant, but not with that wench! The entire household loves and respects her more than they respect me. Make him get rid of her! He will listen to you."

Atenuar shook his head in exasperation. "I cannot do that, Varelia."

"And why not?" Varelia shouted. "This marriage was your doing! I warned you that I would never accept the son of a stonecutter as my husband. A stonecutter!"

"I am aware," Atenuar said, "that you continue to harbor a rage against me because I put an end to your affair with that very handsome and very married Crassius. Well, Senator Crassius had no intentions of ever divorcing his wife and marrying you, and you have never been able to accept that. Septimus is an outstanding man. He knew of your affair with Crassius and he still fell in love with you and married you."

"You were wrong, Father! Crassius had every intention of divorcing his wife. He asked me to be patient and then you interfered!"

"Crassius, my dear, had a reputation for treating beautiful and gullible young women as his toys. He was a scoundrel. The jewels that he showered you with no doubt came from the other women whom he discarded like empty wine sacks. Why do you think he resigned his senate seat and left Rome in haste, and in the middle of the night?"

Varelia laughed sarcastically. "He left Rome because all the disgustingly fat men of the Senate resented him because he was so handsome, and because he was rich and from a noble family. They were conspiring against him and would have no doubt eventually had him in chains. And, if it had not been for you, he would have taken me with him."

Atenuar smiled sadly. "My poor daughter, what ill-advised illusions you had about that man."

Varelia dropped into a couch and grabbed a pillow and fondled it with her long nails. "They were no illusions, Father. We would have been married by now. Instead, I am married to a poor public servant who holds a judicial position, a position you obtained for him. Who respects a magistrate? Who respects his high and mighty morals? Other magistrates have left their offices rich, but your precious Septimus is too honest to reap the rewards of his office."

"For that you fault him?" Atenuar said. "He cannot be bribed and for that I admire him even more." Atenuar took a deep breath and walked to a table where he kept his finest wines. He poured himself a goblet of wine and drank steadily. "You, my dear, and you alone drove your husband into the arms of another woman and you want me to do something about that now, now when it is too late? Besides, it is not uncommon for a man to have children with his concubine, especially when his wife will not sleep with him."

"I swear that at times you act more as if he were your son and I a perfect stranger to you," Varelia said.

Atenuar calmly set his goblet down and looked at his daughter. "I have never hidden from you or anyone else how much I love and respect Septimus and how I do indeed wish he had been my son."

Varelia flung the pillow across the room and vaulted from the couch. "They will never get away with this those two!" she shouted. "Never!" She rushed out of the room before Atenuar could speak and stormed out of the house.

Outside, the rain was pouring down in heavy sheets. Varelia's slaves were huddled in one corner of the garden beneath a thick tree.

"On your feet!" She shouted. She stepped into her litter and shouted, "Get me home and be quick about it!"

The rain continued to pour and the streets were beginning to flood. Fortunately, the slaves knew the streets well and avoided the areas that they knew were filled with dangerous potholes. Traffic was scarce, and they made it home quickly. As soon as they entered the garden Varelia demanded that the litter stop. She stepped out of the litter so quickly that she stumbled and nearly fell. When one of the slaves tried to help her, she brushed his hands aside and disappeared into the house through a private entrance that only she used.

To Varelia's dismay, the house was in an uproar. Servants were rushing up and down the halls. Some of them carried cleaning rags and buckets of water, and others carried blankets. They walked quickly past one another without so much as a whisper being shared between them. Varelia stopped one of the servants and demanded to know what was happening. The young girl trembled under Varelia's gaze and powerful grip on her arm. "My lady," the girl stammered, "it is Lady Nameya. She collapsed in the hall, and she began to hemorrhage very badly. The physicians are attending to her this very moment."

"What physicians?" Varelia asked.

"I heard that Lord Septimus summoned Guardo and he brought the Egyptian physician, Maneria, with him."

Varelia stared anxiously at her. "Maneria? Are you certain?"

"Yes, my lady. I saw both men being escorted into Lady Nameya's quarters."

Stunned, Varelia released the girl. "Go," she said. The girl disappeared down the hall and Varelia walked slowly to her quarters. She could hardly believe what she had just been told. Had the gods finally smiled upon her? She knew Maneria well. He was a brilliant physician. Her sister Laecidia had introduced him to her at her house years ago. She had summoned him to attend to one of her favorite slaves. Maneria had discovered a strange bulge in the woman's belly, and the next day, with the entire household looking on, he removed it. Three days later, as if she had never been ill, the young woman was on her feet attending to her duties around the house.

Varelia was greeted at the door to her quarters by two of her maidens.

"Do we prepare your bath, my lady?" one of them asked.

Varelia's mind was still on Maneria and she nodded absently. "Yes," she said, then her eyes lighted. "Before anything else, summon Tura to me at once." Tura was her most trusted slave. Unlike other slaves, he was bright and had some schooling. He could think on his feet, and he was also as muscular and as strong as any of Rome's gladiators. But more importantly, he was completely loyal to her. Varelia once heard some of the other maidens whisper that Tura was so in love with her, he would not hesitate to take a knife in the back for her. There was no one in the household that she trusted more than Tura.

Varelia sat at her desk and quickly wrote out a note, rolled it and tied it with a thin leather strap.

She rose from her chair just as Tura and her maiden entered the room. "Go and see if my bath is ready," she said to the maiden.

"My lady," Tura said, bowing his head slightly. "I trust that your ride into the Palatine was not too disagreeable. Forgive me for not accompanying you. I missed you by seconds."

Varelia shrugged. "Tura, listen to me, a physician by the name of Maneria, along with Septimus's physician Guardo, is attending to Nameya. I want you to wait for them at the gates to the garden, and as soon as Guardo and Maneria go their separate ways, I want you to deliver this scroll to Maneria. Let no one see you give it to him. Do you understand? No one must see you talking to him."

Tura stuffed the scroll into his belt, and bowed. "Of course, my lady. No one will see me deliver the letter to him."

Varelia walked to her balcony and watched Tura's muscular back as he made his way through the garden towards the gates. Her moment of triumph had arrived so swiftly and so unexpectedly that her mind was in a swirl. Yet, her heart was at ease--an ease that had been missing all day. She walked back inside and to her private bath where her maidens helped her to undress. They had filled the room with dim candles and that suited her fine. A young, effeminate boy played the flute for her. She stepped into the water, closed her eyes and relaxed. Tomorrow she would leave first thing in the morning, spend the day at the Forum and perhaps visit her father again and apologize for her ravings. She smiled. He would understand. Her father always understood.

Forty-One

Septimus looked up from the scroll that he held in his hands and frowned angrily at the guard.

"Sire," the guard said, his face flush and nervous. "I know you asked not to be interrupted, but it is Lady Varelia again. She says that she is prepared to camp outside your door until you give her an audience."

Septimus sighed and tossed the scroll onto a table. Ever since Nameya had lost the baby two weeks before, Varelia had been most persistent about seeing him, but he had avoided her. He was in no mood to see anyone, much less the one woman who caused him more problems than anyone in his life. All he could think of was Nameya and how he could help her recover from her loss. It had been boy, a son. Worse, according to the physician the premature and difficult delivery had left Nameya with no hope of ever bearing another child.

Septimus stopped glaring at the guard, after all, Varelia's persistence was not his fault. He realized that the sooner he spoke to her, and dismissed whatever she wanted, the sooner she would leave him alone. "Very well," he said. "Let us be done with this. Let her in."

Varelia had a habit of wearing some of her most elaborate dresses around the house and of adorning her wrists and fingers with her best jewelry, and today was no exception. She wore a dark green dress, tight around the waist, and with an ample amount of cleavage showing. Her long, dark hair was brushed back and a pleasant fragrance preceded her presence. She was a stunning woman. Septimus could not deny that.

"You may leave us," Septimus said to the guard.

Varelia surprised Septimus. As soon as they were alone, she did not begin with a tirade of accusations as he had expected, but rather was uncharacteristically pleasant. She thanked Septimus for allowing her in to see him and she expressed sorrow about the loss of the baby. All of this put Septimus on guard. His wife was not a woman to be trusted.

"Ah," she murmured, "I see that you doubt my sincerity. Well, I cannot deny that I was at first angry about Nameya's pregnancy. How could I not be jealous? I am after all your wife. You cannot blame me for that, especially since—well, since I was never able to bear a child."

"Your decision, not mine," Septimus said curtly.

Varelia smiled weakly. For a moment, she almost looked contrite. Septimus had never seen that expression on her face before.

"I did not come here to quarrel with you, Septimus. I came to offer you my sincere condolences for your loss."

Septimus was only half-listening now. Nothing his wife had to say to him made any difference to him. He had made up his mind. Soon he would advise Atenuar that he was divorcing her. He should have done so years ago.

"Septimus," Varelia said. "Are you listening to me? I have been worried about you. You have not been seen out of this room for days. You have practically abandoned your office and now I can see why. You do not look well at all. You look pale and exhausted. You have not been sleeping well?"

Septimus shrugged and looked at his wife suspiciously. Varelia had never shown the least interest in his health. No, he was not sleeping well and his headaches were getting worse, but this he was not about to discuss with her. "I am fine," he said. "Perhaps a little tired but I am fine."

Varelia lowered herself onto the wide arm of a couch and played with one of the jeweled bracelets that adorned her wrist. "Do not be angry at me for inquiring about your health, Septimus. I am still your wife. Is a woman not entitled to show concern for her husband's health? I assume that you have consulted your physicians, Guardo and Maneria, about your inability to sleep. Have they not helped?"

"Bah, what do they know? Besides, every time Maneria prepares something for me, I feel worse."

Varelia paled but her expression softened. "I—I can hardly blame you for being angry with him." She removed a bracelet from her wrist. It glistened with yellow diamonds and blue emeralds that were embedded in the wide golden band. "Do you recall that Father brought me this bracelet from Egypt? As you know, Cleopatra once owned it. Father was told that she cherished it and that she wore it for protection against evil spirits. It is my favorite bracelet." She set it on a table. "I want Nameya to have it. Consider it a peace offering." She turned to leave.

Septimus stared at the bracelet. In spite of its beauty, and in spite of the fact that Cleopatra had indeed once owned it, Septimus knew that Varelia was lying. It was not her favorite bracelet. Varelia owned more extravagant jewelry, but none compared to the stunning history of this bracelet. It was priceless, but she obviously did not appreciate that nor did she appreciate how elated Atenuar had been when he was able to purchase it for her. He picked it up from the table. "Just a moment, Varelia." He offered her the bracelet. "Take it back. Your father meant for you to have it. Besides, Nameya will never accept it."

Varelia hesitated then took the bracelet back. "Very well, Septimus. At least tell her that I offered her my condolences, and you should consider seeing another physician."

Septimus was completely uneasy as he watched her leave his study. He trusted nothing about Varelia. He returned to his favorite chair and pressed his temples and closed his eyes. Another excruciating headache was developing.

He heard a voice, a soft voice, and he realized that he had dozed off. He opened his eyes and found Nameya bent down holding one of his hands.

"Septimus," she said. "You have grown deathly pale."

Forty-Two

The Palatine Hill was a raging inferno. The fire had started at the Circus Maximus and was now threatening the Esquiline Hill. Buildings and houses were being rapidly consumed by the flames and reduced to smoldering rubble. Neighborhoods were in complete disarray. The wealthy were out on the streets, shouting instructions to their slaves on what belongings to pack from their enormous homes. The poor loaded their arms and carried what they could from their meager shacks. Business owners and their assistants were scrambling to save their wares and inventories.

Varelia and her two sisters, Herminia and Laecidia, watched the fire from the back terrace of Herminia's house. The house was high on the north side of the Caelian Hill, and they had a clear view of distant flames lighting the dark skies of Rome. Varelia suddenly yawned and returned to a couch. Let Rome burn to the ground, what did she care. Horrified by what they were witnessing, Herminia and Laecidia remained at the balcony.

"Nero has announced that the Christians are responsible for this atrocity," Laecidia cried, "and he vowed to punish them."

Varelia laughed from the couch. "You are so gullible, my dear sister. Do you not understand Nero after all these years? Do you not understand that he is deviate and conniving? He turns every Roman tragedy into a political advantage for himself." She laughed again. "That is what politicians do. Why, just earlier this morning Loreno confided in me that Nero had pinned the blame on the Christians as an excuse to arrest and torture them."

"Loreno? Indeed." Herminia said, walking in out of the balcony with Laecidia. "Our newest senator and your latest conquest. You are a disgrace, my dear sister."

Varelia giggled like a school child. She reached for a table and ran her fingers through a fruit bowl with disinterest and selected a small cluster of purple grapes. "Why, am I a disgrace? He is not only terribly handsome, but he is lean and strong and deliciously naughty." She pretended to scrutinize her fingernails. "I wonder how much he is worth. A senate seat is not cheap."

"Herminia is right, Varelia," Laecidia said, "Your conduct is shameful and now you boast about it to us. You are still a married woman."

"If you two parrots are through criticizing me," Varelia said, chewing on a grape, "you might be interested in knowing that my husband's mysterious headaches are getting worse. Why, earlier this week I saw him, and he looked gaunt and weak. He looked positively terrible."

Herminia and Laecidia exchanged looks of horror, and shaking their heads, they stared at Varelia.

"Why do you two stare at me that way? Do you two actually pity him? After what he and that wench put me through with her pregnancy, you have the audacity to pity him?"

"Septimus is a good man," Laecidia said. "He tried very hard to make you happy. No matter how you may feel about him, he is a good man."

Varelia became enraged. "A good man? Why does this entire family worship him so much? Father acts like Septimus is his son and I a petulant daughter-in-law and now you two!" She settled back into the couch and flung the grapes into the bowl. "Septimus does not need my pity. Nameya has not left his side since he collapsed two nights ago. Before that, I had to practically beg him to give me an audience."

Herminia said, "What is wrong with him? Has he seen a physician for treatment?"

"I have no clue and I do not care," Varelia said.

"You speak of your husband as if her were a complete stranger to you," Laecidia said. "Have you no feelings left for him?"

"None!" Varelia cried. She pushed away a pillow and swung her legs around with a hiss. "I despise him, and I despise his little concubine who attends to his every whim as if he were an invalid."

Herminia said, "You were never home, dear sister. What was he supposed to do?"

"Have you considered saving your marriage, Varelia?" Laecidia said. "Stop seeing Loreno. There is something about him that makes me uneasy. You are beautiful. Do you not see that some men prey on beautiful women? A beautiful married woman is a toy to some men."

Varelia tossed her head back and laughed. "Dear, dear sister. How little you know me. I am no one's toy and I never will be! And as for Septimus, even if I did not despise him, well, he is practically on his death bed."

"You say that so casually," Herminia said. "You are heartless. Have you really no feelings for him at all, not even as a human being?"

"None," Varelia snapped. "Besides, if a man can have more than one woman, why cannot a woman have more than one man? Have you ever known me to follow social rules?"

"I do not approve of adultery no matter who commits it," Laecidia said.

Varelia laughed. "You are dreaming, my young naïve sister. Who in Rome does not engage in a little play outside the marriage? Why, there is an orgy somewhere in the city practically every night." Varelia lifted the hem of her tunic and swung her legs back on the couch. "What do you think goes on in the back rooms of the bathhouses? Decadence, my love, that is what. We live in a decadent world where the only thing that really matters is the pleasures of the flesh."

Laecidia folded her arms. "It is disgraceful. That is not the way Father raised us."

"Disgraceful? Would you like to hear the latest gossip about your husband?"

"Really, Varelia!" Herminia screamed. "Is that really necessary?"

"I know Nestor is not a perfect man," Laecidia said, her eyes full of tears. "But, he is my husband."

Varelia squealed with laughter. "I love you, Laecidia. You are as innocent and naïve as a newborn lamb." She leaned forward in a swift motion. "What would happen if Septimus were to die tomorrow?"

"Varelia! How can you even think of such a thing?" Laecidia cried.

"I would be a rich widow." Varelia said. "And Nameya would be out in the streets." Varelia reached for her cloak. "Please summon my litter, Laecidia. I really must be going." She smiled at her two sisters. "The next time you see me, I might be that rich widow."

Forty-Three

Nameya peeked out of her litter as it barreled down the smoke-filled streets of Rome. She coughed and gagged. She could not believe her eyes. Rome looked like a charred forest. Beautiful buildings that were once marble white, were now black and smoldering. Houses, stalls, furniture, tents anything that could burn, had been reduced to piles of ashes. Alas, as soon as they left the southwest sector of the city, the air was much cleaner, more breathable. Soon, the litter came to a halt in front of a large and elegant white house. There was a fountain off to one side of the garden with six small statues of nude women in various positions pouring water from their buckets into the fountain. According to Jenna's instructions and description of the house, this had to be the place. Her slaves lowered the litter and one of them helped her out.

"I believe this is the house you described to us, my lady," he said.

"Yes, I agree," Nameya said.

"Would you like me to summon the master of the house?" the slave asked.

"No," Nameya said. "I will attend to this matter myself. Please just wait for me here."

Canario was too stunned to speak. He had to be dreaming. He blinked, but she was still there, standing at his door, the loveliest woman he had ever seen in his life and perhaps the loveliest woman in all of Rome. He knew very well who she was. He had seen her many times from a distance, but now that she was so close to him and dressed in a sparkling dark green cloak and blue dress, she made his very soul tremble—she was so stunning! What, he wondered, was royalty doing at his house and, at this hour of the night, under these terrible conditions?

"Are you the merchant, Canario Basilio?" she asked.

Her voice was melodious, as sweet as the notes of a lyre, and for an instant Canario remained too dumbfounded to speak.

"Sire," she repeated. "I am looking for the merchant, Canario Basilio."

Canario snapped his head and then bowed slightly. "Lady Nameya," he cried, "forgive me. I must seem a complete fool it is just that ... well, I am indeed Canario Basilio, your humble servant." He bowed his head again. "Forgive me, but what are you, royalty, doing here looking for me?"

"Then you know who I am?"

"But of course, dear lady. Who in Rome does not know you?" His round cheeks became flushed. "Forgive me for saying so, but the first time I saw you I thought you the most beautiful woman in Rome. Now that you are at arm's length from me, I see that I was not wrong. There can be none lovelier than you in the entire empire."

"You are very kind, Canario," Nameya said. She glanced past him. "Are you alone? I have urgent business to discuss with you. It is a private matter."

"I am indeed. My servants have retired to their quarters at the back of the house. But where are my manners? Please come in." He moved to one side.

Nameya stepped into a lavishly decorated hall. Canario led her into an adjacent room that was also lavishly decorated with furniture, rugs, and figurines. Nameya untied her hood and Canario quickly took it from her and laid it across a chair. Her light brown hair cascaded to below her shoulders. She started to speak but hesitated.

Canario lightly touched her elbow. "You have grown pale, my lady." He walked her to a couch. "I was about to pour myself a cup of wine. May I offer you one?"

"Perhaps it will calm my nerves." Nameya looked nervously around while Canario poured the wine.

"You have a lovely home, Canario," she said.

"Ah, thank you, my lady. Please consider this also your home. I am at your disposal anytime you wish to visit."

Nameya took the golden chalice Canario handed her and sipped from the cup. "Jenna, the masseuse, gave me your name. She said I could trust you."

Canario set his cup of wine down and looked most seriously at her. "But of course you can trust me. Jenna is a good friend, and I am most grateful to her for having offered you my name, for whatever matter you wish to discuss with me."

Nameya sipped her wine. "Then it is agreed that our conversation here is strictly confidential?"

Canario touched his heart with both hands. "But of course, dear lady. You have my solemn word. Speak freely. How can I be of service to you?"

Nameya shifted nervously in her seat. "Please do not be angry with Jenna, but she confided in me that once you were very ill, with some mysterious ailment that no physician could cure."

Canario shrugged. "Bah, that was no secret at all. One day I experienced a severe pain on my side. At first, I attributed it to something I ate, but days later it got worse. It got to the point where I could not leave my bed. I could not attend to my affairs. I began to lose customers. I began to lose business. For weeks, physician after physician came to my side, but as you say, none were successful in treating me."

Nameya leaned forward. "Jenna tells me that you finally summoned a different sort of physician."

Canario nodded his head furiously. "I was desperate, and in my business, I know many people, some of whom are envious of my success and may have wanted to harm me. Well, I had heard of a man who was said to possess the capacity to cure ailments that conventional medicines could not cure. I hate to speak of spells, for it sounds childish. But as you well know, there are many kinds of evil in this world." Canario edged closer to her. "Are you here on behalf of our illustrious magistrate, Septimus?"

Nameya set her cup down. "I should not be surprised that you have guessed so quickly. I suppose that people are talking."

"I am afraid so, my lady. He has not been seen for weeks. Some have even begun to speculate on whether he is even alive."

"No!" Nameya cried.

"But do not worry, my lady. At the moment, Rome is preoccupied with smoke and flames."

"The fire is a terrible thing, Canario, but I could not wait another day to see you. Septimus's health is declining rapidly. He gets headaches, and he is not eating well. Something has to be done. Will you help me?"

"I assume that an army of physicians has seen him, but to no avail."

Nameya nodded. "Septimus thought he was being poisoned and took precautions, but that did not help either."

Canario rose from his chair. "Your visit here is truly auspicious. You see, the man who cured me had left Rome but recently returned." Canario nodded sadly. "He returned to Rome right after he lost his wife to a terrible illness while they were on a Roman ship. He himself was lucky to escape alive."

Nameya gasped. "Perhaps this is a very bad time for him."

"No, no do not worry. He is very sad but doing well. The old rascal has very strange beliefs and draws much strength from those beliefs."

"Then you will contact him for me?"

"But of course."

"It must all be very discreet. Do you think he will want to help me?"

"He most certainly will help you, I will see to that. When would you like for him to see Septimus?"

"Tomorrow if possible. Are you familiar with Septimus's estate?"

"Yes, I know where it is."

"I shall wait for you at the south gate at midnight. If for some reason you are not able to make it, please do not try to reach me. I will contact you later."

Canario gave Nameya a guarded smile. "We will be there, but— does Septimus know about this?"

Nameya reached for her cloak. "You are very astute, Canario. He does not know yet, but do not worry. He will receive you."

At the door Nameya paused. "Canario, if there is ever anything that I can ever do for you…"

Canario stared at her. "My lady, I would never think of imposing on you. I shall do this for you and that will not in the least put you in my debt."

Nameya squeezed one of his hands and smiled. "Just the same, we are friends now and friends help each other."

Forty-Four

Canario sliced a piece of cheese, took a whiff of it and placed it in his mouth. He smacked his lips approvingly, then cut another slice and offered it to his friend, Pableus. He refused it politely by raising a hand. Canario shrugged, and then ate it himself.

"Forgive me for summoning you at this late hour, Pableus," Canario said. "But when I disclose to you the nature of our business, you will understand the urgency." He cut another slice of cheese. This time he inspected its texture before he placed it in his mouth. Canario swallowed. "Forgive me. I tend to eat too much when I am nervous, and as you can plainly see I am beside myself." He wiped his mouth. "I have been asked to solicit your services for a special patient."

Pableus unfolded his arms and frowned as he leaned slightly forward. "Oh, and who can that be?"

Canario chewed on another piece of cheese while he spoke. "Septimus."

"Septimus?" Pableus nearly jumped from his chair. "The magistrate?"

Canario stabbed the knife in the air toward Pableus. "The very one. If you were up on the affairs of Rome you would know that he has been conspicuously absent from his post. It is the talk of the forum."

"What is wrong with him?"

"Ah, well according to his lovely mistress Nameya...?"

"You spoke to her?"

Canario set his knife down. "She was here," he whispered. "She was in this house earlier tonight." Canario shook his head. "Her beauty is beyond comparison. Her skin radiates, no, it shines like sweet moisture in the air. Ah, but the Greek gods would be envious of such a Roman beauty."

Pableus frowned. "She was here? But how did she get through the fire?"

"It goes to show you the gravity of the situation." Canario lifted his knife and pointed it at Pableus. "She sat in the very chair where you are now seated."

Pableus stroked his wrinkled face. "I take it that Septimus's physicians have not been able to cure him."

Canario feigned laughter. "Does that surprise you? What have I always said about Roman physicians? They are quacks. They appeal to the gods on behalf of their patients, but who would trust a pillar of cement when the body is in pain?" Canario waved a slice of cheese at Pableus. "You, my dear friend, are going to cure our illustrious magistrate. Now, I realize that it is not good to benefit from the ailments of others, but what can you do when an opportunity drops into your lap? And this is clearly an opportunity of a lifetime for you, dear friend."

"What are his symptoms?"

"He gets headaches."

Pableus rubbed his chin. "That could be anything. Why do you think I can cure him?"

"Nameya believes that you can. She came to me because she heard how you had cured me."

"I cannot work miracles, Canario. I trust that you did not exaggerate my abilities."

Canario's face turned into an expression of horror. "I did nothing of the sort. I am no fool. Nameya seems pleasant enough. She is divine, but I do not know about Septimus."

Canario inspected his block of cheese, which had diminished to half of its size, and winced. "Romans are absolute barbarians when it comes to making cheese. Have we learned nothing from the Greeks?" He washed his mouth with wine and then observed that his friend had grown pale "Do not worry, Pableus. I have faith in you. You will cure Septimus."

Pableus nodded quietly.

"Now," Canario said. "Tomorrow I shall arrive at your house an hour before midnight. Because no one is to know of our visit, my litter will not take us all the way to Septimus's house. We will meet Nameya at midnight at the south gate."

Canario walked Pableus to the door. "Of course, you are not to discuss this matter with another soul."

"Of course, but what if his physicians find out? They will be furious."

Canario laughed. "Ha! If you are successful—and I know you will be—I will tell those scoundrels myself that you cured Septimus, and I will watch them squirm with envy."

Forty-Five

Varelia flung the covers from her bed and threw her pillow across the room. The heat in Rome was unbearable, and for the third straight night she could not sleep. All the house doors, including the terrace doors, were closed to keep the lingering smoke left from the fire from entering into the house. Varelia crawled out of her bed and opened her terrace doors. Fortunately, a light breeze carried the wind in the opposite direction of her room. She stepped out into the terrace and was pleasantly surprised that the air did not smell of smoke. Varelia walked down the terrace steps onto the garden. The air was fresh and cool and it did much to calm her nerves. Even the moon, which had been hidden behind clouds of dark smoke the last few days, was bright and full.

Varelia was about to return to the terrace when a sudden movement at the house caught her attention. A woman had exited the house, and her actions aroused Varelia's curiosity. The woman wore a long hooded cloak, and as she started down the steps toward the garden, she paused a few times and looked around, as if she did not want to be seen.

Varelia hid behind the closest tree and watched her, but amid the trees and tall shrubs, she momentarily lost sight of her. Suddenly, the woman flew by her, and Varelia caught a whiff of her perfume. Lavender. "Nameya," she whispered. Varelia cringed with anger. What was Septimus's concubine doing in the garden at this hour of the night? Nameya headed for the south gate and the whole time she continued looking about her, to make certain she was undetected. When Nameya reached the gate, she did not step out into the street. Instead, she ducked into the shadows and just stood there. Varelia watched and waited and then noticed that the usual guards were not at their post. Where were the guards? Soon, two figures emerged from the street below, and Nameya opened the gate for them. One was a heavy man. The other was a man of small stature and very thin. Nameya hurried them through the garden and into the house from the same door she had exited from.

Varelia stared at the closed door in disbelief. "What are you up to now, Nameya?" she whispered, and clenched her fists so tight her long fingernails nearly cut into her skin.

She slowly walked back to her terrace, and as she walked up the stairs, she became aware of hanging chimes, swaying softly in the wind, emitting musical sounds. She angrily ripped down the chimes and flung them across the terrace.

Septimus sat tight-lipped on a chair and glared at Nameya. How could she have confided in two strangers, neither of whom had any medical training. What could they do for him? At least she had had the sense to bring them here at an hour when the rest of the household was asleep. As an added precaution, he had ordered that the nightly guards be relieved of their duty for the rest of the night. Of course, this left his estate completely unguarded. The house was vulnerable to thieves and derelicts. He stared at Pableus with great interest and some wrath. What could this poor soul do for him that his far better trained physician had not been able to do? Pableus nervously rinsed his hands in a small basin while Canario poured the water from a jug. Both seemed genuinely interested in helping him, but this was risky. There were many tongues in Rome, and the last thing that he needed was more rumors about his condition. Things could not get any worse for him. The cases that he needed to hear were piled high in his office. And, one of his clerks had sent him a message advising him that two senators were calling on him to haul in an unscrupulous business partner of theirs for questioning and that Nero's ever-present spies were hanging around the Forum like buzzards, asking questions about his absence.

Pableus finished drying his hands and sat in front of Septimus. He studied his eyes and face and lifted his hands to touch him but hesitated.

"Go on," Septimus murmured.

Pableus probed Septimus' ears, mouth, stomach, and even the palms of his hands. He asked a few questions about Septimus's recent eating habits. He asked how he was sleeping and other questions. Although he saw no purpose in this line of interrogation, Septimus patiently and quietly answered him. He had answered similar questions for his physician and had gained nothing by it. He glanced from time to time at Nameya, who stood behind Canario looking worried but hopeful.

At last Pableus dropped his hands and stared at Septimus without saying a word. He had requested that a crystal bowl of water be placed on a table next to Septimus, and he now concentrated on the water. This, Septimus had not seen from the other physicians, and even though Nameya had warned him earlier that Pableus was not a typical physician, he grew impatient.

"Why do you stare at the water?" Septimus asked sternly, "will you find the answers to my condition in the water? Are you some sort of astrologer?"

Not offended, Pableus said, "It is my form of concentration, sire." Without taking his eyes away from the water, he added, "It is my window into another world."

Septimus glanced at Nameya. She showed no reaction to the strange words Pableus had just uttered. They did not affect her in the least. Canario, however, squirmed and stared at his friend.

"Hum," Pableus murmured, nodding his head.

"What is it?" Septimus asked. "Are you about to tell me that someone has cast an evil spell on me?"

Pableus eyed him with a sudden flash of discernible anger. "I do not wish to be disrespectful, sire, but some maladies cannot be diagnosed in the usual manner. Did not your physicians fail you? Are you prepared to continue in this declining condition?" Pableus rose to his feet. "The practice of witchcraft has been around for thousands of years, sire. It has existed before physicians became physicians and studied medicine. It is an art form that has been perfected in many countries. Those who know how to use it can be quite dangerous."

Septimus sighed in exasperation. "Forgive my impatience, but I have never given much credence to such beliefs."

"Then are we to believe that you are imagining your headaches?" Pableus asked.

Canario gasped so loudly that everyone turned to look at him. "Forgive me," he said quietly. "Pableus, do you believe someone has hexed our illustrious magistrate, used sorcery on him?"

"I do sense something powerful, something evil," Pableus said. "Plain water in the hands of someone knowledgeable in the craft of darkness can be turned into the deadliest poison."

"How—how can something like that happen?" Nameya asked.

Pableus sighed. "A man can easily ingest food treated and prepared in a special way by evil hands. An effigy can be created and then burned on a stake to destroy an intended victim. There are many ways."

"You can do something?" Nameya asked. She walked to Septimus and took his hand. "Can you help us?"

"I am willing to try," Pableus said. "But, the patient must maintain a positive attitude that he can overcome his condition. If not, we will be wasting our time."

"I am terribly worried about you, Septimus," Nameya said. "Please tell me that you will give Pableus an opportunity to do something for you."

Septimus saw the concerned looked on Nameya's face and his hard face softened. He looked from Nameya to Pableus. "Forgive me for the way I have acted, but you must understand these headaches are getting worse. At times, they have almost paralyzed me. I am getting worse." He sighed. "What will you have me do?"

"Man is an integral part of all of nature, my lord," Pableus said. "All negative, as well as positive forces derive from the same vine. We shall combat what has been heaped upon you by using those natural forces."

"Meaning what?" Septimus asked.

"I shall perform certain rituals at my house on your behalf. I will also prepare oils that you must apply to yourself daily. Drink only water and eat only fruit such as grapes, until we are finished treating you. Finally, I will prepare special candles that must remain lit until you are well. In three days we should know if my efforts are working."

Canario inadvertently clapped his hands. "Excellent! There is a treatment plan in place."

"Hum," Septimus murmured. "That does not sound like much, but very well, I pray that whatever you do works."

Nameya escorted Canario and Pableus to the gate. She thanked them profusely and then left. Canario placed a hand on the shoulder of Pableus. "You were magnificent, my dear friend. I think you finally won the magistrate's favor."

Pableus pensively brushed his chin. "I trust that you are correct. We do not have a moment to lose. This very night I shall start my work. Our illustrious magistrate should have been a corpse by now."

Forty-Six

Varelia loved visiting her friend Sofia, the widow of an old, wealthy senator. Varelia relished her company. Other than Agrippina, Nero's mother, no other woman was more popular in all of Rome. No banquet or festivity of any kind was a social success unless Sofia was in attendance. And of course, nothing of any significance ever occurred in Rome without Sofia being one of the first to know about it. Varelia reached for a goblet of wine. The myriad of bracelets that adorned her wrists dangled noisily as she lifted the cup and sipped from it. She peered over the rim of the cup and looked across the enormous room. The room was noisy with chatter and music and crowded with Roman socialites. It seemed as if all of Rome was here tonight and that suited Varelia well. Of course, by tomorrow her father and husband will know that she had been here with Loreno but that did not matter. What did she care? The music was excellent, the food delicious and creative, and the wine Sofia's best. She reclined back on a couch and placed an affectionate hand on the back of Loreno. Her dress was very low-cut, revealing an ample part of her breasts. She crossed her legs and her diamond-studded sandals glittered in the light. They had been a gift from Loreno. She playfully stroked the back of his neck.

Loreno wildly swung a cup of wine from to side to side while he spoke with another senator. "Bah," he cried. "What is the point of one more Roman conquest? It is a strain on the army. I say that a man should be content with what he has and enjoy the pleasures of life every day and with zeal. Let the devils who insist on spreading the empire man the newly conquered outpost themselves."

The other senator laughed and drunkenly lifted his cup to Loreno. "You are right, my friend, and I say we begin to enjoy the pleasures of life tonight, right now."

"Agreed," Loreno cried. He gulped from his cup of wine. "And another thing, do you realize the strain these military campaigns impose on the treasury? You could not have enough tax collectors to keep up with the expenses."

Varelia stretched forward and whispered into his ear. "Sofia has a lovely back area where we can stretch and enjoy a private bath. What do you say, my pet. Can you sneak away from your politics to enjoy yourself?"

Loreno laughed. "You certainly know how to tempt a man, Varelia." He looked her up and down. "And by the way, as usual, you look spectacular tonight. There is no woman in Rome who is as beautiful as you." He lightly kissed her on the forehead.

Varelia attempted to entice him into a full kiss but Loreno pulled back. "I am indeed a scoundrel to be in the company of a married woman," he said, "but even scoundrel's value their neck. The room must be full of maggots who will no doubt report us to your husband."

"And so what? Do I look worried to you?" Varelia said. "Besides, Septimus is too busy with his headaches and concubine to worry about what I do."

"Varelia, my dear."

Varelia's eyes shifted to her hostess. Sofia looked ravishing in a white, completely transparent gown. She accented it with pearls around her hair, neck, and wrists. While most of her guests had already drunk too much, and even though Sofia usually enjoyed a drink or two, on these occasions, Sofia did not have a drop to drink. Instead, she swept around the room with a cup filled with nothing but water and made certain that her guests were enjoying themselves.

"Well, my dear," Sofia said. "Are you and your handsome man enjoying yourselves?"

"We are indeed," Varelia said. "Why, I am most impressed with your guest list."

"As am I," Loreno said. "I am surprised Nero himself is not here."

Sofia laughed and leaned into their faces. "Maybe he is. The man is a chameleon. Ah, but my lips are sealed. I will never tell." She waved her empty cup at them and danced away.

"Was she jesting?" Varelia said, her voice sounding slightly concerned. "Nero is a dangerous man. He is the biggest gossip in Rome."

"Hum," Loreno murmured. His eyes scoured the far corners of the enormous room. "Earlier, I did happen upon a few of his personal guards. I just assumed they were here on their own time."

Loreno set his cup of wine down. He took Varelia's hand and helped her to her feet. "I think it is time we slip away and enjoy ourselves somewhere else."

"I agree," Varelia whispered. "Suddenly I am suffocating."

Forty-Seven

Canario and Pableus stood just outside the gates of Septimus's house and watched in silence as Nameya disappeared back into the garden. Under a moonless night, the dark cloak she wore was barely visible. When she completely disappeared from sight, Canario placed an arm around Pableus. "Well, my dear friend?" he said. "Did I not tell you that you could do it? Did I not tell you that you would cure Septimus?" Canario nodded contently. "In just three days, you accomplished what his physicians had been trying to do for weeks, for months. The color returned to our illustrious magistrate's face. He has never looked this well."

Pableus sighed. "We were most fortunate," he said. "I never know how these things are going to turn out."

"Nonsense. I never doubted you," Canario said. He clapped his hands. "And did you see the look on Nameya's face? She was elated." He looked back through the gates to where she had stood. "Ah, but I shall miss seeing the loveliness of her."

Pableus shook his head and smiled. "Come, it is late and I am tired."

"Tired? Nonsense," Canario said. He started forward with his arm once again around the shoulders of Pableus. "We are going straight to my house and open one of my finest wines. We must celebrate and do not worry about the late hour. Tonight you shall be my guest for the night."

They reached an intersection and paused to let a well-guarded litter pass by them. The soldiers who followed the litter slowed their horses and stared at them. Then without saying a word they caught up to the slaves who carried the litter.

"Did you see the way they stared at us?" Canario said. "I ask you, do we look like a pair of thieves, Pableus?"

Pableus waved a hand. "I am not at all surprised, Canario. We are in the Palatine. Strangers are not welcomed in these wealthy neighborhoods at night."

"You mean these pompous neighborhoods."

Pableus laughed. "You are a rich man, Canario, and you have a beautiful home, but you could easily afford to live here in one of these bigger homes."

"Bah, I do not need such extravagances that do nothing but draw the envy of those less fortunate. Besides, to me a man who wears silk togas is no better than a decent man who wears the garbs of a slave."

"Ah, but if only more men thought as you, my dear friend," Pableus said. He paused to admire a large fountain that was situated in the middle of another intersection.

Canario dipped his hand into the water. It was cool and refreshing. "Romans are creative plumbers. Are they not?" He took a whiff of the air and coughed. "Bah, I still smell smoke."

They started to walk again. "That reminds me," Canario said. He handed Pableus the purse of money Nameya had given him. "Add this to your wages. You heard me refuse it. I do not need it."

Pableus protested but Canario ignored him. He stuffed the purse into Pableus's belt while they walked.

At the following corner, which was darker than the others, Canario slowed down.

"What is it?" Pableus asked.

"It might be my nerves," Canario whispered. "But I think we are being followed. Keep walking."

Canario fumbled for his dagger and cursed the excessive cloaks that he wore. But it was too late. The full weight of a man knocked him off his feet, and a second man wrestled Pableus to the ground. Canario caught a blow to the side of his face, and everything became blurred. All of a sudden powerful arms lifted him to his knees and pulled his arms back. Dazed and bleeding, Canario, nevertheless, made out a dagger being waved in front of his face. He grabbed the man's hand and prepared for a struggle but the man suddenly flew backwards. He then stumbled forward, dropped the dagger and fell at Canario's feet. Canario froze. A muscular man swiftly lifted his would-be assailant to his feet, wrapped a powerful arm around his neck and broke it. It was only then that Canario noticed that two other men were sprawled on the ground obviously dead. Pableus was struggling to his feet.

"You are not hurt? Neither one of you?" the man who had saved them asked. He was breathing hard and perspiring, but otherwise he was unhurt.

"Pableus," Canario asked, "are you alright?"

"I am fine, just a little dazed," he said.

"My friend and I are most fortunate that you came along when you did," Canario said to the man. "Who are you? I cannot believe how quickly you disposed of these three men."

"I was not quick enough. Those men should never have touched you, for that I am sorry."

"I do not understand?" Canario said. "Are you trying to say that you were protecting us?"

The man put away his dagger. "I have followed you home each of the last three nights."

"But—how? We never heard a thing," Pableus said.

"You were not supposed to notice me," the man said. "We did not want you to be frightened."

"Nameya?" Canario whispered. "Did she put you up to this?"

The man nodded. "You are fortunate that she did."

Canario stared at the three dead men. "And who do you suppose sent them after us?"

"That I do not know," the man said. "We should be on our way."

Canario said, "We were going to celebrate with a bottle of wine at my house. Perhaps you will join us."

The man shook his head. "Lady Nameya waits each night for my report that you have arrived safely to your homes. I cannot keep her waiting."

"Indeed, Canario said. "She is even a greater lady than I imagined. I pray that the gods will always protect her. She is truly a diamond.

Forty-Eight

Sofia glared impatiently at her two slaves who were serving drinks and fruits and oysters on a table. "Hurry," she said to them. "You are taking too long. I wish to be alone with my guest."

The two young girls hurriedly finished what they were doing and rushed out of the room.

Sofia rolled her eyes and then handed Varelia a chalice of wine. "I thought they would never leave us alone." She stretched out a hand and affectionately touched Varelia on the elbow. "You looked lovely last night, Varelia," she said, "You turned more male heads than any other woman in the house."

Varelia smiled and sipped from her wine. "A woman must take care of herself. After all, a good set of hips can topple an empire. Witness Cleopatra. Had she been a little more astute she might have conquered Rome."

Sofia laughed and raised the cup to her lips. "By the way," she said. "Nero personally invited me to his house next week for another one of his all-night banquets. Care to join me? I have already procured an invitation for you and anyone you care to take with you."

"Ah, need you ask, Sofia? Of course I would love to go. I would not miss it for anything in the world." She placed a mushroom between her lips and nibbled it.

"Who knows who will be sharing Nero's couch, his wife, a prostitute, or maybe one of his little boys," Sofia said, giggling. "It should be quite entertaining."

"Indeed, my dear," Varelia said. "We can always count on Nero to entertain and amuse his guests." She sighed. "Now tell me, my dear friend. Why did you summon me here so early in the morning? What is this urgent business you wish to discuss with me? Did one of your guests threaten to give my husband a detailed account of what I did last night?"

"No," Sofia said shaking her head. She sipped from her wine and then drew her breath. "I am afraid it is more serious than that."

"Oh?" Varelia murmured. She set her cup down and stared at Sofia. "You have me intrigued, my dear friend. What is it?"

Sofia also set her cup down and leaned forward. "Last night after everyone left, I inadvertently discovered something about Loreno. I do not know if it is true or not, but I thought you would want to know."

Varelia frowned in surprise. "This is about Loreno? What is it?"

"First let me explain something," Sofia said. "As you can imagine, when I have so many guests in my house, the house is left in an utter mess. Occasionally, I permit my servants to enjoy some wine while they clean the house. Last night after all my guests had departed I did that. I warn them not to drink excessively, but last night one of them did just that. She got drunk and the wine loosened her tongue. When I realized what she was saying, I immediately silenced her before the others could understand what she was babbling about. I took her into my private chambers, and after I gave her a tongue lashing, I interrogated her about what she had started to tell the other servants."

"And what was that?" Varelia said, edging closer to Sofia. "What was she blabbing about?"

"I would rather you heard it directly from her," Sofia said. She clapped her hands and a male servant appeared at the door and bowed his head.

"Summon Elinia," Sofia said to him.

The servant bowed his head again, turned around and left the room. A moment later he returned with a young woman in her early twenties and then left. The woman was slightly heavy, but attractive, and she wore the white simple tunic of a slave. She stood with her eyes fixed on the floor and her hands clasped in front of her. Sofia rose from her seat and circled around the woman slowly as she spoke.

"You may sit, Elinia," she said.

The girl looked around uncomfortably and lowered herself on one corner of a couch.

"Now, Elinia," Sofia said, "tell my good friend Varelia what you told me last night, and leave nothing out."

The girl glanced briefly at Varelia and then dropped her gaze again. "Of course, my lady," she said, in a low, trembling voice. "Years ago I was taken to a big house full of Roman soldiers. There was music. Women were dancing and everyone was drinking wine." Elinia paused and blushed.

Sofia glared at her. "Go on."

Elinia stared at her trembling hands. "I was young and naïve, and I had never seen such things. The men got drunk and everyone started to take their clothes off. Men began to tug at my clothes too, and I became frightened and hid in one corner of one of the rooms of the house. Then a most peculiar thing happened. I saw a man. He was fully dressed and looked very distressed. He walked about the room obviously looking for someone. Suddenly, he looked straight at me. At least that is what I thought. I froze when he started toward me, but he stopped a few paces in front of me where a couple was lying together. He suddenly grabbed the young soldier who was with the woman, lifted him into the air and pushed him so hard in my direction that the young soldier crashed into me and we both fell to the floor. What happened next shocked me. The young soldier was quite drunk, and while he struggled to get to his feet a man stepped in from behind us and drove a sword through his back. I screamed. I screamed so loud that the room fell silent and everyone turned to look at me and then at the young soldier who lay dead at my feet. All of a sudden, the man who had struck him pointed to the man who had pushed the young soldier and accused him of the murder. Other soldiers then attacked the innocent man but the man managed to get away." Elinia glanced briefly at Varelia then lowered her gaze again. "Later, I tried to tell the lady who took me to that house what I had seen, but she slapped me and told me that the young man who had been mur-dered was the nephew of an important magistrate in Rome and that I was to keep quiet and to never speak about it again. I tried to for-get the incident, and in time I did until…" Elinia lifted her eyes again and again looked at Varelia, who had slowly gotten to her feet and had her hands clutching her midsection.

"Until what? Speak!" Varelia cried.

"Until I saw that man again, the one who killed the young sol-dier." Elinia's eyes filled with tears. "He was here last night."

Varelia glared at Elinia with eyes wide, cold, and ablaze. "Go on," Varelia cried. "Who was he?"

Elinia looked tearfully at Varelia. "My lady, he was the man who was with you."

Varelia clutched the edge of the couch to steady herself. Loreno a murderer? Had her lover killed her beloved Halius? Why? She lowered herself on the couch. Sofia was speaking to her but Varelia did not hear a word. Instead, she tried to think. She tried to make sense of this madness. How was any of this possible?

"Varelia," Sofia whispered. She was now seated beside Varelia and had taken her hand. "My dear, you are positively pale. Forgive me for bringing this to your attention. I see that you are terribly upset."

Varelia looked at her with a blank expression on her face but then, regaining her composure, she turned to Elinia. "How can you be so certain that the man who accompanied me last night is the same man you saw that night? It was many years ago. How can you be certain?"

Elinia glanced at her then dropped her gaze.

"Answer me!" Varelia shouted. "How can you be so certain that it was him?"

"Because, my lady. Earlier that evening I saw him and the young soldier arguing."

"Did you hear what they arguing about?"

"A debt, I think. The young soldier was demanding repayment."

Varelia trembled with anger. "Who else knows about this? Whom have you told?"

"No one!" Elinia cried. "I swear."

"What about the woman who took you to that house? What became of her?"

"She left Rome years ago, and that night she refused to know who the murderer was."

Sofia motioned to Elinia. "Leave us."

"No!" Varelia shouted. "Let her stay." Filled with rage and confusion Varelia tried to think. "Elinia," she suddenly said, "Is it necessary that I have your tongue removed? You babbled about this once when you were drunk. How do I know you will not do it again?"

Elinia jumped from the couch. "I promise! I promise you that I will never touch another drop of wine as long as I live. I will never speak about this to anyone ever again. Never."

Varelia reached for her cloak. "Sofia," she said, "will you walk with me?" She took Sofia by the arm. "No one must know about this, do you understand?"

Sofia nodded furiously. "Of course, Varelia. If that is your wish, but need I remind you that your husband condemned the wrong man for the murder of Halius? An innocent man has been banished from Rome because of Loreno."

"I am aware of that!" Varelia cried. "But is that my fault? What matters to me is that Loreno has made a fool of me. Do you not see that?"

"Of course I see that," Sofia said. "He must be tried for his crime. There must be justice."

"What?" Varelia cried. "You sound like my husband. Well, I have no faith in Roman justice. What would we gain by accusing Loreno now? Even if Septimus believed Elinia and reopened the case, Loreno's lawyers would surely destroy her testimony. And then what would become of us? Would Loreno seek revenge against us?"

Sofia gasped. "I had not considered that. Then, then what do you intend to do?"

Varelia sighed. "Are you certain that no one else in your household knows about this?"

"I am positive."

Varelia glanced past Sofia and looked at Elinia. She had not moved from where she stood. "Our problem for the moment is what to do about her?"

"What do you mean?" Sofia said.

Varelia tied her cloak. "What do I mean? Did you really believe her when she said that she would never drink again, that she would never gossip about this? Well, I do not believe her. She spoke about this once and she will do it again."

Sofia stared nervously at Varelia. "What do you propose we do?"

Varelia sighed again. "One thing is certain. I will not feel safe about what she knows unless she is by my side. How much do you want for her?"

Shaken, Sofia said, "Take her, Varelia. I want nothing for her. She is yours."

"Good. Do you know if she has any family or relatives in Rome?"

"She has never spoken about any family." Sofia said. She summoned Elinia to her side. "Elinia," she said. "Go for your cloak. You are leaving with Varelia. You shall attend to all of her needs and serve her as well as you have served me."

Pale and trembling, Elinia nodded. "Of course, my lady. I shall get my cloak and my things."

"You need only your cloak," Varelia said curtly. "You will be provided with everything else that you need. Now hurry."

Sofia and Varelia quietly watched Elinia get into Varelia's litter and then Sofia turned and hugged Varelia.

"Please," she said. "Let me know if there is anything else that I can do for you."

"Yes, thank you," Varelia said quietly.

Perhaps it had been her nerves but Sofia detected a subtle stiffness in Varelia, and she had the strangest look on her face. A look Sofia had never seen before.

As Varelia got into her litter she whispered to one of her slaves. The muscular slave, clad only in a loincloth, nodded then gave Sofia a glance, and then to Sofia's horror, just as Varelia disappeared into the litter, she paused and glanced at her. It was a cutting stare that instantly filled Sofia with fear and terror. As the men lifted the litter and pulled away, she staggered backwards, realizing that she had committed the gravest blunder of her life. Sofia looked after the litter until it disappeared into the late afternoon traffic. Carts and people got in her line of vision, but she remained transfixed at her door. She pitied Elinia and she pitied herself. They had inadvertently become enemies of Varelia, and if she knew one thing about Varelia it was that she had a reputation for acting swiftly and mercilessly against those whom she mistrusted.

Sofia walked slowly back into her house, and for the first time in a long while she observed the simple things around her house that she enjoyed: a marble table, gold upholstered chairs, a dark maroon couch. She poured herself a cup of wine and sipped from it, savoring every drop. She considered leaving, but where would she go? Besides, she would always live in fear that in the next dark corner she would encounter her fate. She rose and committed another seemingly unpardonable act. She ordered the servants out of the house, and for the first time in her life she bathed without the benefit of assistance. She dressed, and then rested upon her bed, to await her fate.

Varelia leaned against the wall of her litter and stared at the lifeless body of Elinia, sprawled in the middle of the litter with eyes and mouth wide open. She pulled the dagger from the woman's breast and wiped it clean. She then stuck her head out of the litter and ordered it to halt.

She staggered out of the litter, feigning shock and fear. "Have a look," she cried. "Sofia's foolish slave attacked me, and I had to defend myself." One by one the slaves peered into the litter.

They were on a street that had been badly damaged by the fire and no one was around "Take her out of my litter and bury her underneath those ashes," she said, pointing to a pile of rubble. She walked to the other side of the litter and asked her slave Tura to join her. She spoke to him in whispers and then said in a normal voice, "Go, do it now."

Tura nodded without an expression. "I shall not be long," he said.

He started back to Sofia's house in a swift trot. Varelia watched him for a moment. His muscular back and legs were moist with sweat. He looked as strong as a prized stallion running down the street. No doubt he would be swift and efficient and cause Sofia little pain. She leaned against her litter and tried to think. For a fleeting moment she did indeed consider the plight of the merchant, but he was not her problem. He had killed other soldiers. Her real problem was Loreno. Why had he, a rich man, borrowed money from Halius? She could expose Loreno to Nestor, but Nestor was impulsive. If he acted recklessly against a senator he could endanger the whole family. She suddenly realized what she had to do, and it surprised her at how easily she arrived at that conclusion.

The litter was ready to leave. Varelia got into the litter and tried to relax, but the slaves had been careless in taking out the body of Elinia. In one corner of her luxurious box there was a heavy stain of blood, and it nauseated Varelia. When the slaves lifted the litter and started to carry it away, she hung her head out of the litter and became sick.

Forty-Nine

"The man is an imbecile, Septimus," Atenuar said, his voiced filled with exasperation. "I get him an appointment in Judea and what does he do? He and Gessius Florus do nothing but agitate the Jews."

Septimus stood with his back to the open portico doors of his house. He folded his arms and nodded in agreement. Atenuar was absolutely correct. Nestor was an imbecile, but he completely understood why he continued to try and help him. "I know that there is nothing you would not do for your daughter, Atenuar. Do not blame yourself for the holes Nestor digs for himself."

Atenuar drank absently from his chalice of wine. "Yes, yes, you know me well. There is nothing I would not do for them." He paused and smiled to himself. "Well, short of strangling myself politically, there is nothing I would not do for them. Of course, with this appointment, I may have given Nero reason never to trust my judgment again. Yesterday when I had dinner with him, he barely touched his food he was in such a foul mood."

"I was just about to ask you what kind of mood he was in these days."

"I will tell you. Ever since he started building his new Golden House he has obsessed about nothing else. He has even temporarily stopped torturing the Christians, whom he blamed for the great fire, as you well know."

"Ah, yes his golden palace. He is going to break Rome with the expense of that monstrosity that he is erecting."

"It is just as you say," Atenuar said. "Yesterday he was walking around with a battery of architects and painters at his side, shouting out orders and instructions, and then he changed his mind about everything he said and started all over again. It was only after one of the architects mentioned the rave reviews the actor Paris received at some performance last night that he threw all the architects out of the house screaming that he was a much better singer than that miserable, effeminate, second-rate actor. It was only then that I was able to discuss Judea and Syria with him.

"What did you tell him?"

"I told him that the zealots were embarrassing the empire. Which brings me to the point of why I asked you here today, Septimus. Nero has appointed Vespasian to crush the Hebrew revolt in Judea."

"An excellent choice," Septimus said. "Under Aulus Platius, and even under Claudius, Vespasian distinguished himself in Britain. He fought and won many difficult battles."

Atenuar nodded approvingly. "I am pleased that you think so highly of him. He speaks the same way about you."

"Oh? You have spoken to Vespasian lately?" Septimus asked.

"I have, and I can tell you that he is assembling an impressive army of two legions. His oldest son, Titus, will be his right-hand man, and…." Atenuar drank heartily from his cup and set it down with deliberate gestures. He then stared at Septimus. "He would like for you to join him as one of his commanders."

Septimus showed no reaction, but when he realized that Atenuar was quite serious, he chuckled nervously. The suggestion was ludicrous. "You cannot be serious, Atenuar. I have not worn a military uniform in years, much less led an army into battle. Surely Vespasian was pulling your leg?"

Atenuar studied the cuffs of his cloak, adjusted them as he spoke. "I can assure you that he was quite serious."

Septimus frowned incredulously. "What can Vespasian possibly be thinking? I repeat it has been years since I have worn a uniform and gone into battle. I know nothing about modern military tactics and strategies."

"Bah! You were a brilliant field commander, Septimus! What can anyone teach you about winning battles? Besides, Vespasian prefers a man with experience, a man who will not charge into battle without thought and planning. Titus is an exception. He is young, but then, Vespasian himself trained him."

His mind now in a quandary, Septimus turned slightly away from Atenuar. How could he possibly leave Nameya? How could he possibly leave his position? Besides, he was in no condition, physically or emotionally, to do this. Surely Vespasian would understand.

"Listen to me, Septimus," Atenuar said. "I have a feeling about Vespasian. His troops worship him. The people of Rome applaud his every move. Think of it. With Nero's popularity declining, if Vespasian successfully squashes the revolt—well, he will have Rome at his feet." Atenuar gave his thin head a shake. "Mark my words, Nero will not be emperor much longer. And, when that happens, who do you think is likely to succeed him? What man do you think the army will support? Whose name will the masses in Rome shout out to be the new emperor?"

Septimus listened pensively and alertly. No one understood Roman politics like Atenuar, and that is why he had been so influential under four emperors starting with Tiberius. Nevertheless, this was a shock to him.

Atenuar said, "I realize that this is quite sudden and unexpected…" He suddenly paused. "Look, I am aware that your marriage to my daughter has become a sham and that it will be Nameya that you must tear away from, but I do not believe that you will be gone long."

Septimus placed a hand on the shoulder of Atenuar and then dropped it. "Actually, when I received your message this morning that you had an urgent matter to discuss with me, I thought this would also be an opportune moment for me to discuss a matter with you."

"Ah," Atenuar said, "do not say a word. It is written all over your face. My daughter is driving you mad."

Septimus gazed sadly at the man he owed so much to and wondered how it was possible that Varelia was the daughter of such a wise and noble man. "It is time that Varelia and I divorce, Atenuar."

Atenuar frowned, and the heavy lines around his eyes deepened. "I am not surprised. I knew that sooner or later I would hear those words coming from you. I am nevertheless devastated. "

"It has never been a marriage, Atenuar. I tried to make it work, but Varelia detests me. With Nameya, I have found happiness and peace. I cannot deny that."

"Nameya," Atenuar said. "I cannot blame you. She is a lovely woman. She is everything my daughter is not. She is kind and thoughtful, almost to a fault. No, I cannot blame you for being in love with her."

"And I think you know that there is no point in continuing a marriage like this," Septimus said. "Varelia is quite public about her liaisons. It has become an embarrassment to both of us. We must put an end to this folly. Varelia has her life, and I have mine. "

"Of course," Atenuar muttered, shaking his head. "If your decision is final, I will handle the matter with the lawyers. You have important business to attend to and I do not want this to interfere with that. Have you advised Varelia?"

"I told her just as I was coming over here. After she threw a tantrum, she laughed."

Atenuar sighed. "At times, I do not know my own daughter, but enough about her. What do you think, Septimus? Vespasian will be victorious, and I can see you and Titus marching into Rome at his side." Atenuar shrugged. "On the other hand, would you seriously consider turning down the future emperor of Rome?"

Septimus stared through the open portico doors with folded arms. He could make out the dim outline of hills in the distance and a road that led to his faraway home in the countryside, a home that he wished to occupy with Nameya at his side. Never had he been so happy with Nameya. He turned and looked at his father-in-law. "Atenuar," he said, "had Vespasian sent anyone but you, I might have had the courage to turn him down."

Atenuar clapped his hands. "Excellent, Septimus. I am inclined to go and fight myself, but then what enemy would take this old man seriously?"

Septimus laughed and then shook his head. He knew his father-in-law well. It was not past Atenuar to engage in a devious deed or two when it came to politics. "Atenuar," he said, raising an eyebrow and feigning anger. "I would not at all be surprised if you have already committed me to Vespasian. Tell me, am I correct?"

Atenuar sheepishly grinned. "You are like a son to me, Septimus, and a father who loves his son knows him well. Surely you cannot fault me for knowing that you would accept. Besides, you cannot be angry at a father who wishes to advance the political status of his son."

"And so…" Septimus murmured.

Atenuar grinned again. "And so, your ships, along with your troops, await you at Brundisium. You leave as soon as you get there."

Fifty

Varelia knew Loreno's habits and routine well. At sundown she watched him arrive at his apartment from the shadows of the building across the street. Loreno detested walking the streets of Rome late at night for fear that he would be recognized as a senator and possibly be robbed by those less fortunate than he. She knew that he had just left his favorite tavern and was full of wine. Modest in size, and probably occupied by people of average income, the building was west of the Forum. Loreno had explained to her that these were only his temporary quarters and that his villa was under heavy repair, repairs that had been repeatedly delayed. This apartment, he claimed, was his rental property recently abandoned by his tenants. All of it was a lie. The investigator that she had hired had exposed him as a con artist who loved to gamble and was heavily in debt. He had no villa. This was his home. Of course, the investigator also told her that he was trying very hard to swindle his way into a nicer neighborhood, but so far those efforts were getting nowhere. She had also learned that his real fear of walking the streets of Rome was because he owed every-one money, including prostitutes. He was afraid that one day someone was going to put a dagger in his back.

It sickened her to see him wear a senatorial tunic with its purple stripe. Loreno was not just a con artist he was a murderer.

The moment he disappeared into his tenement building Varelia stepped out of the shadows and walked across the street. She entered the building through the same door Loreno had used. She climbed two flights of stairs, and on the third floor she knocked on the fifth door to her left.

Loreno was drunk. His blood-shot eyes at first flashed with anger. He had made it clear from the beginning of their relationship that she was never to visit without an appointment. But Varelia had loosened her cloak and his eyes widened with lust when he saw her fully exposed cleavage.

"Loreno," she said, "Are you not happy to see me? Are you angry with me because I had business in the neighborhood and decided to drop by?"

"No, no of course I am not angry, my pet," he mumbled. "I—you just surprised me."

She playfully jabbed at his chest. "Are you going to invite me in?"

"Of course, of course, Varelia come in." He staggered to one side.

She had not noticed, but he held an open bottle of wine in one hand. Using the hand that held the bottle, he waved her in with one sweeping jester and then drank heavily from it.

The apartment was spacious and very well decorated. She in fact had decorated it for him and she seethed at the thought of the money she had spent on the rugs and furniture.

Loreno again drank from the wine. "I—I just saw your husband leaving the Forum not more than twenty minutes ago. Several lawyers accompanied him. What a fool he is. What fools they all are."

Varelia leaned in his direction and laughed. "Do you mean my soon-to-be ex-husband? He is divorcing me and leaving Rome with his precious little concubine." She removed her cloak to reveal that she wore a flimsy dress that clung to her figure. She sat on a dark green couch and raised the hem of her dress to well above her knees. "Are we going to talk about my husband, Senator, or are you going to properly greet me?"

Loreno emptied the bottle of wine with one long swig and then let the bottle slip from his hands. He laughed and dropped to his knees in front of her. He caressed her thighs. "These," he said, "are the most beautiful legs in all of Rome."

Varelia playfully pushed his hands away. "Liar, I am certain that you have been with women who have much more beautiful legs than I have."

"Nay!" Loreno cried, still struggling to touch her legs. Septimus must be mad to be divorcing such a beautiful woman."

"Well then," Varelia said. "Carry me to your bed and prove to me how beautiful you think I am. Of course, if you are too drunk…?"

"Nonsense!" Loreno cried. He sprang to his feet and swept her off the couch and into his arms.

Varelia giggled and kicked her feet. "Do not drop me."

On the bed Loreno smothered her lips and face with wild kisses. Varelia laughed and playfully pushed him away. "Get on your back," she whispered and close your eyes."

Loreno stopped kissing her and smiled wildly. "What are you gong to do to me?" he laughed. "Are you going to hurt me? Are you going to tie my hands and hurt me?"

"Shh," Varelia murmured. "Now close your eyes and do not open them." She began to kiss his neck.

Loreno squirmed. "Yes, I like it. Do not stop," he said. "Never stop."

Varelia crawled on top of him and slowly moved her hips back and forth. Loreno sighed. He opened his eyes and tried to reach for her but she chastised him. "Keep your eyes closed," she whispered. From her garments she produced a dagger and placed its tip on his chest.

Loreno winced but smiled when Varelia began to playfully rip the front of his toga with the knife. "What is the price of one toga for your love," Loreno said. He started to open his eyes, but gig-gling, Varelia placed a hand over them. Suddenly she leaned across his chest and placed her lips to his ears. "I am about to avenge the murder of Halius, Loreno."

The eyes of Loreno flew open. He tried to say something, but Varelia pressed down on the dagger with all of her weight and his words drowned into a piercing cry. Loreno bolted from the bed and knocked them both to the floor. He tried to stand, but blood poured from his chest. He dropped to his knees clutching his chest. "You despicable witch!" he cried. "What have you done?" He in-spected his chest then looked at Varelia. "Varelia," he cried. "There is time. Summon a physician. I implore you. I do not want to die!"

Varelia got to her feet and calmly began to fix her dress. She put on her cloak. "Silence, Loreno, and die like a man," she said. "Halius tried to help you and you betrayed his good nature. You murdered him so that you would not have to repay your debt to him, and look at you, after all these years you are still in debt!"

Loreno dropped to his elbows and tried to crawl toward her, coughing blood and moaning. He cursed, and just as he was about to reach her feet he gasped and stopped moving. Varelia rolled him onto his back and removed her dagger. She searched Loreno for his dagger, and when she found it she placed it in his hand and buried the dagger into his chest. Suicides were quite common in Rome, and this one would be easy to understand. Loreno was no rich senator. He was nothing but a common free man who had been living a lie. He had shrewdly fooled all of Rome by saying that he was from a rich family who had investments in northern Italy. Bankers and other businessmen believed him and extended him credit that he could not repay. Thus, he had chosen to end his life before being exposed. Her only regret, as she left his apartment and stepped out into the night, was that he had died so quickly. Proud of herself, she smiled. Every problem has an easy solution after all.

Fifty-One

❧ MALTA ❧

The Roman fleet looked ominous in the choppy waters of the Mediterranean. Moreover, the multitude of sails told Marcellius that a full-scale military mobilization was in progress. Marcellius was housed in a small castle high up on a hill that overlooked the Mediterranean Sea. As luck would have it, of the six guards who were assigned to guard him, three had served under him when he had been a Roman officer. The other three young men were in awe of him, mostly due to the stories the others had told about Marcellius's heroics in the battlefield. Also in awe of Marcellius was Publius, the governor of Malta. He had heard that Marcellius was a wealthy and successful merchant and implored him to return to Malta upon his release and consider helping him export Malta's popular olive oil. He took such a liking to Marcellius that he urged him to return and visit, regardless of whether they could do business or not. For his part, Marcellius could not deny that Malta was truly a paradise. Were he not a prisoner kept against his will, Marcellius might have enjoyed the beautiful island and beautiful weather.

Marcellius's quarters were on the third floor, and from inside one of the large doors that led into a balcony, Marcellius continued to study the Roman fleet. Several *Quinqueremes*, large Roman warships, with five full-blown sails and scores of oars simultaneously dipping in and out of the water, led the way. It was an imposing sight. Malta was a Roman stronghold and from the looks of it, the Roman fleet was stopping here for supplies. Marcellius stepped out onto the balcony where two guards were stationed.

Flahas, one of the guards said, "Have a look, Marcellius that has to be Vespasian's new legions, headed for Judea."

"It cannot be anything else," Marcellius said. "It is impressive."

"Who would want to face such a powerful army," the other young guard said.

Marcellius watched until several of the ships pulled into the docks, and then he returned to his quarters and reminisced about Rome, about his home. Where were Trulius and Kemnebi? How were Felicia and Gianina doing? It was these memories that kept him in agony and unable to sleep on many nights, and on many of those nights, he would wake up in the middle of the night, confused and perspiring and calling out Servia's name.

Marcellius looked in the direction of the balcony when he heard horses, several of them pulling into the courtyard.

"Welcome, my lord," Marcellius heard a guard say, in a loud clear voice.

There was a slight pause and then Marcellius heard a voice vaguely familiar to him say, "I want to see Marcellius Kaelus Augustus? Where is he?"

Marcellius became apprehensive, and he tried to think. Where had he heard that voice before?

"He is in his quarters, my lord," the guard said. "You can reach him from these outside stairs. They lead to the balcony of his room."

Marcellius stiffened as he placed the voice that had asked for him—but how was that possible?

The guards at the balcony spoke at the same time. "My lord, welcome," they said, and one of them pushed the double doors wide open.

Septimus stepped into Marcellius's room followed by two men. He wore an officer's kilt and purple cloak. Ornamental metal stripes adorned his upper chest plate, identifying him as an officer of the highest rank. An emblem bearing the eye of the tiger was sewn on the shoulder of the chest plate.

"Marcellius," Septimus said, and then he turned to his men. "Leave us."

Septimus looked around the room and nodded approvingly. "I see that you are living well, Marcellius." He looked at Marcellius and nodded again. "You look a bit thin, but you look well."

"These are excellent quarters and for that I am grateful," Marcellius said. "But I am still a prisoner for a crime I did not commit."

Septimus sighed heavily. "We shall get to that in a moment. I can see that you are quite surprised to see me and in a Roman uniform no less."

"I am indeed. The last time I saw you, you wore the toga of a magistrate and now you are here in a military uniform with the emblem of a commander. Are you in command of that fleet?"

Septimus nodded and then spotted a bottle of wine. "I see that you also enjoy some commodities. Care to offer me a drink? I am terribly thirsty."

Marcellius filled two cups of wine and handed one to Septimus. He looked about the room. "I am aware that you authorized these quarters and these perks that I enjoy. I am grateful, but as I say, I am innocent. I should not be here."

Septimus drank from his cup of wine. "You have many friends. I received many letters, including one from the governor of this island, asking for leniency." Septimus set his cup down. "In truth, I figured that banishing you away from Rome and your family was enough punishment. The circumstances of your case and your past service to Rome merited some favorable consideration."

Septimus walked to the balcony doors and motioned for Marcellius to join him.

"That fleet that you see out there," Septimus said, "is going to join forces with Vespasian in a few weeks. We are going to quell the Hebrew revolt once and for all."

Marcellius said nothing and Septimus turned to him. "Would you ever consider wearing a military uniform again like I have done?"

Marcellius quickly glanced at Septimus. "Are you about to offer me a position in your army? I am a prisoner here. Besides, I have never seen a larger legion, surely you do not have a shortage of men."

Septimus turned away from the doors. "You are correct. I have plenty of men, but not men with your experience. Today's Roman soldiers are brave and fight well, but there are few leaders among them. Most think only of completing their military obligation so that they can return home to find some good woman to spend the night with or to perhaps bear them children." He shrugged. "Of course, for that I do not fault them."

"Is this an official offer?" Marcellius asked. "Are you offering me a uniform so that I can get off this island?"

"In truth, Marcellius, I came to set you free," Septimus said. "Two drunk soldiers were recently overheard at a tavern speaking about how you were framed for a murder you did not commit. I summoned Tarian and, well, it is the one and only time that I have ever threatened a witness in order to elicit the truth from him." Septimus sighed and shook his head. "He finally admitted to his complicity in framing you. I am sorry, Septimus."

Marcellius seethed. "Lying bastards! Did I not speak the truth? Did I not tell you I was innocent? I only agreed to be wrongly convicted to spare my family any further grief."

"I admit that I always had my doubts that a man of your reputation and integrity would ever stab a man from behind, but what could I do? The witnesses perjured themselves. You stumbled upon a bad lot of men that night." Septimus removed a rolled document from his chest plate and placed it on a table.

"This document is signed by myself and Nero. It declares you innocent of all charges and grants you an expungement of your criminal record. When I return to Rome we will discuss reparations for the wrong that has been bestowed on you."

Marcellius stared at the document and winced with anger. He slowly shook his head. "I am speechless." He glared at Septimus. "I am speechless at how easily the lies of men can destroy a man."

"Our judicial system is not perfect, Marcellius," Septimus said. "It is premised on the belief that men will do the honorable thing and testify truthfully, but as you have learned not all men adhere to that principle." Septimus paused and then regarded Marcellius with a stern gaze. "Listen to me, Marcellius. Join me. Romans have short memories and they love their war heroes. Fight with me in Judea and your name will no longer be associated with this terrible tragedy. No one will care that you were once accused and convicted of murder if you return to Rome a war hero."

Marcellius grunted. "How can you ask me to join the cowardly soldiers who conspired against me? There was a time when there was an unspoken code of honor among soldiers. We were brothers, and not just in the battlefields, and it did not matter where a man stood politically or socially. Soldiers were brothers!"

"As I have said, that night you stumbled into a bad lot of soldiers. What I am now offering you is an opportunity to completely restore your name, a name that was tarnished by despicable men. Think of your family. Think of your son."

"I think of Tessius Trulius every day, Septimus," Marcellius said, "and I have nothing to prove to anyone, much less my son."

"I understand," Septimus said. "I have asked that a small ship be placed at your disposal. You may return to Rome as soon as you like."

Septimus summoned his squires. Two young men stepped into the room carrying a wooden crate trimmed with leather and set it down. Septimus pointed to one of them. "You may leave." He pointed to the other squire. "You stay."

Septimus looked at Marcellius and then at the wooden crate. "It is not just a Roman uniform, Marcellius, it is an officer's uniform complete with your initials on the shield and sword. Take it with you back to Rome. It is yours."

Septimus paused at the door. "This squire shall remain outside your door to help you with whatever you need. I shall be in my tent if you have anything else to discuss with me."

Alone in his quarters, Marcellius stared angrily at the wooden crate. Septimus had made a point and it troubled him. No, he had nothing to prove to anyone, yet in these difficult times in Rome, a man's reputation was everything. And whether he liked it or not, upon his return to Rome, he would be the object of much gossip behind his back. After all, he would be returning directly from Malta, the place of his incarceration. Marcellius sighed heavily, his heart and mind in turmoil. He had faith that Felicia was taking good care of Gianina, and that Kemnebi and Trulius were safe. Marcellius sighed again and dropped his head into his hands.

The Roman uniform that Marcellius had once worn with pride now had an awkward feel to it. The exaltation of before was missing. Yet, as he walked toward Septimus's tent the soldiers who swirled around him acknowledged him with slight bows of their heads or respectful glances.

At Septimus's tent one of the two guards who stood outside the tent opened the tent flap for him.

"Ah," Septimus said. "The uniform is a perfect fit." He spread his arms and a squire unbuckled his chest plate. "Have a seat, Marcellius," he said. "I just returned from inspecting the troops. They are a good bunch, a bit young but a good bunch."

"So," Marcellius said. "How long do you expect this campaign to last?" he asked.

"No more than fifteen months. At least that is my hope." Septimus removed his chest plate and handed it to the squire. "You may go now," he said. He turned his back to Marcellius while he removed his belt and hung it on a hook. "Much like you I was not expecting this," he said. "Although in your case I can see that the irony of the situation still has you troubled. It is written all over your face."

"You can hardly blame me. Yesterday I was your prisoner and today I am one of your officers. I am not so certain that I am familiar with new field tactics."

Septimus laughed. "I said almost the exact same thing to my former father-in-law back in Rome when he proposed that I join Vespasian, and here I am."

Marcellius clutched the handle of his sword. Ironically, the guards had trusted him well enough to let him handle a sword, and to pass the time they had sparred with him for hours almost daily.

"Come," Septimus said.

Marcellius joined him at a table that was covered with maps. "Vespasian has occupied Galilee and is concentrating on Perea. We are landing in Caesarea, and from there we shall move south with our divisions to take Antipatris." Septimus tapped one of the maps with his finger. "Later Vespasian shall meet us here, at Emmaus."

Marcellius studied the map silently. Long lines representing the Roman army marked the faded and yellowish parchment. No army fought a war like the Romans. Each battle was meticulously planned and executed. "How much resistance do you expect we will encounter?"

"That is difficult to say. The rebels are brave, but their numbers have been unpredictable. At times they have been staggering and at other times they have offered token resistance. You shall command cohorts of infantry, cavalry, and artillery. Your second in command will be a seasoned veteran, Amatius. He is a widower who has lost all three of his sons in Roman campaigns, but he is not a bitter man. Of course, he should have retired years ago, but he knows nothing else but army life. He will serve you well."

"So," Marcellius said. "I postpone my trip back to Rome and you abandon your post in Rome. We again risk our lives for the empire. Are we that patriotic or are we a pair of fools?"

"Undoubtedly both," Septimus said. "Do true soldiers ever really stop being soldiers?"

Marcellius sighed. "Perhaps not, but unless we find another way of settling our disputes, other than the battlefields, the danger always exists that one day we will face an enemy much stronger, more vicious, and better prepared than we are, an enemy with the capacity to rip out the heart of Rome. It is the inevitable fate of every great empire."

Fifty-Two

One evening, after a walk into the wilderness Trulius headed back to Clivus. All that remained of sunlight was a faint patch of red in the eastern sky where the sun sank out of sight behind a mountainous horizon. A pale moon hung high on the opposite side of the sky. This past winter Trulius had turned fifteen. His arms and legs were lean and muscular now, and he wore his hair slightly longer than before and tied back with a leather strap across his forehead. He preferred short togas and riding boots to the long tunics and sandals the others wore. Always strapped to his side was the short sword Lord Gaios had given him.

These were difficult times for Trulius. He was troubled and restless and not even his adventures into the woods to hunt aroused an excitement in him. These days Trulius thought of one thing only, and it occupied his mind day and night. It was time to go home. It was time to return to Rome. Nothing else mattered. He wanted to search for his father, and he wanted to see Gianina and Felicia again. He loved Clivus. But he was no longer a child, and the idea of hiding within the walls of Clivus from the enemies of his father revolted him. It embarrassed him. Trulius clutched the handle of his sword as he walked through the trees and his anger grew. He was not afraid of any man. If anything, he would like to get his hands on the men who had killed his mother, and if his father was indeed still imprisoned, he needed to know.

Trulius was so engrossed in thought that at the next clearing in the trees he nearly stumbled upon a strange scene and barely had time to duck out of sight. It was getting very cold, and yesterday Ezri predicted that they would soon have snow. Yet, at the stream leading into the secret tunnel, all of the men, except for Kemnebi and Tavius, were knee deep in water and they had formed a circle around Farrenthias, who had his upper body exposed. As if engaged in some sort of ritual, Erasmus Harel doused Farrenthias's head with water. Abiel and Ezri held pots of burning incense while Adin and Cerudotus held torches. The thick smoke from the burning incense and torches made the entire scene hazy, almost surreal.

Farrenthias was as tall as Trulius but much thinner. And while he remained respectful and loyal to his beloved Cerudotus, Cerudotus no longer treated him as a child, and more often than not, he deferred to Farrenthias's wisdom, which he often said was now much greater than his own. Farrenthias had not just grown wiser with age, he was also calm and patient, and Trulius had yet to see him lose his temper.

Trulius thought Farrenthias resembled a Greek god as he stood in the water with the dim light of the torches flickering across his shoulder-length yellow hair. He almost looked unrecognizable to him. Trulius loved Farrenthias as never before and the thought of separating from him brought him sadness. He wondered if there was ever a time in a man's life when he would not suffer. Trulius blinked. The thick smoke surrounding Farrenthias made it difficult to see, but he swore that there was the shape of a man standing beyond the stream, on the opposite of side of where he stood. Trulius blinked again and this time there was nothing, and he wondered if it might have been an illusion formed by the smoke.

Erasmus Harel suddenly spoke, and in the stillness of the night, his voice carried through the trees.

"The path to spiritual realization, to truth, is long and arduous, Farrenthias, and it is an unending quest. But by the dedication to your studies and by your unbending thirst for knowledge, you have started down that path. You will journey far and at times you will despair, but you will never be alone, the spirits of those who love and guide you will always accompany you." He doused Farrenthias with water again. "From this day forward you shall be known as Farrenthias Theophilus."

"*Theophilus* means one who is loved by God," Abiel said.

One by one the men filed past Farrenthias and affectionately touched his shoulder. The last was Cerudotus. He put his arm around Farrenthias and together they followed the others out of the water and up the path back to Clivus.

Trulius stood mesmerized for a moment, breathing in the sweet smell of the incense that was left behind, wondering what to make of all of this. He waited until everyone had left and then he set out feeling strangely guilty, feeling as if he had stumbled onto something he should not have witnessed.

The courtyard was quiet. Trulius figured that the men had returned to their private hall. He would have to wait until tomorrow to confront Farrenthias about the matter. Trulius yawned and walked to his room and collapsed onto his bed without bothering to undress. "Theophilus," he whispered. His eyelids grew heavy. "Farrenthias Theophilus, how strange," he whispered again.

Early the next morning Trulius splashed water on his face and dressed in a hurry. He looked out the window. As Ezri had predicted, it had snowed last night. Trulius slipped his dagger and sword into his belt and tossed a cloak across his back and rushed out of the door. He had much on his mind. First, it was settled, today he would tell Kemnebi and Erasmus Harel that it was time that he go home. It was time to leave. He could wait no longer. But first he had to tell Farrenthias of his plans and today was the perfect day. Today Farrenthias was completely free of all his duties, and he and Trulius had planned to spend the day together exploring the woods. Of course, after last night's events, Trulius wondered if Farrenthias was still going to be willing to join him.

The entire courtyard was covered in a foot of snow. "Magnificent," Trulius said, looking around. The roofs of the towers and the tops of the trees were white. All of Clivus was dressed in white. And to Trulius's delight, it started to snow again. Tiny white flakes fluttered to the ground like wingless butterflies, floating without direction or purpose. Trulius opened his hand. A flake landed on his palm and melted into water. "Beautiful," Trulius cried. "Nature is beautiful."

As usual, Trulius was the last to arrive at the hall where they had their meals. He took a seat next to Farrenthias. Kemnebi and Erasmus Harel were at the far end of the long table engaged in conversation. At the opposite end of the table Ezri was making a point to Cerudotus and Abiel about something Pythagoras had said or meant to say, and Adin was at the far end of the room slicing pieces of cheese.

"Well," Trulius excitedly whispered to Farrenthias. "What do you think of the snow? I am so excited I have lost my appetite. I cannot wait to run across the courtyard and get all wet and cold."

Farrenthias laughed. "When I saw the snow this morning you are the first person I thought of, Trulius. I know how much you love snow and the cold."

Trulius bit into a piece of freshly baked bread and washed it down with water. "By the way," he whispered. He glanced around to make certain no one else was listening. "I saw all of you by the stream last night. What kind of ceremony was that?"

Farrenthias sipped from his cup of water and also looked around. "Where were you, Trulius?" he said. "I did not see you."

Trulius again looked across the table before he spoke. The others remained occupied with their private conversations. "Never mind that, I found it all rather strange. Are you still coming with me? It is a magnificent day."

"Of course I am going with you. We had already agreed that to-day we would spend the day together," Farrenthias said. He placed his cup inside his wooden bowl and pulled his chair away from the table. "I am ready if you are."

Trulius jumped to his feet. "I am ready. Who has time to eat when there is so much to do outside?"

Farrenthias said to no one in particular, "Trulius and I are finished. We are going to walk in the snow."

"Cover yourselves well," Adin said. "It is cold outside."

Outside the gates of Clivus, Trulius held out a hand while he and Farrenthias walked and watched snowflakes land on the palm of his hand. "So," he said. "You never told me. What was all that about at the stream anyway? Theophilus? Why were you given a new name?"

"Erasmus Harel was rewarding me for the work I have done, Trulius. It was a baptismal of sorts. A rebirth into a scholarly world." He brushed off the snow that stuck to his cloak.

"I see, well I have something else to tell you. He brushed the snow from his hands and hid them under his cloak to warm them. "Today I plan to tell my uncle and Kemnebi that I wish to go home. I want to return to Rome to look for Father."

Farrenthias stopped walking and stopped Trulius with a hand. "You are leaving Clivus, Trulius? Is it safe? You told me that you were here because your father's enemies might want to hurt you."

Trulius started walking again. "Come on," he said. He started down the path toward the stream where he had seen last night's ceremony. "I am no longer a child, Farrenthias. I cannot hide forever."

Farrenthias walked quietly beside him, his head hung low. "I will miss you terribly and I will miss Kemnebi."

Trulius paused and kicked a pile of snow. "I will miss you too, but I have to leave. I am tired of hiding. Clivus has been my home now for too many years. It is time to return to Rome."

Farrenthias stood quietly shivering and nodding his head. "Clivus will not be the same without you."

"Do you realize, Farrenthias, that you are here by choice? You want to be here because you enjoy all of your scholarly work. Your place is here, mine is not." Trulius broke off a piece of a branch that was sticking out of the snow and handed it to Farrenthias. "You have not done this with me in a long time. I have gotten much better. Want to see?"

Farrenthias stared at the branch. "I suppose we have not spent much time together recently. I am sorry, Trulius."

"Do not be. Maybe one day you can visit me in Rome. Would you like that? I will introduce you to Gianina and Felicia and you can meet my dog Pharaoh. I am sure he is big now."

"I would love to go to Rome," Farrenthias said.

"Then it is settled," Trulius said. "Now throw that branch as hard and as high as you can."

Farrenthias took a few steps away from Trulius, planted his feet, and threw the piece of wood into the air with all of his strength.

Trulius pulled his dagger from his belt and flung it into the air in one motion. The dagger pierced the wood in mid-air.

"Trulius!" Farrenthias cried. "That was fantastic. Let us do it again." He looked around. "Where did the dagger land?"

"Over in those trees," Trulius said. But he froze. There was a man, hidden in the pine trees, looking at them. Only the upper part of his body was visible through the trees, but he was clearly looking in their direction. The rest of his body was hidden behind the tree. Trulius instinctively clutched the handle of his sword. In the next moment, however, the man ducked out of sight and vanished.

"Did you see him?" Trulius whispered. "Did you see that man?"

"I did," Farrenthias said. "Do you think he was lost?"

Trulius stood staring at the spot where the man had stood. "Hum, that was strange. If he was lost he would have spoken to us."

Farrenthias wiped the moisture from his eyes. "Yes, I did not think about that."

"And he did vanish in an awful hurry," Trulius said. He started quietly towards his dagger.

"What are you thinking, Trulius?" Farrenthias said, hurrying to keep up with him. "You look very pensive."

Trulius picked up his dagger and slipped it inside his belt. "Last night, Farrenthias, when I came upon you at the stream, I thought I saw a man standing just beyond the trees. I could not see him clearly for the smoke was so thick. I blinked and he was gone, and I thought that maybe I had imagined him. But now, I am certain that I was not imagining things. Someone was there last night, and it could have been the man we just saw."

Farrenthias looked worriedly around. "What do we do, Trulius?"

Trulius started quickly back toward Clivus. "It could be nothing," he said. "Perhaps just one man hanging around the woods, but just the same I should like to tell Kemnebi and Tavius. They will know what to do."

Fifty-Three

"I do not like it," Kemnebi said. He wrapped a hand around the handle of his dagger. "No, I do not like it." He looked from Trulius and Farrenthias to Erasmus Harel. "I sense danger."

"Why do you think that, Kemnebi?" Erasmus Harel said. "Could it be that the man is curious about who we are and is too frightened to reveal himself?"

Tavius shook his head. "I agree with Kemnebi. I do not like it either. A man with good intentions would have no reason not to approach two young men in the woods and engage them in conversation. He would not have disappeared so suddenly."

"I am concerned," Kemnebi said, "that he could have been a scout sent ahead of a party. There is danger at every turn out here. He could have been a scout for the Romans or the Parthians or some other renegade group of mercenaries. We must take precautions."

Erasmus Harel sighed quietly. "Very well," he said. "What do you suggest?"

"We shall have to watch the gates and the courtyard day and night, for at least a week, maybe ten days," Kemnebi said. "If after that nothing happens then I suppose that we can assume that the man left the area and that he will not return with an army or his friends."

"Agreed," Tavius said. "And I do not think anyone should venture out alone."

"We should go and warn the others," Erasmus Harel said.

"Trulius and I will join you shortly," Kemnebi said. He waited until he and Trulius were alone and then he said, "Trulius, you have been acting very strangely the last few weeks. You have grown restless, am I correct?"

"It has been that obvious?"

"Trulius, I have watched you grow from the moment you were breastfed. I know when you have something on your mind. What is it?"

Trulius clenched the handle of his sword. "I want to go home, Kemnebi," he said. "I am tired of hiding. I want to look for Father."

Kemnebi looked quietly at him for a long moment. "I knew that is what was troubling you," he finally said. He looked in the direction of a window. "This is a paradise, but we do not belong here. I too am anxious to look for him." Kemnebi placed an arm around him and started for the door. As soon as this situation is resolved, I shall have a talk with Erasmus Harel. It is time to leave."

The following morning Trulius was awakened very early by loud, clamoring footsteps out in the corridor. There were whispers just outside his door. Trulius sensed trouble, and he threw the covers from his bed and quickly began to dress. Just as he reached for his boots, the door flew open.

Ezri was standing at the door holding a candle, which lit his face. It was a face full of terror. "Trulius!" Ezri cried. "Hurry! Come with us!"

Farrenthias and Cerudotus suddenly appeared behind him. They looked bewildered and frightened.

"What is it?" Trulius asked, as he finished putting on his boots.

"Parthians!" Ezri cried, "I counted eight of them. They demanded food and water, and when Kemnebi advised them that they could enter but without their weapons, they grew hostile and stormed the gates. I have been ordered by Erasmus Harel to keep you, Farrenthias, and Cerudotus together. We will wait below and must be prepared to make a run for the gates, if it becomes necessary."

Adin came running down the hall. "Ezri," he said, struggling to catch his breath and sweating profusely. "We cannot find Abiel. Erasmus Harel and Quanarious are out looking for him." He looked at the terrified faces of Farrenthias and Cerudotus. "You are taking them below?"

"Yes," Ezri said.

"Good."

Trulius strapped on his dagger and sword. "I am not going anywhere," he said. "Kemnebi and Tavius might need help." He unsheathed his sword. "I must hurry."

"My child," Cerudotus cried. "Are you mad? Parthians are very dangerous. Why, the Romans can barely contain them."

"Cerudotus is right..." Farrenthias said, but sighed in exasperation. "We are not talking you out of this are we?"

Trulius shook his head. "No, now hurry. We are wasting time!"

Trulius stepped out of his cubicle and ran down the hall. He flew down the stairway and bolted out of the door. The scene he encountered was wild and chaotic. Three men had Kemnebi pinned against the courtyard wall. They were swinging swords and mallets wildly and with brute force. They were large, heavy men dressed in loose clothing and strange head coverings. Four men lay scattered on the ground, either dead or mortally wounded. One of them was Tavius. Without breaking his stride, Trulius retrieved his dagger and flung it at one of the men who was attacking Kemnebi. He struck the man squarely in the back. The man spun around and glared at Trulius in disbelief. He made a feeble gesture to lift his sword but Trulius was too quick. He buried his sword into the man's belly and then pulled back and watched the man fall at his feet. He raised his eyes and looked at Kemnebi. He had killed the last two men and was coming to help Trulius, but when he saw that Trulius was fine, he abruptly turned and rushed to help Tavius. Tavius was bleeding profusely from a chest wound and was struggling to breathe.

"I am afraid that I am done for, my dear Egyptian friend," he said with glazed eyes. He glanced at Trulius and barely managed a smile. "You did well, young Trulius. But you two must hurry. Two of those rascals made it into one of the towers. There is still danger."

"You will be fine," Kemnebi said. "We will be back for you."

Trulius raised his eyes to the tower, and for a fleeting moment, he thought he detected a shadow move away from a window. "Kemnebi," he whispered. "They are in Erasmus Harel's quarters. I think they were watching us."

"Cursed," the man at the window cried. "All of our men are down." He walked from the window and pushed Abiel out of the way and took Erasmus Harel by the collar with one hand. "So, you say that no Romans have been through here. Then who is that Egyptian? Egyptians are known to collaborate with Romans."

"I assure you that if you release us, he will do you no harm," Erasmus Harel said. "We live a quiet existence. No one else needs to die."

The man laughed. "A quiet existence? Five hundred of our men are three days march from here. Now tell me, other than the Egyptian and the boy who was with him, are there any other armed men?"

Erasmus Harel shook his head and the man put a dagger to his throat. "Come, let us go and find out how much the Egyptian values your life."

The other Parthian looked at Abiel and Quanarious, who were on the floor gagged and bound. He kicked Quanarious. "What about these two?"

The other man paused. "We take care of the Egyptian and the boy, and then we come back and take care of those two."

The door suddenly flew open and knocking chairs and tables over, Kemnebi and Trulius stormed into the room. Startled, one of the Parthians tried to block Kemenbi with Erasmus Harel's body, but Kemnebi knocked them both down, rolled to his knees and stuck the man's side, killing him. Kemnebi was on his feet again, just in time to see Trulius sidestep a chair and plunge his sword into the belly of the other Parthian.

The room was suddenly utterly still. Erasmus Harel stared incredulously at Trulius without saying a word. "My son," he finally said. "Are you alright?"

Trulius stared at the body of the man he had just killed. The body was contorted and sprawled at his feet, much the same way as the lion he had killed years before. He looked up at Erasmus Harel. "I am fine," he said quietly, solemnly. "It is just that today," he paused. "It is just that today I killed two men and I feel, I feel no remorse. I feel nothing."

Fifty-Four

A light evening rain spilled through the open window and there was a sudden chill in the air, but Erasmus Harel made no move to close the shutters. Instead, he stood silently staring out the window, deep in thought. The water trickled along the windowsill and spilled onto the cement floor. Except for the sound of the sprinkling rain, the room was utterly still, even though every occupant of Clivus was present.

Moments earlier they had buried Tavius in a brief but solemn ceremony, and now Erasmus Harel contemplated their fate and the fate of Clivus. How quickly things can change in a moment. There were still many things to do out in the world, but he certainly believed that Clivus was home, the place they would return to for many years to come. And now how quickly all of that had come to an end.

He turned away from the window and walked to the table where the others sat and took a seat. He stared at the stunned and solemn faces of the men he had come to love, the men who were his family. He sighed and spoke in a soft, thoughtful voice.

"Kemnebi has agreed to escort Cerudotus and Farrenthias back to Syria. Quanarious will go with them." He turned to Ezri. "You and Abiel will join Ya'ir in Jerusalem. Adin and I will travel to Cilicia in Tarsus, and from there we shall board a ship to Alexandria. In time, we will join the rest of you in Jerusalem."

"What of the scrolls?" Ezri said looking from one man to the other. "How do we get them all to Jerusalem?"

Erasmus Harel acknowledged the comment with the shake of his head. He had indeed given the scrolls much thought, especially since he and Adin were not traveling to Jerusalem. The others could not possibly carry them all out of Clivus. "You shall each carry a small satchel filled with what you can, the rest will have to remain here. We shall conceal them in the tunnels below Clivus that Lord Gaios discovered.

"Will they be safe there?" Adin asked.

"I believe they will be," Ezri said. "Before we sealed the entrance we went back down and discovered many hidden crevices where we can hide them."

"In time, we will one day return for them," Erasmus Harel said.

Abiel leaned back with a heavy, prolonged sigh that drew the attention of the others. "I had come to believe that I would die here," he said, almost in a whisper, "and that my ashes would be spread out somewhere in this paradise. And now, now we are leaving."

Adin said, also in a low barely audible voice, "I too thought we would be here forever." He lifted his eyes and looked about the table. "I shall miss Clivus and our time together." He extended a hand across the table towards Farrenthias and Trulius, "and I shall miss you two young lads enormously."

Farrenthias, who had been too subdued to speak, suddenly cleared his throat. He gazed at Cerudotus, not with the eyes of a child but, rather, with the eyes of a young man who loved and respected his tutor and mentor but who could no longer keep quiet about his feelings. "I wish to speak, Cerudotus," he said.

"Of course," Cerudotus said. "What is it?"

Farrenthias addressed Erasmus Harel. "Sire," he said, "I wish to keep learning from all of you. May I join Ezri and Abiel in Jerusalem?"

"Farrenthias," Cerudotus said in a raised voice that expressed surprise. "Perhaps we should wait and obtain your father's permission."

Farrenthias looked intently at him. "I do not believe that Father would object. Do you? Surely he will understand that I wish to continue my studies."

"But," Cerudotus nervously eyed Erasmus Harel. "Sire, what do you say? Would Farrenthias fit in with your plans?"

Erasmus Harel looked tenderly at Farrenthias before he smiled at Cerudotus. "My dear Cerudotus, how can we object when a young man as brilliant and as passionate as Farrenthias wants to join our quest for knowledge?" He turned to Farrenthias. "My child," he said. "You have been an excellent student, and I am very proud of the work you have accomplished here. You have acquired more knowledge than young men twice your age, and you are fluent in languages few men even know exist. Nothing would please us more than to have you permanently join us. But it has been nearly seven years since you have been home. Enjoy your family for as long as you like, and then if you still wish to join us, look for Ya'ir in Jerusalem. He has an apartment near the temple, but he is hardly ever there. He is usually at the temple, or at his at his father's house. His father, Jishu, and his niece, Sedia, have become Christians, and they are very active in a small community of Christians in Jerusalem. Look for Ya'ir at Jishu's house. Ask anyone in that community where Jishu lives and they will direct you to his house. Abiel and Ezri will let Ya'ir know that he should expect you."

Farrenthias nodded. "Thank you, Erasmus Harel. I assure you that I will find him."

Erasmus Harel stood from the table. "It is settled then. Now, let us proceed to the business of the scrolls."

Quanarious wiggled his way into the area behind the warrior statue that concealed the entrance to the tunnels. "I can push from back here," he said.

Kemnebi and Trulius took hold of a different part of the statue, and while Quanarious pushed they pulled. The statue slid slightly across the floor with a terrible screeching sound.

"I think that is enough," Quanarious said. With a blunt dagger he carved along the edges of a large rock until he was able to pry it from the wall. He passed it to Trulius, who had crouched behind him, and then quickly removed a few other smaller rocks until he had created an opening the size of a small window. "That should do it," he said, looking over his shoulder at Erasmus Harel. "Shall I go in?"

Erasmus Harel's eyes fell upon the five vessels they were about to entomb. About three feet high and slightly round at the bottom, they were densely packed with parchments that represented many years of hard work, and, more importantly, the parchments were filled with vast knowledge, words of wisdom from many great men who lived in far regions of the world. He recalled the difficult journeys to the Far East that he and the others had taken. He recalled the search for great masters in snow-covered mountains. They had found great teachers in simple wooden shacks and caves, warmed only by a feeble fire, and also in temples that resembled great palaces. All those visits were now recorded in these scrolls that he hoped would one day find their way into the outside world.

"Shall I go in, sire?" Quanarious repeated.

Erasmus Harel nervously nodded. "Ezri will show you where they are to be stored." He stepped out of the way and watched quietly as Kemnebi and Trulius passed the vessels to Quanarious, and then he quickly vanished into the hole along with Ezri and Farrenthias. Erasmus Harel stood staring at the hole, his heart filled with anxiety. He recalled the words of one great Eastern master, "Not all knowledge is to be shared at once. Man is not yet prepared for that. We must be patient and wait for the right moment."

Erasmus Harel found solace in these words, for this was not yet the time for the words written in these scrolls.

Ezri stopped at the edge of the abyss and pointed to the ladder with his torch. "This is the way down," he said.

Kemnebi edged closer to the edge and studied the drop into the abyss. "Our rope is not long enough," he said. He reached down and tested the strength of the ladder. "It is made of very thick rope. Excellent. Two of us will have to hang from the ladder at the same time in order to get the scrolls down to the bottom." He looked at the others. "Ezri, you go down first. Trulius, you will go next and stay on the ladder near the bottom. Quanarious and I will follow. Farrenthias will hand us the vessels."

Ezri swung around onto the ladder and then slowly made his way down. When he reached the bottom, he waved the torch. Quanarious followed him down. "I'm ready," Quanarious said.

The vessels were lowered with a rope to Quanarious and Ezri. When the last jar was lowered, the three joined Ezri and Quanarious at the bottom.

"This way," Ezri said. He crouched low and set out down a path with the torch.

"This is an amazing natural wonder?" Trulius said. "Who could have found it?"

"Lord Gaios believed that the opening from the outside was discovered first."

At the first bend in the tunnel, Ezri raised the torch to his left, scraped the wall with his hands and when he saw the small faded drawing of the warrior statue, he nodded. "This is it," he said. He loosened two large rocks from an area just below the drawing. Trulius helped him remove them from the wall, and soon they were staring at an opening similar to the one upstairs.

"Have a look," Ezri said, moving to one side. "Lord Gaios and his men also discovered this chamber. He believed that they used to punish prisoners by putting them in here. They found several bowls used for eating in here, but no bones were found inside."

Trulius slipped a torch into the hole and peered in. The chamber was half the size of the room where he slept. "They used to seal men in here?" he asked, looking back at Ezri.

Ezri nodded. "Man has a very cruel imagination when it comes to inflicting punishment, Trulius." He motioned for Trulius to look back into the room. "Look at the far wall, Trulius. See the boards on that wall?"

"Yes, I see them," Trulius said.

"Behind those boards is a slight indentation into the wall. Our vessels will fit perfectly behind them."

Trulius nodded and then crawled into the chamber. The ceiling was so low he could not stand. He set the torch and wiped the sweat from his forehead. Breathing was difficult and it terrified him to imagine being sealed in this room in total darkness. He quickly removed the boards and discovered a large section that had been dug into the wall. "We must hurry," he said to Farrenthias, who was handing him the first jar. "I can barely breath."

Moments later, with the jars secure inside the wall and covered,

Trulius pressed a hand against one of the boards. It was secure and in place. "It is done," he said. He picked up his torch and crawled out of the chamber.

Farrenthias helped him cover the wall with the two large rocks that they had removed. "We are leaving a great deal of knowledge behind," he said. "But I cannot imagine anyone finding this room."

The following afternoon, just outside the gates of Clivus, Erasmus Harel found himself staring at a dried leaf as it blew across the empty courtyard. It rolled and skipped across the courtyard and then awkwardly flew into the sunken steps that led into the hall where they had worked for so many years. The leaf became wedged between the crack of the door and wall. A cold fall wind pressed against it, but the leaf was stuck and went nowhere. This morning at this very gate Trulius had asked the question he had been afraid to ask. "Will we ever see each other again, Uncle?"

Erasmus Harel had smiled bitterly, for he did not know the answer. "We shall have to wait and see, Trulius. Destiny surprised us once. Perhaps it will surprise us again."

Adin interrupted his thoughts. "They were wonderful years," he said, drying his eyes.

Erasmus Harel nodded silently. It saddened him that his brother had not seen Trulius grow from a mischievous boy to a handsome young man, serious but restless. And yet, had he, Erasmus Harel, and Ya'ir deprived the family of Farrenthias of the same thing? Had not both boys grown into young men here at Clivus?

One of the horses snorted and Erasmus Harel turned to find Adin already mounted and holding the reins of the horse Erasmus Harel would ride. Soon they would be at the papyrus pond. Erasmus Harel would always remember it as the place where he had first laid eyes on his beloved nephew. The pond was significant for another reason. It was also the place where Farrenthias and Trulius had first met. Erasmus Harel smiled thoughtfully. Ever since that day he had never been able to shake the feeling that somehow the lives of his two beloved children would forever be intertwined. No matter what path Farrenthias pursued, Erasmus Harel believed that Trulius would not be far behind, and that thought comforted him. The world was full of abomination, and men who traveled extensively faced danger and needed companions.

A strong gust of wind suddenly swept across the courtyard. Leaves swirled upward. Erasmus Harel looked for the trapped leaf that he had been keeping an eye on. It was gone. It had vanished and Erasmus Harel smiled bitterly. Nothing ever remained the same. Life was nothing but a blur, and at times, he worried that it was nothing but a cruel blur. Even he, who had spent a lifetime in deep veneration of God, could not deny that.

Fifty-Five

✦ CAESAREA ✦

matius raced his horse around the sea of tents at the Roman encampment, which had been set up just beyond the shores of Caesarea. Upon arriving at Septimus's tent, he vaulted from his horse. Two guards who recognized him opened the tent flaps for him and stepped out of his way. Inside the tent Septimus was gathered at a table with his commanders, pouring over maps and planning their maneuvers. Amatius planted a fist against his chest in respectful gesture and then looked at Marcellius.

Marcellius stepped away from the table and joined Amatius in a corner of the tent. Marcellius spoke to him in whispers. "What is it, Amatius? You look pale."

"News from one of our scouts, Marcellius. A sizable army of rebels, three maybe four thousand men strong, are camped a half day's march from here. Without a doubt, they are headed this way."

"What? Before Vespasian left here with his divisions yesterday morning he sent out a patrol of scouts. They reported nothing." Marcellius frowned. "Where are they?"

"They are southeast of here."

Marcellius turned in the direction of Septimus and caught his eye.

"What is it, Marcellius?" Septimus asked. "What news does Amatius bring you? You look troubled."

"I am troubled," Marcellius said. "Three maybe four thousand rebels are camped a half day's march from here," he said.

Septimus inspected one of his maps. "How is that possible? Vespasian's scouts reported nothing, and if Vespasian had encountered resistance he would have sent us word."

"Those were my exact words to Amatius, Septimus," Marcellius said. "Those crafty devils must have purposefully hidden from Vespasian so they could try and take Caesarea. Perhaps we should march out to meet them. If we wait for them to reach the city, they could very well have our backs to the sea."

"Surely you do not believe those rascals will push us out to sea, Marcellius," a commander said. "Caesarea is now a Roman stronghold. Let them come. We prepare for them and decimate them here."

"No, they will not push us out to sea," Septimus said. "But Marcellius is right. The rebels are proud. They will fight us for every stone and every step of their amphitheater, and we do not want that. They may not push us out to sea but they may push us to the very shores of the sea." He glanced about the room. "Vespasian considers Caesarea to be his headquarters now. He does not want it destroyed." He motioned Amatius to the table. "Can you tell us on this map exactly where the enemy camp is located?"

Amatius studied the map for a moment. "Here," he said, placing a finger on the map. "According to the scouts they are here."

"Very well," Septimus said. "We must act quickly. Two divisions will leave at once and we surprise the rebels at dawn. We attack from the north and the south. I will lead one of the divisions."

"And with your permission," Marcellius said. "I will lead the other."

"So be it," Septimus said. He looked at the men around the table. "I leave the city to the rest of you. Remain alert. These zealots are capable of anything,"

Just before dawn the following morning, Marcellius was perched on a low hill that overlooked the rebel camp. Resting on one knee, he quietly studied the camp. Dim fires burned throughout the camp, casting shadows on the dark forms of the men who were asleep on the open ground. There were many canopies under which more men slept. Guards, Marcellius noted, were posted at key locations throughout the camp. All seemed quiet. There was nothing out of the ordinary. Yet, something bothered Marcellius. Something nagged at him. Amatius scrambled next to him.

"Marcellius," he whispered. "Septimus and his troops are in position and await your signal."

Marcellius glanced briefly at Amatius in the darkness but said nothing. It had been agreed that, because Marcellius and his men were closer to the rebel camp, they would commence the attack by launching fiery arrows into the camp. Marcellius continued to study the camp.

Amatius followed his gaze. "I am familiar with your silence, Marcellius," he whispered. "You are troubled. Have we not thus far executed our surprise attack perfectly?"

Marcellius shook his head and brushed his chin. "Vespasian is a brilliant general, yet these conniving scoundrels managed to elude him easily enough. And now, here they are just a day from our main camp, and they sleep as quietly as if they were on a training mission. I do not like it. The camp is too quiet." He pushed back and motioned for Amatius to follow him.

"Send a message to Septimus," Marcellius said. "Tell him that my men will storm the camp in two waves and not one as planned, and tell him that I suggest he do the same."

"Two waves? A delayed second wave from each side?" Amatius whispered. He quickly looked at the surrounding hills and frowned. "Do you think, Marcellius, that these scoundrels are trying to out clever us? Do you suspect that they have men hidden in the hills?"

Marcellius shrugged. "My gut feeling tells me we might be walking into a trap. These are their lands and they know them better than we do. We are going to move in cautiously. You will move in first and I will have your rear flank. Pass the word among the men on what we intend to do."

"Very well, I shall send word out to Septimus and prepare our men."

The sky was still very dark and clear and lit with bright glittering stars. This was, Marcellius thought, a beautiful country, and yet its history was filled with wars and bloodshed. Of course, that was not unlike the rest of the world. War. Marcellius wondered if the madness of men would ever stop. Mounted on his horse, he looked to his left and saw that Amatius was ready. Behind him his troops were also ready. Marcellius nodded, and alert squires, who stood next to the archers, immediately lit various fires and stepped out of the way while the archers lit their arrows. Marcellius raised a hand and waited. As soon as the last archer stepped back in line and raised his bow and arrow, Marcellius dropped his hand. Like a firestorm, a volley of fiery arrows lit the sky. Almost immediately, from Septiumus's position, came another firestorm of arrows. Marcellius signaled Amatius and Amatius lunged his stallion forward.

"To battle, Romans!" Amatius shouted. "For Rome and for the emperor!"

Amatius's men charged forward in droves. The rebel camp quickly came to life—almost too quickly, as if they had expected an attack. Yet, even in the chaos it was clear to Marcellius that not every form on the ground came to life. The men who quickly formed a circle around the camp amounted to no more than about a hundred men. "I knew it," Marcellius whispered to himself. He quickly searched the hills and waited. The wait was not long. Dark forms poured out of the hills and rushed down the hill like black lava pouring out of a volcano. The rebels began to spread out, as they got closer to the charging Romans. They now looked like an army of ants swarming down on their enemy.

"Archers!" Marcellius shouted, pointing to the charging rebels. A new volley of arrows covered the sky. Septimus also unleashed a volley of arrows from his position and many rebels began to tumble and drop due to the aerial attack.

Marcellius had seen enough. "Now!" he shouted. Just as the sun broke through the horizon he and his men rushed down the hill.

Marcellius crashed into a wave of rebels and fell from his horse. He rolled to his feet and swung his sword wildly, cutting down one fierce fighting rebel after another. Never had he faced such a tenacious enemy. For every man who fell at his feet three others appeared. He lost track of time, and before he knew it, the sun was high overhead. And it was hot. It had to be around the noon hour and like a swarm of bees, the rebels still fought relentlessly. Marcellius suddenly winced with pain. He glanced down and saw that he was bleeding from his right side. The man who had wounded him was on his knees looking up at Marcellius with the strangest look of terror on his face. Marcellius cut him down, but at the same time Marcellius cringed with pain from a blow to the head. He staggered forward, dropped to his knees and then collapsed forward.

Fifty-Six

Farrenthias looked anxiously across the dry Syrian Desert and rejoiced at the sight of his father's fortress. He was home. However, for a fleeting moment he almost did not recognize his home. It had changed so much. The walls of the fortress were unchanged, but there were now many more palm trees around the walls and there was a large spring where one had not existed before. In fact, the fortress looked like an oasis in the middle of the desert. There were also considerably more small structures outside the main building than he remembered. Farrenthias squinted in the bright sunshine. Men were gathered outside the gates of the fortress. They were wielding their swords and shields and some were engaged in make-believe combat. Farrenthias realized at once that this was their weekly training session. Some things had not changed. His father insisted on these training sessions. He kept his guard ready and prepared at all times. Farrenthias strained harder and looked from man to man until at last he spotted him. There was no mistaking the towering figure his father made.

"Ah," Cerudotus said. "I am elated to be home, but I see that the business of war never ends." He raised a hand to hood his eyes. "Is that Lord Gaios in the middle of that melee that I see out there?"

"It is, Cerudotus," Farrenthias said with a chuckle.

"It is a magnificent fortress," Trulius said. "And I see that the men train hard."

Farrenthias suddenly became despondent. They were bringing sad news to the fortress. Tavius had been one of his father's most loyal guards. Everyone knew and loved him. The news of his death was sure to depress many.

"I see the look in your eyes, Farrenthias," Kemnebi said. "You are thinking of Tavius, are you not?"

Farrenthias nodded. "Like Father, he came from Greece. He had no family. Here he took in a widow with two small children."

"He was a good man," Kemnebi said. "But he was a soldier. We mourn their loss and then honor their lives by recalling their valiant deeds in battle."

"Have a look," Trulius said. "They have spotted us."

Lord Gaios was at the head of the small group of soldiers who began to ride towards them. At first he appeared to be squinting as he approached, but suddenly his eyes lit up when he recognized Farrenthias and the others.

Trulius glanced at Farrenthias. Farrenthias was grinning proudly, and Trulius was happy for him. For an instant he wished he was in Rome being greeted by his father.

"Farrenthias!" Lord Gaios cried. "Welcome home, son." He looked at the others. "All of you are welcome." He abruptly grew silent. "Tavius?" he said. "Where is Tavius?"

"Lord Gaios," Kemnebi said solemnly. "I am afraid that we had trouble at Clivus. We were attacked. Tavius did not make it."

Lord Gaios grew pale. "Was anyone else hurt?"

"No," Kemnebi said.

"I should have left more men behind," Lord Gaios said.

"These times are unpredictable," Kemnebi said, "We had been at Clivus for years without incident. No one could have anticipated what happened."

"Perhaps," Lord Gaios said with a sigh. "Well, we shall mourn Tavius properly. He was a good and loyal man." Lord Gaios now regarded Farrenthias. His golden hair was spread across his shoulders. His face, though youthful and handsome, was no longer the face of the child who had left several years before. "I at first thought that my eyes deceived me," he bellowed. "But alas you have returned, my son." In one quick motion Lord Gaios dismounted and lifted Farrenthias clear off the ground. "Ah, you are still too thin. You are as light as a feather. It is good to see you!"

Lord Gaios gripped the shoulder of Cerudotus. "Welcome home, Cerudotus," he chuckled with a little humor. "It is good to see you in one piece. The women will be delighted to see both of you."

Lord Gaios turned his attention to Trulius. "It is good to see you as well, my son. This is your home, for as long as you like. This is a home to all of you." He sighed heavily. "Tavius had a family. I must go and break the sad news to them. We shall mourn him for nine days, and after that, we shall have a celebration. It will be a celebration to honor his life as well as a celebration to honor the return of Farrenthias and Cerudotus and our new friends."

Late that evening Lord Gaios found his wife seated in their quarters deep in thought and staring at the flame of a glowing candle. He studied her profile. Well into her prime years, she was still more beautiful than ever.

Sensing his presence, Oralia turned slightly and greeted her husband with a faint smile.

"I thought that I would find you in a more cheerful mood," he said. "Instead, I find you alone and contemplative on the day our son has finally returned."

Oralia exhaled softly. "I am beside myself with joy, my lord. But as I sit here thinking how much I love him and have missed him, I cannot help but to think about how much I will miss him again when he leaves."

Lord Gaios took a seat next to her and sighed heavily. "He told you?"

Oralia nodded quietly. "Almost from the moment I first welcomed him home he told me of his plans. He seems very determined."

Lord Gaios sighed again. "What are we to make of it, Oralia? He had not even sat down to rest when he was asking my permission to accompany Trulius to Rome and then to seek out Erasmus Harel in Jerusalem to continue his education. How could I refuse him? As you say, he seems very determined."

Oralia shook her head. "No, my lord, that would not be wise. Our son has grown up and he has chosen his path."

Lord Gaios also knew he could never do that to Farrenthias. This afternoon when they had talked that is all that Farrenthias spoke about. "He also told me that Erasmus Harel traveled extensively and that he too would like to take similar journeys. He talked about quests for knowledge."

"Perhaps we should have expected it," Oralia said, "Does that not remind you of what you did? Did we not leave Greece because you wanted to explore a new world? And look at all that you have accomplished." Oralia sighed. "Still, it is painful. I must confess to you, my lord, that I clung to a sliver of hope that he might choose to stay, at least for a while."

"I will talk to him again," Lord Gaios said. "He can become a teacher like Cerudotus and perhaps teach at Antioch." He paused. "Are you so certain that it would be wrong to forbid him from leaving?"

Oralia looked at her husband with tears in her eyes. "Do you not recognize, my husband, that like you he is driven by his dreams? They are just not the same dreams that you had. It has become clear to me that Farrenthias is driven by something deeper than you and I can possibly comprehend."

"Then, was it a mistake to have left him at Clivus? It all started at Clivus."

Oralia affectionately covered her husband's hand with one of hers. "No, Gaios. It could not have been any other way. And if it will make Farrenthias happy, I think we should encourage him to pursue whatever is in his heart." Oralia forced a smile from her pale, drawn face. "We should be happy that he has found a brother in Trulius. Is Trulius not the second son you have always wanted? He is brave, full of adventure, and very bright. And more importantly, he loves Farrenthias."

Lord Gaios chuckled. "Cerudotus tells me that Trulius was incorrigible at Clivus and that he and Farrenthias could not be more different. Yet, they were inseparable at Clivus, and they appear to be inseparable now."

"I am not surprised," Oralia said. "Trulius is also quite handsome. He has not been here one complete day and already the maidens who have seen him speak of nothing else. Even Erisa and Clisa are quite struck by him." Oralia lowered her eyes and grew pensive. "I suspect that one day Trulius will marry and start a family."

Her voice dropped to a whisper. "I fear that Farrenthias may never marry, though many maidens have their eyes on him as well."

Lord Gaios always respected his wife's instincts and not just her motherly instincts. She had an uncanny ability to understand people, what motivated them and what was deep in their hearts. She had correctly warned him that Farrenthias was never going to want to leave Clivus, as long as they wanted him to stay there. "What are you telling me, Oralia? Are you telling me that our son will choose his books over taking a wife and having his own family? Is that what you are trying to tell me?"

Oralia remained quiet for a long moment. "I suppose that no man is immune from love," she finally said, "but I am beginning to understand more and more men like Cerudotus and men like those that Farrenthias met at Clivus. They may one day love a woman, but there is really no room in their lives for such a love. Consequently, they do not desire to have families of their own, and there is something else."

Lord Gaios raised an eyebrow and stared at his wife. "There is more? Why, you have already shattered my heart with such thoughts about our son."

"Do you not see, my lord, that men like that only really understand each other? It is as if they build emotional walls around themselves, emotional walls that none of us can pierce or even begin to fully understand. Only they truly understand why they choose to abandon everything in their lives in order to pursue the goals they set for themselves."

Lord Gaios sighed sadly. "What you are telling me is that in time our son will even forget us, his family?"

Oralia tapped her husband's hand. "No, my lord, Farrenthias is too good a son for that to happen, but what I do believe is that we will understand him less and less and must learn to simply love him."

"It sounds as though you have thought this all out," Lord Gaios said.

Oralia gripped her husband's hand and squeezed it tightly. "All I know," she whispered, "is that this will never ever be his permanent home again."

Fifty-Seven

"Judea is in full revolt against the Romans," Ya'ir said. He walked briskly through the crowded streets of Jerusalem with Ezri and Abiel struggling to keep in step with him. "The rebel army manages a victory here and there, but I am afraid that it is like a tiny dog trying to keep a lion out of its yard. He sighed bitterly. "It is only a matter of time before the Romans unleash their full strength and sack Jerusalem." He slackened his pace and turned to his companions. "And yet, we continue to argue and fight amongst ourselves. Clearly you can see that Jerusalem is in utter chaos."

"You speak of the zealots, who will kill anyone who gets in their way in their plight against the Romans," Ezri said, "And I suppose that the Sadducees and the Pharisees will never settle their philosophical differences," Ezri said.

Ya'ir stopped momentarily and gripped the arm of Ezri. "Have a look."

A cloud of smoke was rising from somewhere in the direction of the temple.

"Another skirmish," Abiel said. "Since Ezri and I arrived we have witnessed one skirmish after another."

"Unfortunately, they have become quite common," Ya'ir said.

"Jerusalem has a history of violence," Ezri said, "but I do not believe I have ever witnessed anything like this."

"What will become of Jerusalem?" Abiel said. "What will become of the temple?"

"Listen to me, my dear friends," Ya'ir said. He started walking again. "On my return to Jerusalem I convinced the Great Sanhedrin that we must prepare for the inevitable collapse of Jerusalem. Because of my father's activities with the Christians, there were many Sadducees who did not trust me, but in the end they are more concerned with preserving the temple writings and treasures than the religious beliefs of those who disagree with them. It also helped that my brother, Thason, is a brilliant architect. Therefore, I was given authority over a plan to construct a tunnel system beneath the holy temple, and night and day Thason and his men have worked to dig those tunnels and prepare the temple for its inevitable doom. No matter what happens to the temple, it will not be easy to find all of the tunnels that have been constructed beneath its floors. The ground beneath the temple is a fortress of hidden secrets."

"Amazing," Ezri whispered. "Brilliant and amazing."

Ya'ir led them down a narrow street. On the other side of the street a group of zealots marching in the opposite direction stared at them.

"Why do they stare at us?" Abiel asked nervously. "Can they not see that we carry no weapons? Can they not see that we are harmless?"

"Keep your voice down," Ya'ir said, "and make eye contact with no one. These days everyone is looked upon with suspicion. The Romans have many spies among our people as do the Zealots."

"Where do Christians gather in these troubling times?"

Ya'ir looked at him. "You will soon find out. My father has become very generous with his house. You will also get to greet Andreas. He is staying in one of the inner rooms of the house."

"Excellent!!" Abiel said. "How is he doing?"

"I last saw him three weeks ago and he was not doing very well," Ya'ir said. "He was not eating well, but seeing you will surely bring a smile to his face."

"You say you have been out of the city for three weeks?" Ezri asked.

Ya'ir nodded. "I traveled north to Damascus and south to Petra and visited every city and village in between, giving encouragement to our people, telling them not to fear the Romans but to prepare for the worst."

They turned into another narrow street that was crammed on both sides with simple houses. At the end of the street a small group of men were gathered next to the double doors of a courtyard.

The men greeted Ya'ir and his companions and parted to let them pass. More men were gathered in the courtyard. Some of the men sat on benches and others stood around a pair of large oak trees. A few sat on sparse, yellow grass. Jishu stood with a group of men who were at the entrance to the house. He was thin and his face was full of deep lines. His hair was to his shoulders and his beard was cropped close to his chin.

His eyes lit up when he saw Ezri and Abiel in the company of Ya'ir. "Dear friends," he said. "How good it is to see you." He embraced them. "It will surely bring much joy to Andreas to see you." Jishu bent his head slightly toward Ya'ir. "He has been asking for you. But, before you go in to see him, I think you will want to hear what I have to say to our brothers. We were about to begin our discussions."

"Of course," Ya'ir said. "I, too, bring news from Thason, but for now, only for your ears."

"And so I imagined," Jishu said. "Your brother risks his life daily working in those tunnels with his crew of loyal men." He paused to think. "Perhaps not in this lifetime, but someday his work will be highly recognized as will your work and the work of your companions." He turned his attention to the men who were scattered throughout the grounds. "Come, my brothers, gather around me and hear what I have to say." He grew solemn and waited until all the men had formed a tight circle around him. "My brothers, you see for yourselves what has become of Jerusalem," he began. "Well, matters are about to get desperate. A few days ago Vespasian's new legions avoided a well-planned trap and destroyed a rebel army. Even as we speak Vespasian and his son Titus march across our lands towards Jerusalem. No doubt he seeks to avenge the victory the zealots achieved over Cestius Gallius and his troops in the battle of Beth-Horon."

The men turned to one another and broke into loud private conversations. Jishu lifted a hand to silence them. "My advice to you, my brothers, is that those of you who have families should consider leaving the city, before the Romans arrive to retake it. When the battle for Jerusalem commences, it will not be safe for anyone."

One man near the front said, "If we all go in different directions what will become of us, Jishu? What will become of those of us who wish to continue to abide by the words of Yeshua?"

"Ah," Jishu said. "You must think with better foresight, my dear brother. By going in different directions you spread the teachings of the master. Seek out new acquaintances and teach them what you have learned here in Jerusalem. Even when it is safe to return, you may decide that you will stay where you are. You may decide that you have found a new home."

"Perhaps," another man said, "but we have not heard from Cephas in months. Andreas is ill, and the words of Paulous confuse us. I have heard that in Corinth and other cities he has claimed that Yeshua rose from the dead. That is the first I had heard of such a claim."

The men again turned to one another and noisily questioned one another and discussed other rumors they too had heard.

"My brothers," Jishu said, raising both hands to quiet them. "I understand your confusion, but remember, the men who actually walked with Yeshua, men such as Cephas and Andreas, have never spoken to you about such matters. Instead, they tried to teach you the messages of love, compassion and forgiveness that Yeshua taught. Paulous means well. Do not judge him harshly."

"Then," a man said, "you disagree with what Paulous has said?"

The room erupted into loud whispers, and Jishu turned to Ya'ir when Ya'ir placed a hand on his shoulders. He and Jishu had had many private discussions about Paulous. Paulous had begun to preach not just to Hebrews, but to non-Hebrews as well, and he had indeed attributed many miracles to the rabbi.

"Allow me to speak, Father," Ya'ir said. He raised his hands. "My friends, as you well know, I have devoted my life to the pursuit of wisdom. I have studied the words of many wise men from as far as the Far East, and in my travels I encountered great masters who could indeed perform deeds that defied explanation. Perhaps Yeshua possessed such gifts. I do not know. What I do know is that the world is full of diversity. Do not fear it. Embrace it. There is much diversity in knowledge. Do not blind yourself by your own beliefs or the beliefs of others. Possessing knowledge means not being afraid of truths and of understanding that there will be many times when you must indeed question the beliefs of others as well as your own beliefs." He stepped back and nodded at Jishu.

"Go now, my brothers," Jishu said. "Make your plans and may you and your families be safe."

The courtyard grew quiet as the men began to leave. Jishu turned to Ya'ir. "Tell me, Ya'ir. You saw Thason today?"

"I spent the morning with him, Father, before I met with Ezri and Abiel. He has made much progress. He tells me that soon he will show me a secret entrance to the tunnels, an entrance that is not at the temple."

Jishu gripped the forearm of Ya'ir and smiled. "Excellent. Your brother is a very clever architect."

"It will take a great deal of persistence and luck to find the treasures that he has buried down there."

"I believe you," Jishu said. "But, nothing in this world can be kept a secret forever. Sooner or later word of the hidden treasure will spread, and the Romans will no doubt try and find it as will many others."

"No doubt," Ya'ir said with a sigh.

"Ah, but I have kept you from greeting Andreas. Go and take our friends to see him. Sesdia is inside. She is waiting for you."

Sesdia had not yet reached fifteen years of age, and yet she was intelligent and mature beyond her years. She was petite and delicate yet oddly strong, and each time Ya'ir laid eyes on her she reminded him of his younger sister, who had died giving birth to Sesdia. Worse, a few months before her mother's death, Sesdia's father had been killed in an argument with a Roman soldier.

"Uncle," Sesdia cried, seeing Ya'ir at the door. "I saw you in the courtyard. How good to see you." She embraced him and also welcomed Ezri and Abiel also with hugs. "I have told Andreas that you had arrived, Uncle. He is waiting for you."

"Then let us not keep him waiting," Ya'ir said. He paused. "It smells delicious in here."

"Fresh bread," Sesdia said. I just brought it in from the oven. I shall have it ready for you when you are finished visiting with Andreas."

Ya'ir led them down a narrow hallway to a small door. He knocked lightly and then opened the door.

Several oil lamps lit up the small room, which had no windows. One lamp burned dimly on a table next to the cot where Andreas lay. The air was thick with the smell of herbs and other medicines. Ya'ir stepped ahead of the others and approached the bed. The faint flickering light from the lamp danced on the discolored face of Andreas. Ya'ir was astounded. Since the last time he had seen him, his health had declined considerably. He looked like a cadaver. His cheeks were hollow and sunken and his face drawn and discolored. His breathing sounded irregular and raspy.

Ya'ir placed a hand on Andreas's shoulder and the eyes of Andreas slowly opened. At first, his eyes were blank and then a trace of a faint smile formed around the edges of his dry, wrinkled lips.

"Ya'ir," he whispered in a barely audible voice. "You are back."

"Yes, Andreas, and I have brought old friends who wish to see you." He moved to one side and allowed Abiel and Ezri to step forward.

Andreas's eyes widened. "Abiel, Ezri," he whispered. "You have returned from Clivus." He cleared his throat with great difficulty. "Is Erasmus Harel with you?"

"No old friend," Abiel said. "He is in Egypt."

"Egypt?"

"Yes, Andreas," Abiel said. "He went to the Alexandria library."

"I see."

Abiel sat down on a stool that Ya'ir scooted in his direction.

"Then who remained at Clivus?" Andreas asked

Abiel frowned. "I am afraid that we had to abandon Clivus, Andreas. We all left."

Andreas showed no reaction but grew pensive. "You had trouble?"

Abiel looked at Ezri.

Ezri recounted for Andreas everything that had happened, including the sad death of Tavius. "Everyone else made it out alive," Ezri said.

"I shall pray for the soul of your friend," Andreas said, and then he lay quietly for a few moments. "What about your work? What about the scrolls?"

"We have brought some with us, and we shall deliver them to Thason tonight."

Andreas slowly shifted his eyes toward Ya'ir. "Have you seen Thason since your return to Jerusalem? The temple—the work goes well?"

Ya'ir nodded. "The moment I crossed the gates to the city I went straight to see Thason. He and his men have been working non-stop, day and night. The work is almost complete. We are prepared for whatever the Romans do."

"Excellent," Andreas murmured. "Excellent. The Romans will surely destroy it, but everything must remain in the sacred ground. Nothing can be taken away." Andreas grew pensive and then said, "I recall the first time Bartholomaios returned from Armenia. He was excited about having discovered Clivus. He said Armenia was a beautiful country and that he had accidentally discovered a structure that was built in the clouds."

"We were most fortunate that Bartholomaios discovered it," Abiel said. "It served us well for many years."

Andreas slowly reached up with a frail and thin hand and brushed his chin. "Ya'ir spoke about a remarkable child that joined you at Clivus. What happened to him?"

"You speak about Farrenthias Theophilus," Abiel said. "Erasmus Harel told us privately many times that it was no coincidence that such a devoted and brilliant young man happened upon Clivus. Erasmus Harel sent him home to Syria to see his family. But we expect that he will soon join us here in Jerusalem before too long. We believe that he is now one of us."

"Hum," Andreas murmured. "Erasmus Harel is an excellent judge of character. I am pleased that he allowed the young man to join you."

Andreas suddenly eyed Ya'ir with pale and sad eyes. "Every day that you have been gone, I have asked for news about Cephas but no one seems to have heard from him. What are we to think?"

Ya'ir knew how Andreas felt about Cephas. Cephas was like an older brother to those who traveled and studied with the great master Yahweh, and when Andreas learned that he had gone to Rome, he feared that he would never see him again. Nero was an unpredictable brute. He was a man to be feared. At any time he was likely to resume his persecution of Christians.

"Obviously he is too preoccupied to send us word of his well-being," Ya'ir said. "But we must have faith that his trip to Rome has not been in vain."

"Had I not fallen ill, I would have traveled to Rome with him," Andreas said, his voice barely a whisper. "Rome is too big of a city even for one as gifted as Cephas." He gazed at Ya'ir with a knowing frown. "The men who were gathered here, did they speak of Paulous? Did they ask you about him?"

"They did indeed," Ya'ir said.

"What did you tell them?"

"As you and others have requested, I refused to openly criticize him." Ya'ir said. "But you know very well that I am troubled by his impassioned rhetoric. I am equally troubled by our silence about things we know to be true about Yeshua but do not speak about, Andreas."

The wrinkled face of Andreas remained expressionless, but the hurt was evident in his eyes. "Perhaps you are right, Ya'ir. I know how you feel, but not all men are as wise as you, Erasmus Harel, Abiel or Ezri. Paulous is doing what he thinks he must do." He paused and then said, "Man needs laws to live by. He needs principles and Paulous speaks about what he believes Yeshua taught."

"Still," Ya'ir said. "I do not believe that Yeshua intended for his life to be shrouded in so much mystery. But I do understand. At times I believe that man is deaf and blind and that he lacks courage to accept responsibility for his own misdeeds. He would rather attribute his shortcomings to the will of the divine rather than search his own soul and rectify his actions."

Andreas closed his eyes. "There was a time when I thought such talk was too cynical, but now as I lie here so close to death, and with Jerusalem in the brink of ruins, I do wonder what truly lies in the heart of man? Why is it that he is so bent on destroying himself?"

Abiel, who had remained quiet, now spoke in a pensive voice. "I fear that we shall never have the answers to such questions, dear friend."

"Perhaps not," Andreas whispered. "But let us try and be optimistic. We have acquired much written knowledge from all over the world, and devoted young men such as Farrenthias Theophilus will carry our work forward when we are long gone."

Andreas closed his eyes again and this time Ya'ir lightly tapped his hand. "It shall be as you say. Now rest, dear friend. We shall resume our talk tomorrow."

Fifty-Eight

L ord Gaios beamed with delight. Seven days earlier the mourning period for Tavius had ended, and he now sat at a table, with his wife at his side, admiring the three hundred guests who filled the great hall where he usually greeted dignitaries from other lands. As he had promised, the festive gathering was to properly celebrate the life of Tavius and the return of Farrenthias and his friends. Walls had been scrubbed and decorated with ribbons and plaques. Tables and chairs had been dusted and polished, and the stone floors had been scrubbed and also polished.

For the occasion, the women wore their finest linens and silks and whatever extravagant jewels filled their jewelry boxes. Their hair was decorated with ribbons and other glittering accessories. Their skin, which had been carefully oiled and perfumed, glistened in the flickering lights that filled the great hall. The men wore freshly cleaned togas and polished leather sandals. The muscular men wore wide, tight leather belts that accentuated their broad and muscular backs. Music by the finest musicians from Antioch filled the room and vibrated against the walls, and to the delight of the guests, a troupe of lovely maidens graced the center of the room with their dancing.

A cheer rose from the floor and the dancing maidens stopped dancing and joined in the clapping and chanting when Farrenthias and Trulius entered the hall.

Oralia squeezed her husband's arm. "Have a look at how our friends greet Farrenthias and Tessius Trulius," she said. "All eyes have turned to admire them, especially the young maidens."

Trulius wore a long, sparkling, white silk toga. Wound tightly around his thin waist was a wide dark blue girdle embroidered in gold along the edges. His dark hair had been cropped and brushed back. He wore a wide golden bracelet on each wrist. Farrenthias wore a beige toga, and around his waist he wore a purple girdle. Like Trulius, his golden hair had been brushed back, but much to Oralia's amusement rather than dismay, the servants that Oralia had sent to dress them both reported to her that Farrenthias had refused to wear jewelry.

Oralia beamed with pride. "My lord, Cerudotus tells me that Farrenthias made enormous progress with his studies at Clivus. He now speaks languages I have never heard of."

"I am not surprised," Lord Gaios said. "I have learned not to be surprised by anything our son accomplishes."

"I agree," Oralia said. "Yesterday he pulled out a papyrus scroll from a satchel and showed it to me. I was amazed at how well he read and understood it."

"I am aware that the men at Clivus left quite an impression on him. He speaks of nothing else," Lord Gaios said. "What I do find strange is that Cerudotus tells me that those men bestowed a new name on Farrenthias. They have added the name Theophilus to his name."

"Farrenthias proudly told me about that," Oralia said. "He is quite proud of that name."

"I suppose that it is only fitting that those mysterious men would ceremoniously do such a thing," Lord Gaios said. "Unfortunately, I no longer know what Farrenthias believes. There was a time when Greeks were Greeks and Romans were Romans in their beliefs. The Hebrew have their beliefs. Now, new sects are appearing everywhere. Why, Cerudotus tells me that Erasmus Harel, a well-traveled man, even exposed Farrenthias to the philosophy of the East. The philosophy of the East! What are we to make of all that?"

Oralia smiled at her husband and then turned and watched Farrenthias admiringly as he slowly moved through the crowd, stopping often to greet old friends and looking and acting much older than his young years. Physically, he looked nothing like his father. But there was no mistaking the similar mannerisms and gestures. She affectionately caressed her husband's arm. "Farrenthias tells me that you have given him permission to travel to Rome with Trulius and Kemnebi. As I have said, it saddens me to see him go, but it pleases me that you have allowed it. We have a wonderful son who is deserving of our full support, my lord." Oralia's attention was suddenly drawn to the entrance to the hall. Her two young daughters were being escorted in by a group of maidens. Both suddenly stopped, and clinging on to each other, they looked around the room, then froze and then broke into childish giggles. Oralia followed their gaze, and when she saw whom they were staring at, she smiled. It was no surprise that they were staring at the handsome Trulius.

Lord Gaios tapped his wife's hand. "You have the strangest look on your face, Oralia."

Oralia knew her husband's moods well and sensed the opportunity to speak frankly. "I was admiring your lovely daughters, my lord. They are truly beautiful."

Lord Gaios started to speak, but Oralia continued, "Next year they will be thirteen years old. I was fourteen when you and I were married."

Lord Gaios tightened his jaw. "What are you suggesting? Erisa and Clisa are but children. These are different times. At their age you were much more mature."

"Perhaps, my husband. Just the same, I am confident that when the time is right you will choose an appropriate husband for each one of them."

"Bah! I am in no hurry to see my daughters married, especially since I have yet to see a young man worthy of their hand." Lord Gaios glared at his wife, "unless you have spotted two young men who will grow up and love and take care of them as well as I do."

Oralia laughed. "That, my lord is impossible. In the meantime, have a look at how they admire Trulius. They have truly enjoyed having their brother back and his guest. In the last couple of days they have taken extensive walks with Farrenthias and Trulius."

"Trulius is truly a remarkable young man. It pleases me that he and Farrenthias have remained good friends," Lord Gaios said.

"Indeed," Oralia said. "It is unfortunate that they leave the day after tomorrow."

Kemnebi sipped from his cup of wine and then waved the cup in the direction of Trulius. "I do not particularly like wine. Beer, now that is a man's drink, especially when Egyptians brew it," he said. "But I salute Lord Gaios for this excellent feast."

Trulius chuckled. "I must confess to you Kemnebi that the few times that I have tasted wine, well it just tastes like strange sweet water to me. I do not care for it."

Kemnebi laughed. "In a few days when we are home, we shall

drink a Roman beer together. Now tell me, Trulius, are you enjoying yourself?"

Trulius picked a grape from the table and played with it before he put it in his mouth. "Of course I am enjoying myself. I have never seen so many joyous and happy people in my life. He looked at the musicians. "And I did not realize how much I enjoy music."

"Music?" Kemnebi said with a wide grin. "You are enjoying the music? How about the lovely ladies? Are they not the most beautiful things you have ever seen?"

Trulius blushed. He and Kemnebi had never discussed such matters. "What do I know about lovely ladies, Kemnebi?"

"Bah! You shall learn soon enough, my dear child. Why yesterday Farrenthias's two lovely sisters asked me many questions about you, Trulius."

"Ah, they are truly sweet are they not?"

Kemnebi nodded and smiled. "Have a look. They have just entered this great palace and they cannot take their eyes off of you. I can see that you will break many hearts." Kemnebi set his cup down and regarded Trulius with a frown. "Of course, you will have to be careful with this whole business of love and women. Women are so much more clever than a man when it comes to love." Kemnebi raised his cup again and drank from it. "Roman law favors a man, but that is foolish. A woman, if she knows how to do it, can manipulate and toy with a man all she wants, for as long as she wants."

Trulius grimaced. "I do not know what you mean, Kemnebi. "

Kemnebi sipped more wine and chuckled. "Precisely, but you shall learn soon enough."

"I am never going to fall in love," Trulius said. "Men who fall in love are fools."

Kemnebi laughed heartily. "Do you not know that all men at one time or another make fools of themselves, and there are no exceptions."

Trulius suddenly grew serious, "If I may ask, why did you not ever take a wife, Kemnebi?"

Kemnebi stretched back and stared sadly at the golden cup that he held in his hands. "I almost did once. She was a slave girl in your grandfather's house. She was as beautiful as this jeweled cup. Kemnebi looked at Trulius and sighed. "Your grandfather, the wonderful man that he was, saw my interest in her and was going to make her a freed-woman. But…" Kemnebi fell silent and stared at his cup again.

"What happened, Kemnebi?"

Kemnebi cast his eyes down. Even after all these years, the memory was still painful when he talked about it. "One day, on a trip to one of the fountains, she was abducted." He unconsciously clenched a fist. "Rome has always been full of travelers, many in caravans who pass through the city after conducting business. Your father and I suspected that one of those scoundrels took her. We searched Rome for months, but I never saw her again."

"I—I am sorry, Kemnebi. What was her name?"

"Gali." Kemnebi shifted his weight and raised his eyes. "Enough about Gali. In a few days we will be back in Rome and I want you to be prepared for whatever we discover. We have been gone for years." He became pensive. "It is likely that your father was banished from Rome for a period. Perhaps his properties were confiscated and we have no place to return to. I have no idea what we will find, but I want you to be prepared."

Trulius clenched his jaw in anger. "I understand," he said.

Kemnebi gave him an encouraging tap on the hand. "On the other hand, your father is a resourceful man, and even though he rejects the gods, I have always believed that they favor him."

"What about Gianina and Felicia?" Trulius said. "Do you think they are well?"

Kemnebi drank from his cup of wine. "Felicia. Now there is a resourceful woman. In a battle of wits against any man, I would bet my last piece of gold on Felicia. She is a shrewd woman and would let nothing happen to Gianina." He looked in the direction of where Lord Gaios and Lady Oralia sat. Farrenthias had just joined them. "Is it settled? Are Farrenthias and Quanarious coming to Rome with us?"

"They are," Trulius said, also looking at Farrenthias. "I wish Farrenthias would stay in Rome with us, but he has other plans."

"He still plans to go to Jerusalem and look for Ya'ir?" Kemnebi said.

Trulius poured himself a cup of water from a pitcher. "Yes, nothing can keep him from his plans."

"Hum," Kemnebi murmured. "What about Cerudotus?"

"According to Farrenthias Cerudotus is now going to be the main tutor for the his sisters. Lord Gaios wants his daughters educated."

The room suddenly erupted into cheers and people started to clap. Trulius whirled around to see what the commotion was about.

A train of servants started across the room with trays filled with food. The first trays to arrive at the tables had dozens of roasted piglets brushed with oils, spices, and other delicate sauces. Next came roasted wild ducks and other game in marinated wine sauces. Dozens of trays filled with a variety of freshly steamed vegetables followed, along with trays of freshly baked loaves of bread. Another set of servants arrived with trays filled with every variety of fruit and nuts and imported cheeses.

"I have never seen so much food," Trulius said.

"The Greeks are excellent cooks," Kemnebi said. "We are certainly going to have a feast."

"Trulius!" Farrenthias said, approaching the table. "There you are. One moment you were beside me, and the next moment you were gone. Come, Father wishes to see you and Kemnebi before you start your meal."

The music suddenly grew louder, and more dancing maidens, dressed in loose thin dresses, took to the floor and began to dance. Trulius and Kemnebi followed Farrenthias through the crowd and into a side room that Trulius had not noticed before. The room was small but fixed with beautiful couches and chairs. Lord Gaios was standing next to a couch where Lady Oralia sat along with Erisa and Clisa. On the opposite side of the couch stood Cerudotus, with his hands clasped behind his back. Lord Gaios held a bundle in his hands.

"My lord," Oralia said, "Do not take too long, the food has been served."

"Yes, of course," Lord Gaios said. "Trulius," Lord Gaios said, his face beaming with delight. "Tell me what you think about this?" He handed the bundle to Trulius.

Trulius unwrapped the bundle and gasped. It was a sword, sheathed in a beautiful sculptured leather sheathe. Its handle was carved in gold. A single, dark blue, hexagonal gem surrounded by diamonds adorned the end of the handle. "My lord," Trulius cried, "I have never seen a more magnificent sword."

"Bah, you have seen nothing yet, Trulius. Go on, pull it out and see how it feels," Lord Gaios said.

Trulius slipped the sword out of its sheathe and sliced the air with it. It was light yet balanced. It felt much better than any sword he had ever held in his hands. He inspected its sharp blade closely.

It was very thin but looked solid. "Only a man as great as you, Lord Gaios, is worthy of such a thing of beauty," Trulius said.

Lord Gaios laughed. "When I was about your age it was given to me by my grandfather. I learned that he had it made especially for me when I was born. I used it sparingly for a few years then put it away. I had it completely restored when Farrenthias was born." Lord Gaios looked at Farrenthias. "Farrenthias has asked that I give it to you. And, I could not be more proud to do that. It is yours, Trulius."

Trulius lowered the sword and stared at Lord Gaios. Then he looked at Farrenthias, who quietly nodded. Trulius shook his head. "Sire," he said looking at Lord Gaios again. "I cannot accept such a valuable treasure, such a valuable heirloom that belongs in your family."

Farrenthias gripped the arm of Trulius. "It is staying in our family, Trulius. Are we not brothers?"

Trulius swallowed hard. "We, we certainly are, Farrenthias. But I am unworthy of such a sword."

"Nonsense!" Lord Gaios cried. "You most certainly are. It is settled. The sword is yours. Now, I am very hungry and the food is getting cold. Strap on your sword and let us go and eat."

Trulius turned to Lady Oralia, and she nodded. "I am happy that Gaios chose to give it to you, Trulius," she said. "And I agree with Farrenthias, the sword is staying in the family."

"I assure all of you," Trulius said, "that I will always cherish it and wear it with pride."

Cerudotus cleared his throat. "I, too, agree that Trulius is most worthy to wear such an heirloom and I also agree with you—I am famished. Shall we return to the banquet room and fill our bellies with all that magnificent food?"

"Indeed," Lord Gaios said. "There is much food to eat." He beckoned his wife and daughters to his side. "Shall we go? I have a feeling that this is going to be a long night."

Fifty-Nine

Marcellius opened his eyes and stared into the dark eyes of a bearded man whose face was inches from his nose.

"You are awake," the physician said. He turned to a young boy who was seated on the floor of the tent. "Summon Septimus at once. Tell him Marcellius is awake."

The young boy jumped to his feet and flew out of the tent without saying a word.

"How do you feel?" the physician asked Marcellius.

Marcellius felt the surprisingly soft hands of the physician probe his eyes and ears and nose.

"I have an excruciating headache, otherwise I feel fine," he said.

"You suffered a severe blow to the head, but there has been no fluid leaking from your ears or nose and there has been no vomiting. Those are good signs that there is no brain injury. How is your vision?"

"I can see fine. I suppose I was blindsided with a mallet."

"I understand it was a sledge hammer," the physician said. "You are fortunate that it did not crack your skull. He lifted a finger and moved it

369

from side to side in front of Marcellius. "Follow my finger without moving your head." The physician nodded approvingly. "Any blurriness?"

"No." Marcellius attempted to raise himself but winced with a pain. He looked down at himself. He right side was covered with bandages. "What is this?"

"The head blow was not the only injury you suffered," the physician said. "You have two fractured ribs."

"I have two broken ribs?" Marcellius said angrily.

"Two broken ribs," the physician repeated, "and I suggest that you let them heal properly before you return to the field."

"How long will that take?"

"Three to four weeks."

The flap of the tent flew open and Septimus and Amatius stepped into the small cubicle.

"Marcellius," Septimus said. He removed his helmet and held it under his arm. "How do you feel? Amatius tells me that it took two of those devils to take you down."

"I feel fine." Marcellius winced with pain as he scooted himself to his elbows.

Septimus looked at the physician. "How long is it going to take for those ribs to heal?"

"My advice is that he stay away from wearing armor at least for three weeks."

"Bah, broken ribs are nothing," Marcellius said. "Give me a day or two and I shall be ready to ride."

Septimus laughed but ignored him. "What about his head injury?" he said to the physician.

"It could have been worse. I do not believe he has suffered any brain injury. The gash at the back of his head should heal properly. I was very careful closing the wound. There will be no scarring."

Septimus smiled. "So there you have it, Marcellius. You must give yourself time to heal. Amatius tells me you are fortunate to be alive."

"I was not far from you," Amatius said. "I saw you going down and rushed to help, but somehow, even after you were struck in the ribs and head, you managed to kill one of your attackers. I took care of the other one."

Septimus shifted his helmet from one arm to the other. "In any case, we won an excellent victory because of your brilliant assessment of the situation and your brilliant strategies. First, you correctly anticipated the trap the rebels set for us and then when you attacked, you left a pile of rebels all over the field. It is quite apparent that your skills as a field commander have not diminished in the least. You are a born soldier, a born leader."

"Our victory was decisive," Amatius said. "What was left of their army scattered into the hills."

"What now?" Marcellius asked.

Septimus's expression became serious and dark. "We have disturbing news from Rome. The city is on the brink of internal chaos. Word has reached Vespasian that the days of Nero are numbered. There are multiple plots to dethrone him."

Marcellius stared at Septimus. He had never cared for Nero and it was only a matter of time before his bizarre antics caught up with him. But this was worrisome. With every change in power, there was always the potential for civil unrest and civil unrest in Rome placed a strain on military campaigns abroad. "If there is a change in power, I hope it happens quickly. Fighting in Rome is not good for our troops."

"I agree," Septimus said, "And I will tell you this, Vespasian commands deep respect from his men and already some of them are calling for him to return to Rome at once and claim the crown."

"I have always suspected that given the right circumstance the crown of Rome was his for the asking," Marcellius said. "It sounds as though that moment has arrived."

"I also agree with that," Septimus said. "But in the meantime, you know very well that as professional soldiers our loyalty is to the crown of Rome, no matter who wears it."

"What happens now?" Marcellius said.

"Vespasian has thanked his troops but advised them that at the moment it would be premature for him to abandon his post and return to Rome. So, he is continuing his campaign against the rebels. He has ordered me to join Titus, who is flanking Vespasian to the south as he marches across the country crushing any opposition to Rome."

"When are you leaving?" Marcellius said.

Septimus placed his helmet back on. "I leave first thing in the morning. I shall expect you to join me when you are well enough to ride. I leave five hundred men at your command, Marcellius." He looked at Amatius. "Of course, Amatius will stay with you. He will remain your second in command."

"I shall be at your side in less than two weeks," Marcellius said.

"I trust that will happen." Septimus said. He turned to leave and then paused. "Couriers are on their way to Rome with written details of our battles. Your name is not only completely restored, it is eminently displayed next to that of Vespasian and Titus." He bowed his head slightly in salutation and then left.

Sixty

After two weeks at sea and with stops at Myra, Salmone in Crete, Malta, Syracuse, and Rhegium, they finally arrived at Puteoli, and the moment Trulius set foot on Italian soil, he was like a man possessed. Unlike the first time they had been at Puteoli when he had been a child in the care of Kemnebi, Trulius now took charge. He walked with a purpose ahead of Kemnebi and Farrenthias. Only Quanarious kept up with him by nearly running beside him. The morning was still hours away and it was very dark. Still, a handful of merchants greeted the ship. With lanterns dangling from their tired hands, some offered to lead them to an inn, while others offered to sell them food to eat.

"Horses," Trulius said to a man who carried a basket full of confections. "Where do we buy horses?"

The man shot him a puzzled look. "At this hour?" he said. "Impossible. You will not find anyone awake to sell you horses." He raised his lantern to have a better look at Trulius, and he saw the wild expression on his face. He then turned to look at the others. "Ah, you are all exhausted but in quite a hurry. No doubt you are on your way to Rome." He lowered his lantern and in the darkness he brushed his chin. "Perhaps there is something I can do for you. Follow me."

The merchant banged at the door of a small house, located one street from the docks. "Bolano!" he shouted. "Wake up you lazy imbecile. I bring you customers."

He banged on the door repeatedly until at last the door slowly opened, and a sleepy man peaked out of the house. The merchant raised his lantern so the man could see his face.

"I thought I recognized your voice, Bolano," the man said. "Are you mad? Do you realize what time it is? Do you not sleep?"

"Sleep? Bah! I bring you four good customers who want to buy four stallions from you, and I expect a good commission. Now get dressed and meet us at your stables."

Kemnebi placed his hand on the mane of the last of the four horses and nodded. "They are good animals." He looked at the owner. "They look slightly underfed, but they are good horses."

The owner of the stables yawned and brushed his eyes. "Do we have a deal?"

"We have a deal," Kemnebi said. He reached into this money purse and paid the man.

Trulius immediately helped Farrenthias and Quanarious mount their horses and within minutes they were riding out of the city and on their way to Rome.

Before the dim lights of Puteoli vanished behind them, Trulius looked back and recalled the terrible experience aboard the ship and vaguely recalled being lowered down from the ship while they made their escape. But that was now part of his past. He quickened his pace. "Kemnebi," he said. "If we ride straight without stopping, we will reach the house by nightfall."

"And so it shall be," Kemnebi said. "I am as anxious as you are to reach the house."

Trulius set the pace and it was fast. Armenia had been beautiful but so was the Italian countryside. The morning came and went, and in every direction that Trulius turned, he saw trees and vast green valleys that looked as if they had been groomed. The sky, a clear gray that threatened a slight rain, added to the beauty of the region. All this beauty is what Trulius remembered and missed. They rode mostly in silence, and by late in the evening, the green hills that surrounded the back of his house came into view. Amid his jubilation a sudden wild fear seized Trulius. What if the house had been sold? What if they had to search not just for his father but also for Gianina and Felicia? Unaware that he had slowed down, Trulius suddenly became aware that Farrenthias was riding beside him.

"You look pale, Trulius," Farrenthias said. "Have faith that you shall soon find that all is well at your house." Farrenthias smiled at him. "Will it so, Trulius. Abandon any doubts you might have."

"Faith," Trulius repeated. "You know very well how I feel about faith, Farrenthias."

"I am aware," Farrenthias said, "that you believe that people who petition the heavenly bodies for help are weak and uninformed. Nevertheless, I cannot help but to believe that there is a divine hand in all this beauty that surrounds us. "

Trulius frowned. "I must admit that, at times such as these when I have much on my mind about what my family has gone through, well, it is easy to believe in divine intervention," Trulius said. "Now hurry, we are practically there." He increased his pace again and soon they were on the road that led directly to the house. When Trulius reached the arch that marked the beginning of his father's property, he abruptly stopped to wait for the others. He nervously studied the grounds and was struck by what he saw. The statues that aligned the path to the house looked to be in perfect condition. Beyond the statues the trees that he and Gianina had climbed as children looked exactly as he remembered them. They were a dim yellow but otherwise full of life, with their long branches full of leaves.

Kemnebi reached Trulius. "We are not expected," he said, "so we must proceed cautiously from here, lest we startle Felicia and Gianina, if they are indeed home."

They rode slowly down the path, and because winter was fast approaching, the gardens were not full of vibrant flowers. But otherwise, the grounds were groomed and clean. Stone benches were upright and in excellent condition. Water gushed from the large fountain. The house was also in excellent condition. The white walls were clean, the columns sparkled, and not one dark orange tile was missing from the roof.

"I have never seen a more magnificent house," Farrenthias whispered to Trulius.

"Trulius," Kemnebi said. "Have a look." Kemnebi pointed to a second floor window from which a short, thick rope hung to one side of the window. Kemnebi smiled. "Do you see the knot on that rope? It is a sign your father devised. One knot meant that it was safe to enter, two knots meant trouble."

Trulius studied the window again. Clearly there was only one knot on the rope. "Very clever," Trulius said.

"Aside from your father, only myself, your mother and Felicia knew about it." Kemnebi said.

"You and Farrenthias go on into the house," Kemnebi said. "Quanarious and I will put the horses in the stables."

Trulius dismounted and walked to the front door of the house. He found himself terribly excited but oddly nervous. He could not believe that just beyond the door he was going to find Gianina and finally see her after all these years. He placed his hands on the thick, shiny brass door handles, and closed his eyes. An image of his beautiful mother standing at this very spot, calling out his name, came to him. He also recalled running out of these doors many times at the sound of his father's horse, and of being tossed into the air repeatedly by his father until his belly ached from laughter. Trulius opened his eyes and looked at his hands. He pulled down on the handles. They were locked, but that was not a problem. He removed his dagger and slid its tip inside the door and pried the wooden lock until it opened. He pushed the door open and was immediately struck by the pleasant aroma coming from inside the house. "Come on, Farrenthias," he said. "We are home."

"Incense," Farrenthias said. "Myrrh," he whispered. "Erasmus Harel's favorite scent. Remember how we helped him make it from gum resin and spices?"

Trulius bit his lower lip. "We never burned incense in this house before. Who would be burning it now?"

He cautiously stepped in. The house was dark, but enough light spilled in from the roofless atrium so that he was able to see that everything was exactly as he had last seen it. Nothing had changed, not the furniture, not the curtains, not the rugs, not the life-size statues, not the figurines, and not the vast pool. Moreover, the white marble floor sparkled as if it had just recently been polished.

A dog barked loudly and a lamp suddenly flickered on the other side of the pool. Its dim light outlined the slim figure of the young woman who was holding it. "How dare you break into this house!"

she said in a frightened yet firm voice. Beside her a large dog barked wildly, ready to charge, but she held the dog back with a tight leash.

Trulius held his breath and stared in disbelief at the slender dark outline of her figure. Her head was covered and her dress was long, and even though she had been a child when he had left, there was no mistaking her voice, or the manner in which she spoke. After all these years, finally, standing across from him was the little girl who had run around these halls chasing him and whom he had thought of every day of his life at Clivus.

"Gianina!" Trulius said. He took a step forward, but Gianina drew back. "Gianina," he repeated. "Do not be afraid. It is I, Trulius."

The dog stopped barking, and there was a moment of silence. And then, in a voice that quivered with emotion, Gianina said, "Trulius? Trulius, is it really you? It cannot be!"

"It is me, Gianina," Trulius said. "Is that Pharaoh that you are holding?"

Gianina looked down at Pharaoh. Pharaoh was staring anxiously at Trulius. His tail was wagging wildly, and he was trying desperately to pull away from Gianina. Gianina released him, and Pharaoh charged at Trulius and jumped into his arms.

Gianina drew her breath. "Trulius!" she cried.

Trulius walked slowly around the pool, barely able to contain his excitement. "Gianina," he said. "I am so happy to see you. Since I left Rome I have thought about you every day." He reached her and she lifted the lamp to his face. A flood of tears filled her eyes and she staggered forward. Trulius caught her and caught the lamp that nearly slipped from her hands. She was fragile and lithe but surprisingly strong. She composed herself quickly and Trulius stared at her almost in disbelief. Her eyes sparkled and her cheeks were thin, her hair was long and neatly tied to one side. She was stunning.

"Gianina," he said. "You are so beautiful!" He looked at the water. "Do you recall the last time you and I swam in this pool? We took all our clothes off, and it took three servants to fish us out of the water."

Gianina blushed. "I remember. I have prayed every day to the gods for your safe return, Trulius, and for the return of your father and Kemnebi."

"Have you news of him?" Trulius cried.

"He is safe, Trulius. Mother shall give you the details. She will be so happy to see you." She suddenly turned to look at Farrenthias, who had remained quietly in the background. "But where is Kemnebi?"

Trulius looked at Farrenthias. "Farrenthias!" he cried. "Come around the pool." He turned to Gianina. "Kemnebi is putting the horses away." He waved a hand in the direction of Farrenthias. "Gianina," he said, "this is my good friend Farrenthias Theophilus. He is the brother I always wanted."

"Hum," Kemnebi murmured. "Septimus has left his post to join the campaign in Judea?"

Trulius, who was petting Pharaoh looked at Felicia then at Kemnebi. "Now what? How will we learn news about Father?"

Felicia set a bowl of dates, apples, and grapes on the table. "There is one man who might be able to help us," Felicia said, "Septimus's father-in-law, Atenuar. He has a villa at the northern outskirts of Rome."

"Atenuar," Kemnebi said, "but of course, he would know. I shall have to pay him a visit tomorrow."

"Indeed," Felicia said, "He has been gone for months but returned just a week ago. The talk at the Forum is that he is hosting a group of senators and dignitaries beginning tomorrow afternoon. The last time he did that as many as fifty men spent three drunken nights at his villa."

"Then I shall have to pay him a visit before they all start losing their minds," Kemnebi said.

Trulius leaned toward Kemnebi. "Let me go, Kemnebi," he said. "It is time that Father's friends and enemies know that he has a son who will speak for him."

"If you like I can go with you," Quanarious said.

"No, Quanarious," Trulius said. "Kemnebi might need you here."

Kemnebi looked at Trulius in surprise. "I do not know what to say. There might still be danger out there for you and you are asking me to let you go by yourself?"

"I am no longer a child," Kemnebi. "I am not afraid to venture into the city without you. It is time that I am seen alone."

Kemnebi unconsciously looked at Felicia who was smiling back at him.

"I think that Trulius has a point, Kemnebi," Felicia said. "Everyone in Rome should know that Marcellius's son has grown into a brave and handsome young man, worthy of the house of Marcellius."

"Besides," Trulius said. "I will not be completely alone. Farrenthias will go with me. It will give me an opportunity to show him the city. What do you say, Kemnebi?"

Kemnebi frowned deeply. "It is odd," he said. "We left for your protection and now you wish to venture off on your own."

"Not so odd," Trulius said with a wry grin. "I am no longer a child. I can take care of myself."

Kemnebi sighed. "Yes, I no longer doubt that. Nevertheless, be careful. Rome has always been full of mischievous characters."

Kemnebi turned abruptly to Felicia. "Now that we have settled that, tell us Felicia how did you manage to keep this house free from the scoundrels in Rome?"

Felicia pressed her thin lips together and stared at her hands while she thought a moment. "Well, where do I start? It was not easy, Kemnebi," she said. "Fortunately, Marcellius has always enjoyed the fierce loyalty of a few brilliant men. We owe a great deal to Farron, Marcellius's accountant and banker, and the merchant Canario. Together they helped me maneuver accounts and conceal property from Nero's bankers, tax collectors, and as you say, scoundrels." Felicia shook her head. "We would only move merchandise in the middle of the night or before dawn to keep Nero's spies from discovering what we were doing. One day we managed to empty a warehouse and move the merchandize just hours before Nero's men arrived. Finally, we had enough money to buy the house back from the Greek investor who bought it at auction. It helped that he was an acquaintance of Marcellius."

"I am amazed and pleased," Kemnebi said. "I have always known that both of them are true friends." He stood. "Well, I suppose we should get some rest. We have had a long journey."

Sixty-One

The house of Atenuar was filled with politicians, dignitaries, businessmen, and high-ranking soldiers, and Atenuar knew them all personally. The chatter was loud, and as Atenuar circulated among his guests, he noted that most of the conversations were political gossip. He walked from room to room of his expansive house and made sure that all was going according to his meticulous plans. He had instructed his servants to serve only the finest wines and freshest appetizers. Therefore, trays of fresh oysters, caviar, cheeses, and fresh fruits were stationed throughout the house, and servants circulated among the guests filling their chalices and mugs with wine. Musicians, playing harps and lyres, provided background music. Even Nero had planned to attend, but he lost his voice the previous weekend and had to cancel at the last minute, disappointed that he was not going to be able to sing. Nevertheless, he sent a squire to express his regrets and to read a letter he personally scripted acknowledging the importance of the advice Atenuar always provided to him and how much he esteemed him.

Only one guest particularly annoyed Atenuar. His name was Benaro Sariante. Benaro was neither a politician nor official. Instead, he was the father of Rome's much-heralded wrestler, Fomars Moress Sariante. Fomars was here because Atenuar loved wrestling, as did most Romans. Fomars was loud-mouthed but amusing. Benaro was also loud-mouthed, but unlike his likable son, he was annoying. People generally found him to be obnoxious, as did Atenuar. At the moment, Benaro had a group of senators mesmerized with a wild tale about one of his son's matches. While Benaro talked, Fomars flexed his muscles, and acting like school children, wide-eyed senators poked his muscles as though he were a statue of Mars. Atenuar discreetly shook his head and prayed for the fate of Rome. He stepped into the atrium and paused near the front door.

Guards, many of whom had accompanied the senators, had formed a tight wall across the front door of the house. One of them was engaged in a heated argument with a young man who obviously wanted into the house.

"I do not care what your business is," the guard said. "You are not a guest. Leave. Come back tomorrow or we will throw you and your companion out on the street."

"I should like to see you try," the young man said. "I am asking you kindly to at least announce me to Atenuar. If he will not see me, then I will leave and return another day, but I am not leaving until you let him know that I wish to speak to him on an urgent matter."

Curious, Atenuar weaved his way through the throng of guards until he saw the young man. He was handsome and quite composed for one so young. His companion was not so composed. He looked nervous and frightened, but he stood next to his friend without saying a word.

"What urgent business could you possibly have with me, young man," Atenuar suddenly said. "I have never seen you before."

The young man looked at him. "Sire, my name is Tessius Trulius and this is my companion, Farrenthias Theophilus. I beg your forgiveness for my aggressiveness, but I am the son of Marcellius Kaelus Augustus. I am looking for news of my father, and I am told that you might be able to help me."

Like all of Rome, Atenuar was well acquainted with the banishment of Marcellius to Malta, as well as the tale of the missing son and the rumors of the price on his head that Nestor had placed on him. He expressed surprise. "You are the son Marcellius sent into hiding?"

A flash of fear rippled across the back of Tessius Trulius as the guards scrutinized him with renewed interest. "That is correct, sire," he said, staring back at the guards. "I am he."

"I see," Atenuar said. "I also see that you are a brave young man, coming here as you have. Well, I do indeed have news of your father." He motioned for the guards to step away from Trulius and Farrenthias. "Follow me to my quarters," he said.

Trulius gripped the sides of the chair in which he sat and edged forward. "What?" he cried, his face flushed with disbelief. "But how is that possible? My father was convicted and then exiled, and now what is it that you say?"

Atenuar lifted his empty chalice in the direction of an attentive servant who quickly filled it with red wine. He then cast his eyes on Trulius. "It is exactly as I say, young one. Your father is no longer in exile. He is now a commander in the Roman army." Atenuar chuckled to himself as though delighted by the effect his words were having on Trulius. "And there is more." Atenuar sipped from his chalice of wine and then set it down and crossed his hands in front of him. "It appears that your father has already distinguished himself in the field of battle. He anticipated an ambush and foiled it for the enemy. He was even wounded, but do not worry it was not serious. What that means is that the next time he sets foot at the Forum he will no doubt be besieged and congratulated by well-wishers who will fall over themselves just to touch his cloak and hear about his heroics in battle."

Trulius fell back in his chair shaking his head. "I am speechless!" he said. He looked at Farrenthias. "Farrenthias, did you hear that?"

Farrenthias nodded enthusiastically. "That is extraordinary news, Trulius. You should be very proud of your father."

Trulius stared at Atenuar with a blank expression on his face. His mind raced in every direction, as he tried to think about the consequences of this news. "Tell me, sire," he said. "Do you know how long Septimus intends to keep Father in his army?"

"That is difficult to say," Atenuar said, "but if I were to guess, it cannot be less than a year."

Utterly disappointed, Trulius barely whispered, "I was afraid of that." He slowly rose to his feet. "Well, sire, we have taken enough of your time. Farrenthias and I should let you get back to your guests."

"Bah," Atenuar said, reaching for his chalice and also getting to his feet. "While it is true that as the host I should mingle with my guests, it is also true that most of the men in my house are quite content with the excellent wine that I am serving them and with the excellent food that has been prepared for their enjoyment. They do not need me to mingle with them."

He gripped the arm of Trulius affectionately and then released it. "Now that you know about your father, what do you intend to do?"

Trulius thought a moment then looked at Farrenthias. "Hum, in a few weeks I was to see my friend Farrenthias off on a ship to Jerusalem, now I think that I will accompany him and then go and search for Father."

Atenuar shook his head with a smile on his face. "I am not surprised. Begin your search in Caesarea, that is where Vespasian has his headquarters." He walked to the door and opened it. The room filled with the noise of laughter and chatter coming from the rest of the house. "We have plenty of food," Atenuar said. "I will not hear of you leaving my house without enjoying a full plate of food."

"Thank you, sire," Trulius said. "But I think Farrenthias and I should get going."

"Very well," Atenuar said. He led them out of the room but abruptly stopped. A crowd was gathered around Fomars, making it impossible to move. They cheered when Fomars lifted a young dancing girl and twirled her in the air. Trulius ducked out of the way and attempted to push Farrenthias out of the way, but was too late. The girl's legs struck Farrenthias, and Farrenthias stumbled backwards into Benaro knocking a cup of wine out of his hands.

"Imbecile!" Benaro shouted. "Look what you've done! I'm drenched with wine. You have stained my toga!" He stared at Farrenthias. "Why, you are not Roman you clumsy fool. You are Greek."

Fomars grabbed Farrenthias by the collar and lifted him off the ground with one hand and backhanded him. "Look what you did to Father's toga, you fool," he said.

Farrenthias tried to free himself, but Fomars held a tight grip on him. "Forgive me, sire," Farrenthias said. Blood seeped from the corner of Farrenthias's mouth. "It was an accident."

Fomars attempted to slap him again but Trulius caught his hand with a powerful grip and stared into Fomar's eyes. "Strike my friend again, sire, and I will break your arm. Now let him go!"

A collective gasp rippled through the room. Fomars turned a deep red and quickly wrestled his hand back from Trulius. He released Farrenthias. "Me apologize? Do you know who I am? I am going to break your little bastard neck."

Atenuar stepped between Trulius and Fomars. "Enough, Fomars!" he shouted. "Are you blind? This was your fault. You should have carried out your little antics outside. Besides, Farrenthias apologized. I shall have one of my servants provide your father with a fresh, dry tunic, and I shall have his cleaned and pressed."

Fomars looked around the quiet room. "Perhaps I did lose my temper and overreacted, but after all, I am quick as a cobra." He pointed a finger at Trulius. "You, you are fortunate that Atenuar stepped in, or I would have broken your little neck in two."

Trulius glared at him. "You, break my neck? I should like to see you try! You are twice my size, but I bet I could teach you a thing or two about wrestling."

A collective gasp rippled across the room again and then there was nervous silence.

"Teach me?" Fomars cried, seething like a wild lion. "Teach me? Let me show you why I rule the wrestling venues of Rome." He charged Trulius, but his father blocked his path, and a group of men helped restrain him.

"Atenuar!" Benaro shouted, while he struggled to pull Fomars back. "I do not know who this young man is, but he has now insulted Fomars twice! I demand that we all step outside and let him stand by his words."

"Yes!" Fomars shouted. "Let us settle this outside!"

"Calm yourself," Atenuar said. He gave Trulius a worried look. "Trulius," he said. "I admire your valor and your willingness to defend the honor of your friend, but I have seen what Fomars has done to his opponents. Some have never walked again." He studied Trulius. "He is older than you, has more experience, and he is about thirty pounds heavier. He could seriously hurt you."

Farrenthias tugged at the sleeve of Trulius. "Please, Trulius," he whispered. "Drop the matter."

Trulius looked at him and then at Atenuar. "Forgive me for the trouble that I have caused, sire, but I cannot believe that this is the Rome that I have returned to, a Rome where loudmouths strike innocent people at their will. Well, this loudmouth needs to be taught a lesson in humility, lest the next time, he might try to strike a woman."

Fomars again charged at Trulius and again a group of men restrained him.

"Very well, Trulius," Atenuar said. "You shall have your wish." He summoned the guards. "Take our guests to the south lawn between the back wall and the pool."

Trulius turned his back to Fomars, who had stripped down to a loincloth and was flexing his heavily muscled physique to loud cheers. Amid the cheers, men began to bet on the outcome of the match. One bet was how long Trulius would last, and another man was taking bets on how many of Trulius's bones Fomars was going to break.

Ashen, Farrenthias whispered to Trulius, "I have never doubted your bravery, Trulius, or your skills. But I must confess to you that I am terrified. He is twice your size. He is the size of an oak tree. He could seriously hurt you. Are you not worried about that?"

Trulius handed his outer tunic to Farrenthias. "Of course I am nervous, but Kemnebi taught me something Father used to say and that is that a man who goes into battle without any fear is a fool. He will be reckless and risk serious injury or death quicker than a man who knows that one wrong move can cost him his life."

"Well said, but you do not have to do this," Farrenthias said. "I would rather endure more insults than see you get hurt."

Trulius looked over his shoulder at Fomars. "And I would rather suffer a broken neck than let a man strike you in my presence."

Farrenthias placed a hand on the shoulder of Trulius and pleaded with him. "Were we not taught at Clivus to forgive? I have forgiven him."

Trulius sighed. "Had he grabbed me by the collar I might have forgiven him too, but as long as I am around no one is ever going to lay a hand on you, Farrenthias, especially a Roman. They have caused me enough grief."

The cheers grew in intensity when Fomars walked to the middle of the circle and beckoned Trulius with the wave of a hand. Trulius clenched his fists, crouched low, and started toward Fomars. He focused on Fomar's eyes, his feet, and his arms, looking for some sign of attack. None gave him a clue of what to expect. Yet, Fomars hurled himself with so much speed and agility and strength that, before Trulius could react, Fomars had easily wrapped an arm around his chest from behind, lifted him off his feet, and slammed him to the ground. Stunned by the blow, Trulius managed one deep breath before Fomars dragged him to his feet and lifted him clean off the ground and discarded him as a child discards a rag doll. Trulius hit the ground hard. Dazed and paralyzed by the pain, Trulius could not move. He became aware of the thunderous cheers for Fomars, and as he struggled to roll over, he caught a glimpse of

Fomars parading around in a circle with his arms lifted high, taunting the crowd to cheer louder. The sight of his arrogance not only incensed Trulius, it reinvigorated him. As he dragged himself to his knees and brushed the dirt and blood from his face, he told himself that this fight was far from over.

Fomars lowered his arms and walked casually toward Trulius, and pointed at him. "You are done!" he cried. "Do you hear me? You are finished!" He tried to kick Trulius, but Trulius pinned his foot with his hands and then wrapped his legs around the legs of Fomars and rolled hard to his left. Surprised by the move, Fomars lost his balance and hit the ground. But Fomars did not stay down long. He quickly jumped to his feet, more embarrassed than hurt, for the crowd had gasped at the sight of him on the ground. Furious, he charged at Trulius. This time Trulius was ready. Just as Fomars got close to him, Trulius somersaulted forward into a handstand and pinned a surprised Fomars by the neck with his legs. Trulius then twisted around hard, and the stunned crowd watched Fomars hit the ground a second time. Fomars angrily slammed a fist into the dirt, jumped to his feet, and like a wild bull, he bolted toward Trulius again.

Trulius was again ready. This time, he jumped into the air with his knees tucked against his chest, and just as Fomars reached him, he fully extended his legs with all of his strength. His feet slammed into Fomar's chest with a powerful blow. Fomars flew backwards and landed hard on his back. Flustered and disoriented, Fomars struggled to his feet and staggered towards Trulius. He swung wildly at Trulius, and when he missed he spun around almost in a full circle in front of Trulius. Trulius grabbed Fomars around the waist from behind and cleanly lifted him high over his head. He then arched his back as far as he could until they both began to fall backwards. A stunned Fomars held out his arm to break the impact of the fall, but with his weight and the force that Trulius was applying, he shouted in agony as his arm hit the ground and shattered beneath him. The crowd fell utterly silent as Fomars lay moaning and holding his arm.

Farrenthias rushed to Trulius, who was on his knees breathing hard, and helped him to his feet. "Trulius," he cried. "Are you alright?" He looked down at Fomars. "I am speechless, Trulius. I saw you practice that move many times with Kemnebi but never thought it was possible for you to apply it to a man his size. And it is such a dangerous move. You could have broken your back, or split your head open. "

Trulius wiped the blood from the side of his mouth and started to answer Farrenthias when a hand fell on his shoulder.

Atenuar shook his head over and over. "I am stunned. I am amazed." He pointed to the crowd of men who were gathered around Fomars. "They are stunned and they are amazed at what they just saw. Have you any idea how many men he has utterly destroyed in the arena?" He frowned and nodded. "Truly, you are of your father's house, young man. You are brave and skilled, just like your father."

"Sire," Trulius said. "I did not mean to break his arm. I trust the people of Rome will forgive me for having hurt their idol." He gave Farrenthias a subtle smile. "In the meantime, if your offer is still good, I am famished."

Trulius impatiently scraped the meat from an oyster shell and placed it in his mouth. He loved oysters but found them tedious to eat. "Yes, yes," he said to Farrenthias, speaking with a full mouth. "I promise you that the next time I will better control my temper." He swallowed and drank water. "But you must admit, the man needed to be humbled."

Farrenthias nibbled on a piece of fish. "Violence settles matters only temporarily, Trulius. Remember that."

Trulius pointed at Farrenthias with another oyster shell. "I promise you that I will never look for trouble. And I will consider turning the other cheek if I am struck, but no one had better strike you in my presence."

Atenuar joined them at the table where they took their meal and smiled. "Ah! But sports spectators are fickle," he said. "Everyone is shouting praises about you, Trulius, even though all bets were against you. Even Fomars sends his congratulations. You have tamed the wild beast. Fortunately three of my guests are physicians. They are setting his broken bones as we speak. What do you say to that?"

Trulius shrugged and picked oysters from Farrenthias's plate. "I was fortunate, sire. I can see why Fomars boasts. He is an excellent wrestler. I would not want to face him ever again."

"I regret that my actions caused so much trouble," Farrenthias said. He pushed his plate toward Trulius.

"You do not strike me as a typical Greek, Farrenthias," Atenuar said.

Trulius gulped some water and set the cup down. "He is not. He has many beliefs."

"I see," Atenuar said. "Rome is known for people of many beliefs. It is the Christians I feel sorry for. Nero has made a sport of terrorizing them."

"It is not right that men be put to death because of their beliefs," Farrenthias said.

Atenuar shrugged his shoulders. "I agree, but mine is only one man's opinion. What can I say about the actions of our Emperor? He governs based on the mood he is in."

Trulius wiped his mouth with a small cloth and stood. "I thank you for the delicious meal, sire, and your hospitality. This time we are really leaving."

"But you must be exhausted after such a difficult match. Stay and rest. Spend the night if you like."

"I thank you for the offer, but no, we must go," Trulius said.

"Very well then," Atenuar said. He summoned a guard and instructed him to get the horses. He then escorted Trulius and Farrenthias to the front portico. "You are two fine young men and you have made a friend in me," he said. He turned to Trulius. "When your father returns, I shall invite him to my house for a good meal and wine, and I sill expect you to accompany him. In the meantime, may the gods travel with the both of you and keep you safe."

Sixty-Two

Trulius exited the back door of the house, with Pharaoh anxiously walking beside him. Like every other morning since he had arrived back in Rome, he paused at the steps overlooking the garden and admired the way the early morning light shimmered across the tops of the maple and oak trees that filled the garden. He had loved the cool and bright mornings at Clivus, but now he realized that mornings here in Italy were no less beautiful.

"Trulius."

Pharaoh barked at the sound of the dulcet voice that was familiar to him. Trulius squinted. Gianina, hidden almost out of sight by the early morning shadows, sat on the ledge of one of the fountains. She waved him over. She wore a light-colored green dress accented with gold lace. Her dark brown eyes sparkled like glistening raindrops on leaves, and her long brown hair, with a dark green ribbon weaved through it, lay against one shoulder. Her olive skin sparkled like early morning dew on the petals of roses. Trulius was still amazed at how beautiful she was. He could hardly believe that she was the little girl that used to climb trees with him.

Unfortunately, this morning her eyes were swollen from crying, and she looked subdued. Trulius knew very well he was to blame. Since his return from Atenuar's house seven days ago, Trulius had announced that he was leaving to Jerusalem with Farrenthias—a week earlier than planned, and that he was not going to return to Rome unless his father accompanied him. He and Kemnebi had quarreled about the matter, but Trulius had made up his mind. He was going to look for his father, and he thought it best that Kemnebi remain in Rome to take care of the women and also to look after his father's business interests. Kemnebi finally agreed, but Gianina was another matter. She was inconsolable.

Gianina forced a smile and stretched out a hand to greet him. "Trulius," she said. "I am surprised to see you out here. Since you leave at dawn I thought you would sleep late this morning."

Trulius caught a subtle whiff of the pleasant fragrance that she wore, and as it always did, it brought a tremendous joy to his heart. "I would not pass the opportunity to spend another morning with you, Gianina," he said. "Besides, I thought I would visit Mother's grave one last time before I leave."

"How very thoughtful of you, Trulius." She lifted a rose from a basket of beautiful flowers that sat beside her. "These are for her," she said. "I collected them this morning."

Pharaoh suddenly nudged Gianina's knee with his nose and she laughed and petted him. "It is a wonder that Pharaoh wants me to pet him. Do you realize, Trulius, that he has not left your side since you arrived? He is going to miss you no doubt as much as I will."

Trulius chuckled and also petted Pharaoh. "Is that true, boy? Are you going to miss me?"

Gianina raised a hand and gently inspected the scratches on the side of his face. "What am I to think, Trulius? You have been here barely a week and all of Rome is talking about you. Mother said that yesterday at the Forum, Kemnebi was stopped more than once by several senators who recounted to him the entire wrestling match you had with Fomars."

"Bah, what I have learned is that men are worse gossips then women," Trulius said.

"It was no small feat what you did," Gianina said. "I have never seen Fomars, but I have heard plenty of stories about him." She shook her head again. "And from what I have heard, he could have hurt you."

The sun peeked over the trees and cast a dim light across the beautiful face of Gianina. Her eyes were moist again. "Promise me that you will be careful, Trulius," she said. "It is a very dangerous world we live in. There is so much violence and there is so much killing." She wiped her eyes. "I never stopped counting the days when you would return and now," she sighed in sadness, "and now you are leaving again. I do not know what I would do if something were to happen to you."

Trulius took her hand into his. "I too could not wait to come back to see you, Gianina. I will be careful, I promise you," he said. "Shall we go?"

Gianina picked up the basket of flowers and slipped her free arm through his. Together they walked out of the garden and into a trail through the trees.

"Your mother loved the garden," Gianina suddenly said. "Do you remember how she would spend hours with us out here?"

Trulius nodded silently. Indeed he remembered many things about his mother. He especially remembered with detail the last time he saw her. It was in the early afternoon of the day before he and Kemnebi had left. She was sitting alone in her chambers brushing her hair when he had peeked in. He had almost talked her into spending the afternoon with him and Gianina out in the garden. Instead, one of the servants interrupted them to tell her that three ladies had come to see her. She cupped Trulius's chin with one of her soft hands and smiled. "You and Gianina go out and play," she said. "Perhaps I will join you later." He never saw her again.

"I remember," he said curtly to Gianina.

Sensing his change in mood, Gianina grew quiet. At a slightly sparse area she stopped next to a tall tree with a wide trunk. Next to the trunk was a vase full of colorful wild flowers. Gianina began to replace the flowers in the vase with the flowers she had brought, and Trulius sat on the ground and rested his back against the tree trunk.

Trulius stared at his mother's grave. He struggled not to cry as he had done the first day that Gianina had brought him here. He watched Gianina quietly work at her flower arrangement.

"I missed you terribly all these years, Gianina," Trulius suddenly said.

Gianina paused and looked at him with tender eyes that watered. "I too missed you terribly, Trulius." She looked around. "We used to climb these trees together—do you remember?"

Trulius smiled. Of course he remembered. How could he ever forget those memories?" We used to have great times out here," he said. "At Clivus, I would think about that almost every day."

He and Gianina turned at the sound of footsteps. Kemnebi and Quanarious were walking towards them.

"Ah," Kemnebi said. "I knew we would find you two here. Felicia has baked fresh bread this morning for breakfast." He sighed as he stood over Servia's grave. "Servia was am amazing woman. She was kind and beautiful. She was also very bright. And she loved both of you very much." He winced. "Memories can be beautiful, but they can also inflict a great deal of pain." He turned to Trulius. "I came to tell you that I could not sleep last night worrying about you leaving without me. I know that I have agreed to your plans, but I was thinking that perhaps Quanarious should go with you and Farrenthias."

Trulius shook his head. "It makes more sense for Quanarious to stay here and help you look after Felicia and Gianina," he said. "Besides, there is much to do around here."

"I knew that would be your answer," Kemnebi said. "I believe that you will find your father. I just hope he does not get angry with me for allowing you to leave alone."

"I shall be fine," Trulius said. "Father will surely see that I am no longer a child and that I can take care of myself."

Quanarious petted Pharaoh. "If you change your mind, Trulius," he said. "I am ready to go with you."

"Not necessary, Quanarious," Trulius said. "As I said, I would feel better if you stayed here to help Kemnebi."

"Very well then," Kemnebi said. "Let us go and have breakfast. Felicia and Farrenthias must be wondering where we are."

Sixty-Three

From a hill overlooking Jerusalem, Trulius watched how guards posted at the gates to the city meticulously searched the satchels and bags of everyone passing though the gates. The lines of people, animals and carts were disorderly and long. The morning traffic was a mess.

"Why are they searching all those people," Farrenthias asked. "What are they looking for?"

"Weapons," an old man said. He had paused next to Trulius and Farrenthias to also observe the commotion. "Of course, if they find anything thing else that suits them they will take it."

"Weapons?" Trulius said, suddenly aware of his prized sword, which hung at his side.

The old man looked carefully at Trulius and then at Farrenthias. "You two young men are not from around here. Well, it happens that three men are fighting for control of the city, John of Gischala, a man by the name of Eleazar, and Simon, son of Giora. Who knows to whom those guards owe allegiance." He looked straight ahead. "If you ask me, it is the Romans whom those scoundrels should be worried about, not the people of Jerusalem." He nodded slightly at Trulius and Farrenthias and then started slowly down the hill.

Trulius removed his satchel and then his cloak. He then removed his sword and tied it across the back of his neck so that it hung straight down his back. He then put his cloak and satchel back on. "Let us go, Farrenthias," he said. "I hope they will still let a Roman into the city."

"Hum," Farrenthias said. "Perhaps those men are more interested in enriching themselves with trinkets than with who enters the city."

Half way down the hill Farrenthias stopped Trulius. "Have a look at these magnificent olive trees, " he said.

Trulius placed a hand on the trunk of one of the trees. "They are magnificent trees," he said. "How old do you suppose they are?"

"They are ancient," Farrenthias said. He looked around. "Do you notice that in spite of all the chaos down there, there is a strange peacefulness up here."

Trulius also looked around. "I had not noticed, but you are right."

"I fear," Farrenthias said, "that if men do not settle their differences they will destroy this beautiful country."

"As far as I am concerned," Trulius said, as he started down the hill again, "man is very good at destroying himself and the cities he builds."

At the bottom of the hill Trulius and Farrenthias joined the end of the line, but in just moments, families with camels, asses, and other animals lined up behind them. The line moved slowly, and just as they nearly approached the gates, two guards roughly dragged several young men out of line and refused to let them into the city despite their loud protests that they were merely carpenters working on a private house.

"To whom is your allegiance?" one of the guards demanded of one of the young men.

"Sire," the young man said, as he lifted his satchel. "Have a look, I carry only my tools. I am a stonemason. My only allegiance is to my family and my work."

The guard pulled a hammer out of the satchel and pretended to inspect it. "This can very well be used as a weapon." He tossed it into a wooden box that was placed near his feet. "Move along," he said. The young man began to protest, but the guard grabbed him by the collar. "Keep talking and you do not get in."

Trulius noticed that he had caught the eye of the same guard. As he approached him, the guard seemed to move out of his way, but suddenly Trulius felt the flat end of a short stick press against his back.

"Stop, you two!" the guard said. He stared at Trulius with a smirk on his face and then he looked at Farrenthias. "What is your business in Jerusalem?" he asked, directing his words at Farrenthias.

"I am here to meet my teacher, and my friend is accompanying me."

The guard turned his attention to Trulius, but with his stick, he tapped the satchel that Farrenthias carried. "What is in the satchel?"

"Scrolls, sire," Farrenthias said.

"Scrolls," the guard repeated. He tapped Trulius on the chest with his stick. "You are Roman are you not?"

"I am," Trulius said.

"Maybe you are a spy."

"I am no spy," Trulius said. "I only recently returned to Rome after a long absence. I would not know who to spy for."

The man chuckled dryly without humor and then reached into Farrenthias's satchel. "Maybe this is some sort of propaganda that you are going to use to insight people into a revolt."

"These are historical documents," Farrenthias said.

"Then perhaps they have some value," the man said. "I have a mind to confiscate them."

"Sire," Farrenthias. "I assure you that they have no value to the man on the street."

"Bah," the guard said. He took a step back. "Go on. You are wasting my time. And you," he said pointing to Trulius, "be careful. Romans are no longer feared around here. They are despised and not welcomed."

Trulius and Farrenthias fell in step behind a man who carried a wooden cage on his back that was filled with chickens, and next to him walked a man who led three camels. Trulius discreetly looked back. The guard had summoned two men to his side, and as he spoke to them, he pointed to Trulius and Farrenthias. The two men nodded then quickly set out towards Trulius and Farrenthias. At first they were discreet, weaving slowly through the crowd, but soon they were pushing people out of their way. One of them even flashed a dagger.

Trulius fell a step behind Farrenthias. "Farrenthias," he whispered, "do not look back, and whatever you do, do not stop walking."

Farrenthias nodded nervously. "What is it, Trulius?" He whispered. "Are we being followed?"

"Just keep walking," Trulius said. He looked back. One of the two men was upon him. Trulius casually shifted his satchel from his back to his side and then slowed his step. The man was now upon the reach of Trulius, and Trulius calmly reached back and quickly flung his cloak to one side and pulled down on the handle of his sword until the sword lifted from his back. He then thrust himself backwards, striking the man in the lower chest with the tip of his sword. The bewildered man toppled to the ground. He moaned and grasped his chest. The people behind the man did not slow down. They briskly stepped around him, but the man's sprawled body startled a train of camels that came upon him. The camels went wild and trampled the man before their master took control of them. The man's companion dropped to his knees beside the mangled body of his friend and stared at him in disbelief. He angrily got to his feet and barely avoided also getting trampled by another group of camels. He looked down the street, searched for Trulius and Farrenthias, and when he did not see them, he angrily shook his head. He started back towards the gates, wondering how he was going to explain to the guard how his companion, a trained assassin, had lost his step and had been trampled by camels.

Trulius looked over his shoulder. There was chaos in the street, but he could no longer see the other man who had also been following them. "I think we are safe now," he said. "You can slow down, Farrenthias."

Farrenthias stopped to catch his breath. He looked wearily around. "What just happened, Trulius? What was all the shouting about? Were we being followed?"

Trulius wiped the sweat from his brow. "Two men were following us. The guard who stopped us at the gate sent them after us. Perhaps it was me they wanted to kill, because I am Roman." He removed his sword and wiped it on the ground. "It was my intention to protect you with this sword. Instead, I fear that my presence here has placed you in danger."

"Do not be so quick to blame yourself, Trulius," Farrenthias said. "From what we just witnessed at the entrance to the city, we could not have arrived at a worse time."

Two old men were slowly coming up the street.

"I have no idea where we are," Trulius said. "Should we ask those two men for directions?"

"I will ask them," Farrenthias said. He raised a hand in salutation as the two men reached them. "Sires," he said, "my friend and I just arrived in the city. We are looking for a man by the name of Jishu. Have you heard of him?"

The taller and younger looking man looked at his companion, who used a walking stick. The older man looked carefully at Farrenthias and then at Trulius. "Do you follow the Christian beliefs?"

Farrenthias hesitated. "I study all beliefs including the beliefs of the Christians. I am actually here in Jerusalem looking for the son of Jishu. He is one of my former teachers."

The old man's eyes lit up. "Ah, you are looking for Ya'ir, the great scholar."

"Ya'ir disappears for weeks and months and sometimes years," the younger man said, "and then he suddenly returns in the middle of the night. And before all of his acquaintances have had an opportunity to greet him, he is gone again." He nodded at the old man. "Is that not true?"

"It is true," the old man said. "Ya'ir is as elusive as a fly, but you are fortunate. He is in the city. I sense that you two young men are on a special mission." He lifted his walking stick and pointed it in the direction from where he and his companion had just come. "Keep along this street and soon you will come to a dead end. Go left and stay on that street until you reach an intersection where you will find a merchant selling fruit. He will show you where Jishu lives."

Farrenthias thanked the two men, and he and Trulius set out down the street. They reached the dead end and made a left and soon, as the old man had said, they reached an intersection where a merchant, with a cart full of vegetables and fruits, was waving at a woman who had just filled her basket with fruit.

"Sire," Farrenthias said, "we were told that you could direct us to the house of Jishu. We are looking for Ya'ir."

The merchant quietly scrutinized Farrenthias and then Trulius. "Your friend, he is Roman," the man said to Farrenthias, "and you are Geek. It is good to see that people from different countries still get along. Are you acquainted with Ya'ir, or are you looking to meet him for the first time?"

"Ya'ir was a teacher to us both, Farrenthias said."

The old man nodded. "But of course, Ya'ir is an excellent teacher." He looked at Trulius. "Even a Roman can learn a thing or two from Ya'ir."

Trulius smiled. "It is as you say."

"Ya'ir's niece, Sesdia, was just here," the merchant said. "That pretty little angel bought a libra of cheese from me." He pointed to an alley down the street and then leaned in closer to them. "Jishu's house can actually be reached by going into that alley. It is an entrance rarely used, but Ya'ir himself gave me permission to direct his friends to it at my discretion. "

Farrenthias bowed slightly. "Thank you, sire," he said. "My companion and I shall be on our way."

Farrenthias and Trulius walked into the alley and discovered a simple wooden door at the far end of the alley.

"This must be it," Farrenthias said. He knocked on the door. There was no answer, and Farrenthias waited before he knocked on the door again.

"Who is it?" A female voice finally asked through the closed door.

"I am looking for Ya'ir," Farrenthias said. "He is a former teacher of mine and I am told that he lives here."

"Who told you to knock on this door?" The female asked.

"A merchant from across the street," Farrenthias said.

The bolt to the door snapped and the door cracked open. A pair of dark eyes gazed at Farrenthias. The eyes looked past him to Trulius and then returned to Farrenthias again. "Are you Farrenthias Theophilus?"

Startled by her question, Farrenthias nodded excitedly. "I am, but how did you know that?"

She again looked at Trulius. "And your companion, he must be Tessius Trulius."

Farrenthias followed her gaze and looked at Trulius. "He is indeed."

She opened the door wider and Farrenthias found himself staring at her. Her brown scarf, draped carefully around her head and thin shoulders, barely concealed a beautiful, youthful face. She was petite and had long black hair and unlike Ya'ir, whose skin was pale, her skin was a light olive brown. Farrenthias thought her to be the most beautiful young girl he had ever seen.

"My uncle has spoken quite a bit about you. He has been expecting you," she said. Her voice was sweet but surprisingly firm.

Farrenthias was seized with strange emotions he had never experienced before.

"I am Sesdia," she said. "My uncle will be very happy to see you both."

Farrenthias became aware that he had been staring at her and that she had grown silent, and he blushed. "Forgive me," he said. "Is Ya'ir here?"

"No," Sesdia said, "but I expect him shortly. In the meantime you can meet my grandfather, Jishu. He too has heard of you."

Ya'ir grinned with delight, and then he leaned across the table and first gripped the hands of Farrenthias and then those of Trulius. "I am overjoyed to see you both. The last time I saw you two you were but children and now look at you. You are both handsome young men." He leaned back while Sesdia placed three large plates on the table. One had slices of cheese and fruit, the other hot bread and the third boiled vegetables. "What a treat you are about to enjoy," Ya'ir said. "My niece is an excellent cook. She has totally spoiled me with her delicious breads."

They ate in silence for a few moments and then Trulius leaned forward across the table and whispered to Ya'ir, "Sire, what is happening in the city? There are guards and armed men on all the streets." He recounted to Ya'ir what had happened at the gates and Ya'ir listened intently with a frown on his face. "And so," Trulius said. "As a Roman, I am afraid that I have placed Farrenthias in danger."

Ya'ir shook his head. "There are still many Romans in the city, Trulius. Many of our people predict that sooner or later the city will fall to the empire. In the meantime, as you have discovered, the streets are no longer safe for anybody."

There was silence and then Ya'ir spoke again. "I am surprised, Trulius, that you did not stay in Rome. Did you receive news about your father?"

"I did, sire, and it was very strange news. I learned that Father was exiled, and that years later, he was asked to join the Roman army to come here to fight the rebels. I agreed to accompany Farrenthias here to Jerusalem, but tomorrow I shall leave for Caesarea to search for him."

"I see," Ya'ir said. He frowned thoughtfully. "I still have much work to do here, but just this morning I advised my father and

Sesdia that I will be making arrangements for them to leave the city. They were not happy, but it must be done."

Ya'ir ate very little and then silently watched Farrenthias and Trulius finish their meal. He then momentarily disappeared into a small adjacent room to visit his father. When he re-appeared he silently sipped from a cup of wine that Sesdia had served him.

"I was told by Ezri," he said, "that three short vessels were left behind, hidden beneath Clivus."

"Yes," Farrenthias said. He placed the satchel filled with scrolls on the table. "I brought these scrolls with me. What are you going to do with them?"

Ya'ir looked at the satchel. "Excellent. I shall tell you what we are going to do with these scrolls." He looked out the window. Dusk was upon them. He lit two lamps with the help of Sesdia and then returned to the table. "These scrolls shall become a part of a hidden library beneath the temple," he said.

Farrenthias looked surprised. "A hidden library? Beneath the temple?"

Ya'ir leaned toward Farrenthias. "What is hidden beneath the temple would shock many pious men, and men of greed would kill just to have a look at the hidden treasure," he said proudly.

Trulius said, "Is your library and treasure safe? If the Romans take the city, they will plunder it and search for spoils to take back to Rome. They will interrogate prisoners and make them talk. Surely they will learn about what lies beneath the temple."

Ya'ir eyed Trulius. "You are more correct than you realize, Trulius. We believe that the Romans have already heard about the temple treasure, and we believe that they will leave no stone un-turned looking for it. That is why we have been making preparations for just such an event." Ya'ir frowned. "Of course, nothing is completely safe, but all known precautions have been taken. The rest we leave to what will come to pass—that is all that we can do."

"Are we allowed to see this library?" Farrenthias asked.

Ya'ir grinned ever so slightly. "My dear Farrenthias, it has always been our deepest desire that one day you would travel here to Jerusalem and want to see the library."

Farrenthias stared at Ya'ir. "I do not understand," he said.

Ya'ir clasped his hands and leaned back on his chair. "As you learned at Clivus, Farrenthias, we have all traveled extensively, especially Erasmus Harel. Some of those journeys were long and perilous, but we gained much from them. Yet, our work is incomplete." Ya'ir paused and motioned to Sesdia. She disappeared from the room and quickly returned with a small satchel, which she handed to Ya'ir. Ya'ir opened the satchel and set its contents on the table. "Do you recall these three fragments of papyrus, Farrenthias?"

Farrenthias recognized the pieces instantly. "I do. They speak about Yeshua."

"Indeed," Ya'ir said. "Now let me tell you the complete story of how these scraps of papyrus came into our hands. Remember that Erasmus Harel took three trips to the East? Each trip was several years apart, and on each trip he went further east. I accompanied him on his last trip when we were given these papyri. We had spent some time high in the Himalayas, and on the night before we were to depart, a high priest summoned us to a temple we had not seen before. The temple was well hidden between two mountains that overlapped each other. Inside the temple we were taken to a dark room, where fires burned and a sweet fragrance graced the air. A short, thin priest suddenly appeared. "I bid you welcome to this part of the world and to this temple," he said. "It is my hope that your journey has been fruitful." He then handed us the fragments. "These belong in the hands of men from the west, men who ponder knowledge." Then he said, "One day you shall have to return, for within these peaks lies much wisdom. "He smiled at us, wished us luck on our journey back, and then disappeared behind a curtain.

Erasmus Harel and I immediately inspected the fragments and when we realized that they spoke about the journey Yeshua took to the East, we were astonished. We were aware that Yeshua had traveled to the East, of course, but we were unaware that a written account of that trip existed. By then it was too late to postpone our trip back, and besides, we were exhausted. Our search for the roots of those papyri would have to wait for another trip." Ya'ir paused and momentarily watched Sesdia as she replenished one of the pitchers with water. "Trips to the Far East," Ya'ir continued, "are difficult and can be dangerous, and above all, they can be very exhaustive. But to those of us who wish to learn about the secret lives of the masters and their beliefs, such trips are not only necessary they are indispensable. As we learned, there are many hidden temples in the Himalayas and the men who occupy those temples possess incredible knowledge and spiritual gifts, which they unselfishly share with others." Ya'ir paused and thought a moment. "Erasmus Harel and I never stopped thinking about that next trip that we would have to take to the Himalayas, and then something occurred to both of us after you arrived at Clivus. Not only did you express a deep love for a spiritual life, you also possessed an amazing gift for learning languages." Ya'ir exhaled softly. "It occurred to us, Farrenthias, that perhaps you would one day make that trip with one of us."

Farrenthias stared at Ya'ir. "Am I worthy of making such a trip? Why was I not told of this at Clivus?"

Ya'ir tapped the hand of Farrenthias. "Because, my dear Farrenthias, when you arrived at Clivus you were too young to be burdened with such matters. But more importantly, we had to wait. We had to wait for you to return to your home. Perhaps you would have decided to stay. We had to wait and see whether you were truly committed to our way of life."

Farrenthias lifted one of the pieces of papyrus. "I asked Erasmus Harel many times to tell me more about these papyrus and I recall that each time he would patiently tell me that I would learn more about them in due time." He set the piece down and picked up another one. "Now I understand," he said. "The first time I read these papyri I concluded that Yeshua was not just a great master, he was a brilliant and wise teacher whose life was an example of kindness and compassion."

"And," Ya'ir said. "He was an unbiased seeker of truths, and that accounts for why he would travel such distances to learn from other wise men. Men who perhaps had different beliefs than his."

Farrenthias sighed. "Erasmus Harel cautioned me many times to be an independent thinker. 'Man,' he would often say, 'was often guilty of imposing his own beliefs on others by trying to convince them that they were divine tenets.'"

Ya'ir nodded silently. "It was one of his favorite sayings."

Trulius cleared his throat and then spoke. "Even I remember hearing that from my uncle many times."

"I would like to travel to the Himalayas, Ya'ir," Farrenthias said. "Nothing would please me more than to pursue that quest."

"In time that will happen, but first there is another matter. Tonight, before I take you to the temple, I shall show you a house, a house where a man by the name of Akiva once lived."

"Akiva?" Farrenthias said. "Who was he?"

"He was an interesting and yet mysterious man. We know that he was from Petra," Ya'ir said. "One day he suddenly appeared here in Jerusalem. I will show you where he lived. He stayed at that house for about a year. His neighbors considered him a loner since they never saw him in the company of anyone and since he rarely spoke to anyone. But there was one man that Akiva would speak to. He was an old man who was known to be a Christian and a man who loved to talk about the teachings of Yeshua. One day Akiva surprised the man by telling him that he knew things about Yeshua that few people knew. Surprised but intrigued, the old man asked him what he meant by that, and Akiva told him that Yeshua had traveled to many far away lands and had acquired many of the principles he believed in from great masters from those far away lands." Ya'ir paused. "Akiva told the old man that Yeshua had spent many months in the snow-covered peaks of the Himalayas."

"Those lands must truly hold the key to many mysteries," Farrenthias said.

Ya'ir brushed his chin thoughtfully. "Indeed, but hear me out. There was another intriguing fact about Akiva. One day Akiva and his neighbor walked to the market square together, and by chance, they encountered a man from Petra. He had apparently known Akiva since childhood. The encounter was very strange because upon seeing Akiva the man was quite taken back by Akiva's appearance. He immediately asked him about the terrible deformity that had once almost covered his right eye. The man was further perplexed when he did not see any trace of a surgeon's knife on the eye of Akiva. The man lifted Akiva's chin and inspected the eye. 'I have never seen such work by a surgeon. What is his name?'

'This was not the work of a surgeon,' Akiva said curtly. 'I was cured by the divine hand of a master.'

The friend shook his head. 'I do not know if I believe in such things, but I know what I see. The man looked carefully at Akiva and then shook his head again. 'I am on my way to Petra tonight. I will certainly tell your old friends that you have rid yourself of the terrible scar.' "

"Akiva," Farrenthias whispered, deep in thought.

"What happened to him?" Trulius asked.

"Yes," Farrenthias said. "What happened to Akiva?"

Ya'ir drummed the table with his fingers. "When I show you his house, we shall resume this story, and I will tell you one more interesting fact about Akiva."

"Uncle," Sesdia said, as she entered the room. "Thason sent word that all is clear for your visit to the temple through the fields."

"Ah," Ya'ir said "Excellent news and what propitious timing. It will be dark soon, so we should prepare to leave at once."

He rose to his feet. "Tonight, you shall not only see the secret tunnels, you shall also see the secret entrance." He reached for the scrolls from Clivus. "And, tonight these will take their place beside the other great scrolls housed in the temple." He flung the small satchel across his back. "It would please Erasmus Harel to know that these are in the hands of Thason."

Sixty-Four

These days the streets of Jerusalem were unsafe, no matter the hour. Merchants and pedestrians knew that the potential for death loomed with every step and at every corner. Idle conversations with acquaintances were kept to a minimum and business transactions were handled expeditiously and with minimal bartering. No one wished to be on the streets longer than was necessary. Empty alleys and lots were avoided at all cost.

Ya'ir was well aware of the risks. He walked swiftly and with purpose, especially since Farrenthias and Trulius and Sesdia accompanied him. He was pleased that for some odd reason there was an unusual amount of people still out in the streets. Many carried small torches and others had oil lamps hanging from their carts. Even as darkness enveloped the city, the city was well lit.

Ya'ir turned onto a street that sloped down severely. A group of masons, who had been repairing a wall, were putting away their tools for the evening. A few of them stopped to momentarily look at them. Ya'ir took note of their actions and breathed more easily when the men returned to the task of putting away their tools. Ya'ir slowed down. "The house is at the end of this street," he said. Farrenthias, who walked beside him, looked over his shoulder at Trulius and Sesdia. "We are almost there."

"Yes, Sesdia said. "I have seen the house many times."

Ya'ir stopped in front of a small house. An alley separated the house from a two-story tenement building. Its doors and two front windows were boarded. "This is it," he said.

Farrenthias pressed a hand against the boards on one of the windows. He tried to imagine Akiva standing at the window peering down the street.

"Now let me tell you more about what we know," Ya'ir said. "This was actually once the house of a carpenter by the name of Jarek. He had his shop out in the back. Jarek used to build crossbars used on crosses for the Romans. Rumor has it that he built the crossbar the Romans used when they crucified Yeshua. As the story goes, Jarek and his wife had no children, but one day a child suddenly appeared and started living with them. No one knew the child's name or where he came from." Ya'ir looked around at the neighboring houses. "According to his neighbors, a few days after the crucifixion, Jarek packed his belongings, boarded the house and left with his wife and the child. They never returned." Ya'ir also pressed his hand against one of the boards. "The house stayed boarded for many years, until one day the neighbors woke up to find Akiva living here. When the authorities became aware that someone had occupied the house, they showed up to make inquiries and collect taxes. Akiva produced a deed to the property and settled the taxes."

"Hum," Trulius said. "Could this Akiva have been the child who lived with Jarek and his wife?"

"That is what people believe," Sesdia said.

"Indeed, that is the conclusion reached by many," Ya'ir said.

"If he was that child," Farrenthias said, "he might have witnessed the crucifixion of Yeshua."

Ya'ir nodded pensively. "Erasmus Harel and I have always wondered about that."

"What happened to him?" Farrenthias asked.

"Just as Akiva suddenly appeared overnight one day, that is how he also disappeared. One morning, the house was boarded and he was gone. It has been years and that is the way this house has remained."

Ya'ir watched silently as Trulius pried at the boards with his hands.

"These boards look like they have been here for many years," Trulius said.

"Ya'ir," Farrenthias said anxiously. "Has anyone looked for him? Has anyone traveled to Petra to look for him? He may have much to tell."

"We know that years ago Akiva returned to Petra, spent a short time with a sister that he had there, and then he vanished. The last time Erasmus Harel was in Jerusalem we passed by this house, and he expressed a desire to personally travel to Petra to meet her. Unfortunately, other matters prevented him from making that trip."

"Perhaps I should go and see her," Farrenthias suddenly said. "Perhaps she has heard from Akiva recently. When was the last time someone spoke to her?"

"I have no idea if someone has spoken to her recently. But, you have never been to Petra, Farrenthias. It would be dangerous to go alone."

"I will go with Farrenthias," Trulius said.

"No, Trulius!" Farrenthias cried. "You must not change your plans on my account. You must look for your father and return to Rome as quickly as possible. Gianina waits for you. Besides," Farrenthias now turned his attention to Ya'ir. "I am old enough to do this alone. This is one of many journeys that I must take alone if I am to succeed at what I was trained to do at Clivus."

Ya'ir stared silently at Farrenthias. He wondered what Erasmus Harel might think of such a proposal, but then like he, Erasmus Harel was a fearless wondering spirit when it came to the pursuit of creative ideas. Ya'ir sighed. "I was about your age when I left Jerusalem alone to spend time in Damascus with a teacher I knew very little about. But are you certain you want to do this?"

Farrenthias gave an eager nod. "I am."

"I know of a caravan of merchants that leaves for Petra in the morning. I will make arrangements for you to accompany them, but once you arrive at Petra you shall be alone and on your own."

"I understand," Farrenthias said. "I can do this." He gazed at Trulius, who had grown pale but who did not say a word.

Ya'ir pressed the hand of Farrenthias and gave him a reassuring look, and then he motioned that they should get going. "Thason awaits us," he said.

They walked in silence until they reached a wide, wooded area, well lit by a full moon and millions of bright stars. Straight ahead, just beyond the tops of the trees, the towers of the Antonia Fortress were visible. "I believe this is it," Ya'ir said, more to himself than anyone else.

Suddenly, a young boy of about twelve dropped out of the trees and landed behind them.

Before the boy could utter a word, in one swift move, Trulius had him on the ground with the point of his dagger at the boy's throat.

"Do not hurt him!" Sesdia screamed. "Thason sent him to meet us."

Trulius withdrew his dagger and helped the boy to his feet. "Forgive me," he said. "You startled me."

The boy stared at Trulius and excitedly placed a hand to his throat where Trulius had pricked it with the tip of his dagger. "I—I have never seen anyone move so quickly, sire" he said. "I wish I was as skillful with a dagger as you."

"Come now," Ya'ir whispered to the boy. "Enough of that. Let us not keep Thason waiting."

The boy took his eyes away from Trulius and placed his hands to his mouth and mimicked the sound of an owl. Almost immediately a similar sound was heard a short distance away.

"It is safe," the boy whispered. From behind a tree he quickly retrieved a rope and tied one end to the tree trunk and stepped into a nearby cluster of bushes and dropped to his knees. He pushed aside a boulder and then scraped a layer of dirt away from the ground. He removed two short wooden boards and looked into the hole that he had uncovered. "Thason is there," he said. "He waits for you."

Ya'ir placed a hand on Sesdia. "I wanted you to see this entrance, and now that you know where it is, as soon as we are down there and the boy covers it, he will escort you to the temple. We shall see you there in few moments."

"Yes, Uncle," she said. She gave Farrenthias a subtle smile and then quickly stepped to one side.

The boy dropped the rope into the hole and helped Farrenthias down first.

A short, heavy man was holding the rope, and as soon as Farrenthias reached him, he released the rope. Farrenthias hit the ground, and the man grabbed the rope for Trulius, who was already on his way down.

A taller man, holding a torch stepped out of the shadows. "Welcome, young man. You must be Farrenthias Theophilis," he said.

"I am, sire," Farrenthias said. He was struck by how much he resembled Ya'ir in appearance—only this man had much longer hair that was tied in a knot behind his neck.

"Have a look, Thason," the short man said, looking up at Trulius. "The young man is a Roman. I never dreamed that one day we would be showing these tunnels to a Roman."

"That must be Tessius Trulius," Thason said. "Ya'ir tells me that he can be trusted."

"He would never betray any of your secrets," Farrenthias said. "I bet my life on it."

As soon as Ya'ir joined them, Thason took two torches from a wall and handed one to Farrenthias and one to Trulius. A third torch he kept for himself and raised it slightly.

"What do you think about this entrance, Ya'ir?" Thason said. "Depending on what happens to the temple, this may be the only way back into the tunnels."

Ya'ir looked up at the hole from where he had just dropped down. Thason and his team of excavators and architects had put much work into the tunnels, but in truth, nothing in this world was ever completely safe from thieves. The Egyptians spent a great deal of effort hiding their tombs, and yet grave robbers always seemed to find them, whether by luck or pure persistence. Still, the effort had to be made. The Jerusalem treasure and the scrolls were priceless. "I think it was an excellent idea, Thason. How far from the temple are we?"

"Ten maybe twelve street blocks."

"Ten or twelve blocks?" Farrenthias said. "How many tunnels do you have down here?"

"We could build a whole city down here, my young friend. Some of the tunnels have existed for hundreds of years. We extended some of them and sealed others. We have also added many others. We have created a maze." Thason paused. "A maze that can very easily be a tomb to a man who has no business being down here." Thason raised his torch. "Shall we proceed?" He ducked into the low opening and motioned for everyone to follow.

The tunnel they were in had many narrow turns and descents. In some places the ceiling became so low that they had to crouch nearly to their knees to make it through. Other passages were so narrow that Thason, who was a thin man, had to turn sideways and squeeze through. Breathing was difficult but not impossible, and although the torches dimmed from the lack of air, the flames never extinguished.

Farrenthias frequently turned to Trulius who he knew detested tight and cramped quarters, and each time that he did, Trulius forced a smile.

"I am fine," Trulius whispered to Farrenthias. "I have my claustrophobia under control, but I would give anything if I were outside lying on my back counting the stars. What is it that we are going to see anyway?"

"Patience, Trulius. I am not certain myself."

At last they reached an enormous chamber, where several torches burned from one corner and the sound of pounding hammers against hard rock echoed against the walls.

"The digging continues," Thason said. He raised his torch toward the ceiling. "We are now beneath the temple."

"I have not seen one guard," Trulius said.

"No need for them," Thason said, flashing his white teeth in the dim light. "The entrance from the temple will be permanently sealed by several walls from the inside. That is why we needed an outside entrance, and of course, that entrance will naturally vanish within the terrain." He lowered his torch until the fire danced in his eyes. "Of course, if the Romans or anyone else happen to find the entrance, we arranged it so that the temple would be the worst possible place to descend into the tunnels if you are not familiar with them." His eyes narrowed to two slivers. "Enter here, take a few steps in the wrong direction and you will not find your way back. You will have entered your tomb."

Thason proceeded through another series of tunnels. He moved swiftly and quietly through the dark passages and made one turn after another until Farrenthias, who had tried to make a mental note of what direction they were moving, was completely lost. At last, Thason stopped in front of a narrow opening, a crack in the earth that did not at all look like it led to anywhere. Yet, he turned to the others.

"Through here," he said. He squeezed in and everyone followed him, one by one. The chamber they had entered was so small they could hardly breathe. They stood shoulder to shoulder, with barely enough room for them to move.

Thason dropped to a knee and removed a boulder from the lower section of a wall, and then he stood up. "Come, Farrenthias," he said. "Slip your hand in here and feel the wooden lever."

Farrenthias slipped his hand inside the slight opening and immediately felt a small, wooden lever. "I feel it," he said.

"Excellent," Thason said. "Now push the lever back until you feel it drop into a slot. When that happens push it slightly forward, and without pulling it out of the slot, push hard to the left until you again feel it drop into another slot. Tell me when that happens."

Farrenthias nodded eagerly. He took hold of the lever, pushed it back but did not feel it drop into a slot. He pushed and pushed but nothing happened. At last, the lever gave way and dropped into place. He then continued with Thason's instructions. "There," he cried, "it is done."

"Excellent," Thason said. "Now, it will take the three of us to push the door open."

Thason, Farrenthias, and Trulius leaned into the wall and pushed with all their strength until the door became slightly ajar on the left side. "That is it," Thason said, "that is all that it opens. Let us go inside."

Thason stood in the middle of the room and slowly moved his torch from side to side, thus illuminating rows and rows of clay jars, baskets, wooden bowls, and boxes that were all filled with golden cups, lamps, figurines, different shaped artifacts, ornaments, and golden sticks. Everything was neatly arranged against the walls. Nothing was out of place. Thason reached into one tall basket and pulled out dozens of necklaces, amulets, pins, rings, earrings, and a variety of colorful jewels. "Behold," he said. "When it comes to God, the Hebrew people are quite generous with their offerings," he said.

"I cannot believe the size of this treasure," Trulius said, walking around the baskets. "To whom does all of this belong?"

"To the people of Jerusalem, Trulius," Ya'ir said. "This is their temple. This is where they worship."

Trulius turned in every direction, his eyes in awe. "I cannot believe the size of this treasure," he said again. "I now understand why you have taken so many precautions to keep this treasure hidden."

"Indeed," Thason said. "We have also buried gold throughout various tunnels to fool possible looters into thinking they may have found the temple treasure. No one will ever stumble into this room by accident."

Ya'ir placed a hand on the shoulder of Thason. "Let us show Farrenthias the true treasure that is down here."

"Ah, but of course," Thason said. "Follow me and I shall show you a treasure only a true scholar can appreciate."

He led them to the far wall and then pointed to his right to an opening the size of half a door. A few feet from the opening was a stairwell that led into a lower chamber. "Watch your heads," Thason said. He ducked through the opening and walked down the stairs.

Farrenthias gasped out loud. To his left, against the wall was a row of tall clay jars that extended to well beyond the dim light of the torches.

Ya'ir raised his torch. "Have a look."

On the opposite wall there was another row of jars that also disappeared into the darkness.

"In here you will find scrolls that contain all the knowledge in the world," Ya'ir said.

Farrenthias stood mesmerized by what he saw. Erasmus Harel had told him about a hidden library in Jerusalem, a secret library that contained a great deal of knowledge. Erasmus Harel had also told him that there were only two other places in the world that housed as much knowledge, the library of Alexandria and a secret library beneath the Sphinx.

"Ya'ir," he said in a voice that quivered with excitement. "How many vessels do you have down here?"

Ya'ir started down the room. "The last time we counted them there were three hundred and eighteen." He stopped at the far wall and lowered his torch. The light exposed a large square hole near the bottom of the wall. "Thason," he said. "You have not yet sealed this hole?"

"No," Thason said. "Not yet."

"It is just as well," Ya'ir said. "I think I will show Farrenthias and Trulius what we found in here." Ya'ir bent down and disappeared through the hole. "Come in here," he said from the other side.

The chamber was quite small and the ceiling so low they could barely stand erect. Ya'ir stood next to the far wall with his torch raised close to the wall. "Have a look," he said. The entire wall sparkled under the blaze of the flickering torch.

"Have you ever seen anything so spectacular?" Ya'ir said,

"Is it marble?" Farrenthias said.

"We thought so at first," Thason said, joining them in the crowded chamber. "It certainly resembles it. Yet my best stonemasons could not so much as put a chip into it with hammer and chisel. We have never seen this type of rock, at least not here in Jerusalem."

Trulius stepped up to the wall and pressed his hand against it. "Then what is it?" He scraped the wall with the palm of his hand and turned it for the others to see. Dust sparkled on his hand.

"Odd is it not?" Thason said.

"Is there something on the other side of this magnificent wall?" Farrenthias asked.

Thason shrugged. "We do not know. Not only could we not chip it, we also could not dig around its sides. It is just a solid wall."

Ya'ir lowered his torch. "We should return to the other room and pack the Clivus scrolls into a jar that we have prepared. Sesdia is waiting for us."

Farrenthias was the first to step outside into the temple courtyard. The air was fresh and the night still clear and still full of stars.

Sesdia was seated on a short bench, rocking slowly back and forth. She rushed to Farrenthias when she saw him.

"At last," she cried. "I thought you were never going to come out."

Farrenthias frowned. "What? What do you mean, Sesdia? I lost all track of time, but it did not seem like we were in the tunnels for a very long time."

Sesdia looked at the sky. "The sky is still dark, but I would say that dawn is but two hours away. You were inside the tunnels for a very long time."

"Hmm," Farrenthias murmured.

Trulius was suddenly standing beside him. "Amazing," he said. "The tunnels were amazing."

"Would you care to guess how long we were inside those tunnels?" Farrenthias said.

"Not very long at all," Trulius said.

"Not according to Sesdia," Farrenthias said.

Ya'ir, who had walked out in the company of Thason, nodded. "Sesdia is correct, Farrenthias."

"It is one of the mysteries of the tunnels," Ya'ir said. "When we are down there it is as if time stands still. When we emerge, we discover that we have been down there twice as long as we believed. " He turned to Thason. "You brought it with you?"

"I did," Thason said. He produced a scroll from a small satchel that hung from his shoulder and handed it to Ya'ir.

Ya'ir studied it for a moment then said to Farrenthias, "This is a key to the treasure that you just saw. It is a diagram of the tunnels and a complete description of the hidden treasure. Only three of these documents exit." He offered it to Farrenthias. "Erasmus Harel and I decided that we should entrust you with this copy, Farrenthias."

Farrenthias stared at Ya'ir's outstretched hand without making an effort to take the scroll. "You are entrusting it to me, Ya'ir? But, why? Who am I that I should have such a valuable possession? I am not worthy! Besides, what if I were to lose it? What if someone steals it from me?"

Ya'ir smiled in the darkness. "Take it, my dear Farrenthias. We know more about your mission, your destiny, than you realize."

"But what am I to do with it?"

"In time, you will know," Ya'ir said.

Thason cleared his throat. "It will be light soon and I must get back. I have much work to do." he said.

"Uncle," Sesdia said. "When will your work here be finished? As you know, Ya'ir has ordered Grandfather and me out of the city. Will you be leaving with us?"

Thason hesitated. "It is good that you are leaving," he said, "the sooner the better. But I cannot leave. My work is here."

Sesdia looked desperately at him and then at Ya'ir. Tears flowed from her eyes. "I—I do not understand, Uncle. What are you saying? You cannot possibly stay here. The Romans will destroy everything and kill anyone who tries to stop them."

"It is true," Thason said quietly. "The zealots may enjoy a few victories, but ultimately Jerusalem will fall. But, you must understand, my child, the temple must be defended until the very end."

"Sesdia," Ya'ir said. "I too have tried in vain to persuade Thason to leave with the rest of us, but he refuses to even consider it. Thason believes that his destiny lies here, within these temple walls until the very end. Still, on the day that I leave Jerusalem I promise you that I shall come here and make one last effort to persuade him to leave with me."

"Go now," Thason said. He hugged Sesdia and then gripped the shoulder of Farrenthias and nodded slightly. He shook the hand of Trulius and smiled broadly. "You, my friend, I hope you are the last

Roman who ever sees the tunnels." With those words he turned and disappeared back into the temple.

"Does he ever leave the tunnels?" Farrenthias asked.

"Not anymore," Ya'ir said, shaking his head. "Come, it has gotten late on us. We have no time to waste if you are to join the caravan to Petra."

In the dim light of pre-dawn, Farranthias found himself staring at Sesdia. She was so beautiful and so kind and so full of life. He wondered if he would ever see her again, and the thought that he might not saddened him.

They were on a hill just outside Jerusalem. A short distance away, the caravan that would take him to Petra had gathered. The merchants were loading sacks of grain that they had agreed to take at the last minute for a merchant who could not make the trip. Ya'ir and Trulius were helping them.

"You did not have to accompany us, Sesdia," Farrenthias said. "You should have stayed at home to rest. You have not slept."

Sesdia ignored his comment. Instead, she glanced at him and blushed. "Farrenthias, I wish you had agreed to let Tessius Trulius accompany you. There is so much danger on these roads."

Farrenthias looked over at Trulius. He was single-handedly loading sacks, while the other merchants were working in pairs. Farrenthias smiled.

"Trulius is amazing," Sesdia said. "He is very strong, and I have never seen a young man move so swiftly. I thought he was going to kill that boy last night."

"What you saw him do to that young boy was nothing," Farrenthias said. "While riding his horse at full stride, I have seen him strike a moving target dead center with a dagger. There is nothing Trulius cannot do or master. He is truly amazing." Farrenthias was suddenly overcome with sadness. "I am going to miss him very much, but it is time we go our separate ways. He must return to his family in Rome and I must pursue my mission. Erasmus Harel and Ya'ir are depending on me."

"I understand," Sesdia said, looking more and more despondent. "I also understand that it is very difficult to part with loved ones." Her eyes watered and she turned away.

"What is it, Sesdia?" Farrenthias said. He started to reach for her but realized that he had never touched a girl before, and he let his hand drop. "Why are you crying?"

Sesdia wiped her eyes. "I was just wondering if your family knows what you are going to do?"

"What do you mean?" Farrenthias asked.

"It is just that ever since I can remember, my uncle has been traveling. He leaves for weeks and months, and sometimes years, and it is very painful to see him go. When he is gone, sometimes at night, Grandfather and I sit by a window gazing at the road in the moonlight hoping that he will appear."

Farrenthias was instantly filled with grief and guilt, for there was no doubt in his mind that Sesdia had just described the pain he was inflicting on his mother.

"Forgive me," Sesdia said. "I can see that I have upset you. I should tell you that Grandfather has always told me that there is not a more noble undertaking than the task of sharing knowledge, of teaching others who do not have the time nor the ability to understand the deeper meaning of life."

Sesdia got to her feet. "Have a look, Farrenthias. My uncle is waving us over."

Farrenthias walked quietly with his heart in a quandary. Sesdia had inexplicably become very important to him, but it made no sense. He hardly knew her. How could he have such strong feelings for someone he had just met days earlier?

"The caravan leaves in five minutes," Ya'ir said. He took the hand of Sesdia. "Come, my child. Help me strap Farrenthias's satchel on the ass he will be riding."

Farrenthias stood watching Sesdia and Ya'ir and then he fixed his sad eyes on Trulius. "I confess to you that I have a lump in my throat, Trulius," he said. "I do not know how my life would have turned out had you not arrived at Clivus when you did. You brought so much joy to all of us."

Trulius shrugged. "I was perhaps too mischievous."

"I shall miss you, Trulius," Farrenthias said. "Promise me that you shall take care of yourself and that you will not challenge any more Romans to wrestling matches. It is too dangerous."

Trulius smiled. "I promise. But, it is you who must be careful. There is danger everywhere." He gripped the handle of his sword and frowned. "I could postpone my search for Father and go with you. After all, I know that he is no longer a prisoner."

"No, Trulius," Farrenthias said, in a serious voice. "You cannot look after me the rest of my life. You have your own life to live. Besides, Gianina and Felicia and Kemnebi will be waiting for you. They need you. I must do this alone. I was trained at Clivus to study the manuscripts of scholars, to search for them, to write about them. I must do this alone because I have no idea where those goals will take me."

"It is interesting that you say that, Farrenthias, because last night, as we made our way through those tunnels and I thought about what you and my uncle and the others were doing, I began to wonder when we would ever see each other again?"

"But why do you say that? Of course we will see each other again."

"I say that because my life is in Rome, and you, you are going to travel to who knows where. Where will you live and for how long?"

"The caravan is ready to leave," Ya'ir called out.

Farrenthias gripped the arm of Trulius as they walked toward Ya'ir. "I promise you that at every opportunity I shall write about my whereabouts and look for a way to get my letters to you."

Trulius placed a hand across Farrenthias's shoulders and squeezed his shoulders. "I once heard Erasmus Harel say that a man never bids his brother farewell. He merely sends him on his way and hopes that he will see him soon."

"Those were very wise words from Erasmus Harel," Farrenthias said. "Then I will not say good-bye. I will only say that I hope you find your father soon and that all of your family will be together again."

Trulius motioned to Sesdia who was walking towards them and smiled. "You have truly found an admirer in Sesdia," he said. "I am certain that she will miss you as much as I will, and the two of you just met."

Farrenthias blushed. "I do not know what you mean, Trulius."

Sesdia held out her hands for Farrenthias to take them. "I shall have you in my prayers," she said, squeezing Farrenthias's hands.

Farrenthias awkwardly hugged her. "I, too, will pray for you, Sesdia," he said.

Ya'ir handed Farrenthias a rope that was affixed to an ass. "I shall see you in a week or two, Farrenthias. Be careful."

Trulius helped Farrenthias mount the small animal, much to the embarrassment of Farrenthias.

"I shall never learn how to do this properly," Farrenthias said. He raised a hand in gesture of farewell and followed the small caravan of two wagons, three horses, and two mules down the road. A short distance away he turned and waved again.

Trulius waved back, and even after Farrenthias turned away, the hand of Trulius remained frozen in the air. His eyes remained transfixed on Farrenthias as he road away. He angrily wondered why life had to be so complicated, why things could not be more agreeable.

"Do not despair, Trulius," Ya'ir suddenly said, as if he were reading the mind of Trulius. "I have an odd feeling that life has much in store for the two of you." He looked down the road at the quickly disappearing caravan. "I do indeed, now come my son, let us have one last meal before you set out on your own journey to search for your father."

Sixty-Five

Varelia angrily stopped at a street corner and again adjusted her long dress so that it would not drag along the filthy street. Not even the pleasant afternoon spring weather appeased her revulsion at being in the slums of the Aventine. How dare Maneria summon her to this despicable section of Rome! How dare Maneria summon her at all! Their business had concluded years before, and she had made it very clear that she never wanted to see him again. She set out again. This time she quickened her pace. The sooner she concluded her business with Maneria the sooner she could get out of this deplorable part of the city. She walked down a narrow street, past a row of small abandoned shops. She then turned left and walked between two dilapidated tenement buildings. A few children dirty and with torn clothes were scattered about the street kicking some crude ball. While the children played, a group of women were washing their filthy rags in wooden buckets. Female undergarments, dripping wet, hung from the doors of the tenements. *Rats,* Varelia thought. *These people live like alley rats.* Worse, the stench from the sewage was unbearable. Varelia cursed Maneria again. Why was she meeting him in this seedy neighborhood? Surely he could have met her somewhere else, if this was so urgent. She stopped in front of a building that had a sign dangling from a chipped and faded wall. This was the place. She was certain of it. Following Maneria's instructions she walked to the second floor and knocked on the third door of a long hall. No one answered the door and she could not hear any movement from the other side of the door. She knocked again. Only this time, her knuckles banged aggressively on the door. There was movement from the other side and then the door cracked slightly open and a pair of dark eyes peered out at her.

"Varelia. It is you. Good." The raspy voice was the unmistakable voice of Maneria. Maneria opened the door wider and Varelia stepped into the apartment.

The room was dark, lit only by a dim lantern that sat on top of a feeble wooden table, but even in the faint light, there was no mistaking how wretched the place was. Maneria wore a hood and scarf that was wrapped around his neck. All of his face was covered except for the eyes.

Varelia froze. "Maneria, what is the meaning of this?" she cried in a frightened voice. "Why is the room so dark? Why are you covered?" Her voice trailed off and the back of her hand flew to her mouth. "Maneria!" she screamed, "are you... are you?"

"A leper, Varelia."

Varelia uttered another scream and backed away towards the door. "How dare you expose me like this! Is this why you summoned me, to show me that you live like a rodent and that you are a leper? Am I supposed to pity you?"

Maneria shrugged. "I knew that you would react like this when you discovered that I was a leper. I considered telling you everything in the letter I sent you, but I reconsidered and thought that I should conclude my business with you in person."

"Have you gone mad, Maneria? You and I have nothing to say to each other. Our business concluded a long time ago."

Maneria sighed wearily. "I would offer you a chair and a cup of wine, but I know you will not touch anything in this apartment."

"Why have you summoned me, Maneria? Why am I here?" she said angrily.

Maneria poured himself a cup of wine with bandaged hands and sipped from the cup. "You have not changed in the slightest, Varelia. You are as impetuous and demanding as always." He gulped his wine and poured himself more wine. "It is a funny thing about Rome, no matter the time of day or the place, a man can always hear the latest news. I have kept up with your life and that of your husband and his lovely Nameya."

Varelia angrily pushed aside her cloak. "How dare you speak about such matters? Are you going to attempt to extort money from me? Did I not endure your filthy hands all over me not once but twice? Twice I shared a bed with you and you were also paid handsomely for your deed. What else do you want of me after all of these years?"

Maneria shook his head in disgust. "Those memories also trouble me, Varelia, but for different reasons. I regret that you betrayed your husband with me and I feel no less guilty knowing that I was one of many—but very well, let me get to the point of why I summoned you. I summoned you to let you know that you and I were betrayed."

Varelia frowned. "Betrayed? What do you mean?"

Maneria patiently sipped from his drink. "It is a funny thing about life, Varelia. Those of us who commit terrible deeds somehow wind up paying for them, no matter how much we regret having committed them. We can ask for forgiveness, but there is still a price to pay."

"You are speaking in riddles, Maneria! Get to the point and tell me what you are talking about!"

Maneria stared at his bandaged hands. "The child, the baby boy that I removed from Nameya's womb with these hands, lives, Varelia."

"What?" Varelia cried. "What are you saying? You told me you could trust your friend to kill that child, that child that you so cowardly refused to kill yourself!"

Maneria looked at Varelia and angrily shook his head. "Your insults no longer matter to me, Varelia. But if you must know, I did not lie to you. I did think I could trust him. But after all these years he suddenly appeared at my door about a week ago. He spoke about having joined the Christian sect, and he said he wanted to clear his conscience about the worst deed he had ever committed in his life. He told me that he took the child and that he had every intention of going through with what he promised, but he could not do it. The next day he walked to the edge of the city and stopped a caravan of merchants that were leaving Rome. He gave the child to one of those merchants."

"Bastard!" Varelia screamed. "You are to blame for this! You hired him!" Varelia suddenly glared at Maneria. "Then why was he feeling so guilty if he did not kill the child?"

Maneria shook his head. "You do not understand do you, Varelia? The man had tears in his eyes because he gave away a perfectly normal child to a pair of strangers who were not going to love that child like his real parents. Obviously that does not matter to you, does it?"

"Bah, that coward!" Varelia cried. "And you! I trusted you! When you told me that you could not do it yourself, I knew it was a mistake. I knew it was a mistake to involve someone else."

Maneria groaned and stared silently at Varelia.

"Why do you stare at me that way?" Varelia cried. "What I want to know is what you intend to do about this mess?"

"I have already done something about this mess, Varelia," Maneria said, his voice weak and barely audible. "I lived with the guilt of what I did for too many years, and today as I stand before you, a man ravished by an abominable disease with weeks, perhaps days to live, I have cleared my soul of my misdeeds."

"What are you talking about, Maneria?" Varelia cried. "You are speaking in riddles again."

Maneria walked with difficulty to the window, which was covered with a heavy curtain. He lifted the curtain slightly and a ray of light pierced into the room. He immediately released the curtain. "Even that ray of light that you just saw hurts my eyes, Varelia. I am also going blind. I cannot leave this room, so as we speak, a courier is carrying a letter to Nameya. In that letter I tell her everything, and I ask her for forgiveness."

Varelia felt the blood rush to her face. She clutched her midsection and shook her head over and over again. "No!" she shrieked. "You cowardly deceiving bastard!"

Maneria blinked just in time to see the flash of a dagger in Varelia's hand. Instinctively, he quickly lifted an arm for protection, but it was too late. Varelia slammed into him, burying the dagger into his belly.

"There!" Varelia cried. "That is what you deserve for your stupidity."

Maneria crashed against the window, pulling down the thick curtains as he slumped to the floor. Blood poured from his abdomen.

Varelia plunged her dagger into his belly again. The dagger dropped to the floor. Maneria withered in pain and his lips parted slightly as if he were trying to speak but no words formed. Instead, he seemed to smile as he took his last breath.

The room was now bright and bathed in sunlight. Varelia looked around and saw how truly destitute Maneria had become. There were but a few scattered pieces of furniture about the small room. It did not matter. In these slums, any thief might have made his way into this apartment and murdered its owner. She started to pick up her dagger but then changed her mind. Instead, she kicked it closer to Maneria's bandaged hands, which were covered in his blood. It is more likely that such a sick man took his own life. She smiled at her own cleverness. How dare Maneria think that he would outwit her? How dare he think that she would let him get away with his stupidity?

At the door to the apartment she looked both ways before she stepped out into the hall. Fortunately no one was around. It was a different matter at the front door to the tenement building. Suddenly the street was busy with traffic, but this also worked out well for Varelia. No one seemed to notice her when she stepped out into the flow of the moving traffic. Soon she was just another pedestrian trying to make her way. But Varelia worried. Nameya now knew the truth and soon so would Septimus. She tried to imagine how Septimus might react, what he might think, what he might do, and she worried. Would Septimus have her arrested and charged with some crime? With every step that she took her fear grew worse, but then she thought of her father. She could always count on her father. He would understand her, and he would help her. He would know what to do. She hastened her steps and headed for her father's house feeling, at least for the moment, relieved.

Sixty-Six

ROMAN CAMP NEAR CAESAREA

Septimus read the message from Vespasian and bolted to his feet. He glared at the young soldier who had just delivered it to him. "When did you last see Vespasian?"

"Three days ago, sire."

"Did you witness his departure for Caesarea?"

"I did, sire. Even as he scribbled this letter for you his camp was preparing for an immediate departure."

Septimus waved the young man out of the tent and looked at the quiet faces of his officers. He had summoned them to his tent to strategize their next military move and now this. "Nero is dead," he said. "He took his own life."

There was dead silence inside the tent.

"I suppose we should have expected something like this," one of the officers finally said, "but it could not have come at a worse time for us."

"Indeed," Septimus said. "Morale among the men must not suffer. We must assure them that their families back in Rome are safe and that all of their needs will still be met."

Marcellius said, "Who is running the business of Rome?"

"I am wondering the same thing," another officer said. "Does Rome have a new emperor?"

"According to Vespasian," Septimus said, "Galba is the new emperor."

"Galba!" an officer cried. He looked about the tent in exasperation. "I have not heard anything so ludicrous."

"Has he not the lineage?" another officer said. "And has he not held other posts?"

"Bah," the first officer said. "His family has money. It is that more than anything that accounts for whatever achievements he has accomplished. I do not believe that he has enough loyalty to hold the throne for long, mark my words."

"Perhaps you are right," Septimus said, "The politics of Rome are brutal, and there is much action in the air and behind closed doors. Vespasian has ordered me to Rome to meet with his other son, Domitian, to gauge the political climate. In the meantime, he is gathering with his commanders at Caesarea to assess his campaign here in Judea."

"Excellent," an older officer said. "That can mean only one thing, and I can tell you that Vespasian's troops adore him. The throne is his for the asking."

Septimus said to Marcellius. "You shall return to Rome with me. In the short period that you have been here you have served the empire well. Vespasian will hear...."

A horse thundered up to the opening of the tent and all eyes turned in that direction. The flap of the tent flew open and two soldiers, out of breath stormed in. They removed their helmets and one of them saluted Septimus and spoke. "My lord," he said. "We have spotted a heavily armed army of zealots making their way towards

Caesarea. When one of my scouts reported the news to me, I personally went to confirm the reports. It is yet the largest army the zealots have ever put together. I would estimate that there are ten perhaps fifteen thousand men marching toward the coast."

Septimus glared at the soldier with a clenched jaw. "How much time do we have before they reach Caesarea?"

"My best estimate, sire, is that they can reach it in three days, maybe two, if they march without delay."

Septimus walked to a table and reached for a map. "Show me exactly where they are. We must intercept them before they reach Caesarea, and we must send word at once to Vespasian."

Sixty-Seven

✤ PETRA ✦

The caravan came to a halt at the foot of a series of towering mountains and cliffs. Against a clear sky and glistening sun, the mountains, which were made of red rock looked spectacular. Farrenthias had never seen anything so unique and breathtaking

"It is a sight to behold, is it not?" one of the merchants said to Farrenthias. He pointed to a dark crevice that was carved into the cliffs. "That is the entrance to a passage through the cliffs. Petra is at the other end."

A Bedouin boy was suddenly standing beside them. He was very short and very thin. He wore a light blue vest over a long, heavily stained, white toga. His sandaled feet were black and severely calloused. He smiled through dark, yellow teeth. "I can guide you through the passageway and show you around Petra," he said, "for a coin or two."

The merchant laughed. "I have been through here many times, young lad. But do tell me how has the weather been, hot?"

"Not if you stay in the shade at all times," the boy said, grinning.

The merchant laughed again and this time he tossed the boy a coin, which the boy readily caught with one hand and then quickly put away.

"There is your coin," the merchant said. "There is another group of merchants a short distance away, perhaps you can do business with them."

The young boy bowed his head in gratitude and disappeared just as the caravan started to move forward.

"Is this the first time that you have been to this amazing city?" the merchant asked Farrenthias.

"It is, sire," Farrenthias said. "But I do know that Petra is the capital city of the Nebatean kingdom, and I know that the city is built of solid rocks—solid red rocks."

"Very good," the merchant said. "Petra is an architectural wonder. You will soon see that for yourself, and once the shops open later this morning, you will also discover that no one makes fresh bread like the people of Petra."

As soon as they entered the passageway the sky almost disappeared completely. Farrenthias leaned back on his mule and looked straight up. The walls on either side were enormously high, and there was barely a hint of sunlight piercing through the cracks in the ceiling. It was not enough to light the passageway at this hour of the morning, and it grew very dark. Torches were lit, and the caravan moved slowly through a winding path that narrowed and widened several times. At last, bright light from the other end spilled into the passageway. The torches were extinguished and left at the exit.

Straight ahead, just a few paces away, was a magnificent temple carved of a reddish stone that glistened in the sun.

"Behold this magnificent temple," the merchant who led the caravan said. He turned to the others. "At this beautiful temple we shall part ways. I am returning to Jerusalem in three days," he said. "Those of you who wish to go back with me must meet me here at this very spot in three days at dawn."

He offered to let Farrenthias keep the small animal that he was riding, but Farrenthias jumped down and insisted on walking. As the men left in different directions, Farrenthias stood in front of the temple admiring its columns and windows and the detail given to the edges on all sides. He marveled at how it was carved in stone and was part of the mountain, much like Clivus had been built into the cliffs of Armenia.

Finally, he set out toward the main part of the city, and as he walked, he noted how not just the temple but the entire city seemed to be carved into the cliffs. In every direction that he looked there was a building carved of red stone that made up part of a cliff. Other cliffs had many houses built into small cave-like rooms, and yet, other cliffs had many wooden doors that apparently led into small houses. The hour was still very early, and for the most part, the city was still very quiet.

Farrenthias proceeded along a narrow path, at the end of which he encountered three stray dogs sniffing the ground. They looked frail and thin, too thin. Farrenthias quickly searched his satchel for the one last piece of bread that he had saved. He pulled it apart and tossed the scraps to the dogs. The dogs hungrily pounced on the scraps and quickly ate them all. They then followed Farrenthias with dangling tongues and wagging tails along the path to a public well. Farrenthias lowered the wooden pail that dangled from a crossbar into the well and filled it with water. While he drank the cold water, the dogs clamored around him.

"You are thirsty," Farrenthias said. He quickly dug a hole on the ground and filled it with water.

Farrenthias turned at the sound of a man chuckling. An old man was seated on a nearby stone bench. He wore dark garments and had a long, white beard that was tucked inside the front of his clothing. He waved Farrenthias over.

"I have been watching you, young man," the old man said. "You are very kind to have fed your new friends. What is your name?"

"My name is Farrenthias Theophilus, sire." Farrenthias shrugged. "I had one piece of bread left, but I am afraid that it was not enough to fill their bellies. They look like they have not been fed in days."

"Perhaps you are right," the old man said. "I usually come in the mornings and feed them, but I am afraid that I have been sick and have not been here in days." He looked closely at Farrenthias. "You look as hungry as your new friends."

Farrenthias blushed. "As soon as the shops open I shall buy me something to eat."

"No need to wait," the old man said. "My daughter-in-law made several fresh loaves this morning. Of course, I only brought a few crumbs for our friends, but you are welcome to them since you have already fed them."

"But I did not feed them enough," Farrenthias said. "Please, give it to them. I can wait."

The old man laughed. "Very well, young one." He tossed the crumbs to the ground and the dogs quickly ate them. When they finished the crumbs, the dogs, salivating and wagging their tails, formed a circle around the old man.

"Ah, we must not be greedy," the old man said. "You have had your breakfast. Go now." He gently tapped his walking stick on the ground, and the three dogs scattered.

He eyed Farrenthias while he stroked his beard. "I have never seen you here before," he said. "But if I were to guess, I would say that you are too young to be a merchant, but neither do you look like a slave."

"You are correct, sire. I am no merchant, and even if I were, I would not be a good one. I do not bargain very well, and as far as being a slave, well, what man can honestly say that he is not a slave to someone or to some higher authority?"

The old man burst into laughter. "For one so young you certainly possess a clever tongue, Farrenthias. Are you just visiting Petra?"

"Actually, I have come to your beautiful city in search of a man."

The old man leaned forward, resting his chin on his walking stick. "Petra was even more beautiful before the Romans started arriving. They are everywhere now, and if you ask me, they want to own the whole world." He leaned back. "Now tell me, Farrenthias, who are you looking for? Perhaps I can help you."

"Akiva is his name. I was told he had a sister here in Petra."

The old man grimaced. "Akiva," he whispered. "I would not have guessed that. He eyed Farrenthias with great interest. "You are Greek and you are a well-mannered young man, and you are kind to animals." The old man frowned. "Young men your age are either preparing for military service or are pursuing their studies. You are obviously not preparing for military service, not if you are here searching for Akiva."

"Then you know him?" Farrenthias said.

"Everyone in Petra knows Akiva. Everyone has heard the story of his deformity and mysterious cure. No doubt you seek Akiva so that he can tell you about his encounter with the Hebrew master, Yeshua."

Farrenthias nodded eagerly. "That is exactly why I seek him."

"I see," the old man said. "Unfortunately, my child, Akiva is not here in Petra."

"No?" Farrenthias said, in disappointment.

"No," the old man said. "But I do not believe you have completely wasted your time in coming to Petra."

"Then you know where I can find him?"

The old man brushed his beard again and narrowed his eyes. "Akiva is as elusive as a leaf in the wind, but I have my suspicions."

"What do you mean?" Farrenthias said.

"What I mean is that one day Akiva suddenly appeared," the old man said. "It made his sister very happy, but soon he was gone again." The old man shook his head. "Now, Yehnia spends her lonely days waiting for him to return."

"Surely she must know where he went?" Farrenthias said.

The old man shrugged. "I believe that Yehnia might have some idea, but she will not speak about it. All she says is that one day he will return." The old man struggled to his feet. "Perhaps you will have better luck talking to her."

"Where can I find her, sire?" Farrenthias asked.

The old man smiled. "You are not entirely without luck, Farrenthias. Do not move from here. Yehnia visits that well that you just drank water from every morning. She should be here at any moment, and you will find that, although she is quiet and not very talkative, she is actually a very kind person."

Farrenthias looked across the road at the well. "But how will I know her?"

"She is usually the first one to arrive. She is quite thin and she covers her head with either a dark blue or dark green scarf."

The old man rested a hand on the shoulder of Farrenthias. "You seem like a fine young man and you are certainly well educated. I wish you a long and bright life."

The old man walked away in the opposite direction of the well, with the three dogs trailing behind. He was still within view when a woman caught Farrenthias's attention. Like the old man had said, the woman was thin, and she wore a dark blue scarf and a faded yellow dress. She was nearly at the well when she noticed Farrenthias and hesitated. Farrenthias smiled awkwardly at her and only then did she resume her walk toward the fountain. Her gestures were quick as she filled her pails with water. She watched Farrenthias from the corner of her eyes as he approached her.

"Forgive me if I startled you," Farrenthias said. "My name is Farrenthias Theophilus."

Yehnia looked at him briefly and then resumed the task of pouring water into one of her two clay jars. "You are a stranger," she said, in a low voice. "I have never seen you before."

"I only arrived this morning from Jerusalem," Farrenthias said. He nervously looked in the direction that the old man had taken. "Are you Yehnia?"

Yehnia stopped pouring water. "I saw you talking to the old man. He is kind, and when his daughter-in-law is too ill to bake, he buys bread from me. No doubt he told you my name." She gazed at Farrenthias with a look of distant sadness. "He would not have given you my name if he had not thought you were a decent young man." She resumed the task of filling her jars with water. "Have you come asking about Akiva?"

Surprised, Farrenthias stared at her in silence.

Yehnia set the pail down "I have never been asked about him by one so young." She became slightly pensive and her eyes grew moist.

"Forgive me," Farrenthias said, shyly. "I can see that I have brought back bad memories."

Yehnia dried her eyes with the back of her hand. "No doubt the old man told you that Akiva left Petra years ago."

"I had heard that he vanished, even before I arrived at Petra. I was just hoping that he might have returned or that perhaps you…" He stopped speaking and dejectedly leaned against the well. He quietly looked around. "This is a magnificent city," he said, changing the subject. "My teachers described it to me once, but seeing it in person, I cannot believe how it was so brilliantly built against those hard mountains." He sighed. "Even though I did not find Akiva, I have no regrets about coming here." He stepped away from the well. "Well, I have bothered you long enough. I suppose I should find a place to rest and spend the night. I will leave in the morning."

"You do look very tired and you look pale and thin," Yehnia said. "Have you had breakfast?"

"No," Farrenthias said. "But in truth, I have no appetite."

"But you need your strength if you are going to travel." Yehnia rested a hand on one of her jars. "Perhaps you would like to help me carry my jars home. I have fresh bread coming out of the oven."

Farrenthias immediately reached for one of the jars. "Of course, I will help you, Yehnia, and I was planning on buying breakfast as soon as one of the shops open. I can pay you for a slice of bread."

Yehnia smiled, but there was a sadness to her smile, a distant sadness. "I am not so destitute, Farrenthias, that I cannot be kind to a friendly young man."

Yehnia's house was in a lower section of a cliff far from the main part of the city. It was almost isolated from the other houses. Like some of the other houses he had seen, there was nothing more than a wooden door built into the side of the cliff. Just in front of the door, however, there was a crude fence made of stones, and inside the small fence was an oven built out of a pile of stones. Steady smoke rose from the oven, and the air smelled of fresh bread.

Yehnia pushed opened the brown, faded door. "You can set the jug on the table. I am going to see how the bread is doing."

Farrenthias stepped into the small house. It smelled of fresh dirt, much like the tunnels of Jerusalem. A wooden table with two chairs occupied one corner of the room. A cot with broken legs sat in another corner and draped from the ceiling was a stained curtain that divided the room into two.

Farrenthias heard voices outside and peered out a small circular window. A small child carrying a basket was keeping his balance on one leg while Yehnia filled the basket with bread. The child then handed a few coins to Yehnia and ran off just as another woman also appeared with a basket. The two women talked briefly while Yehnia also filled her basket with bread.

At last Yehnia returned to the house with two small loaves of bread. "Please have a seat, Farrenthias."

She placed a loaf of bread on the table and poured two cups of water. "It is odd," she said, as she cut the loaf of bread into squares and handed one to Farrenthias, "but the moment I saw you, you reminded me of Akiva when he was young. You look nothing like him. It is just that, well, he was always calm and quiet and very polite, but he had this inquisitive manner about him. Of course, the last time I saw him..." She fell silent.

"Please continue," Farrenthias said. "What about this last time you saw him?"

Yehnia nervously brushed her throat. "I almost did not recognize him when he got here. He looked terrible. He was gaunt and emaciated. He ate ravenously, as if he had not eaten for days, and then I led him to a cot where he fell upon it hard. He slept for three nights."

"Why was he in that condition?" Farrenthias asked.

"When he woke up I asked him. He said that he was coming from the Far East, but he did not say much else. He helped me with my chores, and he even delivered orders of bread for me. But he spoke very little, and he seemed to be very contemplative. He was always thinking, as if he was pondering some great dilemma in his life." Yehnia looked at the curtain that divided the room. "He slept in that room, but mostly he would sit in a very rigid position on the floor next to his cot. He would do that for hours, and at times I had to walk up to him and touch him for it seemed as though he was not breathing." Yehnia sighed. "He would also sit by this window for hours, quietly looking out. Sometimes I would sit with him and we would chat about our youth, but mostly he enjoyed sitting in silence. I would not disturb him because he often told me that he believed that a man could accomplish much by contemplating life in total silence."

"The ritual of sitting in a rigid position for hours in total silence that you describe is a ritual that comes from the Far East," Farrenthias said quietly.

Yehnia drank from her cup of water and then sadly looked about her tiny house. "I miss him terribly even though in truth he has hardly spent time with me."

"Did he mention Yeshua to you?" Farrenthias said. "Is it true that he cured Akiva from the terrible scar above one of his eyes?"

Yehnia sighed. "Akiva believed that he did, and after that he became obsessed with finding that Hebrew master, as Akiva referred to him. Akiva knew that there were rumors about men who possessed the power to heal, but he believed that Yeshua was special. He would mention him, and then he would suddenly stop and begin one of his long periods of silence," Yehnia said.

Yehnia stared at the curtain. "Akiva has always been like a son to me. Our mother was afflicted with a terrible disease that made it difficult for her to walk. I took care of him as a child—that is, until he ran away." She dried the tears that had seeped from her eyes and had streamed down her cheeks.

Farrenthias lowered his gaze to allow her a moment of privacy.

"Forgive me," she said.

Farrenthias shifted uneasily in his chair. "You have no idea where he might be?"

Yehnia sighed and her eyes became moist again. "By now he must be back somewhere in the Far East."

"Why do you believe that?"

"He wrote me a letter and told me so. He mentioned some sacred mountains."

"The Himalayas!" Farrenthias cried. "He wrote you a letter and told you that he was going back to the Himalayas?"

Yehnia nodded. "I have the letter. Would you like to see it?"

"I would like that very much," Farrenthias said, his voice filled with excitement.

Yehnia left the room and quickly returned with a thin scroll in her hands. "As you can see, it is a very brief letter." She handed it to Farrenthias. "You may read it if you wish."

Farrenthias quickly unraveled the scroll. It was written in Aramaic, and he was grateful that he had learned the language.

Yehnia- please know that I think of you daily, perhaps every moment of my existence, and please know that I am torn by the guilt of knowing that I am not at your side to take care of you. After all, we only have each other. But you who practically raised me know what a restless soul I have always been. In time I shall share with you all that has happened to me. For now, I tell you only that in my quest to find the Master who cured me, many doors into the true meaning of life have opened before me. This became abundantly clear to me when I reached the sacred mountains of the Far East. There I found the answers to many questions that I had and I was prepared to stay. But I had to come back to see you and to take care of other business. Once I reached Petra and saw you, I was prepared to forget my travels and stay with you, but I could not do it. A force that I cannot explain drives me. It is a force so powerful that I am willing to leave my beloved sister. Peace eludes me, Yehnia. I am in Engedi. This is a paradise, and the men who live here live a quiet and frugal existence in prayer and contemplation. But I cannot stay here, nor can I return to Petra. Soon I shall depart back to the sacred mountains. My work there was not complete when I left. I do not know when I will return but know that I carry you in my heart always and know that one day, whether in this life or the next, we shall be together again. Akiva.

Moved by the powerful words written by Akiva, Farrenthias stared at the letter without saying a word. And then, a shocking revelation struck him like a bolt of lightning. He looked up at Yehnia then down at the letter again. This time he studied the text more carefully, noting how every letter was formed.

"What is it?" Yehnia said. "You have the strangest look on your face, Farrenthias."

Farrenthias looked at her. "Yehnia, I have seen this writing before."

"I do not understand," Yehnia said.

"My teachers, they too traveled to the East and they showed me three pieces of a scroll that was given to them by a priest. The man who wrote that scroll was Akiva. I am certain of it!" Farrenthias sighed. "When did you receive this letter?"

Yehnia quietly wept. "The years, they pass so quickly, Farrenthias. It had to have been two or three years ago, but I cannot be certain."

Farrenthias nodded quietly. Akiva could not possibly be in Engedi. Too much time had passed, but that did not matter. He had to go there. Farrenthias considered his options. Should he return to Jerusalem and report to Ya'ir what he had discovered? What if Ya'ir had already left for Damascus? Should he not waste any time and just head for Engedi? After all, Engedi was much closer to Petra than Jerusalem.

"Farrenthias," Yehnia said. "Are you going to look for Akiva?"

His mind still in a quandary, Farrenthias nodded absently. "I have to try."

"But it has been so long since I received his letter. Is finding Akiva that important to you?"

Farrenthias said, "Yes, I would like very much to meet him and hear from his own lips about his encounter with Yeshua." He rose from the table. "I have troubled you long enough, and the day is still young. I am not going to spend the night in Petra after all. I should like to leave at once. Perhaps I can reach Engedi by tomorrow evening if I maintain a fast pace." He started for the door.

"Just a moment," Yehnia said. She quickly wrapped a loaf of bread and handed it to Farrenthias. "This is not much but it should help keep your strength."

"Thank you, Yehnia," Farrenthias said. "Thank you for sharing so much with me."

"Farrenthias," Yehnia said, "I do not know if I will ever see Akiva again. If you should find him will you tell him that I am well and that he should not worry about me?"

Farrenthias smiled. "Of course, Yehnia. But you should have faith that one day he will return."

Sixty-Eight

Perched high on a hill, Trulius stood next to his horse and watched the spectacle that was unfolding in the valley below. The scene was mesmerizing. Back home he had seen the Roman army march many times along the streets of Rome and it had been an impressive sight. This was different. He had never scene anything like this. The size of this Roman army was staggering. Soldiers dressed in full military regalia stood shoulder to shoulder forming infinite rows of red-feathered golden helmets, red capes, shields, swords, and spears. And not one man was out of line. An armed cavalry flanked the infantry. Those soldiers were mounted on magnificent stallions that were also outfitted with military drapes and straps. Other soldiers carried yellow, white, and red flags and colorful banners with a variety of emblems and insignias.

Across the valley the ranks of an equally impressive army in size were still aligning themselves for battle.

Trulius recalled that, once, Kemnebi had described just such a battle scene to him. The Roman army is the most efficient and ruthless army in the world Kemnebi had said, and like a cobra it is deathly quiet before it strikes. Indeed, in spite of the sheer numbers of men who were gathered on the field, only the sounds of capes, banners, and flags flapping in the wind could be heard.

Trulius wanted a closer look. He mounted his horse and slowly, cautiously, he urged his horse forward. He stopped and from his new location he was now able to see the faces of some of the men. They were intense faces that revealed nothing. Yet some were about to die, and Trulius could not help but to admire the silent manner with which they accepted their fate. Trulius continued to study the first row of Roman soldiers when suddenly his breath left him with a jolt. At first, he could not believe his eyes. He squinted until the image of only one man was in his sight. Tears formed in his eyes. His father had not changed in the slightest, and Trulius stared proudly at him. He sat erect on his horse with his purple officer's cape draped across his shoulders, looking regal in his golden armor and golden armlets. He looked to his left and then to his right, all with the gestures Trulius remembered so well. Yes, Trulius had been told that his father was now a commander with the army, but seeing it with his own eyes, Trulius trembled proudly. And then in a moment of spontaneity Trulius unsheathed his sword and set out down the hill.

"Marcellius," Amatius said. "Have a look. On the hill."

Marcellius followed Amatius's gaze. A lone rider, not in uniform, was boldly riding along the front of the ranks heading in his direction. Marcellius stared for a moment and then he felt the blood drain from his face. The last time he had seen Trulius he had been but a child. He had awakened him in the middle of the night, placed him on a horse, and sent him away from Rome. And now, here he was, riding among the ranks with a sword at hand and a total look of resolution on his face. He was no longer a child.

"Marcellius," Amatius said. "You have grown absolutely pale. Do you know that young man?"

Marcellius cleared his throat with difficulty. "He is my son, Amatius. Tessius Trulius was but a child the last time I saw him."

"He is young but he rides with confidence," Amatius said.

"Indeed," Marcellius said. "I assigned him an excellent teacher. I am certain that he is ready to march into his first battle."

"Of course," Amatius said. "Do not worry about him, Marcellius. I will watch him as if he were my own son. He will need a uniform." He pulled his horse around and whispered to one of his men. The man disappeared and quickly returned with two squires, who carried a chest plate, a red cape, a golden helmet, a shield, and a spear.

Trulius stopped in front of his father. He was too emotional to speak and he was fighting back tears.

Marcellius held out a hand to Trulius and gripped his forearm. "You look well, son," he said. "I cannot fully express to you the joy I feel in my heart to finally see you after all these years."

"Father," Trulius said. "At last."

Marcellius said, "Are you prepared for this?"

"I am, Father. It will be an honor to ride into battle with you," Trulius said.

"Quickly, Trulius," Amatius said, motioning for Trulius to get off his horse so the squires could dress him.

Amatius then maneuvered his horse to allow Trulius to take his place beside his father.

Marcellius stared straight ahead. "Kemnebi?" he whispered.

"With Felicia and Gianina in Rome, Father," Trulius said.

"Excellent," Marcellius said. "The women are well?"

"Yes, Father."

"I am relieved to hear that." He glanced at Trulius. "You hold that spear very well. I can see that Kemnebi did an excellent job of raising you. Are you ready, my son?"

Trulius tightened his grip on his weapons and shield. "I am ready," he said.

Marcellius nodded and then glanced across the field. The enemy was now prepared. They were utterly still and all eyes were focused on Marcellius's army. There was also complete silence. Marcellius had been in this situation many times before and it was at this precise moment, when death was imminent and fear palpable, that a man summoned all of his inner strength in order to march into battle and possibly straight into death. Marcellius looked quickly up and down his ranks. Satisfied that his men were ready, he motioned to Amatius.

Amatius raised a hand and loud trumpets shattered the silence in the air and blared out across the field.

"Young Trulius," Amatius shouted. "We charge into battle beside your father, but stay close to me. You are my responsibility." He reached over and tapped Trulius on his shoulder. "You shall be fine. Today you make your father and Rome proud."

Marcellius motioned again. A cry went out among the ranks and a wave of infantrymen set out in a slow trot with shields raised above their heads. Archers launched a volley of arrows into the air. Within minutes, arrows from both sides pierced high into the sky, temporarily darkening the blue skies.

Marcellius gave another signal and Amatius raised another hand and let it drop. Another cry from the ranks resonated across the valley and a horde of riders ripped across the field with spears ready to be launched.

Marcellius watched the battle rage with a clenched jaw. His troops were too powerful for the zealots. They broke through their ranks all along their lines, yet the enemy fought back valiantly and with determination. They pushed back with rage.

"Now," Marcellius shouted and charged forward in full stride with the rest of the entire army behind him.

Nothing, not his resolve, not his fearless nature, not the rush of adrenaline prepared Trulius for this, his first battle. The pace his father set was maddening, and yet there were men all around him keeping up with him stride for stride, creating clouds of dust, making it difficult to see. Spears were launched at moving targets and swords were drawn, all without missing a beat. Wild-eyed, Trulius also launched his spear, and he kept an eye on Amatius and one on his father. Once they clashed with a wave of the enemy, however, Trulius lost sight of everybody. The enemy swung at him with swords and mallets from all sides. Trulius swung to his left and then to his right, piercing skin and bones. He kicked at a man who was on the ground trying to pull him off his horse. He was suddenly boxed in by two of his own men. They crowded up against him, making it difficult to swing his sword without striking one of them. Hundreds of men dropped to the ground moaning and bleeding and sweating, but that did not seem to stop them. It only slowed them down. Men fought with their last breath. Two men suddenly charged at Trulius. One man was on a horse and the other on the ground. Trulius sparred with both of them, swinging his sword with all of his strength. The man on the ground delivered a blow to his side, and Trulius went crashing down at the man's feet. Trulius never lost sight of the man as he tumbled on the ground. He saw the man lift his mallet to strike him, but the man collapsed from a blow to the side of his face. Trulius then felt a powerful hand lift him to his feet from behind. Amatius nodded at him and tossed him the reins of his horse. "You are doing well, young Trulius. You fight well. Now follow me," he shouted.

Amatius weaved through the sea of fighting men, dust, and chaos until he reached the edge of the fighting. From there, Trulius spotted his father shouting orders at his men. His face and arms and uniform were covered in blood and sweat. Fortunately, the Romans had taken the edge on the fighting, and many of the zealots were running and disappearing behind a hill from where they had come.

"Shall we give chase?" Amatius shouted.

Marcellius looked across the field at a small band of men he had purposefully held back from the fighting. "Send those men in to flush them out," he said to Amatius. "And send word to Septimus that the enemy has been diminished and chased into the hills."

Marcellius sighed and turned to Trullius. "I caught glimpses of you in the battlefield, Trulius. Kemnebi taught you well, but valor in the battlefield cannot be taught. Word has already spread among the men that you are my son and that you fought bravely beside them." He reached out and gripped the shoulder of Trulius. Let us go home. We have much to talk about."

Sixty-Nine

Farrenthias reached down and cupped a handful of water from the dark blue waters of the Dead Sea and splashed it on his face. The heavy salt content in the water burned his dry, cracked lips. Nevertheless, the water refreshed him, if only for a moment, for the desert that surrounded the sea was dry and hot. He had removed his sandals, and as he stood at the water's edge, the salty water also soothed his tired feet. Farrenthias would have liked to have stayed in the water longer, but anxious to reach his destination, he wiped the excessive water from his face, hooded his eyes from the blaring afternoon sun, and studied the brown rocky hills to the west of the Dead Sea. Tucked somewhere inside those hills was the rich oasis known as Engedi. He stepped out of the water, put his sandals back on, and started towards the rocky hills.

As he approached on a well-worn path, Farrenthias began to see trees and green vegetation clinging to otherwise dry desert hills. Soon he found himself in a fertile valley filled with trees, wild tropical plants, and a spring that was being fed by a beautiful waterfall.

Magnificent cliffs surrounded the entire. Farrenthias squinted. Wild deer were calmly grazing on a nearby cliff. One or two of those creatures stopped to look at him. They showed no fear, only curiosity. Farrenthias was so taken by Engedi that he did not at first realize that, aside from the sound of the waterfall and chirping of birds, there was the faint but distinct humming sound of human voices coming from somewhere in the valley.

The voices grew louder. They were softly chanting what sounded like prayers, and soon a group of men in single file emerged from the trees. Like the wild deer he had just seen, Farrenthias felt no fear, even though he was now standing not far from the edge of the spring fully visible to the men. Oddly, the men were so engrossed with their prayers that they did not notice him. Farrenthias watched in fascination as they disrobed down to loincloths, entered the water and engaged in the similar ritual that he had undergone at Clivus when Erasmus Harel had given him his new name of Theophilus.

At the sound of steps behind him Farrenthias whirled around.

"I have startled you," the man said. "Forgive me." He too wore a white toga. His hair was gray and short. He smiled cheerfully and looked in the direction of the spring. "You are a stranger. All strangers are welcomed here. Please, you may refresh yourself in the spring water. It will not bother my brothers."

"I just arrived," Farrenthias said, "and it would be nice to bathe in that fresh water. I am afraid that the Dead Sea was refreshing, but its water left me feeling like I should rinse all that salt off of my skin."

The man smiled. "But of course." He studied Farrenthias with great interest. "My name is Perindious, friend. We are Essenes. We come to Engedi every other day to worship in the water and pray."

"I am Farrenthias Theophilus," Farrenthias said.

Perindious nodded slowly. "A most propitious name, my young friend." He frowned, began to speak and then hesitated. "Forgive me," he finally said, "for it is not in our nature to make unnecessary inquiries of strangers, but I could not help but to notice that the girdle you wear, it was weaved by an Essene. And your name, it is a Greek name commonly given to scholars. If I may ask, why are you in Engedi?"

Farrenthias touched his girdle. Erasmus Harel had given it to him, and he treasured it. "This girdle was given to me by one of my teachers, Farrenthias said. "I came here to inquire about a man who once stayed here. Akiva is his name."

"Akiva, yes he was here but none of us got to know him very well," Perindious said. "He was quiet and he seemed to prefer to be alone. We respected that."

Farrenthias drew his breath. "I understand, but did anyone have any conversations with him?"

"I personally spoke to him on occasion," Perindious said. "I know that he had a sister in Petra. I know that because we arranged to have a letter delivered to her from Akiva."

Farrenthias suddenly became aware that it had gotten quiet, and he looked in the direction of the water. The Essenes had stepped out of the water. Some were still dressing and others were disappearing into the trees one by one.

"Am I keeping you from your companions?" Farrenthias said.

"I am fine," Perindious said. He walked Farrenthias to a pair of fair-sized boulders and invited him to sit. "How do you know about Akiva?"

Farrenthias briefly told Perindious all about Clivus and the mission of the men who lived there."

Perindious raised a finger and stabbed the air with it. "If you are truly committed to your task, you have much to do and far to go, young Farrenthias. Now, there is another man that you should look for. I told Akiva about him. His name is Athinio. Like Akiva, in his youth, he too had an encounter with Yeshua. He used to live in our community but left years ago."

"Where can I find him?"

"He lives in a cave high above the shores of the Red Sea. There was a time when he too would travel considerably. Therefore, I do not know if Akiva ever found him."

"The Red Sea," Farrenthias whispered.

"The Red Sea," Perindious repeated.

Farrenthias looked around. "Where did Akiva stay when he lived here?"

Perindious pointed to several caves just above the waterfall. "He used to live in one of those caves. When we would come to the spring, he would occasionally come down and join us in the water, that is how we got to know him." Perindious smiled. "He got very excited when told that Yehua often bathed in this very spring."

"You have given me much to think about, Perindious," Farrenthias said. He quietly looked around then looked above the waterfall at the caves. "Could you see Akiva from here?"

Perindious nodded. "Yes, he would sit outside the cave for hours, writing."

"Writing?" Farrenthias cried.

Perindious whirled around to look at Farrenthias. Realizing the significance of what he had just said, Perindious looked up at the caves, then at Farrenthias. "He was always writing," he whispered under his breath.

"What do you suppose he was recording?" Farrenthias asked.

"I do not know, but he seemed very committed to his work."

Farrenthias became pensive. *"Could he have been writing about his experiences? Could he have been writing about what he knew about Yeshua?"*

"Farrenthias," Perindious said, slowly getting to his feet. "I bid farewell to Akiva when he left. I have never thought about this before but he carried a small satchel that was filled with dry fruit and bread that we provided for him. He carried a few other items in his satchel and nothing else."

"What about his writings?"

"I recall that he used to wrap his writing scroll in a distinct small, dark brown cloth. That dark brown cloth was not in his satchel when he left!"

"He left it here?" Farrenthias said, looking up ahead toward the cave. "Did he ever return for it?"

"Akiva has never returned. When he left he bid us a heartfelt farewell and said that we would probably never see each other again."

"But, why would he leave his work here?" Farrenthias said, "Why did he not tell you about it?"

"He had his motives I suppose," Perindious said and started up a path. "Come let us go and have a look around his cave. There is a hidden path through the trees."

Farrenthias stepped back from the wall where he had been digging and peeled the moist dirt from his fingers. His face, hair, elbows, and clothes were covered in dirt and dust. He inspected the wall. He could find no other crevice or hole where he could pry his fingers into, or where Akivia might have hidden his manuscript. He sighed in frustration. He and Perindious had been searching for hours, yet the cave was not that large. There were two rooms only.

"Nothing," Perindious said, stepping in from the adjacent room. "Forgive me, Farrenthias," he said, "perhaps Akiva did pack his scroll and I did not see it, or he may have hidden it in some other cave in which case we will never find it."

"That occurred to me, too," Farrenthias said, dejectedly.

"Well, you look terrible, my young friend," Perindious said. "Go outside and catch some fresh air. I shall keep looking."

Farrenthias massaged the back of his neck. "I will only be a moment." He stepped outside and rested against one side of the entrance to the cave. From his position high on a cliff he could clearly see the Dead Sea. It looked like a thin blue ribbon stretched across the pale desert. Farrenthias inhaled deeply. The cool breeze from the waterfall was refreshing and the sound of the water was soothing to his ears. He wondered where Trulius might be this moment. Had he made progress in the search for his father? He also thought of Sesdia, and wondered what she might be doing this very moment. Farrenthias suddenly straightened up and squinted. He had been staring at a moving object far out in the distance. At first, he thought it was nothing more than an illusion created by the heat rising from the hot desert. But no, he realized that it was some sort of pack of animals and they were getting closer. He wondered if it was a herd of wild camels or horses, perhaps. While Farrenthias kept looking, the sight of men riding on horses began to materialize.

"Romans!" Perindious whispered. He was suddenly standing beside Farrenthias. "Every once in a while an army of Romans come through here to refresh themselves and their horses. We do not want to be here when they get here. They are very unpredictable."

"I agree," Farrenthias said. "How much time until they reach Engedi?"

Perindious studied their movement. "They are moving very fast.

I would say that they will be here in no more than twenty minutes, unless they stop at the Dead Sea. But we should take no chances and leave now, Farrenthias."

"Very well, I am just going to walk through the cave one last time."

"I shall wait for you here," Perindious said. "Do not take long."

Farrenthias rushed back into the cave and to the second room, where he had spent less time. He looked desperately around. This room was less lit, and in the dimness he walked with his hand dragging against one of the walls of the cave. Farrenthias suddenly stopped and looked up at what looked like a small protruding rock in one corner of the room, near the ceiling. It formed a small ledge right where two sides of a wall came together. There was a boulder near the wall and Farrenthias tried to climb it in order to reach the ledge. The boulder was not steady, and as he tried to climb on top of it, it wobbled. He was about to shout out to Perindious but Perindious rushed into the cave.

"Farrenthias!" he cried. "What are you doing? The Romans have skirted the Dead Sea, and they are moving fast. They will be here in no time!"

Farrenthias leaned against the boulder and pointed to the ledge above his head. "Perindious, I need to reach that ledge, and then we will go. Please, steady this boulder for me."

Perindious stared at him. "What? But—but, we must get going!"

"Please, Perindious. Hurry. You are wasting time!"

"Very well, but we must hurry." Perindious dropped to one knee and pushed his shoulder against the boulder.

Farrenthias climbed on top of the boulder. He was about to reach for the ledge, when the sound of horses and men's voices startled him. He tried to steady himself but the noises had also startled

Perindious, who suddenly turned toward the entrance of the cave to have a look. The boulder shifted and Farrenthias lost his balance. As he fell, he lunged toward the ledge, gripped it, but it crumbled into pieces in his hands.

Farrenthias fell on top of Perindious with small rocks and dust flying all around them. When the dust settled, Farrenthias and Perindious stared in astonishment at a small satchel that had landed at their feet. Farrenthias grabbed the satchel and quickly looked inside. "It is here!" he cried. "There is a scroll tucked inside this satchel, Perindious. It looks fragile and it may be damaged, but we found it."

"You were meant to find it!" Perindious whispered. "Now hurry, we must go."

Farrenthias and Perindious stopped and stared at each other at the sound of splashing water and of men laughing.

"Good," Perindious cried. "The are in the water. Follow me and stay low."

Farrenthias glanced over his right shoulder as he and Perindious made their way out of the cave. Fortunately, there were enough bushes to hide them from the men below. Still, Farrenthias moved quickly and fearfully. There must have been over a hundred men.

Farrenthias sighed with relief when he and Perindious were safely out of sight.

"You should return to Qumran with me," Perindious said. "You can eat and rest, and you can stay as long as you like."

Farrenthias gripped his forearm. "No, Perindious, I would like to leave at once."

"Where will you go?"

Farrenthias slipped the lip of the satchel through the wrap around his waist. "Egypt."

"Ah, you are going to search for Athinio. Good."

"I also want to see the Great Pyramid and the Sphinx. I have heard and read much about them."

Perindious placed a hand on the shoulder of Farrenthias. "I wish you would stay at least a day or two to rest, but I can see that you are a young man of resolve who does not change his mind easily. I also see something in you that tells me that you will do great things with your life, Farrenthias. But be careful. The world is a dangerous place, and unfortunately, it is an even more dangerous place for those with a kind heart and a long path ahead of them. "

Farrenthias gripped the arm of Perindious. "Thank you for all of your help, Perindious. Perhaps one day I shall return and spend more time with you at Qumran. We have much more to talk about."

Seventy

"It is him I tell you!" The afternoon was cloudy and dim and the road wet and muddy from the early morning showers. The trees that surrounded the road were also still dripping wet and partially obscured the road. Still, from the top of one of the gate walls the guard had a good view of the two riders coming up the road. He wiped the moisture from his face and turned excitedly to Quanarious. "It is my Lord Marcellius Kaelus! There could be hundreds of riders out on that road and I would still be able to tell him apart from the rest. Lord Marcellius has returned and there is another rider with him. A young man."

Quanarious scrambled to a better position on the wall and peered down the road. "Ha!" he cried. "Lord Marcellius I would never recognize because I do not know him, but that is Tessius Trulius riding beside him!"

"Trulius?" The guard hollered. He looked again. "Ah, it is indeed!"

"So," Quanarious shouted. "Father and son have returned." He jumped from the wall and tumbled onto the moist grass. "I must tell Kemnebi," he cried. "Not a day has gone by since Trulius left that he has not worried about him."

He raced across the garden and bolted through the door of Kemnebi's apartment without bothering to knock.

Kemnebi was not alone. Felicia sat at a table with him. They were poring over financial papers Farron had delivered to them yesterday. Kemnebi turned from the table to look at Quanarious who had almost lost his footing at the door.

"What is it, Quanarious?" Kemnebi said. "You are ashen and out of breath." He gripped the handle of his dagger and looked at the door. "Is there danger?"

"No, no," Quanarious cried. "Lord Marcellius and Trulius, they are back!"

"What?" Kemnebi cried. He leaped from the table. "Where are they?"

"They are approaching the gates as we speak."

Felicia gasped out loud. "At last!" she cried. "The gods have answered my prayers." She quickly rose from the table. "I must go at once. There is much to do. Supper needs to be prepared. Baths need to be prepared. Fresh clothing must be laid out."

"Marcellius and Trulius together again," Kemnebi said. "Let us go and greet them, Quanarious. "I have waited for too long for this day to arrive!"

Dressed in a long, freshly pressed toga and polished brown sandals, Marcellius sat with folded arms at one of the back porticos. He was listening intently to Kemnebi, who was seated in front of him, talking about household finances. Yet, Marcellius was momentarily distracted by the sudden presence of Trulius and Gianina in the garden below. They walked around one of the pools and sat down on a bench. Trulius started to pet Pharaoh, while Gianina playfully tossed flower petals into the water.

Aware that Marcellius was no longer paying attention to him, Kemnebi grew quiet and followed Marcellius's gaze. "Ah, those two," he murmured. "Are they not a pair? They have been inseparable since our return to Rome."

"I am not at all surprised," Marcellius said. "Gianina has grown into a lovely young woman. She is beautiful and as kind and sweet as her mother."

"Indeed," Kemnebi said, "and as you can see Trulius is completely in love with her and she with him. She will make him an excellent wife, and they will produce wonderful grandchildren for you, Marcellius. But of course, you and Servia predicted this union even while Gianina was but a child in her mother's arms."

"It was Servia who told me she had a feeling about little Gianina from the moment that Felicia gave birth to her." Marcellius nodded proudly. "You did very well in raising Trulius, Kemnebi."

"I wish I could agree with you, Marcellius, but Erasmus Harel contributed to his upbringing, as well as the other priests at Clivus. It was good that Trulius met his uncle."

"Of course, I am very grateful to my brother, as well. But his fighting skills, you should have seen him on the battlefield, only you could have taught him how to fight like that."

"Bah, again I cannot take full credit for that either. I did nothing but place a sword in his hands. He was born to wield it as expertly as his father."

Marcellius drew his breath. He grew quiet and subdued as he returned his gaze to Trulius and Gianina.

"Ah," Kemnebi whispered. "Do not say a word. I know what troubles you. Nestor."

Marcellius turned slightly toward Kemnebi. "What news do you have of that rat?"

"I cannot lie to you, Marcellius. He remains a threat to our family. He was abroad for some time, but upon his return about a month ago, he immediately made inquiries about you and Trulius. I have men scattered all over the city, men whom we can trust. The moment Nestor or any of his men engage in suspicious activity and head our way, we will know."

Marcellius clenched his jaw tight and nodded silently. He turned away and remained quiet for a long time, but at last he seemed to relax. "Tell me, Kemnebi, will I ever see Erasmus Harel again? Where is my brother now?"

Kemnebi shook his head. "Who knows where he might be. He is completely absorbed with his work, and now that he has left Clivus that means that he will likely travel extensively."

Marcellius drew his attention to the documents Kemnebi had placed on the small table between them. He picked one up and inspected it casually. "And so, what you have been telling me is that I am being taxed to death, but that I am fortunate that the empire did not leave me destitute, am I correct?"

"Perhaps now that you have returned a hero, your next tax bill will be much more fair and equitable," Kemnebi said.

Marcellius laughed. "I fear that my taxes are funding a weak government. Speaking of which, what opinion do you have of Galba? How stable is his hold on the crown of Rome?"

"He is surrounded by very little loyalty. Like most citizens of Rome I also believe that Rome will not be stable again until Vespasian ascends to the throne."

"Trulius! Be careful!" Gianina screamed. "You are going to hurt yourself!"

Marcellius whirled around. Trulius was on a black stallion and was racing around the garden in circles. Marcellius watched in fascination as Trulius easily and expertly rode the horse backwards and then jumped to the ground and back up onto the saddle with ease while the stallion tore through the garden at full speed. Trulius did this while he laughed the whole time. He even waved at Gianina with both hands as he extended his arms into the air to show that he was riding without holding on.

Gianina shrieked and covered her eyes. "Tessius Trulius! Please stop! I cannot bear to watch."

"Behold your wild and reckless son," Kemnebi said, as he and Marcellius walked down the portico steps to join Gianina. "No one can ride a horse like Trulius." He nudged Marcellius with an elbow. "And that is only the beginning of his skills."

Marcellius grimaced with delight. Kemnebi and Felicia swore that Trulius was his complete image, but Marcellius saw much of Servia in his son. His laughter, for example, was identical to his mother's laughter, and his bright penetrating eyes were his mother's eyes.

Trulius thundered to a stop beside his father. "Father!" he said. "Perhaps you ought to invest in a stable of racing horses. With me at the reins of a chariot we could take the Circus Maximus by storm."

"I have no doubt," Marcellius said. "I also have no doubt that if you do this again in front of Gianina you are going to cause her to have a heart attack."

Gianina flashed Marcellius a worried look. "Forgive me, my lord, I should not have screamed. "By now I should be used to Trulius's antics."

Marcellius took her hand and gently pressed it. "Even I was worried that he might fly off the stallion, but if that had happened

I have no doubt that he would have rolled to his feet and jumped back on."

At the table that evening, Marcellius merely picked at his meal and drank sparingly from a cup of wine. The meal Felicia had prepared was excellent. She had served bowls of fresh vegetables and fruits along with roasted poultry served with special sauces. The meal was not the problem. No, Marcellius had other matters on his mind. And then there was the nostalgia that he was feeling. The company of his family overjoyed him, but it also reminded him, in a very painful way, of how much his wife had enjoyed these family moments. Marcellius blinked. Gianina had taken his hand.

"My lord," she whispered. "I miss Lady Servia terribly, but I am comforted that she left us Trulius. She was his joy and I want to love him as much as she did, although I do not think that there is a stronger love than that of a mother and her children."

Surprised and taken back by her wise words, Marcellius could not help but to smile at her and caress her hand. "You are a joy to me, Gianina. You have not only…"

Quanarious stormed into the room panting heavily and sweating profusely. "My lord," he said between gasps, but his eyes shifted to Felicia and Gianina and he hesitated. "I—I do not wish to alarm the ladies, sire," he said. "May I have a word with you in private?"

"Speak freely, Quanarious," Marcellius said. "The women of this household do not frighten easily. Besides, if there is danger I will not keep it from them."

Quanarious took a deep breath and wiped his forehead. "My lord, a few moments ago a rider suddenly appeared at the gates. He asked for Kemnebi. He said that he was coming to warn us that men were headed our way, spies he said. No sooner did he speak those words when we spotted three men prowling around in the trees. We gave chase, and when we caught them, they fought fiercely. We killed two of them. The third man we captured alive."

Marcellius calmly but swiftly got to his feet. "Where do you have him?"

"In the stables, my lord," Quanarious said. He hesitated again.

"What is it?" Marcellius said. He paused and gripped Quanarious by the shoulder. "Is there something else?"

Quanarious looked at Kemnebi and then at Trulius. "One of the guards recognized the man that we captured. He fought like a wild boar. It took four of us to subdue him. I was told that his name is Belfore and that he was a dangerous assassin."

Marcellius glared at Kemnebi as they followed Quanarious out of the house. Neither said a word, but as soon as they were out in the courtyard, Marcellius angrily turned to Kemnebi. "Can you believe that vermin! It is time we settle this matter once and for all. I will not have my family living in fear that at the next corner they will encounter one of Nestor's assassins."

"I agree," Kemnebi said. "As long as Belfore is alive Trulius will never be safe. He must die."

Marcellius paused at the stable doors. "He and Nestor must both die."

Kemnebi nodded. "Let me do it, Marcellius. Do not stain your hands with this rat."

Marcellius shook his head. "It was my actions that got us into this mess in the first place. I shall have to finish it." He started in then paused again. "Of course, no matter what this has cost me and what we have gone through, I am not yet a cold-blooded murderer. Let me have your dagger."

Belfore was on his knees with his hands and feet tied.

He was a much larger man than Marcellius expected. He was

very heavy and his hair was long and tied behind his back. Sweat poured from his brow. There was no fear in his eyes. Instead, there was an expression of defiance, of disrespect.

"Untie him," Marcellius said.

The guard who had been watching him hesitated and Marcellius shouted at him. "Untie him!"

The guard cut the ropes from Belfore's hands and feet and then stepped away.

Marcellius dropped Kemnebi's dagger on the floor and then kicked it in the direction of Belfore.

Belfore looked at the dagger lying at his knees and then glared at Marcellius. He grinned. "I am a dead man, but so are you, Marcellius. Do not blink or I will put this dagger between your eyes before either of your men can cut me down." He grunted. "After you are dead, then your Egyptian brother can kill me. I will be unarmed."

"Are you going to keep babbling like a woman or are you going to make your move," Marcellius said.

Without moving a muscle Belfore lowered his gaze and stared at the dagger. He raised his eyes again. Then, in one swift move he reached for the dagger, grabbed it, and attempted to fling it towards Marcellius but stumbled backwards. His eyes bulged from his face and blood poured from his mouth. He made a feeble effort to reach for the dagger that was buried deep into his throat but his arm dropped and his head fell to the side.

Kemnebi sighed loudly. "The years have not diminished your swiftness or accuracy in the least, Marcellius," he said. "Do we send him back to where he came from?"

Marcellius nodded and turned to leave. "Deliver him to Nestor."

Seventy-One

Upon arriving at the house of Atenuar, Septimus hurled himself from his horse and charged to the door. Since his arrival in Rome three days earlier, he had been here at least a dozen times looking for his former father-in-law, and each time the servants had sent him away, with no news of when Atenuar might return or where he could be found. But alas, just moments ago a messenger had arrived at Septimus's house with news that Atenuar had finally arrived and wished to see him.

At the door Septimus flew past the servants who greeted him and offered to take him to Atenuar. He did not need their help. He knew exactly where to find Atenuar. Septimus swiftly walked down a long corridor, not bothering to pause and search the rooms for Varelia. He had done that on his first visit here and his instincts told him that she did not return with Atenuar. Septimus angrily clenched his fists. In the past, he had always found a way to forgive Varelia for all that she had done to him—but not this time. Her actions were an unpardonable nightmare.

Septimus bolted into Atenuar's private study and then, aghast at what he saw, he froze.

Atenaur was unrecognizable. His skin was pale, his face haggard, and his eyes purple and hollow. He looked utterly frail and completely emaciated. He was in one corner of the room standing over a table filled with wine bottles.

"Septimus," he said, in a low raspy voice that Septimus did not recognize. "I see that my appearance has taken you by complete surprise. You look stunned. Well, you just missed one of my physicians. The imbecile predicted that I would not live another three months. Bah, what does anyone know about when life ends? Although, these days, that would not be so bad." He poured two chalices of wine and offered one to Septimus.

"Tell me Atenuar, what ailment do you have, old friend? Is it the mysterious ailment of the blood?"

"Ah, so there you have it. You are as clever as the physicians, Septimus, and you did not poke around my throat and ears and eyes to reach that conclusion." He winced. "Three months? Bah, I will take my life before that if this pain does not let me sleep." He pointed to a chair. "I would ask you to sit, but I can see that you are in no mood to sit and talk." He winced again. "I do not blame you, my dear Septimus."

Septimus set his chalice of wine down and faced Atenaur with a drawn expression on his face. "I am sorry for your condition, truly I am, Atenuar, but you must forgive me for my abruptness, where is she?"

Atenuar sighed with difficulty. "I am afraid that I have no idea, Septimus. Varelia has vanished. But alas, I do have some information for you." He walked with difficulty to a chair and sat down. "The very day that Varelia spoke to Maneria she came to see me.

She confessed everything to me. I was so revolted by what she told me that I did something I did not believe I was ever capable of doing to my daughter or to any woman. I slapped her so hard she flew across the room. When she got to her feet she quivered and cried like a child." Atenuar shook his head and looked tearfully at Septimus. "In spite of everything, she is still my daughter, Septimus. Oh, I can condemn her actions and I can punish her, but she is still my daughter. If a daughter cannot turn to her father in her darkest moments, whom can she turn to? I took her in my arms and comforted her. We stayed like that for several moments with neither one of us saying a word." Atenuar paused. "But alas, she pressed my hand, wiped the tears from her face, and left without uttering a word. I have not seen her since."

Septimus, who had started to pace, stopped. "What else, Atenuar? You said you had news for me. I have gotten nowhere. I went looking for Maneria, and I was told that he was found in a pool of blood." He shook his head bitterly. "Tell me, Atenuar, is Varelia capable of anything?"

Atenuar lowered his gaze and cleared his throat. "The very next day, after Varelia left this house, I sent an investigator over to Maneria's apartment to look for him. My instructions to the man I hired was to find out all that he could about your child. It was my investigator who found Maneria in a pool of blood. But before he summoned the authorities, he thoroughly searched Maneria's apartment and took a list of what he believed to be a list of Maneria's patients."

"Oh?" Septimus murmured.

"Yes," Atenuar said. "His theory was that maybe one of those patients might have been Maneria's accomplice. He began to trace their whereabouts. It did not take long before he found a man living in the coastal city of Acona. The moment he was approached, the man was only too eager to talk. He was apparently a reformed man who was repentant for his prior bad acts. You already know that he gave your son to an unknown family. But what he told the investigator was that his instructions were to kill the child." Atenuar paused and his lips trembled. "He—he actually placed the tip of his dagger on the child's chest. The dagger pricked the child's left nipple severing a piece of it. The child screamed with so much pain that the man could not go through with his evil deed."

Septimus buried one of his fists into the other hand and glared at Atenuar. "Bastard!" he cried.

Atenuar nodded furiously. "Yes, Septimus. I agree. It was a terrible thing to do to a newborn, but do you not see? That knife caused a permanent disfigurement on the child, but it also identifies him. It identifies your son!"

Septimus lifted his chalice of wine, drank it all in one sip and slammed the cup. "Varelia has done many things to me in the past, Atenuar. You know that. She has always hated me, and she has always hated Nameya. I understand. But this? How can she do such a thing to a child, to an innocent child?"

Atenuar reached out and affectionately gripped the arm of Septimus. "I will not ask you to forgive her. She is unworthy of that. But I do ask you, for the sake of Nameya, the mother of that poor child, do not let this destroy you. Do not let it destroy the love you two share for each other. Go to her. Comfort her. She needs you. Do not become a bitter man."

Septimus sighed heavily. "I can always count on you to give me sound and wise advice, Atenuar. For that I am grateful."

"No, Septimus. It is I who is grateful to you for your friendship. My daughter has done much to try and destroy it."

Septimus gripped the forearm of Atenuar. "This changes nothing between us, old friend, and it never will."

Atenuar exhaled and nodded. "I thank you. Your assurance gives great comfort to my troubled heart." He looked about the room. "There is something else. You should know that I have properly prepared for my death. Upon my death everything that I own will be yours."

"But, Atenuar, you owe me nothing! And if it is because of this…"

"No, it is not because of this, Septimus. It is because you have always been like a son to me. In spite of my many friends and acquaintances, it is only you who has always shown me unconditional loyalty and respect." Atenuar gave his head a reassuring nod. "You have done well for yourself, but I must tell you that upon my death, you will be one of the wealthiest men in Rome."

The extent of Atenuar's wealth did not surprise Septimus in the least. He was well aware that in his own quiet and private way Atenuar was a brilliant businessman.

Atenuar continued. "I have gone through great lengths to keep the extent of my assets a secret. Be careful of the greed and envy of men, my dear Septimus. In that respect, wealth can be a curse." Atenuar sighed. "All the paperwork shall be delivered to you in a few days. Now go, my dear Septimus, and comfort Nameya. The two of you have much to do to find your son."

Septimus stood solemnly over the bed of Nameya, gazing at her while she slept. Dimly lit scattered lamps lighted the room. In spite of the lack of color on her face and her thinness, there remained a remarkable elegance to her face, a quiet beauty. On his instructions that his wife not be left alone, two servants sat quietly in one corner of the room. They were watching him carefully, waiting for any instructions he might give them. Septimus dismissed them with a nod.

He had promised Nameya that upon his return from Atenuar's house he would awaken her, whether he had news or not. He reached down and caressed her cheeks with the back of one hand and Nameya instantly opened her eyes.

Nameya blinked and upon recognizing him, she flung herself into his arms. "Septimus," she cried. "I have been waiting for you. What did Atenuar tell you? Did he have any news for you?"

Septimus forced a tight smile and tried to sound optimistic. "Yes, Nameya. He gave me hope that one day we will find our son."

Nameya pulled away from his arms. "Yes" she whispered. "I know we will find him. I feel it in my heart, but did he tell you anything that would help?"

Septimus did not dare to give her the details of what Atenuar had told him. Instead, he gently pulled her away and lifted her chin. "Atenuar told me of a way to identify our son. He told me of a slight deformity that he was born with, but first you must promise me that you will begin to eat regularly. You must regain your strength. We have much to do to find our son..."

Seventy-Two

A thunderous noise emerged out of nowhere and shattered the stillness of the night. Farrenthias stopped dead in his tracks and looked desperately around. Gratefully, a pale moon hung high in the clear sky. There were also millions of bright stars glittering and flashing. They helped to illuminate an otherwise totally dark desert. Farrenthias whirled around in a circle trying to determine from which direction the noise was coming from, but he could not tell. He knew only that it was getting closer. Then he recognized the sound of hooves tearing into the desert, but he could not tell what animals were making those sounds. Were they horses, or camels perhaps? The sound grew louder and Farrenthias panicked when he realized he might be directly in the path of a stampede of wild animals. He started to back away, unsure in which direction to run, but it was too late. A train of camels thundered by him and knocked him off his feet. Farrenthias hit the ground and rolled several times before he came to a stop on his back. The camels came to an abrupt halt.

"Ha! I see you," an angry voice called out. "Look what you have done. You have frightened my pets." The man's high-pitched voice softened when he spoke to his camels. "Now, now, my children, calm yourselves. It is nothing. There is no danger."

A spark illuminated the darkness, and suddenly a small lamp began to glow.

"Are you alright?" the man cried. "My pets and I, we did not trample you, did we?"

Farrenthias stumbled to his feet and dusted himself off. "I am fine. I am sorry I startled your camels, sire," he said. "But you also frightened me."

"I frightened you, but are you mad?" the man said. "What are you doing out here in the middle of the desert, in the middle of the night, and alone?" He waved the lamp and looked around. "What, no camel? No horse? You are walking?" He raised the lamp to his face. "It is insane trying to cross the desert in pitch darkness on foot. Why, you are even more mad than I am. I am at least riding a camel, but you, how far do you expect to get on foot? The desert is full of danger. Why, not even robbers dare cross this desert at night, unless they are in full flight from the authorities." He lowered his voice. "Are you a criminal? Are you on the run from the authorities?"

"No, no, sire. My name is Farrenthias Theophilus. I am a Greek from Syria."

The man lowered the scarf that covered his chin. "Then what will you do, Farrenthias Theophilus, a Greek from Syria, if a deadly scorpion pricks your skin? Or what if you accidentally stumble into a Bedouin camp and you are mistaken for a thief? Do you know what Bedouins will do to a thief?"

"I must admit that I did not consider those possibilities," Farrenthias said, "but it would not have made any difference, I have to reach Egypt."

"Egypt? On foot? Ha! The Sphinx will crumble to dust before you reach Egypt on foot." The man whispered a command to his camel, and the camel, followed by the other camels, started toward Farrenthias. The old man leaned forward holding the light in front of him to have a better look at Farrenthias. "Bah! Why you are but a child!" He waved the lantern in front of him. "But I see that you have an honest face. No doubt you have been praying for divine help. Well, the gods to whom you have prayed have answered your prayers. They have sent you me, Ja'eleni from Babylonia. In Egypt I plan to sell four of my camels, but I am willing to part with one now, for the right price."

Farrenthias shrugged. "I am afraid, Ja'eleni, that I have very few coins in my purse. At the edge of this desert I came upon a beggar and gave him some of my coins. I cannot afford to buy one of your camels."

"I see, so, you will have to travel on foot to Egypt because you cannot afford a camel because you gave your money away. Well, you do not have a good plan. A man must have a good plan in everything that he does. You must have important business in Egypt to risk walking alone at night."

"Forgive me for asking," Farrenthias said, "but why are you crossing the desert at night?"

"Ah, well my situation is different, young one. Ja'eleni is not so young anymore and the sun and heat bother me. I detest heat. So, even though there is a risk of getting attacked by robbers, I prefer traveling by night so I can catch a cool breeze. Now, enough about me, do you possess anything of value that you wish to sell or trade for a camel, a special dagger or a piece of jewelry perhaps, anything at all?"

Farrenthias looked about his body and then shook his head. "I am afraid I have nothing, Ja'eleni."

"Ah! You are a poor young man all the way around. Well, it is no sin to be poor, but it can be tragic, such as when you are in the middle of the desert at night and you need to buy a camel but you have no money because you gave it away to a beggar." Ja'eleni frowned. "Did I not just say that earlier? Am I repeating myself? I do that often these days."

Farrenthias could not help but laugh. "You are very kind to offer to sell me one of your camels, Ja'eleni." He sighed and looked down the dark road ahead. "I suppose I should be on my way. I have taken enough of your time, and I have a great distance to go."

"Just a moment. No need to rush matters. I am thinking." Ja'eleni flung a short leg around as if he was going to jump down, but he remained aboard his camel. "So I did not strike a good bargain. Bah, what does it matter? Do I look like a man who would leave a poor soul stranded in the desert in the middle of the night? Ja'eleni is a compassionate man, and I suppose that I could use the company. I shall loan you one of my camels, but I warn you I travel fast. I hope you are an experienced rider."

Farrenthias swallowed with difficulty and looked from one camel to the other. They were beautiful animals indeed, but they terrified him even more than horses. "Ja'eleni," he said. "I am afraid that I have never been on a camel before."

"What?" Ja'eleni threw his hands into the air and sighed. "But what is this? Do I have to also give you riding lessons as well?"

"No, no," Farrenthias cried. "I shall walk."

"Nonsense!" Ja'eleni tapped his riding stick against his knee. "Ja'eleni is an excellent teacher. Besides, riding a camel is child's play. After I am through with you, people will swear that you were born a camel driver." He whispered to his camel again and this time the camel lowered itself to its knees, and Ja'eleni jumped out of the saddle. He was very small and thin. His robes dragged as he walked among the other camels mumbling to himself. "Ah!" he cried, pausing before one of the smaller camels. "But of course! Sefone!" He caressed the chin of the small camel. "Sefone, you shall be the one to carry our new friend across the desert. And you must remember to be nice and not toss him off your back. You must behave!"

Ja'eleni waved Farrenthias over. "Come, come," he said. "Sefone is waiting for you. Never keep a lady waiting. She is as docile as a newborn pup. You should have no trouble staying on top of her."

Ja'eleni untied Sefone from the other camels and then lightly tapped her front legs. Sefone kneeled and rested on the sand with its long legs folded beneath her bulky body. "Ah, but if man were only as obedient," Ja'eleni said. "Come, Farrenthias, your ride across the desert is ready."

Farrenthias took a deep breath and then awkwardly flung his leg across Sefone and landed on the saddle. He sighed with relief, but just as he got comfortable, Ja'eleni ordered Sefone to her feet and Farrenthias jerked back and almost fell off.

"Steady now," Ja'eleni said. "You are doing fine. Lesson number one. Do not fall off. Hang on for dear life if you have to, but do not fall. If you fall you could break your neck and then you will never get to Egypt. Now, just whisper the magic words and Sefone will submit to you for life."

"The magic words?" Farrenthias cried, wrapping the reins tightly around his hands.

"Yes, yes, whisper to her, 'lovely is the camel I ride' and then stroke her ears, my child, and she will purr like a kitten."

Ja'eleni mounted his own camel, waved his arm forward and the train of camels charged into the desert. Farrenthias bounced up and down and to the sides. With every stride that Sefone took, it felt to

Farrenthias as if he were about to fall. He was as stiff as a tree. Yet, instinctively, he dug his legs into Sefone and held the reins as tight as he could to steady himself.

"Ah, you are doing wonderfully," Ja'eleni shouted. "Did I not tell you that Ja'eleni was an excellent teacher!"

Farrenthias tried to smile, but instead, he got sick and barely managed to avoid soiling the front of his tunic by hanging his head to his left. Mercifully, Ja'eleni slowed down to almost a walking pace.

"Very well then," he shouted, "that little run was just to make sure my children stay in good condition. What a delight they are, no? I have a mind not to sell any of them."

Farrenthias finally managed a smile and stroked the ears of Sefone. "They are beautiful camels, Ja'eleni."

Farrenthias lost all track of time, and at last a dim ribbon of light across the horizon began to light up the desert.

Ja'eleni was suddenly riding beside Farrenthias. "Ah, my dear friend," he said, "but you look so pale. Are you not enjoying Sefone?" He shouted at the camels, and they slowed and then came to a complete stop. He shouted again, and this time all the camels dropped to their knees.

Farrenthias bent over to one side and became sick again. He had discovered something more disagreeable than riding horses.

"Ah, is that all?" Ja'eleni cried. "You shall be fine." He removed a small pouch from one of his bags and offered it to Farrenthias. "Water. Water is a cure for all ailments."

Farrenthias rinsed his mouth and spit out the water. "I am sorry, Ja'eleni."

Ja'eleni took the pouch and wet his own lips. "Bah, even the most experienced rider must empty his belly from time to time. Sit back and rest against Sefone. I think she has taken a liking to you."

Ja'eleni settled next to Farrenthias, and in the early morning light, Farrenthias got a good look at him. Ja'eleni's dark face was heavily wrinkled, but he was an attractive old man with a thin face and an especially straight nose. He had no beard and he had dark eyes that sparkled and would not stop shifting while he talked. He was almost as small as Quanarious. He was dressed in a pale green robe and bright yellow slippers. A purple turban was wrapped around his head tied with a bright red ruby. In his left hand he wore a ring with a large yellow diamond that he kept twisting around his finger. Aware that he had been staring at Ja'eleni, Farrenthias shyly turned away.

"Ah, do not be embarrassed" Ja'eleni said. "I know what you are thinking. You are thinking that a man like me should have half a dozen servants helping me across the desert with my camels." He stretched his short legs and stared at his yellow slippers. "A man can grow fat and weak if he depends on his servants to do all his work." He pensively sipped from the pouch of water. "In truth, I needed time away from my business associates and friends. They are a strange lot. Money and greed drive them. They are pompous and always have the last word in a discussion. I try to get away from them but they seek me out even when I am at home refusing to attend their functions. Anyway, I am blessed with a lovely daughter and son-in-law. I left them in charge of my businesses." Ja'eleni raised an eyebrow in excitement and raised a finger. He jumped to his feet. "Let me show you something." He retrieved a jeweled box from his camel. "I am going to Alexandria to see Darious, a friend whom I do business with. I buy and sell antiques, relics, and other valuables. Darious buys them from me on behalf of the authorities for a museum." Ja'eleni placed the box between him and Farrenthias and opened it. He picked out a gold ring and admired it. "Rameses

II of Egypt wore this ring every day until the day he died. One of his embalmers removed it and forgot to place it in the basket with the rest of the pharaoh's other jewelry that was placed in his tomb." Ja'eleni looked at Farrenthias and dropped his voice to a whisper. "Bah, a likely story, I think he was caught trying to steal it. I purchased it in Babylonia from a reputable merchant who came by it." Ja'eleni pulled out a dagger and held it up so Farrenthias could see it better. "This killing instrument was actually one of the daggers used in the assassination of Julius Caesar. Morbid, I know, but some will be awed by its history." He set the dagger down and picked up a cup. "Ah, and this precious cup was a favorite of Augustus. On the day he died he was too weak to drink so it had to be placed to his lips with his favorite wine." Ja'eleni shook his head. "Unfortunately, it is rumored that his loving wife, Livia, poisoned many of his children from previous marriages using this very cup."

"Thus guaranteeing that her son Tiberius would become emperor on the death of Augustus," Farrenthias said.

"Ah, you know your history, Farrenthias. Yes, that is exactly correct," Ja'eleni said. "What a mother will not do for her children."

"Speaking of Rome, have you been there?" Farrenthias asked. "I was there not too long ago with a friend of mine."

"But of course," Ja'eleni said. "I have traveled the entire world collecting my treasures. There is no city like Rome in the entire world." He frowned as though stuck by a thought. "What awaits you in Egypt? Is it urgent? Perhaps you and I should board a ship and go back to Rome. I am ready to visit that great city again."

Farrenthias laughed and then thought himself almost foolish for having left Engedi so abruptly. After all, there was indeed no great urgency. "I carry a manuscript with me, and I am in search of the man who wrote it. I am told that there is a man who lives on the shores of the Red Sea who might help me find that man. I also want to go to Giza, to see the Great Pyramid and Sphinx."

"Giza I understand, but what is so important about this manuscript that you carry? Does it have any value?"

Farrenthias could not help but to smile. "Value? I do not believe so. It is about the life of a very wise Hebrew prophet, a rabbi. The Romans crucified him."

Ja'eleni frowned. "Ah, the Romans and their barbaric practices. I can think of no worse way to die. Very cruel indeed." He thought a moment. "Here, I have something to show you."

He walked to his camel and returned with a small pouch.

"A few years back I came upon a man on some desolate road. It was late, and he was seated alone at a campfire, chewing on a piece of bread. He was a man of very few words, but friendly, and he invited me to sit with him. He even offered me a piece of his very small slice of bread. During our conversation I told him that I collected antiques and relics. I showed him some of what I had with me at the time. He seemed very interested but said very little. I could tell that he was troubled and that his money purse was empty, but he was a proud man. He refused the small stipend that I offered him, but he finally accepted it when I pointed out to him that one day when his purse was full again he might consider helping someone in need. Well, the next day when I awoke he was gone and this pouch was lying next to me with a scrap of papyrus upon which he had scribbled a few words."

"What did he write?" Farrenthias asked.

"He wrote that perhaps I could interest some buyer into buying these." Ja'eleni emptied the pouch. "According to the note the Romans nailed a great Hebrew prophet in Jerusalem to a cross with these very nails."

Farrenthias paled, and stared incredulously at the nails. They were long and brown and crooked, as though they had indeed been driven through wood and perhaps flesh and bone.

"But you have paled completely, Farrenthias," Ja'eleni said, and then suddenly his eyebrows narrowed. "Hum," he murmured. "I know what you are thinking but that cannot be possible. The Romans have crucified many men. They have been crucifying men for years."

Farrenthias started to pick up one of the nails but pulled his hand back.

"Go on young one," Ja'eleni said. "Do not be afraid to touch them."

Farrenthias inspected the nails with trembling hands. He was suddenly filled with emotion, filled with wonderment. Was it possible that these were the very nails used to crucify Yeshua? Doubt filled his heart. He shook his head and set them down. "Perhaps you are correct, Ja'eleni," he said. "I am foolish to think they might be the very nails used to crucify the rabbi I speak about."

"Why are you so interested in this Yeshua? Was he no different than any other prophet?"

"That is what I am trying to discover. I am told that he was very wise and knowledgeable, knowledgeable about things few people understand."

"I see, I see," Ja'eleni said, furiously rubbing his chin. He put the nails back into the back. "I am not without my own beliefs," he said. "I am a very superstitious man. Perhaps stumbling into you in the middle of the desert was no coincidence." He handed the bag of nails to Farrenthias. "I do not know if these were the very nails used on Yeshua, but I think you should have them. They are yours."

"But, Ja'eleni, I cannot pay you for them," Farrenthias cried.

Ja'eleni shrugged his shoulders. "What does that matter? Do you realize that these nails have been in my favorite bag since I got them years ago? I never travel without that bag and is it not odd that I never took them out? Is that another strange coincidence?" He got to his feet. "Enough talk about coincidences, it scares me. Now, come, we should go if we ever want to reach Egypt."

Seventy-Three

The dark green waters of the Nile sparkled like a green emerald blazoned on a golden shield. Its grassy banks were filled with palm trees whose wide and long branches draped about, offering welcoming shade from the bright early morning sun. Men, women, and children frolicked naked and half-naked in the water, singing. Dozens of feluccas were moored along the river's banks, and the men aboard them sang along with the masses even as they worked to prepare their feluccas for their departure.

Farrenthias squinted from the glare of the sun. "I have never seen a more beautiful river," he said. "And so many happy people."

"Indeed!" Ja'eleni cried. "There is no other river in the world like the Nile, and we could not have arrived at a more propitious time. The people are in a festive mood. They are celebrating the rising waters by singing praises to the mighty river and to the gods of water and harvest, Sobk and Amon."

Farrenthias looked about. "Where are we? In which direction is Giza?"

Ja'eleni motioned to his right. "Giza is in that direction," he said, and then he pointed to the feluccas. "And there is your next ride." He folded his arms and studied the feluccas. "There!" he cried. "I like that one."

Docked separately from the others was a small felucca with two sails wrapped tightly around two short masts that were positioned at the front and back of a small cabin.

"It looks fine to me," Farrenthias said. "Do you think the man who owns it will take me to Giza?"

"But of course!" Ja'eleni cried. "Ja'eleni is in charge of your passage. Did he not arrange for Sefone to bring you here? Come, let us go and make the arrangements."

Ja'eleni halted the train of camels at the edge of the water and studied the felucca he had chosen. "I have an excellent feeling about this felucca," he said. "Ja'eleni believes that it will carry you safely to Giza and bring you luck. What do you think?"

"I like it too," Farrenthias said. "But I do not see anybody aboard. Where do you think we can find the owner?"

Ja'eleni ordered the camels to kneel, and he stepped off his saddle. "We shall find him."

The great antique dealer from Babylonia waded in the water without hesitation and approached the felucca.

"Well? Who is the master of this vessel?" he shouted. He threw his arms up and then dropped them when there was no response.

"Does this felucca navigate itself or does it have an owner?" he shouted again, but again there was no response.

Farrenthias stepped into the water and stood beside Ja'eleni. "Do you suppose the men are bathing in the water?"

"Obviously," Ja'eleni said. "But it is unusual that not even a guard has been left behind to thwart off potential thieves."

A young boy suddenly emerged from the other side of the cabin. He was on his hands and knees, crawling along the deck of the felucca with his nose close to the wooden floor, as if he were searching for something. He had thick black hair and wore a faded light blue, short toga. He did not look Egyptian. He glanced briefly at Ja'eleni and Farrenthias and then returned to his task. "I thought I heard shouting," he said in Latin.

"Young man," Ja'eleni said. "Where is the owner of this felucca? My friend here needs to purchase a passage to Giza."

The boy's head shot up. His face was dusty and burned from the sun, but he was handsome. He had black hair and dark blue eyes that sparkled with delight. "Giza? You wish to go to Giza? We are leaving for Giza in less than an hour." The boy suddenly dropped down again and began to look around. "Oh, the owner of this felucca is very nice. He will gladly let you ride for free."

"Ah, excellent," Ja'eleni said. "Did I not tell you I had a feeling about this felucca, Farrenthias?"

"You did indeed," Farrenthias said, looking down at the boy who was now on his knees, inspecting his immediate area.

"Have you lost something," Farrenthias said. "Perhaps I can help you look for it."

"There!" the boy shouted. "There it is!" He crawled to the edge of the felucca and triumphantly pulled out an old discolored coin that was wedged between two boards. "My lucky piece!" he cried. "I thought I had lost it." He jumped to his feet and rubbed his knees. "Every man should carry a lucky piece. It brings good luck."

"Ah! A very interesting coin indeed," Ja'eleni said, his eyes fixed on the gold coin the boy held in his hands. "May I look at it?"

The boy hesitated and Ja'eleni held out his hand. "Come, come young man let me see it, perhaps it is more valuable than you imagine."

The boy handed the coin to Ja'eleni and Ja'eleni studied it, quietly making gestures as he turned the coin in his hands. "Just as I thought," he said. "It is a Roman gold coin. Because it is gold, it is not very common. Where did you get this, young man? Have you ever been to Rome?"

The young boy looked at his coin and then at Ja'eleni with a worried expression on his face. "I have never been to Rome, but I did not steal it, sire" he said. "I swear I did not steal it."

"Bah," Ja'eleni said. "I was not accusing you of being a thief."

The boy licked his lips and swallowed. "Oh, well I do not remember where I got it. I have always had it."

Ja'eleni reached into one of his satchels and produced a very small purple pouch with a gold colored string. "This," he said, "is what you use to carry a valuable coin." He put the coin inside the small leather pouch and handed it to the young boy.

The boy stared at the pouch. "It is beautiful, sire. But I cannot pay you for it." His eyes lit up. "I can do a chore for you!"

Ja'eleni laughed. "A young man who likes to work for his keep. I like that. Well, it is a gift. You owe me nothing for it."

"My name is Farrenthias. What is your name?" Farrenthias said.

"Gavinio," the boy said. "My name is Gavinio." He kissed the small pouch and tucked it inside a small bag that hung from his belt. "If you are going to Giza, I can show you around, Farrenthias. I have been there many times. What do you want to see, the Pyramids? I can also show you the Sphinx."

Farrenthias suddenly realized how much Gavinio reminded him of Tessius Trulius when he had first met him, and he suddenly laughed to himself.

"Did I say something funny?" Gavinio said. "I do not lie. I know my way around Egypt."

"I was not laughing at you," Farrenthias said. "It is just that you remind me of a friend of mine when he was about your age."

"Hum," Ja'eleni murmured. "You do not look like a day over seven years old. Are you traveling with your father and mother? Where are they?"

Gavinio's dusty face darkened and he looked away. "I—I do not need a father or a mother. I can take care of myself. I have been up and down the Nile many times. I have been on the Mediterranean, and even the Red Sea, and I have never gotten lost."

Ja'eleni smiled broadly. "Ah, but of course, my child. I can see that your lucky piece has served you well."

Gavinio tapped his purse. "And now that I have it inside a beautiful pouch I will not drop it again."

"You have been to the Red Sea?" Farrenthias asked. "After Giza I am going to the Red Sea. I hope to find a man who lives somewhere by the Red Sea."

Gavinio's eyes widened and he looked excitedly at Farrenthias. "I have been there. I can help you get to the Red Sea. I have a friend at Giza. His name is Jabari. He owns camels. He can take you to the Red Sea, and if you like, I can accompany you. I also know a fisherman. Haji is his name. He owns a fishing felucca on the Red Sea. He knows everyone. I can take you to him."

"Well then, Farrenthias," Ja'eleni said. "I am amazed. Did I not tell you this felucca would bring you luck? Our young new friend here has it all figured out for you. It sounds like you have found a new traveling companion." He searched one side of his belt and then the other. "Ah, here it is," he said. He produced a small moneybag and offered it to Farrenthias.

"I cannot take your money, Ja'eleni," Farrenthias said. "You have already done enough for me and you have given me a priceless gift."

"Bah, do not be silly, Farrenthias," Ja'eleni said. He shoved the purse into Farrenthias's hands. "You are on an important mission and Ja'eleni wants to help. Besides, if you are ever stranded in the desert again you shall now be able to afford a camel. Oh, and as we agreed last night. I shall send a messenger to Jerusalem to look for your friend Ya'ir to inform him of your whereabouts so he will not worry. Who knows, maybe I shall even deliver the message myself. So there! Everything is settled."

"I am very grateful for everything you have done for me, Ja'eleni," Farrenthias said. "I hope that someday we will see each other again."

"But of course we will see each other again!" He placed a hand on Farrenthias's shoulder. "I expect that one day you shall come and visit me in Babylonia. Sefone and I will be waiting." He looked at Gavinio and removed a purple ring that he wore on his smallest finger. He held it up and stared at it. "This once belonged to a Roman senator, but I do not recall his name. Take it, it is yours. Like your lucky piece perhaps it will bring you luck."

Gavinio stared incredulously at the ring. "No one has ever given me a gift. I do not know what to say, sire! Do you really want me to have it?" He tried it on every finger, but the ring was too big.

Ja'eleni laughed. "One day you will grow into it. Perhaps for now you should put it away with your lucky piece?"

"A good idea," Gavinio said. "I thank you for being so kind to me, sire."

In contrast to the alluring blue waters of the Mediterranean, the green waters of the Nile snaked away for as far as Farrenthias could see. He stood at one end of the felucca with Gavinio standing silently beside him. Three men holding long sticks dug their sticks into the shallow water and pushed the felucca along. The felucca, therefore, moved steadily through the peaceful waters of the Nile. The men did not just navigate the felucca along, they also acted as lookouts, keeping an alert eye for hippopotamuses or crocodiles who might venture into the path of the felucca.

Fortunately Gavinio had been right. The captain of the felucca had welcomed Farrenthias as well as a few other passengers who had rushed toward the felucca just as it started to pull away from the bank. The captain had explained that his business was hauling baskets of wheat and barley and other fruits and vegetables up and down the river, and that he enjoyed the good deed of taking passengers when he had room.

"Have a look," Gavinio said, just as everyone on the felucca began to cheer and holler at the farmers who were on the riverbed waving and chanting.

A herd of hippopotamuses were near the bank of the river bathing. Some raised their massive heads and watched the felucca float by. The men with their long poles worked furiously to hurry the felucca along, just in case one of those hippopotamuses got too curious and charged the felucca. "Sometimes the Egyptians are afraid of those huge river horses," Gavinio said. "But mostly they love them."

Farrenthias looked curiously at his new friend. He decided that Gavinio was either a runaway or an orphan who had no family. Either way he was remarkably bright and mature for his tender age. And again, Farrenthias could not help but to be fascinated by how much he reminded him of Trulius. He had dark curly hair and had a strong build for one so young. Were he to guess, he would guess that he was Roman. Both were highly spirited, fearless, and very sure of themselves. *Trulius.* Farrenthias paused to wonder where he might be this very moment. He also wondered when he was ever going to see him again.

"Ha!" Gavinio cried. "Look, Farrenthias! Look carefully way off in the distance, and you can see the very tip of the Great Pyramid between all those palm trees."

Seventy-Four

"**B**ehold!" Gavinio cried, running slightly ahead of Farrenthias. "Have you ever seen anything like it?"

No, Farrenthias thought, I have never seen such magnificence! The three Pyramids were even more spectacular than he imagined. They rose majestically into the sky, one enormous stone on top of another with stunning precision. But the sheer size of the largest one took his breath away. The size of the base, the size of each stone, and the height of the Pyramid made it nearly impossible to comprehend how man could ever erect such a structure of that magnitude and beauty. Farrenthias concluded that the builders must have applied very advanced mathematical principles and impossibly difficult labor to erect such structures. A train of camels walked past the Pyramid, and Farrenthias stared at them in amazement. Against the enormous Pyramid the camels looked like nothing more than a trail of ants walking by.

Oddly, Farrenthias was suddenly overcome with a strange sense of familiarity not just with the Pyramids but also with the entire area. It made no sense. He had never been to Egypt before. Yet, he recalled that even at Clivus he had been fascinated, almost obsessed, with stories about Egypt and the Pyramids. He had asked Erasmus Harel many questions about the great structures, and Erasmus Harel had never tired of telling him about them—and now here he was.

"Well? What do you think?" Gavinio said. "Are they not amazing? The Bedouins say they are tombs for the pharaohs."

"Yes, that is exactly correct," Farrenthias said. "There was a man, Imhotep was his name. He was a brilliant architect. He designed the first Pyramid for King Zoser," Farrenthias said. "That Pyramid is not far from here. Now, it is believed that the largest of these Pyramids was built for Khufu. The next one in size was built for Khafre, and the smallest one for Khafre's son, Menkaure."

Gavinio scratched his head. "I thought you had never been to Egypt before? How do you know all that?"

Farrenthias laughed. "I learned from studying about Egypt, Gavinio. Now hurry. I am anxious to get close…" Farrenthias abruptly gasped. He had been so busy admiring the Pyramids that he had forgotten about the Sphinx, the statue that has the body of an animal and face of a man. "Do you see that, Gavinio? Do you see the Sphinx?"

"Of course, I see it," Gavinio said. "I have seen it many times. Is it not the strangest thing you have ever seen? It is so large."

"It is magnificent," Farrenthias said. "It is another one of the mysterious figures of Egypt. Not much is known about who built it and why."

"There!" Gavinio cried. "There is my friend Jabari. Do you see him feeding his camels?"

Jabari was dressed all in long, white clothing. The turban on his head was rolled high and a part of it drooped across his shoulders.

Six camels that were loosely tied together surrounded him. They were chewing greens that Jabari was feeding them from a wooden bucket.

"Jabari," Gavinio cried. "I am back."

Jabari beamed with delight. "You are indeed, my little rascal friend, and this time you bring a friend." He smiled at Farrenthias through yellow, crooked teeth that contrasted brightly against his dark skin. "Greetings," he said to Farrenthias. "You are in good company."

Farrenthias greeted Jabari in his native tongue and Jabari nodded. "It is a joy to hear a non-Egyptian speak our language," he said. " You speak it very well."

"And he knows a lot about your country," Gavinio said. "He is a very bright young man."

Jabari laughed. "Then you are both bright young men. Have you come to see the Pyramids and the Sphinx?" he asked Farrenthias.

"Yes, but I have other business." Farrenthias explained to Jabari that he and Gavinio needed to get to the Red Sea as soon as possible.

"Of course, that is not a problem at all," Jabari said. "But I will have to charge you a bit more than what I charge for a tour around Giza." He grinned. "But it will not be much." His grin widened. "Otherwise, Gavinio will get mad at me."

"Good, thank you," Farrenthias said, looking past Jabari and fixing his eyes on the Pyramids.

Jabari grinned again. "You would like to explore the Great Pyramid and the animal god before we leave, of course. A trip to Giza is never complete until you visit our great monuments."

Farrenthias stood staring at the Great Pyramid. He recalled that Erasmus Harel had told him that on his first trip to Giza he had been shown an entrance into the Great Pyramid, an entrance that was kept hidden from visitors. The men who had shown it to him, however, had only allowed him to step inside for a few moments before they rushed him out and sealed the entrance for fear of getting caught by the authorities. On his second trip, Erasmus Harel was determined to go inside again, but upon arriving, he had fallen ill for weeks and had to leave Egypt.

"Sire," Farrenthias said, his eyes shifting back and forth between Jabari and the Great Pyramid. "I know about the hidden entrance. Do you know where it is? I would like to go inside the Pyramid."

Jabari winced and then he too eyed the Great Pyramid. "The hidden entrance is not totally a secret anymore," he said, still looking at the Pyramid. "At times the authorities have allowed limited access to it, but at other times, they refuse to allow anyone to go in. They fear that looters will find their way into secret chambers and loot what they find or scribble on the walls of the passages." He looked at Farrenthias and slowly shook his head. "I am afraid that no one has been allowed inside the Pyramid for more than a year."

"Hum," Farrenthias murmured, with great disappointment. "Have you been inside?"

"Many times," Jabari said. "The passage is difficult to get through." His eyes grew wide and expressive. "It is very tight in there. You cannot stand. You must crawl, and that is difficult to do when you are holding a torch. It is difficult to breathe in there, and it is infested with bugs and vermin and who knows what else." He frowned and shook his head. "I do not know what the authorities fear. The passage leads to nowhere. There is nothing to see. There is nothing to loot." He paused and thought a moment. "It is true that in recent years government diggers successfully removed a section of the left wall at the end of the passage, but that led to nothing more than a small chamber you can barely crawl into." He looked at the Great Pyramid again. "Of course, there is talk of many secret chambers and the Pharaoh's treasure, but the walls are very thick. Even an expert thief would find it difficult to pierce through those thick walls."

Farrenthias sighed in exasperation. He had come too far not to go inside the Great Pyramid. "Jabari," he whispered. "I want to go in. Please, help me to go inside."

There was a long moment of silence, during which Jabari studied Farrenthias's intense face. He then turned several times to look at the Great Pyramid. "Hum," he finally murmured. His face eased into a subtle smile. "I can see that you are quite determined." He hooded his eyes with both hands and gazed at the Pyramid. "The guards are no longer at the entrance all day ever since the authorities began to spread what I believe to be false rumors that the ceiling to the passage was weak and that it could collapse at any moment, trapping those inside."

Gavinio gasped out loud, and Farrenthias became aware that the young boy had taken his hand and had squeezed it hard.

What if the rumors are true," Gavinio said. "Do not go inside, Farrenthias. It is too dangerous. Besides, I have heard that some men begin to choke inside because it is so difficult to breathe."

"Gavinio is right," Jabari said. "Many men have crawled in and out, but there have also been those who had to be dragged out of there pale and gasping for air."

"I understand," Farrenthias said, "but I have to do this."

"Very well," Jabari said. "Some say these monuments have a strange effect on some people, perhaps you will have no trouble at all." He looked around. "I will get my tools and we shall be on our way."

Jabari paused at the north base of the Pyramid and looked casually around and scratched the back of his neck. "Strange," he whispered.

"I have never seen so few people here at this time of day. I consider that a good omen."

Indeed, there were a few vendors walking around with open boxes of wares and some people walking aimlessly around looking up at the Pyramid. Several merchants were seated off in the short distance tending to their camels. No one seemed to notice them.

Jabari motioned with his head. "The entrance is up there." He placed a hand on an enormous block of limestone and scraped it until particles of stone dropped away. "These limestone blocks are not difficult to climb, but you must be careful. They can be slippery. Stay close behind me. The entrance is not far from here."

Farrenthias inhaled deeply and was so excited his feet trembled when he took the first step onto the Pyramid. *At last he thought. At last I am climbing the Great Pyramid at Giza and soon I shall be inside.* For the moment he forgot his quest to find Athinio. For now all he could think about was how fortunate he was to finally fulfill his dream of being here. Jabari had been right. Farrenthias did not even break a sweat before Jabari stopped climbing and announced that they had arrived.

"I told you it was not far from the bottom. We are here."

Fortunately there was a ledge wide enough to allow Jabari to kneel down and spread out his tools. Farrenthias gazed across the Nile Valley. It was a beautiful day, and even though the sun was shining brightly, it was not terribly hot. The valley was rich with vegetation in some sections and dry and desolate in others. It was, he decided, a beautiful country. A few Bedouins at the bottom of the Pyramid would occasionally look up at them, but for the most part, they seemed uninterested.

Jabari looked down at the Bedouins. "It is good that there are no elders down there," he said, while he kneeled and began to pry a stone with his finger. "Some of the elders say we violate the sacredness of these tombs when we enter them. Perhaps they are right, but I also believe that these ancient monuments have to be explored before thieves loot them."

Jabari picked out a very thin tool that resembled a dagger and slipped it across the bottom right side of a large block of stone. The instrument slipped in with little difficulty. "This block is actually cracked here," Jabari said, while he worked the instrument back and forth across the bottom corner. "This lower section has been removed many times, that is why I was able to slip this instrument in so easily," he said. He pointed to a set of instruments with his free hand. "Each of you take one of those and pry it into the side of this section."

Jabari waited until Farrenthias and Gavinio had wedged their instruments into the side as he had instructed. "Now slip your fingers in," he said.

Farrenthias slipped one and then two and then all of his fingers inside the crack. Gavinio who was kneeled beside him did the same.

"Now both of you pull!" Jabari whispered excitedly, while he also pulled from the top of the cracked section. "Pull with all your strength! This section has to slip out."

Farrenthias pulled so hard his arms stiffened and burned with pain. But nothing happened.

"Again," Jabari said, "only this time pull harder!"

But again, nothing happened, and the three of them collapsed back. At the sound of voices they turned to see that two Bedouin men had climbed up to them.

"Jabari, you rascal," one of them said. "What are you up to? That entrance has not been opened in over a year."

"I am aware of that," Jabari said. "But my young friend here is a guest in our country and he wishes to go inside."

The men stared at Farrenthias.

"Has Jabari told you how dangerous it is in there?" one of them said.

"Of course I warned him," Jabari said. "But he insists on going in. Now are you two going to help us, or are you just going to waste our time?"

The two men waved at Farrenthias and Gavinio to step out of the way. They then rolled up their sleeves and positioned themselves next to Jabari. Farrenthias watched in fascination as the three men pulled a lower right section of the block out.

"That should be enough," one of the Bedouins said. "The lad is not very big. He can make it through."

Jabari moved out of the way. "Have a look, my young friend," he said. "There is your entrance. As you can see, you will have to slip in sideways. Once you are inside, I will hand you a torch." Jabari paused and looked intently at Farrenthias. "Unless you have changed your mind about going in."

"No, no," Farrenthias said. "I am going in."

"Very well," Jabari said. "I just hope that you are not too disappointed. There is not much to see."

Gavinio kneeled in front of the crack they had created and peered in. "It is very dark in there, Farrenthias. Be very careful. I would not want something to happen to you before we get to the Red Sea."

Jabari lit a torch. "Go slow. In some places it is a very tight squeeze, and the deeper you go in, the harder it will be for you to breathe. The lack of air will cause your torch to dim but do not panic. There are tiny pockets of air inside. The torch will not go out, but if it does, just crawl straight back."

"I understand," Farrenthias said. He glanced up at the peak of the Pyramid and then down to its base. Its size was staggering. "This structure is a masterpiece," he said, "but it suddenly occurs to me that perhaps it cost many lives to erect. I would not doubt it if somewhere out here there is a cemetery full of laborers."

"You are very observant," Jabari said. "Many of us also believe that many builders must have lost their lives out here. These blocks are extremely large and heavy. It must have taken enormous human effort to move them into place."

Farrenthias inhaled deeply. He felt calm and confident. He turned sideways and slipped into the entrance. He emerged into total darkness, and he could not fully stand. It was so dark he could not see any part of his body, and not even the sliver of the entrance provided enough light to see a few paces in front of him. The air felt thick and stale. He reclined back against the entrance and spread out his hands. Not only was the ceiling very low, the passage was also very narrow. He closed his eyes and then opened them. It made no difference. The darkness was thick and heavy. Fortunately, he experienced neither nervousness nor a shortness of breath. In fact, he was quite eager to set out down the tunnel.

"Are you all right?" Jabari called from the other side.

"I am fine," Farrenthias said.

The area where Farrenthias stood lit up as Jabari slipped halfway in with a torch and handed it to Farrenthias. "Are you sure you are alright? Are you feeling strange in any way? Are you breathing fine?"

"I am fine," Farrenthias said. "I shall return shortly."

"Very well," Jabari said, "and remember, if the torch goes out do not panic. Just turn around and come straight back."

Farrenthias took two steps and then was forced to drop to his knees. Crawling was difficult while holding the torch, but Farrenthias quickly adjusted. The sliver of light from the opening quickly disappeared behind him, and when that happened he became aware of how utterly silent it had become. The only sound was the sound of his feet and knees as they dragged deeper and deeper into the darkness of the passage. The light from the torch flickered and danced beside his face. He paused and studied the walls on both sides. It was astonishing to see how well the blocks interlocked. They were so precise. The wall looked smooth. He paused when he saw what he at first thought were hieroglyphics written on the wall to his left, but upon closer inspection he realized that someone had written Roman and Greek inscriptions, mostly names and nonsensical sayings. No doubt they had been inscribed in haste by visitors and written with what looked like crude rocks. He moved on and suddenly became aware that he was moving slightly downward. The torch dimmed and the passage felt cooler. He also became aware that he was now taking shorter breaths and that a slight perspiration had covered his forehead. The torch dimmed again, and he was now moving in almost total darkness. And then he reached a dead end.

He found himself strangely at ease in spite of the thick, heavy darkness and utter stillness. The space where he rested was so cramped he could barely maneuver his arms and legs. Nevertheless, he explored the dead-end wall with his fingers and tried to imagine who might have labored inside these cramped spaces to erect such perfection. Jabari had said something about a small chamber to the left. Farrenthias shifted his position within the tight space and explored the wall to his left. He discovered a slight crack at the lower part of the wall and slipped his hand through it. He tugged and pulled at the rock until it gave way. The space was very confined but Farrenthias managed to push the stone that he had removed out of his way so he could see what he had uncovered. His heart was pounding wildly as he thrust the torch forward. It was a small chamber. He crawled inside and was quite surprised to discover that he could stand. But, the chamber was so narrow his shoulders scraped the sides. He could barely turn and twist around inside. Oddly, but much to his relief, he experienced a slight draft coming from somewhere. The torch flickered brightly for an instant before it dimmed again. Farrenthias lifted the torch and inspected the walls. They were solid. He was about to lower the torch when something on the wall where the entrance was located caught his attention. Farrenthias held the torch close to the wall. There was a depiction of the Great Pyramid and of the Sphinx. There were measurements all around the Great Pyramid and lines reaching into the sky. There was something else. Fascinated, Farrenthias edged even closer to the wall and raised the torch. Just below the drawing of the Great Pyramid there were four names. The inscriptions were so small they were barely legible. Farrenthias ran his fingers along the writing and pronounced each name out loud. "Katunda, Phali, Saroniu, and Harim." Just then the torch flickered and burned out.

Panic seized Farrenthias. A paralyzing fear followed. He could not move and he could not breathe. It also felt as if the walls were pressing in on him. He quickly closed his eyes and inhaled deeply and slowly until he was calm again. He opened his eyes, and in total darkness he hurried out of the chamber and somehow was able to replace the stone that he had removed to get into the chamber.

The darkness enveloped every part of his body, and for a brief moment he had no sense of direction. He had also lost all concept of time, and the panic that he had felt moments before was beginning to return. Without another moment to lose Farrenthias lowered his head and moved swiftly in the only direction that he could go. He crawled and scrambled along as quickly as he could even when his legs threatened to collapse from the lack of air to breathe. It was an eternity, but at last he detected a dim light just ahead moving towards him.

"Farrenthias!" Gavinio cried. "There you are!"

Farrenthias gasped for air. "What are you doing in here, Gavinio? You should not be in here!"

"Jabari could not squeeze through the entrance, and the men who helped us left a long time ago. Are you all right? I see that you lost your torch."

"Go, Gavinio," Farrenthias said. "I could use some fresh air."

Gavinio started out of the entrance. "Yes, let us get out of this place, it scares me."

Breathing hard, Farrenthias collapsed at the feet of Jabari.

"You have lost all your color," Jabari said. "Stay down and breath slowly. You will be fine."

Farrenthias raised himself to a sitting position. The sun was much lower than when he had entered the Pyramid. "How long was I in there?" he asked.

"At least an hour," Jabari said. "You had us worried. Unfortunately, my friends left at around the time that you went in, and for the last hour Gavinio and I have been trying to move this block of stone so I could squeeze in to look for you. When our efforts failed I finally let Gavinio go in to look for you." Jabari lowered himself and sat next to Farrenthias. "Well, what do you think? Was it worth it?"

"It was fascinating, Jabari," Farrenthias said. "It was fascinating."

Jabari got to his feet, gazed across the plateau at the other structures and then looked at Farrenthias. "You look tired, Farrenthias. I think we have done enough exploring for one day. What do you think?"

"I agree," Farrenthias said. "The Sphinx will have to wait for another trip. If it is agreeable with you, I would like to start on our journey to the Red Sea."

"That is a good plan," Jabari said. "It will not take me long to pack a few things and we shall be on our way."

Seventy-Five

Farrenthias stood at the bow of Haji's ship with his hands clasped on the ship's railing and his eyes fixed on the cliffs. The ship was moored at the foot of a wall of cliffs. Gavinio was high up on a mast hollering down at Haji that he could see nothing so far.

"Patience, my good little friend," Haji said, while he worked on a fishing net. "Patience. You will see him soon enough."

Farrenthias smiled. Gavinio amazed him. Not only did he know his way around these lands, it seemed as though everyone knew him well and liked him. Yesterday when they had arrived, much like Jabari in Giza, Haji had been delighted to see Gavinio. Farrenthias recalled how Ja'eleni had predicted that boarding the felucca where he had met Gavinio would bring him good luck. So far it had. Not only had Haji quickly agreed to help, it turned out that he knew exactly where to find Athinio, and upon his departure Jabari had absolutely refused payment for his services. He had expressed admiration for the way Farrenthias had entered the Great Pyramid without hesitation and wished him good fortune in his life.

"There!" Gavinio hollered. "I see a man, Haji! He has just come out of a cave. Is that the man we are looking for?"

Haji joined Farrenthias at the railing. "Do you see him, Farrenthias? That is him. That is Athinio. He can sit for hours outside of his cave with his eyes closed. I have fished at this very spot on many occasions, and the first time I saw him he was so still that I thought I was imagining a man sitting on a stone."

Athinio was small and thin and he wore a long white toga wrapped around his body with one shoulder exposed. He had a white beard and long, white hair. Farrenthias could not make out his face clearly, but he seemed to be looking at them. He suddenly waved and Haji waved back.

"Have you ever spoken to him?" Farrenthias asked.

"Two maybe three times, when he has come down to bathe in the water. He is quiet but friendly. Obviously the man prefers to be completely alone."

"He is an Essene, Haji," Farrenthias said. "Some Essenes pursue purity by living in the wilderness in solitude."

Farrenthias studied the terrain. The cliffs were shear towering walls. They looked impenetrable. "How do I reach him?"

"Not by climbing those towering walls. The first time I saw him in the water I asked him how he got down. He pointed to that dark area," Haji said, pointing to an area to the right of the ship. "Do you see it?"

Farrenthias nodded. "What is it?"

"In that dark area you will find a path that cuts through the cliffs and leads to the very top. According to Athinio, it is not a difficult climb."

Farrenthias turned his attention to Gavinio, who was noisily making his way down from the mast. "How long have you known Gavinio," Farrenthias suddenly asked.

"Gavinio?" Haji said, looking at the mast. "I first spotted him on the docks about two years ago."

"He has been roaming around that long? All Alone?" Farrenthias asked. "He is so young. Is he not afraid to be alone?"

Haji laughed. "Gavinio is afraid of nothing. I, too, worried about him when I realized that he had no father and mother that were looking after him. He will not talk about where he is from. But I quickly realized that he was very bright and not like other boys his age who have no homes and run around the streets stealing to get by. Do you know that the first time I met him, rather than beg for money, he asked me if he could work around the ship for a few coins?" Haji chuckled. "I immediately liked him so much I asked him to stay on the ship with me and learn how to fish, but he laughed and said he could not stay, that he had the world to explore. How about you? Where did you meet him?"

"I just met him in Egypt. He was on a felucca that was moored on the bank of the Nile." Farrenthias sighed and looked nervously at Gavinio. He was on one knee adjusting the straps of his sandals. "I think it is best if he returns to the port with you."

"Oh? I thought that you two were traveling together. He seems to be very excited to be in your company."

"Yes, but..."

Gavinio hollered at Farrenthias as he ran towards him. "He is still there, Farrenthias! What are we waiting for? We should hurry before he disappears into his cave again."

Farrenthias folded his arms and leaned back against the ship's railing. He asked Gavinio to take a seat on a wooden box that happened to be at his feet.

"But, why?" Gavinio cried. "Are we not leaving? We have a long climb ahead of us." He snapped his head back and glared at Farrenthias with a smile. "Are you afraid of heights, Farrenthias? Is that what you are trying to tell me?"

"No, it is not that," Farrenthias said, nervously glancing at Haji. "It is just that I do not know how long I am going to stay here or where I am going next. I was thinking that you should return to port with Haji."

Gavinio's eyes watered, and he slowly got to his feet. "What? But what are you saying, Farrenthias? I do not understand. I thought we were friends? I thought I was going with you? Did we not go to the Great Pyramid together?"

Gavinio's sudden emotion took Farrenthias by complete surprise. He tried to speak, but the sudden lump at his throat made it difficult. He cleared his throat several times before he was able to find his voice. "Of course we are friends, Gavinio. But for now, this is the end of our journey together. From here I must travel alone. I do not plan on staying here for very long—and after that I have no idea where my travels will take me."

Gavinio's eyes widened with wild hope. "But I do not care where you are going. I will go with you. I can help you! I will carry your satchel, and at nights, I will keep an eye out for thieves and dangerous animals. I am not afraid. I sleep very little at night."

Farrenthias turned desperately to Haji, who understood him though no words were spoken between them.

"Gavinio," Haji said, his soft voice full of compassion. "What Farrenthias is trying to tell you is that it would be too difficult to travel with him. He has no idea where he is going or what is going to happen. Why do you not stay here on this ship with me? I could always use the help around here. This ship can be your permanent home."

Tears streamed down Gavinio's face and he quickly dried them and turned away in embarrassment. "Neither one of you has to worry about me. I can take care of myself."

"Gavinio, listen to me," Farrenthias said. "If you do not want to stay with Haji, I could write Father a letter asking him to welcome you into our family in Syria. You would have your own quarters, your own soft bed, and you could play with children your age. You could even study with Cerudotus, my childhood tutor, and when you are not studying, you can ride horses. You will get your very own horse. Would you not like that?"

Gavinio looked away. "I do not care about any tutor or about any soft bed. I—I thought you and I were friends. If you do not want to be friends, then do not worry about me. I will go away."

"Gavinio listen to Farrenthias," Haji said. "You are very young. We are concerned about you. You need a home. You need a place where you will be cared for. Besides, why would you not want to ride your very own horse and play with children your age?"

"I can ride a horse anytime I want," Gavinio said. "I have friends who have horses, and I do not need anyone to care for me. I have always looked after myself." More tears streamed down his cheeks, and he brushed them away with the back of his hand. "Maybe I will go to Rome. I have been told that I am Roman."

Farrenthias sighed wearily. If he changed his mind, how could he be responsible for such a young child? He hardly knew what was to become of his own life. Still, it pained him to see Gavinio cry. Worse, he reminded him so much of Trulius it was like having Trulius at his side again and how could he say no to that? He sighed again. "Gavinio," he said. "An education is very important for a young boy like you. If you stay with me you shall have to study, and you shall have to learn to read and write Latin and Greek. A boy your age should learn those things. Are you willing to do that?"

"I promise, Farrenthias!" Gavinio shouted. He took out his

lucky piece and kissed it. "I promise to do anything you ask me to do! I swear by my lucky piece!"

Farrenthias glanced at Haji, who wiped a tear from his eyes. "I am glad we settled that," he said. "But two children traveling alone together? You shall both have to be very careful and take care of each other."

Farrenthias looked over the railing of the ship at the dark green and blue water. "How do we get to shore?"

"We swim," Gavinio laughed.

Farrenthias paled. "I—I do not know how to swim."

Haji also laughed. "Do not worry. I have a small raft hanging from the port side of the ship. "I will take you ashore."

Farrenthias studied Athinio's profile while he related to him why he had sought him out. Athinio's cheeks were bony beneath his beard, and his nose was long and straight, giving him a regal appearance. He was very thin, but seemed quite healthy and strong. He was pensive as he listened to Farrenthias. He stared at the sea, though his dark eyes had a far away look. Occasionally he would brush his beard and nod to himself even as his eyes remained locked on the sea.

At last Farrenthias finished speaking and there was a long moment of silence before Athinio finally spoke.

"It is good to study and contemplate life in a quiet place such as Clivus. There is also no better quest in the world than the pursuit of truths." He paused and regarded Farrenthias with intense eyes. "Knowledge is the true source of all enlightenment and although it is not the destiny of all men to pursue and embrace it in this lifetime, in time all men will come to seek it." Athinio paused again, and then said, "It speaks highly of you that you have begun your quest at such a tender age, but your path will not be an easy one."

Farrenthias nodded "I must confess to you that I am often troubled by my decision to leave my family and follow what lies in my heart."

"Do not be afraid, my child. Self-doubt is all a part of the learning process. You must also be prepared for what you might discover. Wisdom and knowledge bring many unexpected tribulations for the enlightened."

Athinio watched silently as Gavinio picked through a basket of dates he had placed in front of him. "Akiva," he said. "I am afraid that I have never crossed paths with him, but I wish I had. He sounds like a driven man." Athinio inhaled. "Unfortunately, from what you have told me about him, it sounds as though his life's journey has not been easy." Athinio reflected quietly. "According to the letter Yehnia showed you, he was on his way back to the sacred mountains, you say?"

Farrenthias nodded. "That is what the letter said."

"Hum," Athinio murmured and reclined back. "There was a time when Yeshua walked easily among those who followed his teachings. After the crucifixion, he became more elusive, as Akiva discovered." Athinio paused. "Even as a child he was quite remarkable. According to my father Yeshua lived with the Essenes for a small period of time." Athinio looked at Gavinio, who was quietly resting against a boulder. "I suppose that he was no bigger than Gavinio. He and Father played together, although that was rare since Yeshua was not like the other boys. He was polite but preferred to be off by himself. He would sit for hours in some corner watching others play, but mostly he seemed to be constantly deep in thought." Athinio brushed his chin. "Yeshua traveled to Egypt several times. It is said that when he first visited the Great Pyramid as a child, he went inside and disappeared for hours."

"He did?" Gavinio cried. "Sire, forgive me for interrupting you, but we were just at the Great Pyramid a few days ago. Farrenthias went inside."

Athinio gazed at Farrenthias. "Some sages believe that the Great Pyramid can bring good luck to those who enter it."

"It was a remarkable experience," Farrenthias said. "It is terribly dark and tight in there, but I sensed that it was a very special place. Did Yeshua ever discuss his experience inside the Pyramid?"

Athinio grimaced. "I do not know. He imparted knowledge and wisdom, but as I say, he was also very quiet about other matters."

"Did you ever meet him?" Farrenthias asked.

Athinio reflected quietly. "It was but a brief encounter and quite by accident, and even though I was just a child, I have always re-membered that night with a great deal of fondness," he said. "One night Father and I were camped outside the borders of Babylonia. Father had been asked by some traders to look for a new route to the East. I remember it being a very dark night. No moon, but many stars filled the sky. Father was by the campfire, and I had my feet dangling in a cool stream. Suddenly I heard Father gasp. I turned around and saw a stranger standing in the darkness, just beyond the light of our campfire.

'Sire,' Father said. 'Are you lost?'

'Leyhman,' the man replied, 'Do you not recognize me?'

Father rose slowly to his feet and stared at the lone figure. Even in the darkness I could see the joy in Father's eyes when he recog-nized the man. 'Yeshua?' Father said. 'Is that you? Why, I have not seen you in years. What are you doing out here in the middle of the desert?'

'Then you do recognize me, Leyhman,' Yeshua said. 'How good to see you.' He sighed and looked over his shoulder. 'What am I doing out here in the middle of the night?' His face grew serious. 'It is a long story, Leyhman.'

He stepped into the light of the campfire and I was able to see him better. He looked exhausted, but I could see that he was a youthful man. His long hair was dark and light depending on where he stood in the light. His face appeared to be burned from the sun. Something about him, perhaps his gestures or his soft-spoken voice, made a big impression on me. But what I remember the most were his eyes. They were sad and dark and penetrating. They expressed pain one moment, uncertainty the next, and determination the next. After he had greeted Father he turned to me with those incredible eyes. 'Your son, Leyhman?'

'Yes, Athinio is my only son. Come, Yeshua, let us join him in the stream. You look as though you could use some cool water.'

Yeshua relaxed beside me and then he put his arm around me. 'I have known your father since we were both children,' he said.

Father quietly started to remove Yeshua's sandals, but Yeshua protested. 'I can do that, Leyhman.' Father ignored him, and when he saw that his feet were red and swollen, he massaged them in the cool water. I was so moved by what Father was doing that I reached down and began to help him.

'You are a good man, Leyhman, and I see that your child is as noble as you are.'

'I have thought of you often, Yeshua,' Father said, 'especially when I heard what Herod did to your cousin Yochanan. I remember Yochanan running around the hills of Qumran begging you to climb with him.'

The face of Yeshua became drawn, the pain evident in his eyes. 'Yochanan was a good man,' he said. 'He served God well.'

He protested when Father removed his own sandals and placed them on his feet and put on the worn ones. 'Leyhman, do not deprive yourself on my account,' Yeshua said. 'But I will tell you this. One kind gesture to a man in need is more valuable than hours spent in a synagogue prostrated in prayer.'

Suddenly he was on his feet again. 'I must be going, Leyhman,' he said.

Father protested. 'Now?' he said, also getting to his feet. 'But it is so late. You are tired and your feet are swollen. Stay and rest. You can leave at sunrise.'

'That is the prudent thing to do,' Yeshua said, 'but I am afraid I would not sleep. I am quite anxious to reach Galilee. I have been gone too long, and I have much to do.'

'Where have you been, Yeshua?'

'I am returning from faraway lands that are covered in ice and snow, faraway lands where the sun hardly shines.' He looked at Father and then looked at his feet. 'I roamed across endless deserts, traversed vast seas, and climbed the highest mountains on the sandals that you now wear. Some of the places I had seen before, while others were new to me.' He looked down the road in the direction that he was headed. 'It is time to return and reveal the lessons that I have learned to those who will listen.' He thought a moment. 'Of course, I shall have to be patient. After all, we would not ask a child to read a verse and understand it before he even knows that a language exists which he must first master?'

He touched my head, squeezed my father's arm, and then disappeared into the night like a sudden, unexpected breeze. I never saw him again."

Farrenthias sank back. "Roamed across endless deserts, traversed vast seas and climbed the highest mountains," he whispered. "I shall have to be patient." He eyed Athinio. "What are we to make of those words, Athinio?"

Athinio regarded Farrenthias with a keen and thoughtful eye. "Those were the words of a very wise man who did not tire of learning and of imparting his knowledge."

Farrenthias pondered those words for a long moment and then he removed the satchel that contained Akiva's scroll from around his neck. He placed it in front of him. "Athinio," he said, "Let me tell you about this scroll and how I came to possess it."

Seventy-Six

January was a busy time of the year in Rome. The new year always brought changes. The Senate was busy with the business of the government, the Forum was teeming with new businesses, and the streets were packed with an influx of new residents. The city was also in utter political turmoil. Galba, who had assumed the crown of emperor seven months before, had just been assassinated, and two men, Otho and Vitellius, and their factions were in a desperate fight to replace him. The streets were not safe. Killings and assassinations were rampant at every street corner. Deadly scuffles erupted throughout the day. Still, the business of the day could not be postponed. At mid-day Trulius and Kemnebi were at the family warehouses taking inventory of newly arrived merchandise, but Trulius could not concentrate on the task at hand. He was worried. Marcellius and Gianina were at the Forum shopping for much needed household essentials that Felicia had requested. True, Marcellius had his well-armed guards, but that type of protection meant very little against soldiers who marched in large numbers or wild mobs that killed indiscriminately.

Trulius kept his eyes on the street corner hoping that at any moment his father's entourage would appear, safe and unharmed. Trulius jumped when the unexpected hand of Kemnebi dropped on his shoulder. "Kemnebi," he cried, "you startled me!"

"Of course, I did," Kemnebi said. "You have not taken your eyes off of that street corner." He set his writing tablet down. "Do not worry, Trulius. Gianina is safe. Do you not realize that ever since your father returned from the battlefields he is more recognized and respected than ever? Besides, Marcellius has remained neutral in this fight for the crown. Chaos or no chaos, no one would dare launch an aggression against a hero of Rome, and even if they did I would not want to be at the other end of Marcellius's sword."

"There!" Trulius cried. "There they are!"

Four guards led the entourage, and the moment Gianina's litter rounded the corner, she hung her head out of the small window and waved at Trulius. Trulius was overcome by a strange surge of excitement, a strange surge of excitement that he only felt when she was in his company. Gianina was more beautiful than ever, and she seemed to grow more beautiful every day. There was nothing that gave Trulius more joy than to spend time with her. Of course, life with Gianina was not like before, when she would climb trees with him and chase Pharaoh around the woods. These days during their long walks they engaged in serious conversations. She was not just beautiful, she was intelligent, and for a Roman woman, she was educated and opinionated. Gianina loved to hear about his life at Clivus, and she would speak about Rome and everything that had occurred while he was gone. Trulius would listen intently and many times he would shake his head in disgust when she would speak about the corrupt politicians in the city. Gianina had also taken on an important role in the household. Felicia allowed her to make many household decisions, and Gianina embraced her new responsibilities with a great deal of enthusiasm. Every member of the household loved her, not just because she was like a daughter to Marcellius, but because she was kind and gentle and caring, even when chastising servants when they did not do their work properly. Trulius suddenly jumped. Kemnebi had dropped a hand on his shoulder again.

Kemnebi laughed. "I startled you again, Trulius," he said. "You look like you have been struck by a bolt of lightening and I can see why. Our precious Gianina has blossomed into a stunning young woman. Perhaps she is the loveliest maiden in all of Rome." He laughed again. "You should see yourself every time you are around her. It is a wonder you can find your way around the house."

"Kemnebi," Trulius said, his face flush and his eyes aglow with embarrassment. "You should warn me any time you think I am making a fool of myself. Have I not asked you that before? What will Father think if he sees his son behaving like a foolish child?"

Kemnebi smiled shrewdly and looked at the entourage as it approached. "Your father could not be more pleased with both of you." Kemnebi frowned and his eyes narrowed as he looked up and down the street. "Speaking of your father, I do not see him."

Trulius looked quickly past the guards and litter and wagons. His father was indeed nowhere to be seen. "Perhaps Gianina sent him back to the Forum for something she might have forgotten," he said.

"Perhaps," Kemnebi said.

Gianina's litter came to a halt and Trulius helped her out of the litter. She wore a simple, light green dress that clung to her narrow waistline. Her sandals were brown and they matched a shawl that partially covered her head and her shoulders. She wore a green ring in each hand and a matching green necklace. Her scent was a sweet mixture of flowers and plants from an imported perfume from the East.

"Trulius," she said excitedly. "Have a look. I purchased enough food and supplies to last us a month."

"I can see," Trulius said.

"Mother ordered new beddings for all the beds. Tonight you sleep in the finest linens from the East. Oh, and I purchased material for new togas, which Mother and I are going to sew for you, Lord Marcellius, Kemnebi, and Quanarious."

"Where is Father?" Trulius said.

Gianina was about to answer, but a loud commotion erupted at the other end of the street. A small group of mounted soldiers had turned the corner and were coming down the street. A mob of men, women, and children followed them. The men taunted the soldiers with clubs and sticks, but the well-trained soldiers, in their shiny golden helmets and red capes, ignored them. The soldiers rode rigidly, seemingly oblivious of the mob.

"Assassins!" a man shouted at the soldiers. "Assassins!"

"Which one of you cowards murdered Galba?" another yelled, and the crowd responded by shouting that they demanded answers.

A tall, thick man emerged out of the crowd and practically bumped one of the horses. "Which one of you maggots beheaded him?" he shouted. "Is that how you got your man Otho to become emperor, by beheading Galba?"

A soldier glared down at him. "I warn you. Keep your distance, or you will be trampled," he said.

Trulius tensed and gripped the handle of his sword. "What do you make of that news, Kemnebi?" he said, his eyes glued on the raucous crowd.

"What do I think? I think Otho will not be emperor for very long," Kemnebi said, shaking his head. "He may enjoy the support of his loyal troops, but as you can clearly see not everyone approves of him."

"Then you do not believe that all this chaos will end soon?" Trulius said. "You do not believe things will improve in Rome?"

Kemnebi grunted. "Things are far from settled, Trulius. If I were to guess, I would say that even as we speak Vitellius is plotting his move to take the crown from Otho, and then there is Vespasian. You know what you father thinks. He thinks Vespasian stands a better chance to emerge as the true emperor of Rome." He turned to Gianina. "Speaking of Marcellius, where did you leave him, Gianina?"

"He left us just as we were about to turn the corner. He said that he had unfinished business to take care of and that he would join us at the house."

Kemnebi flashed his eyes towards the corner. "I see," he said. "Very well then," he said. He stepped way from the litter. "Go home with Gianina, Trulius. I shall finish here."

Trulius did not like the look on Kemnebi's face. He shook his head. "I think I will stay with you, Kemnebi," he said. "The guards can escort Gianina to the house."

Kemnebi was about to protest, but he had heard that determined voice before, and he knew that any argument that he made would be in vain. "Fine," Kemnebi said. "We still have work to do around here."

Trulius made a move to help Gianina back into the litter, but Gianina did not move. "Are you two worried about Lord Marcellius?" she said. "I can see it in both of your faces." She looked over her shoulder. "The streets are rather chaotic back there."

"Our little pearl is too perceptive for her own good," Kemnebi said. "I am certain that we have nothing to worry about. Marcellius will be fine. "

Trulius helped Gianina into the litter and she immediately hung her head out of the window. "I have a feeling you two are going to go look for Lord Marcellius. "Perhaps he went to see his Farron or Canario. Please be careful."

As soon as the guards surrounded the litter and began to pull away, Trulius turned to Kemnebi. "What is it, Kemnebi?" He asked. "Do you know where Father went?"

"Hurry," Kemnebi said, walking hastily toward the horses. "It may be nothing, but for days Marcellius has spoken about the need to have a word with Nestor."

"Nestor?" Trulius cried as they got on their horses and headed down the street. "Have you not told me that he is a madman? Father cannot reason with that man."

Kemnebi glanced at Trulius. "Exactly. I think your father knows that and that is exactly what I am afraid of."

Marcellius waited impatiently in the unmoving traffic. Just past the northeast corner of the Circus Maximus, where the Via Ostiensis and Via Appia intersected, a train of carts loaded with broken racing chariots lost two of its chariots. They were scattered across the street and were causing a traffic nightmare. To make matters worse, a line of soldiers were keeping two wild mobs from each other. One shouted support for Otho and cheered the death of Galba, and the other shouted that Vitellius would soon be the new emperor. Marcellius had enough. He backed his stallion away and turned around. The throngs of people made it difficult to maneuver, but at last he freed himself from the crowds and headed down a narrow alley. He took several side streets that were also heavily filled with traffic, but at least the traffic was moving. He finally reached the edge of the Palatine.

In the Palatine the neighborhoods were surprisingly quiet, in contrast to what he had just left behind. The houses were simple in design, but large and with manicured gardens and fountains, all indicative of modest wealth. Marcellius knew exactly what house he was looking for. At his request, Farron had personally shown him the house weeks before. The house had two white columns on both sides of a wide door and a balcony on each of the four windows that faced the street. The house itself was set back, separated from the street by its garden. Marcellius felt the blood rush hotly through his veins as he tied his stallion to an isolated tree. He rushed to the front door and banged loudly on the door.

A male servant quickly opened the door. The thin man took one look at Marcellius and by his expression it was obvious that he recognized Marcellius. "My lord," he said, his voice trembling slightly. "May I assist you?"

"Summon your master at once," Marcellius said curtly.

The sternness with which Marcellius had spoken unsettled the servant even further. "I—he is in his quarters resting, and when he is in there at this hour, he is not to be disturbed. Perhaps you can return at a later time of the day."

Marcellius pushed him aside and stepped into the house. "The choice is yours. Either get him down here now, or I will drag him out of his bed."

Aghast, the servant took a step backwards and spread his arms. "No, no, my lord! I beg you!" he cried. "I shall go and get him for you. I shall tell him that the honorable Marcellius Kaelus Augustus wishes to see him at once."

"Good," Marcellius said, "and be quick about it."

"Of course, my lord," the servant stammered. He turned and rushed down a dark hall.

Marcellius looked around. The house was splendidly decorated. The rooms that he could see were filled with expensive furniture and an array of beautiful rugs and accessories. Marcellius knew very well that Nestor had nothing to do with how well he was living. He saw the hand of his wife and father-in-law, Atenuar, in everything that Nestor owned.

A small group of servants had gathered behind one of the columns, no doubt they had been roused by his loud voice. They were watching him intently, but there was no fear in their eyes, only curiosity. He was not surprised. By now everyone in Rome was well aware of his plight. Marcellius pitied the servants. Working for a man like Nestor had to be a living inferno.

Marcellius turned at the sound of scuffling of feet coming from the hall. Nestor was not alone. Two armed guards walked beside him.

"Marcellius," he said, feigning surprise. "At first, I did not believe my servant but I see that it is true. Our military hero has decided to pay me an unexpected visit."

Marcellius glared at him. "Spare me your stupidity, Nestor. You knew very well that sooner or later I would come and make you pay for the way you hounded my son, and sent an assassin to my house. My house! Where my family eats and sleeps."

Nestor raised his hands to show that he carried no weapons. "I do not know what you are talking about, Marcellius. I have done nothing to your family, and as you can see I am unarmed."

Marcellius angrily gazed at him. "You are a liar, Nestor, and a madman." He looked at the guards, "and from what I can see, you are also a coward."

"Me a madman? A coward? Bah! You are the one who has barged into my house like a madman making wild accusations." Nestor smiled. "Tomorrow the word on the streets will be that Marcellius Kaelus, their war hero, was killed when he barged into the house of a citizen of Rome and tried to assassinate him in front of all his servants. How does that sound, Marcellius?"

"You are a fool, Nestor," Marcellius said. He removed a scroll from his belt and tossed it onto the floor. "I am not here to kill you. That is a summons signed by your brother-in-law Septimus. He has returned to his post as a magistrate, and he has ordered that you appear before him tomorrow to answer to the charges that you hired assassins to kill my son and that you hired assassins to come to my house to kill me and other members of my family. I have witnesses who will testify to that. Witnesses who heard you admit to all of this and laugh about it. "

Nestor glanced at the scroll and laughed. "You can prove nothing against me. Besides, is this how a Roman soldier, a returning hero of Rome, settles his disputes? He hides behind the authorities like a coward. Well, I am here to tell you that my servants shall mop your blood from my floor with that scroll signed by my precious brother-in-law. What do you think about that?"

Marcellius winced. "Septimus and I both agreed that you would react this way, but I promised him that I would at least try and settle the score between us in front of him."

Nestor spat on the floor. "We settle our score here and now, Marcellius." He unsheathed his sword. "Spread out," he said to the guards. "I go in first."

Herminia suddenly appeared and leaped at her husband from behind. She tried to restrain him. "Nestor!" she cried. "What are you doing? Marcellius has come in peace! Do not kill him. All of Rome now knows that he was not responsible for the death of Halius."

Nestor roughly gripped one of her wrists. "I do not care what all of Rome thinks. Do you not see that this is not just about Halius?

Men like Marcellius think that they can do what they please with their wealth and education. I detest the fat and rich men who govern this city and I detest what Rome has become. Perhaps after I am through with Marcellius I will plunge a sword into Septimus and your father as well. After all, Herminia, your father has always protected Septimus and together they turned this merchant into a hero of Rome!"

Herminia clung to Nestor. "Do not do this out of hatred for my father or jealousy of Septimus, Nestor. Please!"

Nestor roughly pushed her aside. "Get out of my way!"

Marcellius drew his own sword and took a step back. "Think about your actions, Nestor. I repeat, I did not come here to kill you but I will if I have to."

Nestor laughed. "The only man who dies today is you, Marcellius." He gripped his sword with both hands and charged at Marcellius, swinging wildly. Marcellius tightened his grip on his sword and braced himself. Men such as Nestor who fought awkwardly but had a powerful swing were difficult to handle. They clashed in the middle of the room. Nestor was relentless. He thrust his entire weight behind every swing of his sword and almost lost his balance with every step that he took. They knocked chairs, tables, vases, and cups to the floor. Servants scattered in every direction, screaming, and ducking for cover. It took every move that Marcellius could muster to hold off Nestor's wild aggression. Marcellius moved in a tight circle, and in spite of Nestor's wild and erratic style of fighting, Marcellius managed to pierce Nestor's defense and rip his tunic and graze his side, causing his white tunic to turn red with blood.

"Say, the word, Nestor," one of his guards shouted, his eyes wild with anticipation, "and he is a dead man."

"Imbeciles!" Nestor shouted. "Do I need to die before your eyes? Kill him! Kill him! A bag of gold to who ever kills him!"

The two guards charged at Marcellius. They were not as powerful as Nestor, but they were quick and agile, and they were relentless. With Nestor still swinging wildly, the three men managed to back Marcellius out of the front door and into the garden and onto the street.

Nestor's entire household and some of his neighbors poured out into the street and watched in stunned silence as the four men fought.

Neither Nestor nor his guards possessed Marcellius's skills, yet they fought surprisingly well together. They knew each other's moves and they attacked like a pack of wild wolves that skillfully hunt and kill their prey as a single unit.

Sweat poured from Marcellius's brow as he skillfully defended himself. He turned and swung and ducked in every direction. The men were relentless, however, and it was apparent that they meant to wear him out and then move in for the kill. Marcellius had faced such odds before, but never against a man as powerful and as driven as Nestor. He was about to launch a full assault against Nestor in the hopes of slowing him down when a disturbance behind him momentarily distracted him.

The small crowd that had formed on the street scattered and two horses crashed out of the raucous. Trulius lunged toward one of the guards with so much force that he sent them both tumbling to the ground. The guard barely managed to get to his feet in time to avoid the sword of Trulius from slicing his throat. The second guard easily intercepted Kemnebi's sword but overlooked the dagger Kemnebi held in his other hand until it was too late. Kemnebi buried it deep into the man's chest.

Nestor incomprehensibly winced with pain. He had seen Marcellius thrust his sword, and even though it had been like a blur, he could have sworn that Marcellius had not touched him. Yet, he tried to swing his sword but his knees buckled and he stumbled forward. Marcellius side- stepped him and turned to his right but thrust his sword to his left, taking Nestor by complete surprise. The sword pierced the right side of Nestor's chest, just below the heart. Nestor crumbled to his knees, stared momentarily at Marcellius, and then slumped forward.

The guard, who was fending off Trulius's repeated attacks, suddenly backed away and dropped his weapon. "Enough!" he shouted. "Nestor is dead. Marcellius, I have no quarrel against you, my lord."

Trulius placed the tip of his sword at the man's throat. "Father?" he cried.

Marcellius wearily shook his head. "Let him go, Trulius. There has been enough killing this day."

"Father," Trulius said, sheathing his sword and rushing to Marcellius. "You are bleeding."

Marcellius looked down at himself. A smudge of blood had soaked through his tunic, but after years in the battlefields, he was quite familiar with the types of pain associated with serious wounds. "It is nothing," he said. "It is only a scratch." He placed a hand on the shoulder of Trulius. "Your skills continue to amaze me. You fight like a seasoned soldier."

"It is in his blood," Kemnebi said."

"And you, Kemnebi," Marcellius said. "The years have not diminished your skills. I have never seen a faster kill. I am fortunate that you both came along when you did."

The three mounted their horses and Marcellius looked over his shoulder. A group of women and men had gathered at the body of

Nestor, but only his wife wept. She looked up at Marcellius, but there was no hatred in her eyes only a strange look of resignation, as if she knew that this day would one day arrive.

A small group of soldiers arrived and dismounted. One of them approached Marcellius. "Are you all right, my lord?"

Marcellius nodded and the soldier looked at the body of Nestor and the guard.

"Clear the street of these bodies," he said to Nestor's household, "or we will."

"Let us go home," Marcellius said, looking at Trulius and Kemnebi. "Our business here is finished."

Seventy-Seven

Farrenthias carefully scrutinized Akiva's scroll. The material was dry and brittle, and he worried that it would crumble in his hands.

"Do not be afraid," Athinio said, seeing the fear in Farrenthias's eyes. "The material is much stronger than you realize."

They were seated inside Athinio's cave, where a fire burned hot and bright. Outside the wind howled and the ocean hurled waves against the rocky shoreline. The night was exceptionally cold and dark, and to keep warm Athinio had helped Gavinio light the fire.

"I suppose you are right, " Farrenthias said. "It cannot be as frail as it looks."

To avoid getting dirt on the scroll, Farrenthias had spread out two mats made of tree leaves that Athinio had weaved together and that he usually used to sit on, and he placed the scroll on the mats.

Gavinio was lying on his belly next to the campfire. He raised himself and looked at the scroll. "Do you have enough light, Farrenthias? Shall I add more wood to the fire?"

"That is not necessary, Gavinio, I have plenty of light," Farrenthias said. He held his breath and began to unravel the scroll. There were many smudges on the papyrus, and the writing was faded in many places, as if it had once been wet. He lowered his head and studied the first few words. He instantly recognized the style of writing that he had also seen in the letter to Yehnia. "It is written in Aramaic," he whispered, without looking up. "There are many smudges and the writing is faded in many places, but overall it is in good condition," he said glancing at Athinio, who sat on the other side of the fire, the flames of the fire dancing across his dark, wrinkled face.

"No telling where the scroll has been," Athinio said. "We are fortunate to have it."

A gentle breeze, filled with moisture, rippled through the cave causing the fire to flicker. Gavinio scrambled to his knees and eased toward the fire. "Do not worry, Farrenthias," he said. "I will not let the fire die down."

"I smell rain," Farrenthias said.

"Indeed," Athinio murmured. "It is that time of the season, when the winds make the cave tremble and bring much rain, but we are safe in here."

"And we will not be in the dark," Gavinio said. "I collected plenty of wood."

Farrenthias lowered his eyes and studied the scroll again. "Very well then," he said. "I cannot make out the first few lines. They are too smudged, but here is what follows."

I waited for the storm to pass, and by the time I got to Golgotha, there were but a few stragglers left on the hill. Even the Roman guard had dwindled down to half a dozen men. The sky remained dark and filled with heavy clouds but a slight cool breeze was moving those clouds slowly away. The entire area was wet and eerily silent. As I approached the hill, I was sickened by what I saw. Three men were hanging from three crosses. I instantly recognized the man on the middle cross. It was Yeshua. The Romans had carried out their threat to have him crucified. Green vines were wrapped up and down the stake on which he was crucified. He had been crucified on a tree. A handful of people, mostly women, huddled at the foot of his cross. They all wept quietly.

"At least the crowds have left. Moments ago you could not walk through here it was so crowded." A man who was suddenly standing beside me whispered those words to me. He spoke with a strange accent that I did not recognize. He was neither Roman nor Hebrew. He was tall with powerful arms and broad shoulders. His clothes and long dark hair were drenched.

"What pleasure can there possibly be in watching a man die?" he said.

I did not say anything, but he suddenly tapped me on the shoulder to draw my attention to Yeshua's cross. "You see the crossbar on the middle cross? It is called a patibulum. I am not proud of it, but I carved it out for the Romans."

"You made it?" I said.

The man looked miserable. "I said I am not proud of it, that is why I am here. I came to see what my evil work has done."

Farrenthias stopped reading. The cruelty of the scene moved him nearly to tears. He stared at the flames of the fire and at the shadows of the flames that danced against the dark walls of the cave.

"Do you find the cruelty of man troubling, Farrenthias?" Athinio asked. "Is it not amazing what he is capable of?"

Farrenthias sighed. "Tell me, wise one," he said, "what crime is worthy of such a barbaric punishment?" Farrenthias sighed again. "I learned about Yeshua at Clivus and I still do not understand his crime."

"You ask wise and difficult questions, Farrenthias," Athinio said. "Now let me ask you a question. Suppose Yeshua had been a murderer. Does a murderer deserve to die in such a cruel manner?"

Farrenthias slowly shook his head. "I do not know how to answer that, Athinio. I know only that I am saddened by man killing man under any circumstance."

Athinio brushed his chin. "The degree of punishment that a man deserves for his crimes can pose quite a dilemma, especially if that crime is murder. On the one hand, man can be quite barbaric. Killing is in his nature. He is also a master at justifying his actions. He will charge into unnecessary wars, and in the battlefield he will kill at will and without remorse in the name of his king or emperor. Man will also kill in the name of the god that he worships and claim that his god willed it. He will kill those who violate his laws and claim that such is the will of the people."

Gavinio, who had been quietly listening, raised himself to a sitting position. "Will the killing ever stop, Athinio?"

Athinio grimaced. "I fear that man cannot change his nature, but we cannot lose hope that he will learn some lessons in life." He turned to Farrenthias. "Go on, my son. Keep reading."

Farrenthias cleared his throat and continued to read out loud.

A centurion mounted on a black stallion approached us. "Jarek," he said to my new friend. "You are still here. Well, as you can see, the patibulum you built is very sturdy. It is holding very well."

"Petronius," Jarek said, brushing the moisture from his forehead. "I am sick to my stomach at what you have done to those men. And I am sick to my stomach that I helped you."

Petronius laughed. "Did you not see the size of the earlier crowds, Jarek? People love a good spectacle." He leaned back on his horse and stared at the three crosses. "Sometimes I wonder if these public executions are more for the benefit of the public than for the integrity of the laws of the state. Perhaps both."

"Sire." A short, heavy man dressed in elegant robes and waving a scroll approached the centurion. He was followed by a parade of slaves. "Sire, I have here a proclamation from Governor Pilate," he said. "It states that Yeshua is to be given to me at once."

Petronius grunted and ripped the document from the man's hands. He quickly read it and then he looked at the man. "You are Yousef of Arimethea?"

Yousef bowed his head slightly. "I am, sire." He pointed to the entourage that accompanied him, men with ropes and ladders. "I came prepared. With your permission, we will bring Yeshua down and take him with us."

Petronius inspected the proclamation again. "These orders are unclear to me," he said. "You see, the governor also ordered the death of the Hebrew and he cannot possibly be dead yet. Perhaps what the governor meant is that I am to release the body to you at once. The dead body."

"No, no," Yousef cried. "The proclamation is quite clear. There is no mention of a body. I am to take custody of Yeshua at once, no matter his condition. Would you disobey the governor's orders?"

Petronius glared at him and at the same time he shouted at one of his soldiers. "Longinus!"

Longinus, who was on one knee chatting with a small group of soldiers, jumped to his feet. "Commander," he said.

Petronius motioned to the crosses. "The Hebrew, he has not moved for some time, but I cannot tell if he is dead. Take a spear and prick him in the ribs. I want to know if he is still alive."

"Sire!" Yousef cried. "I beg you. Do not do this!"

While Yousef continued to protest, Longinus moved quickly. He ripped a spear from the hands of one of his men and poked Yeshua in the ribs. Yeshua moaned and blood trickled from the wound.

"Bah, he is barely alive," Petronius said. "He will not see the next sunrise." He tapped his thigh with the rolled proclamation and then tossed it to Yousef. "Very well, take him, and be quick about it. The sooner this matter is cleared the better."

Yousef turned to his men and clapped his hands. While the men raised ladders and untangled ropes, the women and men at the foot of the cross, who knew Yousef very well, moved quickly out of the way. Before I knew it, Jarek was on one of the ladders. No one argued with him, for he towered in size over everyone else on the hill. Jarek removed the nail from Yeshua's left wrist with a short instrument that he produced from a side pouch strapped to his belt. The arm dropped and dangled lifelessly. A man on the other ladder removed the nail from the other wrist and the wilted body of Yeshua collapsed into the arms of Jarek. The men on the ground removed the nail from his feet, and once Yeshua was completely free from the cross, Jarek lowered his body into the arms of Yousef and his slaves. Weeping quietly, the women wrapped Yeshua in linens and helped place him on a cart. The entire entourage then quickly disappeared into a nearby wooded area.

"Was he dead?" I asked Jarek, struggling to hold back tears.

"I think he was," Jarek said, "but I could not be sure. His body felt warm to me."

"Where do you think they are taking him?" I asked.

Jarek shrugged. Then he gave me a strange look. "Why are you so interested, young one? Did you know him?"

I touched my eyebrow and told him the story.

Jarek stared at my face and then he looked in the direction in which the procession had left. "I have heard of men who possess such powers. What do you think, should we go and see where they are taking him?"

"Yes," I cried. "I would like that very much!"

"Then let us go, before we lose them," Jarek said.

Farrenthias quietly mumbled a few words and then brushed the papyrus with the sleeve of his tunic. He shook his head in exasperation. "I cannot make out the next few lines. They are too faded but here is what follows."

Three torches were planted into the ground around a slab of stone on which the body of Yeshua lay. The small chamber smelled of spices and incense and aloe. A woman slowly applied some type of ointment to his wounds. Yousef and another man and two other women watched silently. From where I was hidden I could not see any of their faces. As soon as the woman finished treating Yeshua, they covered his wounds and changed his linens.

The man who had been standing next to Yousef then placed an ear to Yeshua's chest. "Nothing," he said bitterly. "He is not breathing."

"You are certain, Nicodemus?" Yousef asked.

Still looking at Yeshua, Nicodemus nodded sadly. "I am afraid that he is gone." He turned to Yousef. "We have lost him."

Yousef sighed heavily and then addressed the women, who were quietly weeping and comforting each other. "I am sorry. Truly I am sorry, but I suggest that we quickly proceed as planned. We do not want his enemies causing more trouble."

One of the women nodded. "Of course," she said, crying softly. "We do not want his body disturbed."

The wagon is still outside," Nicodemus said. "I shall go at once and speak to the men."

The women gathered around the body of Yeshua and quietly wept. One of them touched his forehead and seemed to offer a quiet prayer.

Nicodemus quickly returned with two men. "It is quiet outside. Shall we proceed?"

Yousef nodded, and I watched in complete fascination as the two men who accompanied Nicodemus carried the body of Yeshua out of the tomb and loaded him onto a cart.

Farrenthias stopped reading and frustratingly thrust his hands in the air. "There is another terribly smudged section here," he said more to himself than anyone else. "I cannot make out what it says."

Gavinio suddenly spoke. "What happened to Jarek?" he said. "Why was he not mentioned?"

"He must have left," Athinio said, "that was probably covered in the earlier section that Farrenthias could not read."

Farrenthias rubbed his eyes. "Here is what follows."

Yeshua had been placed on a stretcher and men dressed in long hooded robes and uttering incantations carried his body down a long descending passage. Holding a torch in each hand, Yousef and Nicodemus led they way. I wondered if the men were the followers of Yeshua, the men who had been with him on the hill, but I had no way of knowing that. Finally, after taking several winding turns, they arrived at a small chamber. They placed Yeshua on a pallet of straw and then one by one the hooded men filed past the body as they left the room.

"Summon Jacob and his mother, Nicodemus," Yousef said. "Tell them we have completed the move."

I was well hidden and Nicodemus passed right by me without seeing me. I was now determined to stay and to see what else was going to happen, but I did not realize how tired I was. Soon my eyes grew heavy, and I struggled to stay awake. I began to doze off, and my head kept dropping forward. Then one of the times that I caught myself falling asleep I snapped by head back and gasped. I found myself staring at a pair of feet. I slowly raised my eyes. Yousef stood over me, holding a torch above his head and shaking his head.

"Who are you, child? What are you doing here?" His voice was not raised in anger, but rather he seemed quite amused that I was there.

"Forgive me, sire," I said. "I should not have followed you. It is just that..." I suddenly looked around.

"Why did you bring him into this tunnel? Where are we?"

Amused by my daring question Yousef leaned into my face until I could feel his hot breath on my face. "This is holy ground. This is where the great master must come to rest. Now tell me, who are you and why did you follow us in here?"

"Holy ground?" Gavinio blurted out loudly. "What does that mean?

Farrenthias glanced at Athinio. "Holy ground," he murmured. "Is it possible that they are somewhere beneath The Temple of Solomon?"

"It cannot be any other place," Athinio said.

Farrenthias stretched his arms, exhaled and continued to read.

I told Yousef my story and he slowly nodded as he pondered what I had told him. "Great masters like Yeshua develop certain mysterious gifts," he said. "I have no doubt that he cured you." He sighed and then tapped my hands. "Now, it is time that you run along, young one, and you must not speak about what you have seen to anyone. Do you understand?"

"I understand," I said sadly, for I wanted to stay. He helped me to my feet and then we both froze. Yeshua had moaned.

"Did you hear that?" Yousef cried. "Hurry, lad, come with me."

I held a torch while Yousef cleaned and gently applied more ointment to Yeshua's wounds. Several times he had to steady my hand, because I trembled when I saw the holes the nails had made in Yeshua's wrists and feet. I even touched one of the wounds when I helped Yousef clean it. Yousef then produced a small wooden cup and wrung the cloth he had been using over the cup. Blood poured into the cup.

"We do not want his blood spilled all over the place," Yousef said. Once no more blood could be drained from the cloth, he put away the cup and applied new bandages. At last he and I reclined back against a wall and stared at Yeshua in silence. He appeared to be resting as comfortably as possible given the serious wounds he had suffered. "You did well," Yousef said to me.

"Will he be all right?" I asked him.

He looked at Yeshua. "He has gone through quite an ordeal. We shall see," he said pensively. "We shall see." He handed me a small skin of wine. "In the meantime, drink some of this and rest for a few moments."

What happened after that is unclear to me. Sometime later I thought I heard voices, but I was too drowsy to open my eyes. Apparently I fell into a heavy sleep, and when I finally did come around, I found that I was still in the mysterious chamber but was completely alone. Oddly, a lamp burned beside me. I staggered to my feet with a terrible headache. Even the pallet of straw where they had laid Yeshua was gone, but I did notice something I had not seen before. A beautiful wall that glittered was just beyond where the pallet of straw had been. I walked to the wall to inspect it more closely but had to steady myself against it, for I was still very drowsy. I slid down on the very spot where I stood and fell into another deep sleep again.

The next time I opened my eyes, Jarek was leaning over me.

"Jarek?" I whispered. "Is that you?" I raised my head and discovered that I was on the floor of a carpenter's shop. "Where am I, Jarek? How did I get here?"

"This is my shop," he said. "I brought you here."

"But I do not understand," I said.

"Of course you do not understand," he said. "A few hours after I left you I decided to go back and have a look around, and it is a good thing that I did. I found you fast asleep beneath a tree. I could not just leave you there so I decided to bring you here."

"Beneath a tree?" I cried. "But I do not recall falling asleep beneath a tree."

Jarek shrugged. "That is where I found you, beneath a tree very near the spot where I last saw you."

A woman entered the room. "Ah," she said. "Our little guest is awake. Good. He needs warm milk. It will do him good. I shall get it," she said and left the room.

"That was my wife Lezinia," Jarek said. "How do you feel?"

"I feel fine, I think," I said, rubbing the back of my neck. "I just have a headache."

Jarek folded his heavy arms and smiled. "You need rest. Lezinia and I have discussed it and we both think that you should stay here until you are well."

Jarek then asked me what had happened after he left me. I wanted to tell him everything that I had seen, but I remembered that I had promised Yousef that I would not talk about it. Fortunately, when I hesitated to answer him, Jarek assumed that I could not remember. He never asked me again and for that I was grateful. Yet, I was extremely curious about the final outcome of those events. Had Yeshua survived? What happened to Yousef and Nicodemus?

I was fine by the next day, but Lezinia insisted that I stay in bed two full days. Finally, she let me accompany Jarek around the city while he took care of his business. I was quietly pleased when Jarek mentioned the crucifixion to a group of men who were gathered in a public square. I eagerly waited for their answer, but all they could tell us was that many of the followers of the crucified rabbi had vanished.

That night, Jarek and Lezinia sat me down and told

me that they were leaving Jerusalem and that they wanted me to go with them. Their plans were to travel to Babylonia, where Jarek said he could find work. At first I said no, but Jarek asked me to please reconsider. "What will you do by yourself here in Jerusalem?" he said. "Come with us and I will turn you into the best carpenter in all of Judea?"

Jarek was right. What would I do here? I was tired of being alone, and I was not yet ready to return to my home in Petra. I reluctantly agreed, and the next day I helped them pack. It took us all day to pack and that night we slept in an empty house. We left very early the following morning, but just beyond the gates of the city we had a strange and unintentional encounter with an old man. It changed my life. The old man was stranded on the main road leading out of the city. His cart had a broken wheel. The old man looked down the road. "I was traveling too fast and did not see the pothole until it was too late. I should have been more careful."

Jarek inspected the wheel and then nodded confidently. "You are fortunate that I am a carpenter. I have all the tools that I need to repair this wheel. I shall have you on your way in no time," he said. He removed his outer cloak, and in his short tunic he immediately went to work fixing the wheel.

"Excellent," the old man cried. "My luck has already changed. Of course, I shall pay you for your trouble."

"No need to do that," Jarek said. "A man must do a good deed every once in a while and not expect compensation for it."

"Well, I hope that I do not delay you too long," the old man said. "Where are you and your family headed?"

"Babylonia," Jarek said. "And you?"

"Damascus," the old man said. He leaned a hand against his cart. "I have wool rugs to deliver." He brushed his chin and his face darkened as he momentarily appeared to be lost in thought. "Of course, it is also an excellent opportunity for me to confirm a rumor I had heard."

"A rumor?" Jarek said, without taking his eyes away from the pin he was hammering into place. "What rumor?"

The old man's voice became quietly excited as he spoke. "I do not know if you ever heard of the wise prophet, Yeshua. Even though the Romans crucified him days ago, people swear that he is not dead. They say that he and some of his followers slipped out of Jerusalem in the middle of the night, to protect him from the Romans and those who wanted to have him killed. You ever hear of him?"

Jarek stopped hammering and whirled around to look at me. I had kneeled beside Jarek, but upon hearing this stunning revelation, I jumped to my feet. "Yes!" I cried. "We have heard of him. He is alive?"

"They say that he has been seen alive in Damascus," the old man said.

Jarek swung his hammer one more time and then stepped back from the cart. "Your wheel is fine now. The damage was not as bad as it looked."

"Ah," the old man bellowed, "I am eternally grateful to you. Please, let me pay you for your trouble. Perhaps I can offer you one of my fine rugs as payment for your labor."

"You owe me nothing," Jarek said. "I am happy that I was able to help you." He put on his cloak and put away his tools.

"Then I thank you again," the old man said.

Lezinia joined us, and the three of us watched the old man pull away.

"I heard what he said about Yeshua," Lezinia said. She caressed my cheeks and took me under her arms. "Jarek," she said, "I think that we should postpone our trip to Babylonia and spend a few days in Damascus. I think Akiva would like that. Am I correct, Akiva?"

I eagerly nodded. "There is nothing that I would like more than to see Yeshua again."

We reached Damascus at dusk three days later and took a simple room at an inn. Early the next day Jarek and I set out on our search for Yeshua. We roamed the streets and visited market squares. We visited food establishments and inns, and everywhere that we went we discreetly asked for news of Yeshua. To my bitter disappointment we got nowhere on our search. A few people who had heard of Yeshua told us that they had heard that the Romans had put him to death in Jerusalem, and others did not know whom we were talking about. We searched for two days until nightfall with similar results. Exhausted and frustrated, Jarek, nevertheless, agreed to search one more day. On that final day we again set out early. Jarek and I again visit-ed inns, taverns, and neighborhoods, but once again we got nowhere. I wondered if there had been any truth to the rumor that Yeshua was alive and that he had been seen in Damascus. At noon we reluctantly decided to end our search and head back to the inn, where Lezinia waited. Jarek had instructed her to be packed and ready to leave Damascus upon our return. But then, everything changed. We were walking down a side street and came upon a small inn that we had not seen before. As we approached the inn, I looked through a large window that was facing the street, and my heart stopped. At the head of a long rectangular table with a group of men sat Yousef of Arimethea. I could not believe my eyes. Seated next to him was none other than the old man Jarek had helped with a broken wheel. Jarek and I watched in amazement as the men chatted and partook of bread and wine.

Jarek cleared his throat and tugged at my shoulder. "What are we waiting for? Let us go in and have a word with Yousef and our friend. They will certainly have news of Yeshua."

The old man saw us enter the inn and immediately left the table to greet us. "Ah, my new friends," he said. "But what are you doing here in Damascus? I thought you were on your way to Babylonia."

"I wanted to see Yeshua," I blurted out.

The old man smiled affectionately at me. "But of course, my child, I too wanted to see him, but unfortunately, we just missed him. He was here in this very inn just last night, but he left before sunrise."

"But how is that possible?" Jarek asked. "We have

been asking about him for days. Some swore that he was dead and others had no idea what we were talking about."

The old man brushed his chin and looked sadly at us. "I am told that it was his wish that no one know that he was here. He quietly entered the city. He did not preach nor gather with too many people. He stayed a few days and then quietly left. Few knew that he was even here."

"But where did he go?" I cried.

"Yes," Jarek said. "Where did he go?"

"No one knows," the old man said.

Jarek looked over the old man's shoulder at Yousef. "He has to know the whereabouts of Yeshua. After all, he is responsible for taking him down from the cross."

The old man looked at Yousef. He had reclined back in his chair and was gazing out the window. "Yousef does not know. I have asked him, and all that he has told me is the Yeshua told him that he needed to finish a quest he had started years ago."

My eyes filled with tears. "But, but what does that mean?" I cried.

The old man took pity on me and took my hand. "Come join us at the table, my son. There is plenty of food and I was about to ask Yousef that very question."

Yousef was very surprised to see us, and he greeted us warmly. He affectionately rested a hand on my shoulder. "This is a special young man," he announced to the others at the table. "Tell me young one, what brings you and your friend to Damascus?"

"Like myself they wanted to see Yeshua," the old man said to Yousef.

"I see," Yousef said. He shook his head sadly. "I suppose that our friend here has just advised you that he is gone."

"But to where?" Jarek asked. "In which direction did he go?"

Yousef sighed and gazed out the window again. "Truly, I cannot say. I have been sitting here staring out that window wondering that myself. When I asked him, his last words to me were, 'Yousef, I would tell you where I was going, but I am not quite certain myself. I know only that I still have much work to do, and that to accomplish it I must travel far. And, I must travel alone.'" Yousef lifted his cup and sipped from it. "I have asked his followers not to pursue him but rather to wait, to wait patiently for his return."

I was stunned. I could not believe that we had missed him by a day, but Jarek and I politely remained at the table for a bit longer while the men talked and ate. I was tired and hungry but could not eat. Finally, Jarek explained that he and I needed to leave. Yousef thanked Jarek for his assistance back in Jerusalem, and then he took both of my hands and smiled at me even as he studied me with intense eyes. He started to say something, but instead he abruptly cleared his throat and then said simply, "Go in peace, my child. It was good to see you again."

I fought back tears as I walked out of that inn with Jarek, and when we arrived back at the inn, I was still fighting back tears.

Jarek told Lezinia all that had just occurred and she took me in her arms. It was then that I could no longer hold back my tears, and I quietly wept.

"I wanted to become one of his followers," I said, stepping out of Lezinia's arms. "Even if all I had done was take him water when he was thirsty."

"I understand," Jarek said sadly. He glanced at Lezinia. "Akiva, Lezinia and I have grown very fond of you. We can legally adopt you or you can just stay with us for as long as you like. I will set up a new shop in Babylonia and it will be yours when I die."

"Listen to Jarek, Akiva," Lezinia said. "It is what we both want."

I wiped my face with the back of my hand and stood awkwardly between them. "You have both been very kind to me," I said, "but it is just that I cannot explain how I feel. I want to go and look for Yeshua."

"But you heard Yousef," Jarek said. "You must be patient and wait for him to return. Besides, where would you look for him?"

I shrugged my shoulders. "I-I do not know, but I have to try."

Lezinia wept and took me in her arms again. "You are too young to be roaming the country alone. Please reconsider."

"Forgive me," I said, tears still flowing down my face. "I must do this."

Lezinia sighed. "Then promise me that you will be careful. And if you ever change your mind, you can find us in Babylonia."

"Look for a carpenter's shop," Jarek said. "We should be easy to find." He went outside to the packed cart and quickly returned with a small pouch. "I thought you might want to have these," he said. He emptied the contents of the pouch into one of his hands. "Remember, I removed one of these from Yeshua's hand, the other two I found on the ground. I stared at the three long, crooked nails, almost afraid to touch them. Yet, even though I hated what they had done to him with these nails, I was glad that Jarek had saved them. Jarek put them back in the pouch and handed the pouch to me.

I bid farewell to them and left. Thus began my long and lonely quest to find the man who had so profoundly touched my life at a tender age. Sometimes I would go for months without finding one single person who had even heard of him. On other days, I would hear a rumor of a sighting, and with renewed enthusiasm and hope, I would set out in pursuit of that rumor, only to be disappointed. I took odd jobs to feed myself, but stayed a very short time at any one place. And whenever I happened upon a stranger on a lonely road, I anxiously searched his face. I hoped that it would be the face of Yeshua, but it never was. I lost track of the years and gradually slowed my search. Then one day, when I was ready to abandon my quest altogether, I heard about a caravan that had trickled out of Egypt toward the Far East. I heard that a man of wise words traveled with that caravan curing the ill. Could they have been speaking about Yeshua? I did not know, for by then, the land was full of stories about prophets and magicians. Still, although

I was tired and had been at the point of giving up, I was reinvigorated by this news. I once again had the desire to keep searching, and to not give up. I packed my frugal belongings in a satchel and set out again, only to be disappointed again. I visited my sister Yehnia in Petra and considered staying there but neither she nor the profound love I had for her could keep me from my mission to find Yeshua. When I found my way to Engedi, I stayed for a period of time and learned many things from the men with whom Yeshua had once lived. Engedi was a paradise and I was tempted to abandon my quest and just stay there to live permanently. But in the end, I could not contain my restless soul, and I set out again. I had to continue....

Farrenthias stared numbly at the document in silence. Finally, he looked up in exasperation and shrugged his shoulders. "It abruptly ends there. There is no more." He exhaled and slumped back in a daze. Akiva's story was fascinating and compelling. But it left many questions unanswered. What happened to Yeshua? Where did he go after he left Damascus? Did Akiva ever find him? If he did, was it in the Far East? Where in the Far East? And what happened to Akiva? Why has no one heard from him again?

Gavinio scrambled to a sitting position with his legs crossed in front of him. "The story is not finished," he said, dismally.

"No," Farrenthias said. "It is not." He turned to Athinio. "Sire, now that you have heard what Akiva wrote, and according to the letter he wrote to his sister, is there any doubt in your mind that he returned to the Himalayas?"

Athinio frowned and looked intensely at Farrenthias. "None."

"The Himalayas." Farrenthias whispered, as he rolled the scroll and put it away.

"I was taken there as a child," Athinio said, "but I recall every detail of that journey. Once you reach those peaks and the hidden monasteries…" he drew his breath. "Depending on what you seek, it can change your life forever."

"Is it true," Farrenthias asked, "that in those snow-covered mountains there are hidden communities where many masters live and study in seclusion."

"It is true," Athinio said. "It is also said that all who travel to those lands and meditate and pray are blessed with special knowledge. There are many mysteries there."

Farrenthias pondered Athinio's words, trying to make sense of them. "Why is life so full of mysteries, Athinio? Why so many riddles?" He looked at Athinio, shaking his head.

Athinio smiled patiently. "You are beginning to understand the challenges man faces when he contemplates his existence." He inhaled and his expression turned solemn. "Is it all futile? I think not. Even though we may never fully resolve some mysteries, there is still much value in the quest for answers. It is what gives us hope in one day understanding the cruelties and the unfairness of life. It is also what distinguishes man from the rest of the animals that roam the land, animals that occupy their daily existence solely in the pursuit of a meal and a mate to breed with."

Farrenthias sighed. "Truly, those are words of wisdom, Athinio, but at the moment they give me little comfort. I am in a quandary about what to do next. Do I return to Jerusalem with an incomplete document that chronicles one man's search for Yeshua, or do I set out on my own quest to the Himalayas? "

Athinio sighed heavily. "An interesting dilemma, indeed, by dear young Farrenthias. But I caution you. A trip to those mountains would take you many months. It is not an easy journey. You would endure hardships and danger." He looked about his cave. "Of course, if you decided to go I could provide you with adequate clothing and a travel sack for what you will need."

Farrenthias wondered if he would truly dare to take such a trip on his own without the blessing of Ya'ir or Erasmus Harel and why would he even consider it in the first place? Was there a rush to undertake such an important endeavor? Of course there was something else, a sign perhaps?

"There is something else I must show you, Athinio," he said. He produced the pouch containing the three nails Ja'eleni had given him. "One night in the middle of the desert in Egypt, I came upon a rich merchant by the name of Ja'eleni and his train of camels. In truth, he rescued me from having to walk across the desert. During our journey I told him about Yeshua and how the Romans crucified him. He then showed me these and gave them to me to keep." Farrenthias produced the nails. "They were given to Ja'eleni by a man who claimed that a great Hebrew prophet was crucified in Jerusalem with these nails. He and I marveled at the possibility that these might be the very nails used to nail Yeshua to the tree. And I of course wondered if the man who gave these to Ja'eleni might have been Akiva."

Gavinio quietly crawled around the fire for a closer look at the nails. "I would not like one of these to prick my skin," he said. "It would hurt terribly."

"Is it not a strange coincidence," Farrenthias said, "that I would encounter a man in the middle of the Egyptian desert who would give me these?"

"Nothing in life is a coincidence, Farrenthias," Athinio said, looking at the nails. "Life has a strange way of expressing itself.

There is a purpose to everything. We merely have to learn to understand what is revealed to us and act on it, accept our fate."

With those words Farrenthias got to his feet and stretched his arms. "You have given me much to think about, wise one. I do not know if I can sleep, but I think that I shall huddle in a corner and try."

"Rest peacefully," Athinio said. "Tomorrow your mind will be clearer and then perhaps you can make decisions. Be patient, however, the answers that you seek may not come as quickly as you would like, but they will come to you. Remember this, sometimes it is better to be driven by our feelings than our thoughts. As such, you can never be completely wrong about what decisions you make and what steps in life you take."

Early the following morning, Farrenthias stood alone at the edge of the sea. He watched a group of white seagulls land on the sand. They pecked at a dead fish that had washed ashore. When they finished their meal, they spread their wings, lifted into the air, and soared away in a tight organized group, towards an orange sun that had barely cleared the horizon.

Farrenthias watched the well-organized migration just as a lone eagle appeared high overhead. The lone predator made several low passes along the shore before it too headed towards the horizon, disappointed no doubt that it found no prey.

As Farrenthias watched the eagle he recalled the words Athinio had spoken last night. Animals lived a simple existence he had said. They hunt to eat and stay alive and they reproduce their species. That was the whole purpose of their existence. Perhaps there were many men who also lived such simple lives but that could never be his life. No, his life was much more complicated. Like the men at

Clivus he had chosen a much more complex path, a path that would lead him down many roads, some empty and unfulfilling perhaps, and, hopefully, some rewarding and gratifying. Akiva had also chosen such a path. Akiva. Where was he? What became of his life?

He heard footsteps behind him and turned to find Gavinio cheerfully walking towards him and stripping off his clothes as he walked. "Farrenthias," he called out. "I did not hear you leave the cave. Is the water cold?"

Farrenthias laughed. "It is cold out here so I am certain that the water is also cold. Are you not cold?"

"No, I am fine. I am jumping in the water. Are you getting in?"

"I suppose that I must, bathing is important."

"Athinio said that it is good to bathe in water right after it has rained. He said it was good for the soul," Gavinio said. "He is on his way down."

"Then let us get in the water," Farrenthias said as he started to remove his toga. "Of course, I can only go so deep. I do not know how to swim very well."

"Ha, then I shall have to teach you." Gavinio said. " I can swim as well as a fish."

He scratched a small purple scar on what remained of his left nipple.

"Does that hurt?" Farrenthias asked.

Gavinio looked down at his chest. "This old scar. Nah, but sometime it itches. Anyway, it used to be darker but it keeps getting smaller." He bolted toward the water. "Hurry, Farrenthias, catch me if you can," he yelled.

"You were up early this morning," Athinio said, joining Farrenthias at the edge of the water. He looked at him and nodded.

"I am delighted that you look rested and at peace. I think you have found your answers."

"I have, Athinio," Farrenthias said.

Athinio took Farrenthias's arm and gripped it affectionately. "Excellent, my son, then let us join our young lad in the water. Cold water always refreshes my old bones."

Epilogue

Letter from Farrenthias Theophilus to Tessius Trulius in Rome

Noble Trulius, I trust that this letter finds you well and in the company of all of your loved ones in Rome. I write you this letter in haste to apprise you of recent events in my life and to ask you to consider certain matters of importance that concern me. First, I should tell you that by the time this letter reaches you I will be well on my way to the Himalayas. Why the Himalayas is a long and complicated story, which I will gladly share with you one day. What I will find and when will I return I do not know. I know only that I have to go. Of course, by now my actions should not surprise you in the least, you being my dearest and closest friend and one who knows me so well. You know very well that I enthusiastically embraced the calling and task, which the noblemen of Clivus chose and revealed to me. In truth, to follow their steps was not even a conscious decision, Trulius. I am convinced that I was born to a life of contemplation and devotion. As such, I am well aware that I have and will continue to forfeit many aspects of my life, including the company of those who I love. It is my hope that Cerudotus will comfort my family as they struggle to accept my absence. I tell you all of this for an important reason. Although your life is in Rome, I hope that you shall always consider that you also have a family in Syria as well. My father and mother and sisters love you, and it is my hope and desire that one day Father will name you heir to everything that I would have otherwise been entitled to by inheritance. I have written Father and made this request of him and I am certain that he will agree to it. I wish not to burden you with our family matters, but I must confess to you that knowing that Father took to you with so much love relieved me of the burden of knowing that as his son I failed him in many ways. On another matter, in Egypt I befriended a charming young boy of barely six or seven years old. His name is Gavinio. He is homeless, and you will be amused to learn that he is Roman. When and how he came to Egypt is a mystery, but I should tell you that he reminds me very much of you when you were his age. He is witty and mischievous and very bright. At his insistence he has become my traveling companion. He is accompanying me on this long and difficult journey. I hope that one day Gavinio will return to Syria with me. I am certain that my family will welcome him but I should also like for you to meet him. Perhaps

Gavinio and I will one day travel to Rome. I am certain that you will like him and it would be good if you taught him all the skills that you possess. As a Roman, he will one day need them.

I close this letter by telling you that it has brought joy to my heart to know that you have found love and happiness with Gianina. I shall never know such happiness, not even with a young girl as lovely and kind and understanding as Sesdia. No, my destiny has taken me in a different direction, and as I have already stated, it is a destiny, which I fully embrace and accept.

My warmest regards to you and your entire family, my dear friend. Farrenthias Theophilus.

THE END

ABOUT THE AUTHOR

Roberto J Ramos was born in El Paso, Texas. He has practiced law for over thirty years and is currently employed as a prosecutor in the El Paso District Attorney's Office. *Plight of the Lions* is his first novel. It is the first step towards fulfilling a lifelong dream of becoming a novelist.

For an update on future novels visit Roberto on Facebook: facebook.com/robertojramos111 or his webpage: www.robertojramos.com

www.ingramcontent.com/pod-product-compliance
Lightning Source LLC
Chambersburg PA
CBHW071331020726
47502CB00001B/61